CW00798991

To. Pat
Love and Best
wishes. Amy

April 2010

The Brook Runs Free

Book 2 of 2

The War Changes Everything

Amy Lecouteur

AuthorHouse™ UK Ltd.
500 Avebury Boulevard
Central Milton Keynes, MK9 2BE
www.authorhouse.co.uk
Phone: 08001974150

First published by AuthorHouse 1/13/2010

ISBN: 978-1-4490-5362-8 (sc)

This book is printed on acid-free paper.

Amy's Profile

Amy is born and bred in Shropshire where she still lives; although not in the area of her origin, which is the beautiful area under the Wrekin.

Her early life was taken up with her father's farm and she left school with no significant qualifications.

Because of the war years she was unable to achieve her dream of being a teacher. Amy settled for married life and took up residence at the Wrekin Cottage. (known as the Half Way House) Situated on the Wrekin itself.

After fourteen years of marriage she broke with the area and moved away to start a new life finding her vocation as a driving instructor, continuing for over twenty years until she forced to retire due to ill health.

It was during this time that the idea for this book became fruition and was the driving force while she battled through so many dark days

She now enjoys hobbies of painting, writing and gardening.

Dedication

I would like to deicate this book to my late parents who like so many other farming families worked so hard during the war years to help provide food for the country.

Acknowledgements

I gratefully acknowledge and give special thanks to my Son Tony Harper and Beryl Evans for their effort, devotion and help during the creation of this work.

Also to David, Anne and Paul for their patience and technical help with the working of the computer. Also to my immediate family for their support.

CONTENTS

Chapter 1

ALL WORK AND NO PLAY

Fred and Dorothy Thomas were coping but only just. They were farming their farm one hundred and four acres the best that they could with only the family to help with the colossal amount of work that there was to do to keep the farm going, but it was hard going and they both were extremely tired. Their nights sleep seemed to them to become shorter. The hours went by so quickly, no sooner than they had retired to bed the alarm clock would be ringing to say that it was time to rise and start another day's hard toil.

The ministry were asking for every available field to be ploughed and sown with cereal crops and potatoes Etc; to help feed the country. However the Ministry did not reveal to the country how the food stocks were dwindling.

Wireless broadcasts and news papers were appealing for everyone to do their bit. They called it Dig for Victory. Plant your gardens with potatoes and other vegetables and not to have lawns of grass. It was amazing how the people responded.

Fred and Dorothy's family of six girls were now doing all that they could to help their parents. Each had their own chores to do as this was the only way that they could cope, and so the work was fairly shared between them.

Dorothy still wished that they could have been born boys instead of girls, it would have made the work load so much easier, especially for her but she now knew that she must not complain, they must all get on with it they had to keep the farm going it was their living and if she and Fred did not do as the Ministry ordered they would be turned out on the road to fend for them selves. She had no sympathy for the girls what so ever, she had to work hard when she had been a girl on her father's farm and had to work hard along side Fred when she had married him. There was a difference in those days she had not had to be responsible for the cooking and washing as well as working outside on the farm.

More forms arrived from the Ministry of Food and Fisheries. There was a lot to fill in. Fred left it to Dorothy. She had to give details of the stock, the number of milking cows, sheep, pigs, goats, horses, ducks, geese, hens and so on, the use the fields were put to and the acreage.

"What will there be forms for next?" Dorothy grumbled to Fred as she opened another brown envelope after the postman had left.

"To go to the lavvy I'd say," Fred answered as he took a yellow invoice from the mantle shelf and tore a strip off it to light his pipe. He had to save his matches for lighting his pipe out of doors,

Mary was working feeding most days now. Rebecca was always up at the crack of dawn as soon as she heard Fred setting the fire in the range. She went and let the fowl out and did some feeding and was usually washed and changed ready for breakfast with Grace and Hanna. Lizzy got up with Mary and made breakfast for herself and her sisters, and also the sandwiches that they needed at lunch time she then went to school, staying with them till the top of the bank and then she ran on ahead. She would be leaving school next year but she still worried about being late.

Dorothy was becoming worried. Britain had sent troops to France at the beginning of the hostilities but no more had happened. She was concerned at the constant warnings over the wireless about being vigilant. And the civil defence reminders. To make matters worse, the girls were coming home telling her how they must not talk to strangers and must report anything suspicious.

Russia had invaded Finland.

"What are those Germans up to?" she said to Fred, "you can't tell me that they drop bombs on us then do nothing."

"You know more than me," he said, "I have no idea."

"They're saying that if we see any strangers they could be German spies, we are not to talk to them but we must tell the authorities. Well I ask you, what authorities do we run to from our place?"

"I'll not bother with the authorities if I see any strangers on the bank," Fred answered, "I'll run the bloody pitchfork through them and if I'm out with the gun they will get a blast from the twelve bore and no questions asked."

"Now don't you go talking so daft, you can't just shoot someone because you think they are a spy, what if they were some one from the Ministry an official and you killed them? You would be locked up for murder and what then? Hung. What am I supposed to do when you are not here, Stop and think Fred what would I do then?"

"Yes you are right, with the young ones and such a big place we may have to think about this a bit more."

"How about the gun? Do you think I could handle it?" she said

"But you've never even picked one up," he replied, quite astonished at the idea of Dorothy using a gun.

"I think it's about time I did." She continued. "You've got two guns and I think that we should make sure there are plenty of cartridges handy in case we may need them."

Fred was surprised at her tenacity; Dorothy had never shown interest in the guns before and they were both twelve bore, double-barrelled guns. They were propped up in the back larder. He made sure they were always unloaded before he put them away after going out shooting.

"I don't know about this, "he said, not sure how to continue, the guns were his, and no one ever touched them.

"I think we should be looking to the guns for protection especially without Sam around. I don't feel very safe around the house when you are working in the fields from morning to night."

For a moment Fred was quiet.

"Can we talk about this tomorrow Dot?" He wanted out of the conversation and needed time to think things over.

"Well you give it some thought Fred Thomas. I'll not hesitate to use one of those guns if it comes to it if any beggar puts me or the kids at risk." Her anger was boiling up

"I do believe you would Dot. Put the kettle on and make a pot of tea and let's have a drink." He was hoping to drop the subject.

Next day she had not forgotten.

"When can I have a go with the gun?" she asked.

"I don't know Dot, what if you were to hurt yourself?"

"Don't talk so daft Fred Thomas. Do you think I'm that stupid? I've watched you shoot enough and I can't see why I should not be able to do the same. It would look a lot better if I didn't show that I was nervous of the thing so how about some practice?"

Fred hesitated, not sure what to say.

"I think that if you put some sacks on posts down the field there," she pointed towards the bottom field, "I could stand by the garage and take some shots at them."

"Aye, all right then." He gave in; she was right as usual. "Shall I paint faces on them?"

"Don't be soft Fred Thomas; it won't take long to set up. I'll make you a cup of tea."

"I reckon you are right Dot. OK then, we will have a go tomorrow while the girls are at school."

Fred set two posts a short distance in the field; each had a piece of wood nailed to it to form a 'T'. He then hung up a sack with a grim face painted in mud on it. Later he brought out a gun and some cartridges then he went and shut up the dogs just in case. Dorothy joined him and he instructed her about safety and the gun.

"I know all that," she said, "for goodness sake load it and let me have a go!"

She was taken aback by the kick when she pulled the trigger. It hurt her shoulder a bit. The blast was louder than she expected. Fred was surprised, she was quite a good shot she had hit one of the sacks.

"That is with one barrel," he said, "do you want to try two?"

She grinned. "Oh yes, and I'll load it myself," she said as she released the barrel and removed the spent cartridge, She practised for a while. She soon got used to the kick, firing one barrel after the other; she held the gun tighter to her shoulder as Fred instructed her to do. "I'll feel a lot safer now I know I can use that," she said, handing the gun to Fred. "That will do for now, no sense in wasting any more cartridges. We are going to need them to shoot a rabbit or two for dinner if food gets rationed."

He was very pleased; he said that she was to make that gun hers for now; it was the shorter and lighter of the two.

On a cold December morning a group of three men from the War Agricultural committee turned up at the Willowmoor Farm to inspect the entire farm. The committee was made up of prominent local farmers and Ministry advisors. It was their job to look over farms in their area and to determine what crops were to be grown. Mr Jones from Uppington was the farmer who was made responsible for the Wrekin area. Two Ministry men who arrived in a separate car accompanied him. Fred was keen to hear what they had to say.

Mr Jones had a map with him and at first they left Fred out of their conversation. They studied their papers and debated. Fred was annoyed. The war had brought major changes and restrictive tenancy agreements were being swept aside. He wanted to make best use of the acreage he had but he was concerned what demands would be made and how he was going to cope; they were struggling without Sam's help. Mr Jones left the other two and came over to Fred; he seemed a reasonable sort of man. He had with him a map of the farm.

"They are off," he said, "we will take a walk and see what we have here."

They stood at the front gate and looked across the road towards the Wrekin.

"The first field here," he said, "can't plough it."

"But why? It's one of the biggest fields on the bank and is ideal." Fred had seen that field as the best to start ploughing.

That is the only one we can not consider at this time. Apparently it is a Roman burial ground. If the worst comes to the worst I will have to get special permission for you to be allowed to plough it but in the meantime we must concentrate on the other fields like the one behind it.

"It's a what, do you say? A burial ground? Well I never!" This is not a good start thought Fred, the war effort needed all the food it could get and there were the subsidies.

"There was a battle fought on that ground many years ago and orders are that the ground must not be disturbed. Apparently that is how this farm got its name, Willowmoor, Valley of Doom."

"Thanks very bloody much," Fred said, "that's made my bloody day."

Mr Jones smiled.

"Don't be hasty, we should concentrate on which fields can be ploughed and sown with corn. I believe that you have 104 acres. By the look of it, a lot more of it could be put to much better use than you are doing at the moment." He looked at the map. "As I said, you can plough that one." He turned back towards the house, "and what about that one?" He pointed to the very bottom field and referred back to the map. "That is a good size and no mistake."

"Too wet in the spring that one. Only need a bit of snow in the winter months and it is far too wet to get on, the horses get bogged down."

They walked over the farm and returned to the farmyard.

Mary came across with a jug of tea, some cups, milk and sugar.

"Mam sent you this Dad." Mr Jones was impressed.

"I could certainly do with a drink," he said, "how old are you?"

"Twelve," said Mary.

"She is helping out at the moment. Sam our hired hand was called up last month and we have so much stock to feed and water."

"That must be hard on you," he said to Mary.

She looked at her father, not sure what to say. "I suppose," was all she could think of.

Fred gave Mr Jones his tea and they forgot Mary. She hurried back to feeding the horses.

Mr Jones drained his cup.

"Well, I have seen all I need for now. I will make my recommendations."

"When will I hear something?" asked Fred.

"In the New Year and I think you must think seriously about the future. I will try and help you but first you have to help yourselves. Mr Davies at the Wrekin Farm has gone; he saw this coming. There is a new tenant now, Joe Evans; he will be producing milk soon."

Fred and Dorothy had seen a couple of Lorries going to Wrekin Farm. The drivers had to open the gate to cross Fred's field.

"Good lord, Old Morkin has been there for years."

"And that is part of the trouble. This country has got to eat and too much has been imported in the past. It is said that if we had no more imported stuff we could only last from breakfast on Sunday to midday Wednesday. We are farming two million less acres than the end of the last war and have five million more mouths to feed. Do you see the problem?"

"That's the bloody tenancy rules tying the farmer down. I lost my last farm through trying to do better."

"Then you will appreciate the opportunity you have, Mr Thomas. I wish you well. I must move on now. Give my regards to your wife."

Fred was worried. He told Dorothy later what had been said.

"I know Morkin has gone," she said "the postman said he just upped sticks and went." She had not said anything she too was worried for their future

Mid December there was some cheer for the British people; the news was broadcast that the pocket battleship Graf Spee had been sunk, being scuttled off Uruguay.

"At last something to cheer us up," said Fred to the family around the table.

"What does scuttled mean Dad?" asked Hannah, "like a spider?"

"No," he said, "it's when the crew pulls the plug out of the bottom and lets it sink."

"Why do they have a plug in the bottom, that sounds daft and anyway Danny Probin at school said they were going to blow its guts out."

Fred chuckled "Aye lass, our lads certainly would have liked to."

"That's enough," said Dorothy, "where do you get such talk?"

"From Danny Probin," said Grace, "he is horrid""

"Shut up the pair of you"" said Dorothy and they went back to what they were doing.

Fred had seen some farmers selling bundles of holly in the town from their carts; it seemed quiet popular. He started thinking; there were lots of holly trees on his land. There were five growing in the hedge alongside the road.

He mentioned it to Mary when she was helping out with the evening chores.

"What do you reckon lass, we've plenty with berries this year?"

"I can help you Dad if you want but it is prickly stuff. I could wear my gloves though."

"Aye, that's a good idea and it will help to give a bit of cheer to a few who are miserable this Christmas with not having their loved ones at home."

Mary liked the idea and that Sunday at her suggestion, she and Fred took a small ladder and went along the hedge. They cut the pieces which had the most berries and tied it into bunches with string. Mary wore her gloves, keeping warm and prickle free.

Rebecca had seen them down the hedgerow and when she next saw Mary she asked what they had been up to.

"Mind your own business nosy," said Mary, "just helping Dad if you must know."

Fred took the holly to the cattle auction and made a good sale with it. His was some of the best on offer. He was well pleased and was surprised how much he made.

That evening he put some pennies in Mary's hand.

"We will do this again lass. Now take these and get something for you and your sisters when you are next in the shop."

Mary was very pleased but kept it quiet, not telling her sisters until she had bought a big bag of mixed sweets and shared them out. None of them told their mother.

Dorothy had fifteen geese to kill and dress, the girls coped with plucking the feathers despite being more difficult than cockerels or hens.

Jess the dog, so long Sam's companion, withdrew into herself. She lay on the yard and hardly stirred. Jingo tried to make her play but gave up and left her alone. Sadly, on Christmas Eve she died. Fred found her in the morning by the back door still waiting for Sam. He took her gently in his arms and walked to the orchard. He laid her on the grass and fetched a shovel. Rebecca came down and went outside; she knew something was wrong. She went to the orchard and found him fixing a little wooden cross into the ground. They were used to burying dead pigs, calves or sheep but they never got a cross. The tears welled up, she knew it was Jess. Fred saw her and tried to speak but the words wouldn't come out. He saw her tears and he, too, began to sob. Together they finished tidying the grass, saying nothing to each other. It upset the girls terribly; both Sam and Jess were gone, it was the most miserable Christmas ever.

The New Year did nothing to lift the cloud that hung over the family, there was nothing much to look forward to. Lizzy and Mary were kept from school to help with the work. The war was a non starter it seemed. Then rationing came into effect, there were no bread or grocery deliveries. It meant all their provisions had to be fetched from Wellington on Thursday or else Saturday. Dorothy could no longer run her stall. The market was now a food collecting centre. She handled the ration books when they went to town to get their provisions. Fred still slipped off for a pint before loading the float whenever he could but it was still a miserable time, Dorothy grumbled all the way there and all the way back.

All that they produced now had a fixed price. They sold poultry direct to the butcher. The eggs now had to be collected, washed and put in cardboard trays, which then went into wooden crates. These were collected once a week by a van.

They were obliged to complete returns for the Ministry each month. The information they had to give worried Fred, he knew he had to be seen to be doing all that he could to support the war effort. If he could get through the spring he knew he would get help; there was the talk of land girls being sent to work on the farms.

They had heard from the postman that the new tenant at the Wrekin Farm was a Joe Evans and he was already milking several cattle. Fred had noticed the milk lorry now went off up the track after collecting from the platform by the front gate.

A week into January the weather turned bad and overnight several feet of snow fell, all the roads were blocked.

"Looks like we are in trouble this time," Fred said to Mary as he looked through the kitchen window

The girls helped clear the way through the snow to get to the pens. There would be no school again for a while and they had to do so much more. Mary helped with milking the cows; she was slow but it helped save time for her parents.

Lizzy helped with feeding and watering the stock, she was not as sturdy as Mary and felt the cold more. Dorothy did not let her stay out too long. Grace looked after Helen and did household chores while Rebecca and Hannah dealt with the poultry. Dorothy helped Fred with the dairy and tended the sheep. She found she tired easily; she couldn't lift the way Fred could and trudging through snow was heavy work.

The biggest problem was the cold; the temperatures plummeted. They heard later in February that it was the coldest since 1894 and that even the Thames had frozen. All weather news was kept back due to the war.

Fred built a huge wooden box over the pump; it was packed with hay and sacking to keep the pump from freezing.

Night after night the sound of the trains echoed in the woods.

Three days later the milk was building up, they had lost some poultry, several sheep and a calf to the cold. The milk was put in every container and Fred was considering pouring some away. In the mid afternoon Hannah appeared in the stack yard; she had a pair of wellington boots several sizes too big and had clearly fallen over.

"Dad come quick, Mam says you are to come and see."

What on earth! He set off after her as she stumbled through the frozen snow.

She led him round to the garage to where Dorothy was standing. The snow was deep and level; they could just see the top of the hedgerows alongside the road. To their amazement they could see a man astride a tractor at the edge of the wood where the road from the Forest Glen emerged. Snow was being thrown up onto the drifts in front of the tractor.

"Surry they are digging through to us I had better get down there."

He fetched some shovels and with Mary's help they started digging a path through the deep snow. An hour or so later they reached the gate.

They could clearly see that a gang of men were digging a way through throwing the snow either side as they inched forward. Fred stood up on the gate and shouted down to them

"You're doing a grand job have you come for the milk?"

"Aye we have." one shouted back. The snow was over four feet deep between them. Fred sent Mary back to carry on with her work while he started digging towards the men. After a while the men ahead of him disappeared around the back of the tractor and he had to half dig half wade his way through the last few feet. He pushed his way past the Ford tractor to the trailer where the men were sat taking a break. They had a small stove and had brewed tea.

"Surry, you are a sight for sore eyes" said Fred

A heavyset man, clearly the foreman, jumped down "Aye Gaffer, but we have to get through for the milk; can't have you cut off when there's a war to be won."

"Where were you last year when me and my hired hand dug through ourselves?"

"Don't know about that but if you dug it yourselves fair play, it was some achievement! We have been at it two days now, bloody hard going. We will take your milk down with us today but after we have had a break we have to get through to the Evans farm. Can you tell us where it is?"

"Through the wood there," he said pointing.

"Bloody hell, how much further?" he turned to the men on the trailer. "See that gap in the trees over there," they all looked, "well, that's where we are going."

"There is a gate under there that opens onto the track," said Fred pointing at the hedge in front of them. "About twenty foot in front of you where the hedge disappears."

"Right," said the foreman, "Have a brew with us then while you fight your way back we will make a start on that one." We will pick up your churns on the way back. There are a couple of empties under the sheet for you." Fred was enthralled by the tractor, the smell of fuel and oil was strong.

"Surry, she is a beauty," he said.

"Aye, are you still working with horses?" asked one of the men on the trailer.

"Aye, and expect to be for a few years yet."

"Get your subsidies mate and you will soon have one. Don't have to feed it every day, just use it when you want it."

Where is the joy in that? Thought Fred. His horses had personalities; they worked for him willingly. This machine though impressive was soulless. He drank his tea in silence.

Later when the tea was drunk and the men refreshed they gathered in front of the tractor; the foreman stood in the middle

"Right lads, dig!" and they went at it, snow thrown in all directions.

Each day they returned to fetch the milk and they took the eggs when they were ready. Fred had them bring groceries and even the post; he could not afford the time to battle through.

They brought salt and spread it on the road and cleared a way through to Little Wenlock. Soon the milk lorry got through despite the cold.

The news was not good for Britain; shipping was taking heavy losses in the Atlantic; on mainland Europe the British soldiers were waiting alongside the French. There were exchanges of fire with Germany but nothing major.

When the weather picked up the girls went back to school without Mary. She hated seeing the little troop walking down the drive and off up the bank. She had complained to her father repeatedly at first but he had told her to simply wait and see. Now he pointed out to her that there could be help from the land army soon. This pleased her a little but she would be thirteen this year and if the war didn't end she could see herself stuck on the farm; she was by far the sturdiest of all the girls.

Fred really noticed how heavy the work was getting. "Those lasses are worth their weight in gold," he said as he stretched out in front of the range. "I am so tired of fetching and carrying."

"Aye, me too," said Dorothy, "I don't know how we are going to cope come the lambing."

All the extra work and responsibility often caused her to be overtired. When she had gone to the top fields with him to dig some sheep from a snowdrift she was so exhausted by the climb and the cold she passed out, He had to leave the sheep and carry her back to the kitchen and warm her up with hot tea. It was only when he was sure that she was all right that he went back, taking Mary with him this time to rescue the sheep.

Dorothy had also getting little sleep. There was the sow to keep an eye on, she was due to give birth and sometimes if there was no one about she would eat the little ones, pigs were such peculiar animals. The cows too had to be watched in case of a difficult birth. Sometimes the calf would have to be pulled out by its feet because the cow was too exhausted. Dorothy could not rest at such times and would often get up in the night, take the lantern and slip out to check on progress.

Recently she had sat up virtually all night so that Fred could put his head down for an hour or two, only waking him only when necessary. When the girls were rising Dorothy returned to the kitchen completely worn out; Rebecca had started the fire

"Where's Dad?" she asked.

"In the loose box with twin calves, don't bother me. Just get the kettle boiled and shut up."

Dorothy was so overtired she was so short tempered, so the girls knew that it was best to keep out of her way as much as possible and make sure that their work was done.

At the beginning of February Mr Jones called round in his car. He went down to the bottom fields without seeing Fred. When he returned he had mud all up his coat, on his hands and sleeves. His boots were caked with mud making them twice their normal size. Fred mucking out when Mr Jones came into the farmyard saw Fred and said.

"I see what you mean about the wet. I lost my bloody wellington boot trying to get out of that bottom field." Fred couldn't help but laugh.

"You should have let me know you were here I could have warned you."

"Well be that as it may I need a sack to try and get some of this off me before I get back in the car."

"I have heard nothing as yet," said Fred, "what is going on?"

"There are a few irons in the fire. You are not the only farmer round here but do not worry, there will be more help for you later in the year, all being well."

A week later Fred received a letter detailing the results of the Ministry visit. He sat in the kitchen after his breakfast and studied the contents, he whistled softly to himself.

"It says here we can sow spring oats on the one good bottom field and the second field across the road, the one under the Wrekin. Later in the year we can put winter oats on the one halfway up the Willowmoor bank. For every new acre we plough we will get two pounds. We can claim back any money spent on fertiliser. You know, we stand to do all right."

"The money will certainly be very useful, we are almost out of feed again; the cold spell has cost us dear," said Dorothy

"Aye well, there are fixed prices for produce so the market should stay the same, as long as we don't lose much more we should do all right. Some good may come of this war as long as we keep the Germans on the other side of the water."

"Well there are reports of more German aircraft flying over; they could be here before long."

He ignored her concerns, He could see that Willowmoor Farm was about to change for the better. The tenancy rules had been swept aside. He went back to the letter.

"We can have the seed delivered but we will have committed ourselves then. We will have to hope that there isn't too much stone in these fields to be ploughed."

"I don't know if there is enough time to do all of the work as it is," said Dorothy, she was worried that Fred was doing too much. She had not appreciated how strong Sam had been. He made light work of hefting the water and feed and carrying bags. Just shoving a cow out of the way to get through to a trough was hard work for her. Fred did not have Sam's build but he still tried to do the same amount of work. Fred seemed to sense her unease.

"Aye, but if we keep the stock ticking over with the help from the girls and you and I can handle the milking we should be able to get by. We may have to make twice as many trips as Sam would but the result is the same. Come ploughing I am hoping we can get some help from the village. As long as it is not those Bailey boys the girls are always on about," he added.

"Well, I hope we can get through, the subsidy for ploughing will be a great help and if we get paid for the grain as well we can afford to get some help. I hate to say it but this war may do us a lot of good."

Fred thought for a while.

"You are right. Let's get a seed drill now. If there are others doing the same as us then they could be in short supply; are there still sales on in town?"

"Of course." She got up and went to the stack of newspapers and magazines behind Fred's chair

"There was one in last week's Advertiser." She pulled out a paper and went to the kitchen window

"There it is," she said and passed the paper to Fred. "Just up from the bottom," she said, holding her thumb on the column. He saw the advert. "That's it!" he said, "I'll go along to the sale and see if I can buy it

"Don't get too excited, get it first then we can get the seed. Anyway, you shouldn't get too excited we are going to need a binder as well."

"We will have to worry about that when the time comes. I expect that Mr Jones will come up with an idea, it's him that is behind all this."

Fred bought a seed drill from a sale. He had to pay more than he had expected but it was a good one. He tied it to the back of the float with a length of rope to get it home. Dorothy grumbled about the cost, the bills were mounting up.

Mary helped Fred unharness the mare; she was keen to know what the seed drill did. He showed her the wooden box for the seed and the chutes and how the depth was adjusted. "You may get a chance to ride on it one day soon," he said. Mary was pleased, such a responsibility.

"That would be good, maybe I can help fill the box with seed too."

Fred went to the kitchen and lit his pipe.

"I think our Mary is keen on the seed drill, she could probably help out with it." Dorothy was not listening, she was still thinking of the money they had just spent.

"I've told you about tearing those bills up, you know that they have to be paid. A piece off the newspaper would have done to light that pipe of yours. By what I can see in the shops I reckon that it will not be long before there is no tobacco available to be bought for you to smoke."

"Surry Dot, don't you go saying things like that. My bit of tobacco is me only pleasure."

"You talk of pleasures Fred Thomas, what pleasures have I to look forward to? Not many as far as I can see. If this war is not ended quickly it will be Germans coming over the water and killing the lot of us."

"They will never come across the water Dot I reckon they will be stopped before that."

"I only hope that you are right Fred, but none of us can dismiss the possibility. Are you sure you know what you are doing? The work is going to kill us if the Germans don't. We will have lambing to cope with next month, all this extra ploughing and now I can't see us affording to pay anybody to help. What hope have we got?"

"Do not worry lass, this is something we have to do. I will get the seed ordered next time we go down past the Glen. Next time Mr Jones comes around I will ask his advice about the amount of work that has to be done."

Fred could see that she was really worried and knew that there was little that he could do about it. He went and changed into his working clothes. He too had misgivings but kept his thoughts to himself. He knew that he would have to have the girls to help him as this might be the only way to get through.

He would take Mary with him when he next went to the fields to be ploughed.

CHAPTER 2

Help is it hand

One Sunday morning at the beginning of March Lizzy came to work at the Forest Glen as usual. As she hung her coat up Margaret Podmore called out, "Elizabeth, come and sit and have a cup of tea with me before we start work for the day." Lizzy went and sat on one of the chairs at the table. Margaret placed a pot of tea, which she had already made, ready with a plate of toast. She knew that Lizzy would arrive punctually. She was always on time.

"I have been thinking what are you going to do when you officially leave school at Easter?"

"I don't know," Lizzy said, "there is a lot to do at home."

"Well, my husband and I have grown very fond of you and unless you stay at home and work on the farm what else could you do? I would not like to see you having to work in one of those factories making bullets and things." She poured Lizzy a cup of tea and passed the dish of raspberry jam across the table so that she could help herself, which Lizzy did. It was unusual, as the morning break from work was not until eleven o'clock. And then jam was not available, just tea and toast.

Although it was still early in the year customers still came in for afternoon tea. The Podmores main income in the winter months was from dinner dances and wedding receptions.

"My husband and I were thinking, what if you came here to work full time? You would certainly be doing us a favour. What with the forces and the factories taking all our young men and women, it is going to be very difficult for us to get any help."

Margaret made it sound as if Lizzy would be doing them such a favour. But in reality she had thought it out very carefully. Lizzy already knew the running of things and Margaret was pretty sure that she would make a very good waitress. She lived just up the road and walked in so would not require transport like the women who came from Wellington.

Her husband reckoned that there was an opportunity for them to hold dinner dances when they were not doing wedding receptions or special parties. People would look for entertainment to take their minds off the war. With the reputation the Forest Glen had for it's catering he was sure it would be a winner financially.

"Have another cup of tea dear, there is no hurry to start work for a minute or two. Right now we have to give the place a good spring clean before Easter. Perhaps you could talk it over with your mother and see what she says. We would pay you a pound a week and you would get all your food during the daytime, I was thinking you could have all day Tuesday off."

"I will ask tonight when I go home," Lizzy answered enthusiastically. The thought of being paid a pound a week seemed too good to be true and Lizzy did not want to work in a factory or join up for the forces because of the rumours that they could be sent to France to fight the Germans.

Margaret could see by Liz's face that she had taken the bait.

"If your mother and father say that you can come and help us we will register you with the ministry. You will be working for us and then there will no danger of you being called to join the forces or having to go and work in a factory. Now my dear, we must get on or Mrs Green will wonder what we have been doing. I suggest you wash our cups and plates and put them away." She smiled a roguish smile as if to say that they had been very naughty wasting time.

Lizzy was happy throughout the day. She had thought about asking to go full time but had not plucked up the courage to do so. She had made up her mind that she would not stay at home and work for her parents. She knew in her heart that she would never see any pay. Despite all the years of working for her mother she had never been given any pocket money or even a card or present on her birthday, Dorothy had always maintained that she could not afford to throw money away, that having sufficient food and a roof over their heads was enough.

Lizzy helped Mrs Green spring clean what was called the second kitchen and it took them all day. Around five o'clock they had finished, washed dishcloths and dusters were put to dry on the rack that stretched across the big kitchen ceiling. Margaret told them they could both leave early if they wished.

"You never know when I just might want you to stay a little later when we are busy."

Again, she was thinking of herself. One favour deserved another; she would see that Lizzy did not get paid for time not worked.

"Off you go dear before it gets too dark. Thank goodness the evenings are drawing out a little at last. The tea rooms will soon be busy again once the light evenings are here. You too Mrs Green, as soon as my husband returns he will take you back to town."

Lizzy could not wait to get home and ask her Mam and Dad if she could work full time at the Forest Glen. She had been thinking all day how much better it would be to have more money of her own; a whole pound a week. More than she was paid for the two days she worked now.

As she walked home her mind was racing. The first thing she wanted was a bicycle of her own. She had tried riding the bike Sam had used but it was far too big and cumbersome.

She knew there were smaller bikes; she had seen them in the village, girls her build seemed to cope fine. Then there would be no more walking. She would be able to pedal into Wellington. She had never seen the town properly in all the years they had lived there, her mother never let her go. "Well, we will see about that". She said, "I will go on my day off. Oh Lordy, it would be a Tuesday and that was washday.

She thought how best to approach the subject, would it be better to say something as soon as she went in or wait until later in the evening? That would depend on what sort of mood her mother was in. By the time she arrived home she had decided to wait until the little ones were in bed and her Dad had finished outside. If her mother said no her Dad just might stand up for her. It was Sunday and her mother was usually in a good mood after she had listened to the church service on the wireless despite the war still going on.

Helen and Hannah put up no resistance when she prepared them for bed; she washed their hands and faces and checked that their knees and feet were not too dirty. They had been bathed at dinnertime before going to Sunday school. By half past seven they were tired and ready for bed. Grace was in no hurry; she and Rebecca were busy playing snakes and ladders by the light from the lamp on the table. Mary sat opposite them busy knitting mittens on the real knitting needles Lizzy had bought her from the money she had earned at the Forest Glen. Fred had picked them up for her on a market day; she had been so pleased

All was quiet in the kitchen, Fred and Dorothy were sat listening to the wireless.

When she came back from putting Hannah and Helen to bed she decided that if she did not ask now her opportunity would be gone. It would not be long before her mother was ordering the rest of them to get to bed. She went with a jug over to the range to get some warm water to wash the last of the dishes left in the sink. Her mother was poking the fire so she stood and waited Dorothy stopped and looked up. She could see that Lizzy had something on her mind and was dying to speak.

"Mam, Mrs Podmore says I can have a job and work full time at the Glen when I leave school at the end of school term. She said I could train to be a waitress. I was to ask you what you thought and to let her know next weekend. I can, can't I?"

She looked at her standing holding the jug in both hands, a pained look on her thin face. She turned to Fred, he was dozing.

Mary put down her knitting. Grace and Hannah stopped their game.

"Got it all fixed up already have you? What about the work here. I take it you are going to finish the washing up like I told you?"

"Yes Mam, Mrs Podmore said I could be a waitress and wear the black dress and the white lace-trimmed apron and cap. I will have a day off as well. I really want to be a waitress."

Her mother gave the fire a good poke with the poker and adjusted the logs waking Fred...

"We'll have to think this over. What do you say Dad"?

"Aye that's right, think it over," Fred replied, not having heard the conversation but knowing the right response

"What day would you get off? There's still all the washing to do here, the ironing and cleaning as well as little ones to look after. I suppose you will be earning something?" She gave a pause as if she was giving the matter her full attention.

Lizzy was no longer interested in all the work to be done; she had helped with that since she had been old enough to do it.

"I'll tell you what we will do. We will call and have a talk to that Mrs Podmore about you working full time when we come back from shopping on Thursday. Won't we Fred?"

"Aye," said Fred, "that we will on Thursday, no mistake."

Dorothy sat back and Lizzy got her water, she was shaking.

"Look what you are doing, and you three get on with what you are doing or go to bed."

Later, when Mary and Lizzy retired, "I hope they will let me work all week when I leave school, there is little else to do. I can earn real wages."

"And what would you do with it?" asked Mary.

"New clothes and shoes, real girl's shoes and perhaps a bicycle."

"You've got big ideas. I doubt if Mam is going to let you get out of working here, we are all up to our necks with work trying to keep going without Sam."

Mary was not the least bit enthusiastic; she was so tired working out of doors every day. The only break was when she got an occasional day at school and then there were all the taunts from the other children. She was not paid anything for the work she did and probably never would be.

Again, the only bicycle available was her mother's old one. She could not even reach the seat to practice.

As soon as the girls had gone to bed Dorothy filled Fred in on what had transpired.

He was pleased; he had realized that something major had occurred as he woke.

"She should go. She will do well down there," he said.

"We will see, let's not get ahead of ourselves, I need her help here."

They called in at the Forest Glen on Thursday after shopping in town.

Margaret Podmore made them welcome, taking them into the tearoom and having tea brought by one of the waitresses.

Fred had spoken to Lizzy; he thought how nice she would look in the uniform.

It was agreed Lizzy would start work at the end of the current school term. This would suit the Podmores as she would be there for the Easter trade.

Margaret was delighted. She watched as they went on their way then she went into the kitchen to give her husband the good news and tell the other staff. Lizzy was such a hard worker and popular with everyone.

Dorothy had moaned to Fred as he drove the mare and float home.

Dorothy had secretly hoped Lizzy would stay at home after finishing school and carry on working in and around the house. As they made their way up the road she said, "Well, I suppose she will be earning a bit towards her keep and will be all right with the Podmores. I suppose it will be better than us having to keep and provide for her."

Fred was taken aback.

"Working at the Glen will mean that we won't be seeing much of her and we won't be keeping her that much either," he protested.

"We've still got to give her a roof over her head," Dorothy argued back.

"That isn't going to cost that much is it? Leave her be and let's see how it goes. She certainly is not cut out for farm work like Mary. She has no meat on her bones to speak of and I don't want her working in one of those factories."

"But who is going to do the housework?" she asked.

Fred bit his lip, "Look, she will have her own money. A bit can come to us for her keep. She will keep herself in clothes and the Podmores will look after her while she is there."

"That will help a bit I suppose, one less for me to worry about," she gave in

"Worry about!" thought Fred, "you have not worried about Lizzy for a long time. Not since she was a little one and could earn her keep, you've never let her know anything else but work."

"Well, I think Helen can start helping a little more soon."

"She is not even four yet!" he said.

"Well, we'll see. She could start school next spring rather than September. I can do with her help doing a bit of running and carrying for me."

"Aye Dot, you could be right, she is not very big though."

Fred had enough on his plate without arguing with Dorothy about when Helen should start school.

As the weather picked up there was a further visit from the Ministry men Fred had seen in December. They asked him if he had seen Mr Jones and whether he was going to proceed. He took them and proudly showed them the seed drill.

"Very good, you have done well to get one so good and so soon."

"You couldn't have a word with the bank manager for me could you?" he said jokingly.

"That is not our concern Mr Thomas." one of them said.

"It was a joke," said Fred.

"Indeed, well we think you should start ploughing as soon as possible. Mr Jones will be in touch." The seed was delivered and stored in the granary.

Fred was quite excited. He made sure Bonny and Kit were well fed; he would need them soon.

Midway through March Mr Jones turned up unexpectedly with a Ministry man called Clews. Jingo met them at the garage, barking furiously. "Shut up!" said Mr Jones and walked on. Jingo followed behind. Mary was on the back yard, she had been feeding pigs when she had heard the dog barking.

"Shouldn't you be at school?" Clews asked.

"Yes, but my Dad needs me here seeing as how Sam had to go and fight."

"Who is Sam?" asked Clews looking at Mr Jones.

"The hired hand, it's left them struggling a bit."

"Tell your father we are looking around and not to bother coming, we will find him later."

She nodded. People don't normally just walk around the farm so she went and told Fred straight away.

"What is it?" Dorothy wanted to know.

"Jones and the Ministry back again, told Mary that they will see me later."

"They have a nerve, whose farm is this anyway?"

"Best not antagonize them lass, they may help us out."

An hour later the Ministry man wandered down the cowshed.

Dorothy had gone to do the dairy and to keep an eye on Helen.

"Morning," he said, "Don't mind me." He stood and watched as Fred finished the last cow.

"I see you have the seed already Mr Thomas."

"Yes, but as you can see we are short handed at the moment."

"Well, that is sort of why I want a word," he said, "when you have finished join us back at the front gate; we are parked there. Try not to be too long."

"Cheeky beggar!" said Fred after he had left.

Nevertheless he hurried and was down at the gate fifteen minutes later.

The two men were sat in the car eating sandwiches.

"Breakfast," said Mr Jones. "Aye, I've not had mine yet," said Fred.

Well, we had best not keep you. We are setting up a camp for German prisoners of war down the road at Cluddely. It will be one of many such camps to be set up."

"What! Bring the Gerry's that close to us. Is that wise?"

"They are prisoners and under guard. They are to be given work to do and will be ideal as agricultural labour. As I see it they could be put to work draining that bottom field and then we could get some cereal on it."

"What sort of cereal are you talking about?" Fred knew that there would be a good subsidy for ploughing that field.

"Winter oats if it dries out properly."

"I don't know if I can cope with the ploughing on my own."

"You have some time till you sow," said Mr Clews, "you see there is a pressing need to improve our output. The country will need all it can get. There is little coming in with the U-boats sinking so many of our ships. You must make a start as soon as you can; your horses seem in good fettle. You are in for a very busy year Mr Thomas."

Mr Jones spoke up, "I will see you get the first available labour. I think you are only just coping."

"Aye, they took our hired hand last November. We can't cope without keeping the girls from school."

"So we have seen. But if you pull it off, the subsidies will be well worth it. You can improve your lot considerably."

"Aye, I understand you but I don't think the missus would have Gerry's on the bank."

"Your wife will have no choice," said Mr Clews, "and they would be well supervised. There would be no running away into the woods. Anyway, the camp is ready; the first batch should arrive in the next week or so."

"We've been wondering what was being built down the road there. Now we know."

Mr Clews went round the car to the driver's door; he opened it then leant on the roof. "You give this matter a lot of thought, Mr Thomas. They could drain more than one field for you when they arrive. What I have seen here today is promising; we need all the help we can get if we are to get through this war. By the way, have you met Mr Evans, your new neighbours yet?"

"No, been too busy."

"Well, we are off up to his place now," said Mr Jones opening his door. "He has a lot to cope with as well. As for the prisoners, you are not going to have any choice in the matter." He handed Fred some paperwork and forms.

"We must be on our way now. Good luck!" he said and got in. Mr Clews nodded.

"Would you be so kind as to open the gate for me? Saves on petrol you know."

"Aye, gladly," He said and he walked across the road and let them out.

Fred waited till Mary was out of the way before he raised the idea of German prisoners working on the farm.

Dorothy did not respond at first, then she said, "Well, let's think about it, you can't do any more than what you are doing now Fred Thomas. If we agree to them coming and draining the field, what happens then?" They had already agreed to produce cereal crops but with Sam gone he was working too hard. And the thought of German prisoners on the bank was cause for great concern.

"If they were able to do some of the heavy work it would help. You're worn out Fred. Worn out you are. They will be supervised no doubt and they won't have to be any trouble to us."

Fred told her what he had been told by Mr Jones.

"We've no choice lass but to do as we are told. They said they will give us some more help as soon as possible. I think we have to show willing; there are good subsidies to be had at the end of it."

At the thought of getting some help on the farm, she was all for the idea.

"I will go along with what you say but are we taking on too much Fred?" she asked, concerned, "we've only the girls you know, and a hard winter could cripple us."

"Well, we are going to have to try, as I see it we've no choice else if we don't co-operate they will turn us out on the road."

"They can't do that can they?"

"Aye, they can. Remember we are only tenants and after all the country is at war. You had better fill those forms in for us," he said, pointing to the forms he had placed on the table. "Send Lizzy to post them at the Glen."

Fred was tired. He felt the burden of responsibility weighing him down. There were days when he was worn out through working from morning to bedtime.

Dorothy lost no time filling the forms and sending them off. She was aware this would be a tremendous boost for them financially and also with her parents. Cereal production, who would have thought it?

When Mr Jones received notification that the Willowmoor Farm was to be given priority he was pleased, he remarked to his wife, "Here's another one that has seen sense, I am worried how we are going to get him suitable help though and he only has his wife and daughters. Mind you, the one we met seemed capable, not far off a land girl already. I think what Fred Thomas and others are beginning to realize is that if they do not do as asked we will take the farm from them and turn them out onto the road. We will put somebody in who will get on with producing what we need."

"Can you really do that, turn a hard working farmer out on the road?" asked his wife.

"We sure can and we will. It is our job to get the food grown, Thank goodness we have a few old chaps around here to give a hand with the work we have here."

On a Monday morning at the end of March an army lorry pulled up at the back gate of the farm. It was only eight o'clock in the morning. Fred and Dorothy were milking, Mary was outside feeding and Lizzy was in charge of getting the others off to school.

Grace had spotted the lorry parked at the back gate from the bedroom window. She called Hannah and they went to the window in their mother's bedroom where they had a clear view of the scene. A car pulled up and two men got. They went to the front gate and walked towards the farmhouse. One wore an army uniform and carried a briefcase. The other they recognized as Mr Jones.

"This looks official," said Grace.

"What is in the lorry do you think?" asked Hannah

"I don't know. Mary said we will see some men here soon to dig ditches, perhaps it is them."

"Get down the stairs," shouted Lizzy from the bottom of the stairs, "we've got to go to school." She ran back to the kitchen where she had just finished preparing their sandwiches and a breakfast of bread and warm milk but now with hardly any sugar. She had to make sure that Grace, Hannah and Helen were washed and dressed and had clean faces. The girls did not go to school as neat and tidy as they used to, Dorothy had no time to worry about darning socks or if they had washed behind their ears. Instead she was helping with the outside work more and more. The girls were terrified in case Miss Evans carried out her threat to sow carrot seed in their dirty ears.

Rebecca and Mary were still outside. Mary was feeding the stock. She would not be going to school again today. They were going to try and shift some muck later on. Rebecca could see to herself, she was always ready on time.

Lizzy was rushing about in the kitchen when there came a knock at the back door. She stopped what she was doing and hastened to answer it. The two men were taken aback as she opened the door too quickly, causing it to bang against the mangle. The farmhouse had looked calm and serene when they walked up the drive and onto the backyard, not even the collie dog to greet them.

Now they were faced with a young girl who looked as if she had the worries of the world on her shoulders.

"You'll find me Mam and Dad milking. Go round to the side." She pointed them in the general direction of the cowshed; she shut the door on them once again far too quickly. They looked at each other, smiled and set off to find Fred.

Hannah and Grace came down to the kitchen bringing Helen with them.

"There's a big lorry at the gate," said Hannah.

"Just eat your breakfasts and let us get to school please," said Lizzy.

Rebecca came in. "That Mr Jones is here. The one Mary goes on about. He is with a soldier as well, an officer; I think he has a gun. I've just seen it, there could be something going on."

"There is a lorry at the gate," said Lizzy, "get your breakfast and let's get moving."

They all sat and ate then each of them got their coats, scarves, gas masks and bags and stood by the back door.

"Come on Helen!" Lizzy said, taking the child by the hand, "I will be glad when you can come with us."

"You three wait on the back yard for me. We have to get going now or we will be late. Come on Helen, I am taking you to sit in the cow shed until Mam's finished milking. Helen was reluctant to go, she sensed something was happening; the other three were peering through the small kitchen window. "Get moving," Lizzy said and led Helen off to the cow shed.

She sat Helen down on a bundle of hay out of harm's way then went along the shed to find her mother, the smell of dung heavy in the air; there was no sign of the men or her Dad. She found her mother sat between two cows, head bowed busy milking. She was also muttering to herself.

"Mam" Lizzy called. Her mother made no reply.

"Mam!" she shouted loudly.

Her mother glanced round. "What do you want here?" she said abruptly.

"We're off to school now Mam, here is Helen."

"Helen, where? Where've you put her? You stupid girl"

Lizzy was taken aback by her mother's response.

"By the door, down the other end, she is sat on some hay. I have put her coat on her to keep her warm." she replied.

"Good. Those German prisoners are here to start work, who would have believed it?" She stood up and picked up the milking stool. She looked down the cowshed to see Helen sitting quietly alone. She shook her head. "Your Dad's gone off with Mr Jones and that other fellow you sent round. Have you seen them? What do they look like? Are there soldiers with them?"

"Who do you mean, the two men?" Lizzy replied, not knowing where her mother was going with the conversation.

"I mean the Germans, girl. The prisoners. Have you seen them?" her mother snapped.

"No we haven't. They might be in the lorry that is parked at the end of the drive."

"I don't know! Are the rest of you ready for school or are the others messing about gawping through the window looking at them? Are they?"

"We're ready and going now Mam," Lizzy replied.

"Well get off with you then and stop wasting time. I don't know when your Dad is coming back to get this milking finished. I suppose it will be me who will have it all to do. We're running late as it is. Find Mary and tell her to get here, she can milk a couple, it won't hurt her,"

Lizzy turned and ran down the cowshed trying not to step in the cow muck. She paused as she passed Helen to check that her coat was buttoned properly to keep her warm. She stood on the edge of the yard and called "Maaaary" as loudly as she could, then again. "Maaaaaaary." There was a reply, "whaaaaaaaaat?" it came from the stackyard. She ran and met Mary coming out with a bundle of hay in her arms.

Mam wants you to go help with the milking now. I have to get off to school, the others are waiting. There are prisoners at the back gate."

"Terrific," said Mary, "that's all I need," and dropped the hay where she stood.

Lizzy shot off around the farmyard back to the house to get the other girls moving.

Mary walked round to the cowshed; her mother was waiting for her.

"They could have waited till the afternoon to bring prisoners here," she said to Mary when she arrived.

"Are they German?" asked Mary.

"We will see in a while, now have a go on that one there," she said, pointing to a cow which was quiet and yet to be milked.

"Hold that bucket tight with your knees girl in case they kick. We can't afford to lose the milk."

Mary shuffled off to the cow as told while Dorothy carried the full buckets around to the dairy.

What a sight they must have looked; four girls, the oldest not yet fourteen, the youngest seven; as they walked from the gate and past the lorry. They stopped to watch as men in grey cotton jackets and trousers climbed down from the lorry. A man in army uniform carrying a rifle said, "Good morning ladies."

The girls were silent.

"Stand well back, you are quite safe," he said. He held his rifle across his chest, finger by the trigger

The men in grey were lined alongside the lorry. Most of them wore big black boots. Hannah had never seen such big boots. They were being passed spades, long handled shovels and other tools; none of them looked their way.

"Look at those funny hats they are wearing," said Hannah.

"Stop gawping!" Lizzy reprimanded, "Come on and get up that bank."

One of the men turned around to take something off the lorry, revealing a big round patch that was sewn to the back of his jacket. The patch had a number on it.

"Look, he's got a number," squealed Hannah.

"They are prisoners," Rebecca said.

"So that's what prisoners look like," Grace muttered to Rebecca.

"Come on or you will be late." Lizzy was losing her temper. At that the girls ran as fast as they could until halfway up the bank. Only then did they dare to look around to make sure they were not being chased by the men in strange looking clothes.

"What are they going to do?" Hannah wanted to know.

"Work in the fields," Rebecca answered.

"Never mind them, did you let those hens out in the stackyard and give them a bit of corn?"

"Of course we did, and let the ducks go as well as the geese."

"Come on you lot. Stop talking, you are all going to be late," Lizzy shouted.

At the start of every school day a hymn was sung and prayers spoken. The whole class had to recite the Lord's Prayer. And only then could they sit back at their desks, Miss Evans would start the rest of the day, standing in front of the class and asking if there was any news the children had that may be of interest to the rest f the class. It was possible that a child may have seen or heard something that may be important to the war effort. Has any one of you anything new to report.

There was silence then nervously Lizzy raised her hand.

"Have you something important to tell us Elizabeth?" Miss Evans inquired.

"I don't really know if it is important," Lizzy whispered. The whole class was looking at her.

"Well, what is it girl, speak up!"

"A big lorry brought a load of German prisoners to work for my Dad this morning."

"This sounds interesting class," she said going to the blackboard. "And what do these prisoners look like?" She wrote, "German Prisoners of War" on the board in bold letters.

"I don't really know," Lizzy whispered, "I did not get a good look at them."

"Big and strong with big black boots, miss," Rebecca blurted out. Normally Miss Evans would have scolded Rebecca for speaking up for her sister but not today.

She was unaware of this turn of events. Everyone now knew the new camp at Cluddely was for housing prisoners. It was not top secret but for them to be out and about was worrying.

"Why are German prisoners on your farm and who is in charge? Surely they are under guard?"

Lizzy spoke again with more confidence.

"Mr Jones arranged for them to come. He has been around before. There are soldiers with them with guns. We are going to have ditches dug and drains put in miss," Lizzy was gaining her confidence.

"This is news indeed," she wrote 'under armed guard' and 'laying drains'.

The class was silent. Mrs Evans knew that there had only been conflict at sea. So far despite the large number of British soldiers in France there had been only one casualty and no reports of prisoners. It was becoming known as the Phoney war.

"But where have they come from?" she asked. "Do they have uniforms?"

"Sort of. Grey with a big yellow circle on the back and a number. They were in the back of a lorry and they have spades to dig with miss."

"Where have they come from?" she asked as she wrote 'Prison Uniforms' on the board.

"We don't know miss," said Lizzy.

"They will not hurt us because there are soldiers guarding them and if they try to run away they will be shot miss," added Rebecca.

"Shot! Indeed so they should be. Thank you Rebecca Thomas."

She then gave the class a lesson on the Geneva Convention and the Red Cross organisation.

At playtime one of the Bailey boys said, "Gerry lovers," as he bumped into Rebecca

After break when Hannah sat at her desk Danny leant over and whispered, "You have Germans on your farm?"

"Yes," whispered Hannah.

"Oh, wait till I tell my Mam."

"You be quiet Danny Probin. Mrs Hayward is watching us."

At lunchtime and in the afternoon there were more remarks from the boys. Danny pestered Hannah; he wanted to know if the officer carried a revolver and what kind of rifle the soldiers had.

As Lizzy and Rebecca walked into the playground to wait for Grace and Hannah they were set upon. "You've got Gerries on your farm," shouted one of the bigger lads.

"Yes, so what?" said Rebecca.

"You have brought them here. We don't want them; they should be sent somewhere else."

One of the Bailey boys stepped up and pushed Lizzy; a crowd was gathering.

"It must be because you are mates with them. I bet you think Hitler is great, don't you?"

Lizzy ran followed by Rebecca out through the gate and up the road.

"Go on, run away Gerry lovers," shouted the louts, then they spotted Hannah and Grace walking out.

"You scruffy Thomas are Gerry lovers," said one and the crowd turned on them.

The poor girls had their shins kicked and hair pulled. The Bailey boys were the worst.

"Leave them alone or I will cane the lot of you!" It was Miss Evans. She pushed the trouble makers aside. "Who started this?" she demanded.

"They are Gerry lovers. Got Germans working for them," sneered one of the lads.

She rounded on him.

"Dan Bailey! Inside! Three strokes for you." She turned on the group, now shamefaced.

"You will leave these girls alone. Their farm needs work and if our officials chose to help this way we must support them, however strange it may seem. Any one of you I catch picking on them will get the same as Dan Bailey. Get off home you two," she said and hit a boy across the head, "Get out of their way you." She shoved a boy in the back and the girls ran out of the playground.

Once they were well out of reach of the boys, Hannah told Grace, "Wait till I see Danny, I will kick him under the desk for this." They could see Lizzy and Rebecca waiting for them.

"And a fat lot of use those two were. They ran off and left us."

"Those Bailey boys are horrid; I hope they get blown up by a bomb." Said Hannah."

"Those sort never do," said Grace, "they seem to get away with murder."

"I wish they would come down and try to steal from Dad, and then he could have an excuse to shoot them."

"That would be bad; it would mean that he would have to go to prison for the rest of his life or at the worst be hanged for murder."

"He could just shoot their legs then."

"Yes, that would be good."

They told their parents of the problem when they returned. Fred was angry, "Well, these prisoners have started on digging in drains so we can plant on the bottom fields. That will bring more grain for the country. You tell your Miss Evans to sort them Bailey boys or I will come up myself. There is enough to do, they should get on and help instead of poaching other folk's stuff."

The girls were surprised. Rebecca told Miss Evans the following day what her father had to say.

"He is quite right. I have had time to think and it is good that these prisoners are putting something back for all the harm they have done. Today I am going to teach how we must make use of them and get more from the land."

Dan Bailey stayed well away from the girls at playtime but they still felt threatened.

Fred and Dorothy decided that Lizzy would work full time at the Forest Glen when she officially left school at the end of the spring term.

Lizzy was so excited she could hardly wait until she went back to work on Saturday morning. She had missed so much school there was no chance of her being the nurse she had always wanted to be. "I'm not brainy enough," she complained to Mary when they had been sharing confidences.

The prisoners came every day to lay the drains. It was slow going due to the wetness of the ground and it would be next year before the fields could be used. The family got used to the lorry arriving each morning and leaving at five in the evening. They dug a fairly deep trench down the centre of a field and then they dug shallow ones all leading from the outside edges into the centre of the field, forming a herringbone pattern. Drainpipes were stacked by the gate ready for laying.

As soon as he could Fred got some muck onto the fields He was eager to start ploughing so he made a point of walking them whenever possible. When the top fields were dry enough to take the weight of the horses he made a start. It was the Easter break for the girls and Lizzy had started work. He was keen to start on the fields allocated which had not been ploughed before as they would bring the subsidy but they were too wet. Each decent day as soon as the dairy was done and the churns at the gate he would harness the horses and make a start. He left all other work for Dorothy and the girls to take care of. He would not return until teatime. Mary had the majority of the work to do as usual. She was given all the heavy jobs; mucking out, lugging feed and water. The others helped; Hannah liked feeding the calves best of all and would often tag along with Mary when she had to walk the fences around the woods to check that there were no holes the sheep might squeeze through. If they found a hole, they cut hawthorn branches and filled it in. Fetching provisions still had to be done but there was no time for tea at Sidoli's café or a pint in the pub, that day was for catching up around the farm.

When Dorothy prepared dinner she made up a meal to be taken to Fred in the field. She sent separate basins for meat, vegetables and pudding; each had a saucer placed on top to keep the heat in. There was a bottle of tea for him to drink. While they were off school one of the youngsters got to take it to him. Hannah did not mind taking the dinner to the fields; she would sit on the grassy hedge growth alongside her father and watch as he ate his dinner. She would chat away and then when he had finished he would light his pipe and talk to her for a while before she returned to get her own dinner, which would be in the oven.

The horses also enjoyed the break; it gave them a chance to have a bite to eat off the grassy verge. When Fred and the horses were rested it was back to work for them until they returned so he could begin milking. It was Mary and Hannah's job to fetch the cows in and tie them ready for when he returned. Then they took the harness off the horses and turned them out into the field, while their father started the milking. Hannah could not reach to take the bridles and collars off, so she had to climb in a manger to do it; the girls had no fear of the horses.

After milking Fred was usually so exhausted he fell asleep in the chair while everyone else listened to the wireless. Up until early April the war had mainly been focused on Russia's battle with Finland but now Germany had moved on Norway and the British stirred. In the second week there were clashes at sea and the RAF went on the attack. On the fifteenth, news was broadcast of British troops landing in Norway.

"I wonder if Sam is there," said Mary.

"It is very cold but he would soon get used to it," said Grace.

There was so much work to do around the farm the girls were finding it hard going. Mary was washing out the dairy when her mother came in with two blue and white enamel jugs to collect milk for use in the house. "When Dad has finished the top field will he come and give us a hand with some of this work," Mary asked.

"I really don't know," Dorothy replied

Mary threw another bucket of water on the floor and swept it out. "There seems to be no end to all this work. What next is to be done?"

"I will ask him when he comes in tonight, that is if he can stay awake long enough for me to get an answer." She scooped out some milk from a churn and returned to the house. That night Fred was exhausted, Dorothy waited till he was relaxed then asked. "What do you have to do next?"

"I will carry on the top getting the ground ready while the weather holds; we will get lambing over then I will plough the Slang under the Wrekin."

The sheep began lambing and there was little sleep to be had. Mary and Hannah were made to count and check on them every night. Even so Dorothy still asked Fred if he had checked them before she would sit down and relax for the evening. They were always in bed by nine unless there was a crisis with the stock but lambing could keep them up all night. Fred could get little ploughing done until the lambing was finished.

Jingo followed the girls everywhere they went. They had to be careful if a cow had left the herd to give birth. She was liable to charge at the dog and if she did charge, the dog would always run and hide behind whoever was fetching the cows in to be milked. Fred had warned them of this, telling them that it was better to leave the newly calved cow until later and not to go near if they had the dog with them. It had been known to prove fatal to quite a few farmers. In the animal world mothers were very protective of their young and a cow that was usually very docile could turn into a killer.

The top fields had been ploughed in the past but there was always stone to be removed. Fred took extra care to remove obstructions before sowing. As soon as the weather was suitable and the ground was rolled and prepared he took the seed and seed drill to begin. He had let Mary practice leading the horses while he was with her and so while he steered the drill she led the horse up and down the field. He had to keep the box from getting low on seed and make sure the nozzles did not block or get stones jammed between them.

Eventually the field was sown. As they prepared to leave the field he put his arm around Mary's shoulder. "Lass, we have done a grand job. This is the first time oats have been grown here. We should see a good return later in the year as long as the war doesn't change things."

The trenches were being steadily dug across the fields; the first pipes were going in.

Fred had to begin ploughing the field across the road for his root crops. This would be the first of the ground that would bring the subsidy. He had a quiet word in the horse's ear before starting. From the start it was clear he had a problem. The ground was very stony. He had hardly started when the plough was suddenly deflected by a large rock. He was severely jarred and had to wait for the pain to subside. The horses waited patiently as he wrestled the plough out of the furrow.

"Surry that hurt!" He looked at the rock in the ground; it was not huge but enough to cause a problem. He had walked all over the field beforehand as was usual to check for holes the horses might step in. He shifted in front of the rock and with a shout the horses set off again. The plough was pitched left and right as it struck stones and before he had made twenty feet he struck another large rock.

When Mary brought his dinner she could see he was having trouble.

While Fred ate she walked along the furrows. She picked up a couple of small rocks and returned to where he sat.

"This is bad isn't it Dad? There are stones everywhere."

"Aye lass, I feel like I have been through a mincer and I think it is all going to be the same." He struggled on through the afternoon the girls stopped to see him on their way back from school. Fred gave up for the day and they all walked back to the farmyard.

He told Dorothy of the problem and that he would persevere for a while.

"Well, don't you overdo it," she said, "rauling that plough is hard work?"

For the next week with only the day off to fetch provisions he toiled at the plough, Mary had to help milk so he could get to the field earlier.

Joe Evans from the Wrekin Farm stopped by on his way to town.

"How is it going?" he said.

"Very slow, the rock and stone is making this hard work I have never ploughed anything this bad."

"Aye, I am the same, nothing much has been done with this ground for years. We will earn our subsidies by the time we are through."

"Do you have any help?" Fred asked.

"Aye, my son. But you seem to have no help. How so?"

"They took my help Sam to fight last year, only got me daughters now."

"Bloody hell. I'd like to help you but I am in the same boat. I am struggling to get the ground broken; I am dragging a lot out with chains."

"That's the next thing for me to do."

Joe went on his way. Fred was disappointed when he had come across, he was sure he was going to offer some help. He would pay for someone to help right now but paying for the seed and the drill on top of a bad winter had left them in a bad way. He had lost lambs and it would a while before their finances were back on track.

After days of breaking up the ground Fred had done half the field. He took a break; the weather was too wet to continue.

It was then that the news was broadcast that Germany had moved against Holland, Luxembourg and Belgium. "Well we can forget about this being a phoney war now. France could be next."

"Aye, and then us. They have dropped soldiers by parachute in Holland. What is to stop them doing the same here?" grumbled Dorothy.

"What does this mean for us, Dad," asked Mary.

"I think it proves we were right not to trust Hitler. Sinking our ships was bad but he has been planning this for ages. I don't think it will stop yet but we have problems of our own. Right now we are going to have to get the rock out of that field if we are going to be able to use the seed drill. I will start to clear what I've ploughed and see how it goes."

Dorothy had seen what he was dealing with.

"What say the girls all stay off for a day or two and help out? We have the buckets. And some of the heavier pieces can be dragged out by Bonny."

Fred looked at the girls. He thought for a moment. "I know you need your schooling but I need to get these fields ready for sowing. If the weather is good tomorrow we will do as your Mam says."

The next day was fine, much to the girls' dismay. They had to dress in their working clothes and go across to the field with their buckets as soon as they had finished helping Mary with her chores. They trooped through the farmyard and down to the back gate. Dorothy did not like them staring at the prisoners.

They had to walk along the furrows collecting stones in their buckets then emptying them in the hedge.

Fred came along later with iron bars, chains and a spade. Between them they levered the big rocks up and put the chains around it then Bonny dragged it to the outside of the field.

With just a break for dinner they carried on all day. Dorothy brought Helen across in the afternoon and joined in.

That night as they sat at the table with legs and backs aching they heard that Britain had a new government. Chamberlain, who for so long had tried to maintain the peace had resigned, Winston Churchill was Prime Minister. For the next few days the girls stayed off school. Fred harrowed the ground bringing more stone to the surface which they cleared piece by piece.

In the evenings and mornings the wireless was switched on so they could gather the news. It was bad; not only had Britain pulled out of Norway but as British troops were moving with the French to support the hard pressed Belgians and Dutch the Germans smashed into France from the East at the same time, after being bombed mercilessly, Holland capitulated.

"What does that mean Dad?" asked Grace.

"They have surrendered lass; add another one to Hitler's list." The Germans had devastated Rotterdam from the air

"We had better stock up by the sound of it," said Dorothy, "we are short of stuff anyway. Should have gone today."

"Aye, we will go down tomorrow. I think we have done well; I want to call in on Joe Drury and set up a date for dipping those sheep."

"I had not forgotten," Dorothy said, "I thought it best not to meither you with it just yet."

He got up from the table and stretched, the wireless was talking of fighting and bombing.

He lit his pipe and stood warming his back by the fire. "You girls can go to school tomorrow. It is Friday but at least you will have shown your faces."

"Can't we stay at home and have a rest?" asked Grace.

"No you can't. Day off indeed!" said Dorothy.

The next day it rained so anyway the field was too wet for them.

"Marvellous!" said Grace as they trudged to school, "now I will be damp all morning, they could have let us stay at home today."

"I don't want to stay at home," said Hannah, "I want to go to a big school. Mary did too, but now she has no chance."

"None of us may have a chance the way this war is going," said Rebecca.

Mrs Hayward was pleased to see Hannah, she was sure she would do well.

Danny wasted no time in telling her his version of the German attacks.

"Blitzkrieg, lightning war," Danny told her. His father had gone to work at High Ercall and Danny was worried they might have to move.

In the afternoon there was air raid practice. "Especially for you Thomas girls," said Mrs Hayward to Hannah.

Fred and Dorothy did not stay long in town. There were even more sandbags in front of important buildings and they had every window was taped up. Dorothy couldn't see what all the fuss was about and she never even got the tape.

And so as the weeks continued the girls helped carry the stones to the hedge whenever they were free. As the nights drew out they carried on into the dusk; they had some help from two men who cycled past after finishing work in town, they helped for a couple of hours before going on their way. All the effort paid off. The ground was cultivated and despite heavy showers the field was harrowed and rolled ready for sowing at the end of May. Fred was keeping an ear to the wireless whenever he could; the British were fighting in France again. Air attacks on English towns now began in Yorkshire and Essex causing Dorothy great concern; she made the girls carry their gas masks everywhere they went.

"I am not taking mine into the lavvy," said Grace, "it will get mucky, and it is horrible in there."

"Put it on, it will help with the smell," said Mary, laughing.

Grace thought on that for a while. The next time she went she put her mask on before she sat on the hole. She tapped her heels and hummed but before long she was steamed up and the rubbery smell was making her feel sick. In future it stayed outside the door unless it was raining.

The sheep had to be dipped ready for shearing and so with the field finished, Fred had the girls take a day off to help with herding them to John Drury's. It was a welcome break and an adventure as all the girls went along and even a few locals joined in, blocking off entrances. They all had their gas masks with them and any planes flying overhead made them nervous. Fred met a Mr York when the sheep were being pushed through the water. He offered to come and help with the shearing. He was too old to do heavy work but he could turn the handle and help with the fleeces.

In the evening the news of the Belgian surrender shocked Fred. He had been particularly interested as the British were fighting with the French and Belgians in places he had been himself in the Great War. He was expecting the armies to dig in as before but now the British were wide open to attack from north and south. They were pulling back to the coast.

The Germans had reached Boulogne and Calais already.

To take his mind off things Fred got the muck shifted off the farmyard and prepared for sowing the potatoes. He made sure they went to town when it was wet so the day wasn't wasted. Dorothy was not impressed. The old tarpaulin draped over them did nothing for her appearance as they plodded through the town.

On the Saturday the weather was fine and Fred had arranged help through the two men who had helped in the previous weeks. Ben arrived early; he was keen to help with the milking so Fred left him with Dorothy and Mary to carry on while he got the bags of seed potatoes across the road to the field. He was pleased that for once he did not have to worry about Dot lifting the buckets of milk. He placed the bags at intervals around the headland then went back to fetch the ridging plough. Later, the second of the two men arrived with some lads from Little Wenlock, each brought a bucket. Fred had made a good start; the ridging plough cut a deep furrow. The girls came across to help, they recognized the boys. "That's Billy Jones and his stupid brother," said Rebecca.

"And George Stapleton; his sister sits in the next desk from me," said Grace.

"I know him, he is in my class and he smells."

"I wonder if Danny is going to come down?" said Hannah.

"I doubt it, probably off flying Spitfires with his Dad from what you've told us."

Each girl had a bucket and along with the others they put as many seed potatoes in it as they could carry. Then they had to walk between the ridges their father had made with the plough putting a seed potato at a distance of every two shoe lengths. The furrows were so narrow in the bottom the soil would fall off the ridge into their shoes and make it hurtful to walk. They had to persevere, often emptying their shoes when they refilled their buckets. When a length of field was completed, Fred would return and split the ridge, covering the potatoes, safe from the crows and pigeons hovering in the trees nearby.

When it was time for a break the girls sat with the village boys. It was quite a social occasion. The boys had brought lunch with them.

"So, is all this land yours?" asked Billy.

"Of course didn't you know?"

"Well, sort of but I never seen you here, always passing through see. How come you're so scruffy then," he said with a grin.

I'll lay you out with this bucket," said Mary.

He put his hands up

"Just teasing'"

"Give us a drink of your tea," said Grace.

"Get your own."

And so the banter continued until Fred stirred the horses. Nothing was said but everyone returned to work.

That evening the girls retired to the far room. They had lots to talk over, the day had been really good and they had laughed and joked like never before.

Lizzy joined them and she too had to laugh.

"Are they coming back?" she asked Mary.

"I doubt it, but you never know we need the help right now."

Fred and Dorothy listened to the radio. The evacuation of the British troops from Dunkirk was well underway despite repeated attack.

"Poor beggars, what a way to come home," said Fred. "This past month has certainly been bad as far as the war is concerned."

"Aye, and it's getting worse but we have to think of ourselves. There's the sheep to shear and the hay to get in soon, we couldn't have got this lot done today without the help."

"Aye, I will start on the hay as soon as I can. We still have swedes to get in around the edge of the top field and maybe a strip or two of mangolds."

Mr Jones called in to see how the work was progressing. He came early to be sure of catching Fred before he went up the fields.

Mary carried on milking while the two men went to see how the drains were coming on.

"Doing a grand job they are," said Fred as they watched the water tricking from the newly laid pipes. The soil was drying out from the winter much quicker than it would have done in previous years.

"I reckon you could be turning this over next year. But for now I want to see more root crops on the field across the road and then you can plough some more up the back and that half field on the top of the bank."

"Are you sure?" said Fred. The ploughing was wearing him out and he was having second thoughts. "That field has been so difficult, the stone is a nightmare. I have only got the potatoes in as you can see."

"Seed is precious, none can be wasted. We would not have recommended you unless there was a good chance of a reasonable crop being produced. Remember what I said; the end result will be worth it."

"Well, how does it look for the future? With Belgium gone, our lads coming back from Dunkirk, there may not be a future."

"That is not the way to think. We will win through, this is an island and no Germans will set foot in it, unless they are like that lot over there," he nodded to the POWs half-heartedly digging the wet fields.

"That brings me to the second reason I am here. There may be an offer of one or two of those prisoners being allocated to you full time if you wish."

Fred was speechless, he had not expected this.

"Beggars can't be choosers," said Mr Jones with a wry smile.

"Lord knows how I am going to tell the missus, I can not see her agreeing to this."

"Your choice. I will leave you to think on it."

Later, when Fred plucked up enough courage he told Dorothy what Mr Jones had in mind for the land. She became quite alarmed.

"You hold on a minute Fred Thomas, big ideas you are getting. Who is going to help you with all this extra work? You have the hay harvest and you still have to sow the mangolds, turnips and swedes?"

"Well." said Fred looking at the distant fields, "Mr Jones says that the War Office says we can have two of those prisoners every day if we need the help. Something to do with the war effort. He says we are to decide before they finish the drains. I don't want to turn back now lass, we need the subsidies."

"Now just a minute Fred Thomas. Before you go getting big ideas, let's look into it a bit. Do you think those prisoners will be able to milk a cow?" She sensed trouble ahead. Laying a couple of drainpipes didn't make a farm worker in her book.

"Will they be able to milk a cow, I asked?" Dorothy asked more loudly.

"I should think so, I don't see why not. If they can't we can soon teach them. But where we need help right now is with the mucking out and the lugging of feed and water. All the heavy stuff Sam used to do. Our Mary tries hard but she could do with a break, perhaps get some schooling in."

"And what about me?" she retorted, I have better things to do than milking cows. I have my poultry to see to and the house to look after." She did not want Mary to get out of work before she did.

He was surprised that she had not said no to the idea of Germans on the farm.

"Well, it probably wouldn't be for long anyway," he said. "Maybe we will get local help in the future. I think the war is going to go on for quite some time but for now we are out of it."

"Don't be for sure their bombers are coming over, I feel as though we are only seeing the start of our problems France is next to fall by the look of it. We were wrong about being gassed in our beds but the war is not over yet."

"So you think I should say yes then?" he said as he began to fill his pipe.

"Maybe, let me think on it." She could see advantages of having extra help and she knew they certainly could do with it. She decided not to air her misgivings any further.

"I should get some weekend help with the harvest if we give out a little cash. Those lads are keen to come and help a bit more." He didn't let on that they wanted to come again so they could see the girls as well.

"Can't be relied on though," he chuckled. "I must get more ploughing done though. If we don't get some more corn sown we will fall out of favour and so far we are doing all right."

Dorothy was lost in her thoughts. Germans working here every day! In the buildings, the fields and close to the house; the thought made her bite her lip with apprehension. She knew they needed the help, she had seen Fred struggling to get out of his chair to go to bed after a day's work. Great Britain now stood alone in Europe; the great alliances were swept away now France was crumbling under the German assault. Fred knew there was nothing he could do other than carry on with the farm. If all went well he stood to gain as well. Dorothy was worried. In the days that followed she listened intently to the wireless. She was sure the Germans would invade eventually; it was clear that the war in France and the Low Countries such as it had been was now lost.

It was at this time Churchill gave his famous speech in which he said "we shall defend our island whatever the cost may be. We shall fight on the beaches; we shall fight on the landing grounds; we shall fight in the fields and in the streets; we shall fight in the hills. We shall never surrender."

On hearing it Fred sat back and lit his pipe with a slip of paper.

"Now lass, do you hear what he is saying?"

"I do but it sounds desperate to me, I don't like the way this war is going. What on earth will happen to us all if the Germans win?"

"Don't you go thinking about that? I reckon that pushing our men into the sea is only a setback. We are on our home ground now."

"It won't be safe for us to sleep in our beds soon," she said, "so make the most of it. I'm off to bed."

Fred sat a while longer. He knew she was right to be concerned. Germany smashed anything and anyone who stood in her way; a far cry from the stalemate of the Great War.

Fred did not raise the subject of the prisoners again with Dorothy; he had made his mind up that he would make use of them to pay back for all the time he lost through their gas.

A week later Fred was due to shear the sheep. He had sown swedes and mangolds with his small drill around the edge of the potato field using the ground left where the horses had turned.

The sheep had got out up by the Hatch and it had taken a while to get them back so Fred went with Mary and Hannah to make a permanent repair. It was a hot Saturday afternoon, it was Mary's job to hold the post firmly for Fred to hammer into the ground and it was Hannah's job to carry and pass the tools or staples as they were needed. They had a couple of long handled brushing hooks for cutting the thistles while they were there.

Down by the front gate a car pulled up and two men got out.

"I think we've got visitors Dad," said Hannah shielding her eyes from the sun when she caught sight of the black car stopped at the front drive. It was a very long way off and too far away to make out any details. He could just see the two men by the gate.

"Can't make them out from here," said Fred and he scanned across the farm to see if Dorothy or one of the other girls was in view.

"Looks like no one has seen them pull up. I wonder how long they've been there," he said

"Shall I run down and tell Mam?" said Mary dropping the next fencing post to be put into the ground.

"No," sighed Fred, "we'll wait and see. If they want us they can come on up. Beggar, them! I'll bet they're Ministry, but it may be they are checking on the drainage work."

The best part of the lower fields was complete now. There were only five prisoners present; they were supposed to work until five o'clock on Saturdays, but because it was such a fine hot day they were taking things nice and easy.

Their guard was some distance away, sitting on some pipes smoking a cigarette.

Fred was tired; the amount of work that he was trying to cope with was enormous and he only had Dorothy and the girls to help out. She was continually reminding him about how he was overdoing it and the worry of the war. Form filling. Nothing was private any more. Every animal had to be accounted for and it was getting him down.

"They are not coming up the drive," said Mary.

"Well, let's get on with this or we will never get finished."

Down at the gate the two men were Mr Jones and a sergeant who was in charge of the work detail. The army sergeant leant on the gate and watched the prisoners for a while. Mr Jones waited patiently. He was wearing a heavy jacket over a waistcoat and his tie was a bit too tight. He was hot and uncomfortable.

"We may as well go up to the house; at least it looks as if there is some shade there."

The sergeant looked up the drive to the bannut tree. He was in total contrast to Mr Jones. Although in full uniform he appeared cool and relaxed. Under his arm he had a new cardboard file held shut by a loop of thin green string. He straightened up and unchained the gate.

They walked towards the house. Mr Jones took a handkerchief from the top pocket of his jacket and wiped his forehead.

The sergeant stopped and handed him the file. "Hold this for me please, "he said."

The men down the field were moving at a snail's pace. He watched them for a minute or so then cupped his hands to his mouth and shouted, "Get on with it you lazy buggers."

Mr Jones jumped slightly and watched as the guard quickly rose to his feet. Taking stock of the situation he motioned the prisoners with his rifle. Reluctantly they picked up the pace slightly.

The two men carried on up to the house and around the back to the kitchen door which stood open, some hens were wandering about quite contentedly. Mr Jones stepped inside; it was untidy and the air was rank.

The sergeant knocked loudly on the door and called. "Anyone home?" he called. A moment later Rebecca appeared from the front room.

"Where is your Dad lass?" Mr Jones said, staying on the threshold.

"Up the back fields, cutting thistles and fencing."

"We'll go see if we can find him. Is the bull out?"

"No," replied Rebecca simply and went back the way she had come.

They could see the little group at the top of the steep bank.

"I'm not walking all the way up there in this heat just to arrange a bit of help for him," said the sergeant. This surprised Mr Jones who assumed he was not feeling the heat like he was.

"Wait here a minute, I think they have seen us and they will probably come down." He stepped forward and waved for Fred to come down. Mary had seen the two men go to the back door while Fred and Hannah continued with the fencing.

"Dad, I think they're after you," she said.

They looked and could see them standing at the end of the yard by the fence.

"I've not got time lass; if they want me they can come up here."

"It's Mr Jones and a soldier Dad," said Hannah.

She could see Mr Jones waving. "He is waving for you to come down."

Fred shielded his eyes. "Aye, I reckon you are right, maybe I should go down."

This could be about the extra help, he thought, better show willing. He put his tools together and placed them on his shoulder.

"Come along you two, lend a hand; we are finished up here for now."

The girls picked up the brushing hooks and joined him as he set off down the bank to the hedge that ran horizontally along the middle of the steep slope.

"If it's the men from the ministry they could keep me all afternoon," he said as they reached the gate. He dropped the tools to the other side of the gate and clambered over himself. The girls simply threw their tools over the gate without any regard for how they landed. Hannah squeezed through the gap, Mary clambered over after Fred. They exchanged glances and smiled as they retrieved the brushing hooks. Hannah had a small, slender bladed hook set on a light shaft. It was very sharp but she enjoyed cutting the thistles with it.

They could clearly see it was Mr Jones and an officer. "He has been before when they first arrived," said Mary.

"Good, maybe he has some help for us. Lord knows we need it but we will wait and see."

Mary glanced at Hannah she raised her eyebrows and tilted her head back up the field.

The girls smiled at each other, this was a turn up for the books. Their Dad could be busy for the rest of the afternoon, they would be able to go for a walk in the woods where it was cool and quiet and out of Mam's sight. He was getting a good step ahead of them.

"We will keep out of the way then as you will be busy," shouted Mary.

He stopped and turned.

"It's better if you two start feeding early today," he replied, "and if you have finished before we start the milking, you can fork some of the muck out of the top loose box. We may need to put some heifers in there soon,"

"Yes Dad," they chorused and slowed their pace to a slow shuffle.

Fred carried on down to the fence. The girls were forgotten.

"It is just not fair," said Mary. "Just is not fair," she repeated. Shoveling muck would not be pleasant on such a hot afternoon. Still, it was more than they dare do to ignore what their Dad had told them to do. "Well, he didn't say start straight away," said Hannah, "let's go and play in the granary, it's cool up there."

"Afternoon to you gents. What brings you out here?" Fred inquired politely as he approached the two men patiently now waiting on the other side of the gate. He noticed that Grace had come out of the house to see what was going on.

"Fetch us a drink girl," he said pointing at the two standing in the shade. "They look as if they need one."

Mr Jones wiped his face again and put his handkerchief away; he relaxed a little.

"To business Mr Thomas," said the sergeant, "it's these prisoners and your workload that we have come to see you about." He took a piece of paper from his file and handed it to Mr Jones.

"Ah yes. Thank you," he said, scanning the neatly typed document.

"You are being allowed to make use of two prisoners full time for the undertaking of manual labour which will aid in the production of food and in turn support the war effort on the home front as requested by His Majesty's Government. Do you wish to accept, Mr Thomas?"

"I can have two Gerry's to work on the farm every day, is that what you're saying?" Fred replied.

"Correct Mr Thomas," said the sergeant. "Let us go over to the field where they are now."

"I'll just drop these off first and catch you up," said Fred.

He went round to the farmyard and put the tools by the cowshed doors. He could see Mary and Hannah heading to the Granary. Cheeky devils, he thought, but never mind.

He stopped at the kitchen; Rebecca had fetched a large jug of homemade lemonade from the pantry and had removed the cloth put over it to keep the flies out.

"I'll take it lass," he said.

"What are they here for Dad?"

"I am hoping we will get some help soon. Get me three glasses will you?"

She did as she was told then he took the jug and glasses and hurried off and down the field.

He found the two men watching the prisoners. As he arrived the sergeant turned and pointed at them.

"Two of that bunch is yours, if you want them."

"Quite," said Mr Jones holding the sheet of paper out, "If you would care to choose the two you think are best suited from this list we will make the necessary arrangements.

"Have a drink," he said, "then I'll take a look."

They took glasses and Fred poured, he then set the jug down and took the paper; he looked at it and then at Mr Jones.

"I don't know their names," he said, looking at the piece of paper, "I have no idea which are the most suited to farm work. It is not like laying drains so this is of no use to me."

"In that case I suggest you leave it to Mr Jones here and myself to sort out which two would be best for you. Not that there is a lot to choose between the lazy buggers. Won't work if they think they can get out of it. Some of the lazy sods should have been shot and saved the transport and the keeping of them. Still, orders are orders; they can earn their keep." The sergeant closed his file. He looked to Mr Jones who nodded in agreement.

"I agree with the sergeant, we will make sure you get your help, in the meantime they will carry on draining. I will be in touch and let you know the outcome but you will probably be seeing a different fellow from then on who will be in charge of the two that you get and you will see him on a weekly basis. Thank you for the drink, I will say good day to you."

Fred set to cutting the grass on the Monday, the weather was perfect and he made good progress. That evening while milking a Mr Richards turned up. Grace brought him round to the cowshed. He introduced himself; he was a retired army officer who had fought in the last war and was now working in administration. His job would be to monitor two prisoners that were to be allocated to the farm as manual labourers.

Fred referred to him as 'the Boss'. They got on well together; they had shared in the bitter fighting of the last war. He had been told which two prisoners were allocated and was keen for them to start work.

"I will call around tomorrow and we will pull Keppler and Stange from the crew. Have you decided what they are to do?"

"Lifting jobs mainly, feeding, watering and mucking out."

"That sounds good; we can have them hard at it by the end of the week."

The next morning he was there and from the prisoners he called out two of the men. He spoke fluent German to them and together they went to the farmyard. They followed Fred through the milking process and then Fred led them around indicating all the troughs that had to be filled and what with. The Boss wrote details down in a small notebook and described in German what Fred was telling them.

Fred did not want to leave them around the house while he was grass cutting; Dorothy had already looked nervous enough when they had been in the cowshed. He had them come with him to the fields. He explained the business of lugging muck, harvesting, fencing and anything else he could think of, the Boss wrote it down and translated for the prisoners.

"This here is Gunter Stange," said the Boss, "and he asks if he will be able to drive the horses?"

Fred was taken aback. "Not on your life," he said.

The Boss spoke to Gunter who smiled, nodded and said "Danke."

"What did you tell him?"

"I simply told him no, he has to work to prove he can be trusted before he can ask such a question."

"Fair enough," said Fred and nodded to Gunter.

That afternoon the Germans spent their time turning the hay that had been cut the day before. They left the farm with the others when the lorry came to collect them...

The Boss spoke to them at length before they left then told Fred that they would be on their own the next day and that they would do whatever he wanted but not to rush things; let them work steadily for now. He was a busy man and had so many other farms to visit during the week, but he would call on Friday and thereafter on every Monday for an update.

When the draining was complete they would be trusted to walk the three miles to the farm and return to the camp at the end of the day.

Mary was pleased she had seen them during the day and though they were scary she was pleased that they were to help with the work. Dorothy had misgivings, which she kept till the girls were all in bed.

"I do not like this," she said, "they are to have free run of the place, that can't be right."

"I will keep an eye on them, they are under no illusions. They cannot step out of line so we are perfectly safe."

She was not convinced and it was some time before she let it rest.

The next morning the two men appeared on the backyard; Rebecca saw them as she came up the yard with eggs for packing.

"Guten tag junge madchen," said the larger of the two, a smile on his face.

She shot past into the kitchen and shut the door.

Two minutes later Lizzy came out and looked at them.

"Guten tag junge madchen," the man said again.

Lizzy ran past them and off to the cowshed.

"Dad, the prisoners are on the backyard. Beccy's too scared to carry on with the eggs."

"Bloody hell!" he said, "I'm in the middle of milking."

"Well none of the others are going to come out of the house; Grace wants to bolt the door."

He left what he was doing and went around to the backyard. "Guten tag," the two men said.

"They keep talking like that Dad, scared Beccy half to death."

He beckoned to them and led them to the farmyard.

The larger man held out a piece of paper to him and said "Bitte."

Fred looked at it, it was in English and from the Boss it was an itinerary of the work they were to do. At the bottom there was a note 'They have the same only written in German. Good luck.'

"Good," he said and handed it back. The big man smiled.

"Danke, Ich bin Gunter," he indicated the other man, "Klaus," he said

Klaus shrugged and said simply "Ja." Fred instantly took a dislike to him.

"Begin?" said Gunter.

"What?" said Fred, "oh, you want to begin?" Gunter nodded, "Arbeiten, Begin ja?"

Fred trusted to his instincts and nodded.

"Yes you begin, get started, whatever," he had seen that the first item on the list had been water and feed stock. He found them some buckets which they took.

"Danke," and the two headed off to pump water.

Fred followed and went to go in the kitchen but the door was bolted; this had never been done in all the years they had been there. He banged on it and a face appeared at the window.

"Open up!" he shouted. The door opened and there stood Hannah staring past him.

"No more daftness," he said, "get yourselves together and get off to school. Beccy, Mary can finish the eggs so get going."

"We are scared," said Grace

"Yes," said Hannah, "they look dangerous."

"I haven't time for this," he said, "use the front door if you want, but get a move on."

Lizzy says "If we can't bolt the door let's put the mangle across it, then we will hear them if they try to come and get us. Give me push with it" and the girls pushed as hard as they could and soon the mangle was across the door. Fred tried to push the door and it did move slightly.

The two men set about their tasks referring to the paper at regular intervals. There was much debate between them. Fred did not interfere; he decided to let them get on with it. He returned to the cowshed and told Dorothy what had occurred and how they were now fetching water off the backyard.

"I am not going to the dairy while they are there," she said, "You will have to come with me."

"Well, carry on while I take this milk and I will bring Mary back to give you a hand. They can do her feeding while she helps you out."

He took the full buckets down to the dairy, passing a beaming Gunter on the way. He poured the milk and went to the back door – bolted again. He banged on it and Hannah opened it. "Are they coming in here?" she said.

"Don't talk daft, is Mary here?"

"Yes but she doesn't want to come out right now and we are going to go through the front door in a minute."

He went past and called Mary. "Come on out and give your Mam a hand. You lot are driving me mad."

Mary appeared and peeped out onto the yard. "Where are they Dad?"

"They are doing your work lass, so come and give a hand with the milking."

Fred concentrated on the dairy, when he had the churns full he fetched the trolley and beckoned Klaus to lift them on to it. The German came over and manhandled the churn into place while Fred stood back. When the girls left for school they ran from the front door, through the picket fence and down the drive to the back gate. Once on the road they breathed a sigh of relief and set off for school; they only had a few weeks left to go.

The two men followed their list and after the cows were turned out they cleaned out the muck and washed the yard down. As much as possible they kept themselves to themselves.

At lunchtime when the family ate they wandered off back to the work party where there was food for them. After they had eaten they returned and sat down by the pear tree until Fred came out.

They followed him to the fields and carried on turning hay.

The week went well, with their help Fred was able to get in a large part of the hay harvest. The girls helped with the stacking when they returned from school.

On the Monday when the Boss came round he went and sat with them; he had his notebook and wrote in it repeatedly.

"How are they doing?" he asked Fred and Dorothy.

"Well, I think Gunter is fine," Fred said, "but I'm not sure of the other."

"Well, they will stay with you and are happy for now. You could try giving them other work if you wish."

"If I can get them to milk some of those cows it will save the missus having to come out in all weathers."

"That would be fine."

At the thought of no more milking to do Dorothy was pleased. She thought to herself, thank goodness for that. She would be happy if she never had to milk another cow, it was time to take it a bit easier.

Later in the week Fred demonstrated how to milk a cow. Gunter was keen to learn and soon became good at it. Klause was not so keen and showed little interest.

The girls soon settled down, even Helen would sit on the doorstep and watch as they came and went carrying the water to the farmyard. Gunter made an effort to be friendly; he seemed quite an intelligent man and made an effort to learn Basic English. He really seemed to enjoy working in the fresh air.

The family quickly took a liking to Gunter; he stood six feet tall, had short blond hair and blue eyes. Klaus on the other hand was very surly, he made it obvious he was not willing to do manual work, or for that matter any work at all if he could help it. Whenever he used the tools he would not clean and put them away after use, as he had been shown, instead they were left covered with dirt or left on the ground... When being shown what to do, he would just shrug his shoulders and walk away as if he did not understand what was being asked of him. The worst was his attitude to the stock, he had no patience with the animals whatsoever, hitting the cows hard with a stick as he brought them in to be milked the cows he hit seemed to be the ones that always kicked out at him later. On one occasion when he helped Gunter with the milking a cow kicked at him causing him to upset the bucket.

This made him furious and he picked up the kicking strap and hit the cow hard.

Fred saw it and was angry. He went to shout but Gunter was already there. He took the strap from Klaus; there were harsh words between them.

Fred decided Klaus would have to go; he did not like to see anyone taking their spite out on an animal let alone a German. He saw the Boss on the Monday morning and told him of his misgivings.

"No, he's not happy working, not settled down at. He is a military man, can't hack it." He confirmed Fred's suspicions, "I will have him kept in the camp for a bit. Have him doing some kitchen duties and cleaning the lavatories, see how he likes that. Shame they didn't shoot the bastard."

"Well, he knows his place well enough, nowhere to run I suppose but it seems that is as far as it goes. I reckon if it wasn't for that Gunter we would have had real trouble."

"Yes, I believe you are right. Tell me, do you want a replacement, you can have one if you want one."

Fred thought for a moment "No, I can manage with just Gunter, he'll do me."

Gunter arrived daily and did all the heavy jobs, this left Mary to help with the milking. Dorothy took the opportunity to take things easier and soon the schools would shut for the summer break so there would be more help with the poultry, the washing and household chores.

When all the bottom fields were drained the work party was taken to work on another farm. Gunter was trusted to walk to the farm in the morning and return after milking. He still wore the grey prisoner's uniform, no number now, just a round, yellow coloured patch on the back of the jacket like a big sun. He worked alongside Fred and they fetched in a good hay harvest.

Dorothy gave him a mug of tea and two rounds of bread with some fried bacon between them while Fred had breakfast. At dinnertime she gave him a cooked dinner which he ate in the dairy sitting on an old kitchen chair provided. He was always cheerful and did not seem to mind at all the fact that he was not allowed to go into the kitchen unless it was to unload an arm full of logs that he had chopped. When he had finished his work he would keep himself busy tidying, sweeping the yards or fixing things.

They fetched the shopping on a Saturday and at first the girls stayed inside with the doors bolted till they came back.

Mary knew where the gun was and Fred had let her hold it just in case.

All produce had to be accounted for. Dorothy sold her poultry to the butcher or to such as the Podmores who had to account for what they had purchased and what they had used them for.

Fred was concerned about the fact that in a month or so he would be in need of a binder. Dorothy was not keen as already this year he had bought the seed drill. Mr Jones came out to see if he had started ploughing the extra fields. Fred took the opportunity to ask if he should get one of his own.

"You should indeed, there could be a problem borrowing one or else you will have to wait for someone to come round and that is unlikely in this climate."

As a result he wrote a letter of confirmation for Fred to take to his bank manager saying that the subsidy was due on the fields ploughed. This gave him the credit he needed to buy a binder. Farmers with a much larger acreage than Fred's were purchasing bigger, newer harvesters to gain from the subsidies and their older, smaller machines were coming up for sale. It was a good time to buy.

Despite the letter and Mr Simmons agreement, Dorothy was still apprehensive.

"I hope you know what you are doing? Fred Thomas. We've kept out of trouble with the bank all these years. I don't want the worry of Simmons breathing down our necks. If it had not been for my scrimping and scraping to make ends meet, you would not be where you are today."

"Well how else are we going to harvest those oats?" he argued, "If we have to wait our turn until some other farmer can get to cut them for us it will be Christmas, I wouldn't wonder. You know as well as I do all farmers are working flat out to grow as much corn as they can and you can guess why; it's because of the amount of money they are going to get from the subsidies."

She reluctantly gave in and a binder was bought. It was put under cover in the cart shed. It was imperative he get the fields ploughed now. He studied it and sharpened the cutting knife and tried it out on the field as he needed to be sure it would work when required.

With the hay harvest in, Fred began ploughing the new fields Mr Jones had requested to sow winter wheat. Mary would fetch the horses in and harness them ready for Fred when he and Gunter had finished the milking and had some breakfast. Gunter then got on with all the heavy jobs while Fred began ploughing. This left Mary much lighter jobs to do and she was much happier she could take her time with the eggs, washing and packing them in the big wooden box. With the summer holidays the rest of the girls were expected to do lots more; cleaning the kitchen, scrubbing the table and chairs and mopping the floor. They were expected to clean the bedrooms and front room as well. It was at this time that all the road signs disappeared, it did not affect them but as Fred said to Dorothy when they came to the A5, "Funny, I never really thought of the road signs until they took them away and now I miss them."

Ploughing the fields under the Wrekin was a problem from the start as there was still so much stone. Fred struggled terribly to break up the ground then with help from Gunter and the girls they carried and dragged the rocks and stones to the sides. There was not so much pressure this time, only the heat, which left them exhausted at the end of the day. The summer holidays were hard work for the girls but they managed to eventually have the ground prepared.

One half of one of the fields at the top of the Willowmoor bank was another to be sown with winter wheat.

Lizzy worked full time at the Forest Glen. On her one day off Dorothy gave her as much work as possible to do. The Forest Glen was becoming much busier, despite the war there were more dinner dances than ever before, the majority of them were for military personnel and often went on late into the night. Dorothy complained to Fred about it.

"How is it they can have food to entertain and we are kept so short. We are only allowed to have what our ration books will allow."

Fred did not see it that way, he knew there were many in the cities who had nothing to fall back on; his mother and Kathleen were finding it hard as were a good many.

"We do all right Dot, we have the milk and eggs and an odd cockerel or two and that's besides the rabbits we catch, just be thankful, there's a lot worse off than us. Aye surry, some of them pies Margaret Podmore sends home with Lizzy are grand."

"That's only when the greedy beggars have not eaten them all and as for the rabbits, it's only when you have the time these days to catch one for me. I will soon have no boiler fowl left at the rate we are eating them." Dorothy was not going to give in; she was not going to let Fred think that these little extras were making it any easier for her to feed the family. Like every other mother Dorothy found that the rations that they were allowed did not go as far as she would have liked. She had absolutely no cause for complaint, Lizzy often brought home leftover pie or cake and even some of Margaret Podmores trifle.

The Battle of Britain began in the skies over the South of England. The whole nation followed the progress of the RAF Hannah was particularly interested, she and her sisters listened to the news broadcasts every chance they got. Fred and Dorothy tried not to worry; they had more than enough on their plate. Hannah was the most informed she knew the names of the aircraft. She so wanted to go to see one on the ground, Danny had told her so much about them. He had pictures and now he was saying that there might be fighter planes coming to Atcham up the A5.

Harvesting the oats Fred had planted earlier in the year would require the help of all the members of the family and anyone else who would lend a hand. He decided to make a start as soon as the weather turned fine. Hopefully it would stay fine and dry long enough to get the harvest safely stacked in the brick barns. After a short wet spell the forecast was good and so early in the morning he went to cut a swathe around the edge of the field with a scythe. Gunter could keep busy cutting thistles. The corn was still too wet to be tied into stooks. The heads of the corn would go mouldy and would be ruined if stacked. He had to clear a path of about two yards wide ready for the binder. It was to be pulled by horses and he wanted no corn to be trampled under their feet, every grain was valuable, none could be wasted. The temperature rose; it was a muggy day. Fred swung the scythe gracefully. If the sun breaks through, he thought, we might be all right to start tomorrow. He had his shirt sleeves rolled up, sweat was forming on his forehead, and he took his cap off and wiped it. He was going to be at this for a while. He called Gunter over so he could take a turn, see how he managed. Fred heard the noise of an aeroplane; it was distant and it was not unusual except that it seemed different somehow. He looked up, not sure where the sound was coming from. There was still some mist in the air, the Wrekin looked hazy, the sound of the plane was coming from little Wenlock way, it was definitely not right. Then he saw it quite close now. It was twin engine and very low; there was smoke pouring from one of the engines and it was losing height. The wheels were up. Gunter ran up, he had seen it.

"Gott und Himmel!" he said and shaded his eyes.

There was a cough and a bang; the plane lurched. It was right above them, they could see the pilot it was so close. He was looking down as if trying to find somewhere to land.

"Surry, he won't make it," said Fred and dropped the scythe. The plane was falling now towards the far end of the Wrekin but the mist was all around, rising from the woods.

The plane dropped lower and lower, the wheels appeared to be coming down. Pieces were falling away from the burning engine. Then it struck the Wrekin below the Cuckoo's Cup. The pilot may have tried to land in the Wrekin farm fields. There was a loud thud as the sound reached them.

"Surry, it has crashed," said Fred. He could see that a fire was starting. Wreckage was strewn in all directions; it had completely broken up on impact.

"Gunter you go back. Tell Mary to phone police. Quick," he spoke clearly. Gunter understood perfectly.

"Ja, but the men," he said, "I will help."

"No, get going now. I'll go and see if there is anything I can do." They set off in opposite directions.

"Poor beggars, they have no chance of getting out of there alive, no chance at all." Fred was talking to himself as he ran. There was smoke rising lazily, the grass and heather would be damp but a fire could still spread especially if there was fuel spilled. He ran as he had never run before. Down the field to the gate, across the road and off towards the Wrekin he went, across the Slang and into the wood then followed the rough track which led around the bottom of the hill, As he passed Joe Evans' fields he could smell the acrid smoke. He could see the wreckage now above him; pieces had tumbled down to where he was, mostly twisted metal but he recognized a tip of wing or tail. He started to climb up the side, passing other pieces which had been scattered by the impact. The sweat ran down his face, he had seen so many men killed and mangled in the Great War but was still unable to prepare for the task at hand. As he reached the crashed plane he could see the fire was only small and not spreading. The wreckage was everywhere; the plane had been quite big. The ground had been smashed and scattered as well by the impact. The fuselage was recognizable, the tail was elsewhere but the bulk of the plane was there in front of him. He could see where the engines had struck, throwing pieces in all directions. Someone was moving about. "Good lord, he made it!" said Fred but then realized it was Joe Evans from below; he was at the side stamping out the flames.

Fred started towards him then stopped in his tracks. A mans body was lying face down at the side of the wreckage where it looked as though there had been a door. The man was wearing a flying suit and his limbs were at awkward angles. Fred went to help him but as he got closer he noticed blood on the ground. Gently he turned the man over then stood back; there was no hope for this man, his throat was gaping open and he was drenched in blood. Fred laid him gently on the rough ground; there was nothing he could do.

"He is done for," came a voice from behind Fred causing him to turn quickly, it was Joe.

"Surry, you made me jump!"

"Sorry Fred, I was putting the fire out, I did not see you arrive."

"Saw him go overhead and then come down, ran here as fast as I could."

"I just heard the bang and came out to see what was going on. I saw the bits rolling down the hill. The mist has been hanging about a bit today. Do you think he did not see the hill?"

"Nay, his engine was gone, smoke and flames. I think he was just trying to get it down. Is there anyone else in there?" he said, looking at the twisted mess, he could make out the fuselage properly now.

"Haven't looked, just at this one and he has gone."

Fred carefully clambered his way into the wreckage; deep in he found another body tangled in the mess, pressed into what was left of the instrument panel. With great difficulty Fred climbed to check for any sign of life, but there was none. He checked around the area, there appeared to be no others.

"Poor beggars," Fred said to himself, "not a chance." He scrambled back the way he had come.

"Are you all right?" called Joe.

"Aye, let's hope the police get here now. There is nothing we can do for these poor beggars." Fred was quite dismayed, "I sent word to phone them so they should know soon. Surry I feel sorry for these two."

"I am glad you have done that, I was worried that I was the only one to see it."

"I have sent Gunter to tell Mary to go to the Glen and ring for the police. She will take her Mam's bicycle so it should not take long. I suppose the army will also be called out."

"Better we stay here for a while and keep an eye on things then until they come. I doubt anyone saw it go down but you never know." They sat themselves down on a rock to wait.

Dorothy was sitting in Fred's chair listening to the radio when she sensed someone on the back yard. She got up and went to the back door; Gunter was at the dairy, he was flustered.

"Mary please, she must go get police." She looked at him in surprise.

"Why, what is going on?"

Gunter pointed to the Wrekin. "Plane Kaput. Mary to ring for police. Schnell!"

She walked around to the front of the house. Gunter followed, he was clearly worried.

"Where is Fred?" she asked.

"He has gone to help."

She looked across to where she could see smoke rising through the mist.

"Oh my goodness!" she ran to the back yard and began shouting Mary. Gunter called as well.

"Where is she?" She called again "MAAAAAAAARY!"

Mary had been in the barn reading a book. She had been so absorbed in what she was reading she had heard nothing of the crash. Now she heard her mother she put her book down and set off toward the back yard.

As soon as Dorothy saw her she shouted, "You get my bike and go to the Glen. Ask the Podmores to ring for the police; a plane has crashed into the Wrekin. Down by the Wrekin farm." Mary stood open mouthed.

"Get a move on girl, this is serious!" she turned to Gunter. "Thank you, now find something to do and settle down."

Mary went off to the Forest Glen and passed the message on to Margaret Podmore who dialled 999. Half an hour later a car pulled up at the front gate, a man came hurrying up to the farmhouse and Dorothy met him at the garage.

"Can you tell me the quickest way to get to a plane that has crashed around here? I believe you phoned it in. The Wrekin farm I am told."

Dorothy hurriedly pointed towards the crash site. She told him to go through the gate and follow the track to get there. "My Fred has already gone to see if he can be of any help. I expect you will find him there somewhere."

"Thank you very much," the man said and turned on his heels and ran back to his car. "Bugger," he said to himself, when he looked he realized he could see the blackened patch where the fire had been.

"The chap from here has already gone up there," he said to the occupants of the car who were home guard. "One of you will stay here and direct the rest up that track." A man got out, there was a discussion then the car drove off to the Wrekin farm. Soon the police arrived then more and more vehicles. At the site Fred and Joe met them. Joe's wife had been up to look, and returned upset at the news of the airmen. It was a long time before things were sorted. Fred was asked to stay around and answer questions as more and more officials turned up.

Later in the day as the girls came from school they saw the wreckage from the top of the Willowmoor Bank.

"Look!" said Grace to Hannah as they neared, "It looks as if a plane has crashed over there." She pointed to the Wrekin.

"I can see a wing," said Hannah, "up on that bare patch up there. And there are big pieces all around."

They started to run home to find out what was going on.

"Did you see a plane crash Mam?" asked Hannah.

"No, your Dad has gone to it, he sent Gunter back to the yard to get on with the work."

"Come on Grace, let us go and see what is going on."

"You're not going anywhere near that crash," she ordered, "there could be bodies laying everywhere and anyway the army and police are there. Your Dad will tell us all about it when he comes home. Get out of those tidy clothes and start your jobs."

"Bodies!" Hannah gasped. "What, dead men?"

"What else are bodies?" Grace quipped.

"I don't mind seeing a dead man," said Hannah.

"You're not going to young lady," said Dorothy, "go and get changed and I will make you a drink."

Hannah wandered to the window.

"Don't stand there gawping through that window. Get yourselves changed as I've told you. Goodness only knows what time your father will be back."

The girls went upstairs, the view was better from there anyway.

Later, when Fred returned, he gave them the gruesome details of the crash. There had indeed only been two crew aboard. He was weary and sat in his favourite chair to smoke his pipe and drink his tea.

"Can we go and see it Dad?" asked Mary.

"Bloody hell, no you cannot."

"Well, can I go?" asked Hannah.

"None of you are to go near it at all. Leave them to sort it out; there is plenty to do here. Now look lively there is work to do." At that Fred swallowed the remainder of his tea and went outside.

"Don't you girls meither your Dad, he is a bit shook up."

"Well, he would be if there are dead bodies," Grace piped up.

"Ooh bodies," Hannah's big brown eyes opened wide.

"Come on you two," interrupted Mary, "I see that you have got the sticks and coal in, now find something else to do."

For the next few days there was quite a lot of activity; Lorries coming to take the broken plane away, soldiers were left to guard the site until it was all cleared away. Danny Probin was waiting on the schoolyard for Hannah the day after.

"Tell me what happened? What did you see?" he asked eyes wide with excitement.

"Nothing," replied Hannah, "my Dad saw it though and there were two bodies, but he won't talk about it much."

"My mates and I tried to get a look but the army told us to bugger off."

"Well which way did you go to get to it?"

"Down the Spout Lane and through the scout's camp. We have managed to get a few bits and pieces that were scattered in the trees. The soldiers did not see us take them."

"You will be in trouble if you are found out. I would not go boasting around the playground like you usually do if I were you. One of the soldiers told my Dad that there was secret equipment on board and that is why they are guarding the site night and day."

"Secret equipment? What sort of stuff? Was it stuff to bomb the Gerry's with?"

"I don't know it could have been a new gun that blew up other planes."

"Really! I'll bet that's what it was; I will see if my Dad knows about it."

Hannah left him guessing. The site was cleared quite quickly but there were always bits and pieces turning up. They often found bits of the plane as they went collecting chestnuts and hazelnuts later in the year. They took them back to the kitchen to show their mother.

"Throw them away in the woods. They will only bring you bad luck," Dorothy ordered. "Don't bring them in here, those poor men died up there, let them rest in peace."

The two bodies of the men were later buried in a cemetery up north.

Hannah found a piece of Perspex that had been part of a window. She gave it to Gunter and he carved it into a little aeroplane for her. Hannah treasured that little plane; she called it her Wrekin plane and often thought about the two men who had died that day. She found some small pieces that she hid in the hedgerow and gave to Danny when she went to school. He was so grateful and promised to take her to see a real aeroplane one day.

CHAPTER THREE

Reap as you sow

The harvest had to be got in so Fred pushed the crash from his mind. He arranged things quickly to take advantage of the weather. The binder worked perfectly but it needed three horses to pull it. One-eyed Jack from Cluddely lent him a mare. Kit and Bonny were harnessed together and Mary rode on the lead horse. The huge blades revolving were fascinating to the girls, it was the first time they had seen such a machine at work. It had a blade like the mower that swept along cutting the stalks just above the ground. The sheaves were then bundled and tied before falling off the bed to the ground; each bundle was called a stook. Dorothy and the girls helped by putting the stooks into small stacks to be collected on the dray. Hannah was too small for this work; it was her job to look after Helen. Dorothy put them in the long grass by the hedge and left them to play by themselves with an old rag doll and a tennis ball she had found for them. They were ordered to keep out of the way of everyone else. Rebecca and Grace carried the sheaves of corn to Dorothy and Gunter to stand them up. Grace complained bitterly as the sharp points of the stubble left by the freshly cut corn scratched her bare ankles; her old socks had worked down under her feet in the old shoes she had to wear. Each child had only one decent pair of shoes and those had to be kept for going to school. Clothing coupons did not allow any others to be bought. That was the excuse Dorothy gave when any one of the girls complained. Old shoes whatever the size were worn for work around the farm. Rebecca, on the other hand, had pulled old socks of Fred's on her feet and they did protect her legs a little bit. When it was all cut and stacked it was a rush to get it safely carted to the brick bays and stacked. Dorothy led the horse and cart while Fred and Mary threw the stooks up to Gunter who arranged them safely. The weather broke almost as soon as the last stook was in. It would stay in the barn away from the rigours of the weather until Jack Munslow who owned a threshing machine could come and thresh it. Dorothy wrote to give Jack a rough estimate of how much they had harvested. Mr Jones came to see the result of the first crop.

"Well, that is a fine result," he said after looking at the quality of the grain. "That ground has produced a good yield, we can get more fertilizer in next time round, and I will see to it that you get help with that..."

"Well it has certainly been worth the hard graft," said Fred. He was looking forward to the threshing in the winter months this was the first cereal crop to be grown on this farm. Each farm had to wait their turn. It would likely be the first week of February when they got round to the Willowmoor Farm or later if the weather turned against them. Mr Jones looked at the hay stacked in the stack yard.

"I don't know fortune smiled on you this year. How did you dodge the bad weather and fit all this work in?"

"Needs must as the devil drives," said Fred

"Well, I did not think you would get through it all. I am glad you did, that family of yours must take some looking after."

The haystacks had to be covered with straw thatching to keep out the weather. It was too precious and the milk cheque would depend on it during the winter months. Fred had some suitable straw delivered and with the help of Gunter and Mary they made a really good job. Mary was unsure of the wooden ladder; she waited until Gunter had climbed it reasoning if it was to break it would be under his weight. Hannah and Helen were not impressed; they had liked playing in the hay when it was in the brick barns.

"Where can we have our tea parties now Dad?" asked Hannah.

"In the granary before it is full of sacks of oats from this lot," he said, jerking his thumb at the full barn.

William Hollis the gamekeeper was not concerned with farming. His neighbours were a nuisance to him but he put up with them. What he could not stand was town folk or townies as he called them. It was early in the morning, what day of the week didn't concern him. He tapped the barometer with a rough, dirty-nailed finger. Its brass needle stayed in the 'fair to fine' area. It looked like being another fine day, there would be no rain for a day or so he surmised.

There were not many people for miles around who had not heard of William Hollis the gamekeeper to the Johnston's estate. It was mostly wooded but had large open quarries and some disused mineral workings known as the Limekilns. His responsibilities were many: keeping down vermin, maintaining fences and rearing the pheasants for the annual shoot but above all he saw it was his duty to keep everyone else out.

He returned to his favourite chair, it afforded the best view of the path leading to his solitary cottage. His wife was busying herself in the scullery. He had no interest in her activities at all. What was he going to do with himself today, no point trying to catch Fred Thomas poaching the odd pheasant?

"I'll get him one of these days," he said to himself, "I know that bugger gets the odd bird or two."

But it was September, the wrong time of year the birds were a bit too small for anyone to make it worth their while. Another six to eight weeks and the birds would have fattened up a bit. The risk of getting caught was high around here. The penalties could be hard as well, not just fines. If a poacher was also a tenant they could be out on their ear. A breach of tenancy agreement met with little sympathy.

Rules were rules and William was a stickler. He took great pleasure in enforcing them; he saw it as upholding the wishes of the estate manager. He always looked forward to the annual shoot; that was his big day. That's when they thanked him personally and patted his back. He would be top dog of all those who worked elsewhere on the estate and surrounding farms. He would not admit it but he would creep under the dirtiest stone if he had to, just to see his boss smile.

As he gazed across the clearing in front of his cottage watching the early morning birds' going to and fro a thought crossed his mind.

The blackberries are just ready for picking. Nice and ripe, full of juice and I'll bet them townsfolk will be after those down the Limekiln.

The Limekilns were the old lime workings that stretched from above Fred Thomas's fields and beyond the quarry on the town side as he called it. Townsfolk sometimes came over the old Roman road and went up there to gather blackberries and nuts. There were caves, deep holes and it was all over grown. He had scared brats away many times with his stick. But the women who came to take the blackberries were a particular irritation to him. He would rather see the fruit rot than have them take it, worse still he knew that they sold some for profit.

"They know they're trespassing, I'll take a look and see if they're about," he decided, taking dark pleasure in the thought.

He put bread, cheese and a bottle of tea made earlier by his obedient wife into his deep coat pockets. Then, picking up a knobbly rosewood stick he had whittled during the dark winter evenings, he set off.

Today he would change his routine and make the Limekiln his first stop.

He told his two black Labrador dogs "Stay, can't take you two today," as they clamored at the door of their pen. The last thing he wanted was the dog to scare off any trespassers, today he felt lucky.

As he strode out the air felt fresh and cold, early morning mist was still clearing. The late September sunshine felt good, if things went his way today he would put the fear of god into them women.

William Hollis took a familiar short cut through the woods to the old Limekiln. As he expected there were signs of recent activity, the long grass on the pathway was trodden down and there were clear inroads into the mass of tangled briars. However, this was a good year and there was plenty of ripe fruit still to be had.

"They'll be back, they'll be back," he smiled knowingly.

He took a brief look around the old site. The caves where the kids would pretend monsters lived and push each other in daring them not to scream. There were still some shafts in the open space where buildings had long fallen down. He did not venture there, if the town brats were stupid enough to go near them they deserve to fall in. By the path was the steep embankment still with debris visible at the bottom. He moved further along until he could see Limekiln lane and the town in the distance. It was at this point that he spat, cursed, then turned and made off back to his woods. He would give them a while to crawl out of their beds. He knew they would come back, something for nothing.

Later in the day after he had taken his repast he made his way over toward the quarry. It was from here that he could hear faint voices coming from the direction of the Limekiln.

"Right," he said to himself, a surge of anger came over him which he suppressed as he headed towards the 'kilns.

Moving quickly he soon came down through the woods, coming right up to the old workings. As he moved he was well camouflaged by the changing colour of the leaves. William kept himself well hidden from the women picking the ripe juicy berries from the prickly bramble bushes, his grey, and weasel like eyes peering through the hazel bush where he was hidden like a fox watching rabbits at play waiting patiently to pounce for the kill.

He could see a group of women. They were happy picking the berries and putting them into glass jars or enamel cups. When they were full they would return to the path where the wicker baskets stood in the long grass. They chatted amongst themselves completely oblivious of being watched. They had been warned to keep an eye out for the gamekeeper. It was said that he was a horrid little man and living deep in the woods had made him madder than hell. He would have no truck with townsfolk and even despised them. But there was no sign of him being about today. Picking the berries was enjoyable, they knew they were good for the children and with the odd handful of apples made a very tasty pie for the table. And this year with rationing they were especially sought after. In the past they would have sold any surplus to the restaurants and hotels back in town.

William Hollis patiently waited until he thought the baskets were more or less full, and then he made himself known. Surprise and horror showed on the women's faces as he stepped out into the open only yards from where they were picking.

"And what are you good ladies doing?" He inquired in the most sinister voice he could muster.

"Minding our own business!" answered one of them bravely. She was middle aged and not easily intimidated.

"Now would you believe it?" he said, his weasel like eyes meeting hers, his hackles rising.

"This is my business, you are trespassing." And he took a step toward her.

"And who says so?" she returned.

"I do. You have no bloody right to pick here. I am the gamekeeper here and what I say goes," he shouted and waved his stick in the air.

"There's no law against picking a few blackberries," a new voice said.

"That's what you ignorant townies think is it? I've booted your sort out of here before now so go back to where you came from." He pointed his stick the way they had come.

"You can't stop us," said a woman deep in the patch of briars, battered enamel mug half full in her hand. Saying nothing he moved forward and looked at the nearest full basket of black shiny fruit.

Then to their surprise and before they could utter another word the evil little man lifted up his right boot and kicked the basket down the embankment. The basket emptied and rolled down into the quarry below. The other women realized his intention but before they could gather their baskets and get out of his way he had barged further forward and sent another four baskets rolling down after the first.

"Now bugger off! And don't come back here again," he screamed at them seeming totally out of control. The rosewood stick was flailing in all directions.

The women stood stunned at his behaviour and were speechless.

He turned on his heel and strode away the way he had come, giving an eerie chuckle that echoed through the woods as he went.

The women had heard of the evil little man who kicked the baskets of blackberry pickers down the quarry, now they had met him.

"We've got to fix that little rat," said the woman whose basket had been first to go.

"If my old man had seen that he would have killed him," said another.

"Now that's an idea, let's get our heads together," said the first.

As they walked back home they planned what they could do to pay back that horrible little man. The results of their afternoon's work were disappointing and retrieving the baskets from the bottom of the embankment had been risky in the flat-soled shoes that they wore. They would share out the fruit when they got back to town but there was very little.

Two days later on the Sunday morning, William was out on his own again. He had seen signs of a fox around his feeding boxes and had gone over by the quarry to look further.

He was thunderstruck to hear the sound of voices echoing from the direction of the Limekiln. It was no loss to him and no one from the estate minded the blackberries being picked. However, William got a cold pleasure when he could bully and frighten folk. Kicking the baskets and wasting the fruit was the icing on the cake. He approached as before and hid. There were only four this day. They had their backs to him and scarves covering their heads. They were bent over and were quietly and carefully putting berries into the baskets, which they kept close to them.

"Think your basket's safe do you?" he muttered to himself quietly.

"Time to make myself known."

"Clear off you scrounging old women!" he shouted, waving his rosewood stick and stepping out from the bushes.

The pickers took no notice.

"Do you hear what I said? Clear off, you're trespassing."

Still nothing.

"Bugger off back to town!" he screamed d, moving toward the nearest figure.

Still nothing, he was angry now and was intent on making them pay for their insolence. He was just lifting his foot to boot the first basket when the figure turned and looked at him. William was mortified, before he could step back a strong hand caught hold of him very firmly. He screamed with terror and dropped his precious stick as he was lifted off his feet. Staring at him from beneath the scarf was a man, a very big man who had a face like leather and eyes that cut right through him.

"Now, you evil little bastard, let's see you kick this basket," said the man, his voice was deep and threatening. Looking at the man's dark, weathered face, William was reminded of a prize-fighter he had seen a picture of in a newspaper. His world fell apart in front of his eyes.

The other pickers had come forward and they too were men, further back a group of women were now on the path.

"Kick this one as well," said another of the pickers.

"Or this one, why don't you?" said another.

William had lost his strength. He was hanging from the man's fist like a bag of rags.

"What shall we do with him?" asked the man holding William.

William couldn't speak.

"Bloody kill him here and now," said one of the faces just to William's right.

"Aye, kill the snivelling little rat," said a voice to his left.

As William desperately tried to get control of him he heard a woman's voice in the distance.

"Think how many times this rat has kept food from the table. How many times has he stood and watched the fruit rot rather than let us so-called townies have it?"

"Aye and how big a man is he now that he faces my husband?" joined in another.

"Tell us again about yon law that says we can't pick fruit growing wild." Through his terror William recognized the voice of the woman who had faced up to him two days previous. He tried to form words but nothing came, things were going from bad to worse. The men turned their attention back to him.

"Kill the bugger," said the voice to his right.

"What do we do with the body?" asked another.

"Down the bloody mineshaft with him, nobody will find him when he's at the bottom."

"What a sound idea," said the man holding William, gripping him now with both hands.

William suddenly came to. He was not going down any mineshaft. He struggled but the grip was like a vice, he started to scream with fright.

"You can shout all you want you nasty little bugger. No one can hear you who'll give a damn."

"You wouldn't dare hurt me, I'm the gamekeeper here." William managed to squeeze out the words.

The men started laughing, "And that gives you the right to kick the sprogs' food out of the women's hands does it. Well you won't do it again when we've finished with you." William found himself being pushed backwards toward the wood from where he had come. Through the undergrowth he was propelled until he was thrown down hard against a dead tree trunk covered in moss.

"Who's going to do it then?" said the first man.

"Do what, do what?" whispered William and he pressed himself back against the old dead tree. The four men ignored him. One of the men placed his great hobnailed boot on William's outstretched coat and turned to debate with the others.

"Do what?" repeated William quietly.

The men were talking too low for him to hear clearly but his heart dropped when, pinned to the spot, he heard, "Right, let's kill him here and now, get a good rock and we'll lay him out."

One of the men broke away from the group and moved purposefully toward a hazel thicket as the others turned their attention back to the frightened little man on the ground.

The gamekeeper was weeping; tears were rolling down his face and onto his old jacket.

"Let me go," he said softly.

"I'll do anything you ask, I'll leave the women alone, they can take what they want. Just please let me go, please," sobbed William.

"Sod ye, why should we you evil little bastard?" came back one of the men.

"On my word I promise you may take all the fruit you want; it's yours, just let me go."

The missing man stepped back into the group. He had cut a thin hazel stick about three feet in length. He flicked it through the air a few times and said, "This will make sure you remember your promise." William was hauled up, his trousers removed and he was thrashed soundly with the switch.

They left him in agony huddled back against the dead tree and sobbing uncontrollably. As they went back to the path, all were smiling.

The women were waiting back by the blackberry bushes; they hadn't dared interfere when the gamekeeper was dragged off.

"That'll teach the little bugger," said the first man to emerge from the undergrowth, "now let's get off home with what we've got. You ladies can come and gather some more tomorrow if the weather's fine."

"You won't see him around here tomorrow girls," added another, raising a chuckle. They picked up the baskets and cups, one of the men picked up William's stick, "he won't be in need this for a while," he said and tossed it down the embankment. Just as they were leaving the man who William had first set eyes on grabbed one of his companions.

"Aren't we forgetting something?" he said.

"Surely that was enough," was the reply.

"No, you soft bugger, we can't go back in these dresses; we'll get arrested for sure. Call 'em back and let's get this stuff off."

It was a long while later when William Hollis finally limped back to his cottage deep in the wood to lick his wounds. He did not tell anyone what happened that day, but the hiding had done him good. No more did folk have to fear the little gamekeeper with the rosewood stick whenever they went up the Limekiln lane. The story soon got out and Fred heard a version when he was at the cattle market. He told Dorothy she nodded her head.

"Well he probably had it coming. But I'm sure he will bounce back, his sort always does."

In October they began to clear another field, which was called the Gorses. It was situated directly under the Hatch. Fred was hoping to plant the ground with potatoes the next spring.

This field presented them with a particular problem; the field had only known sheep for years and was named the Gorses because of the thick patches interspersed with ash and alder trees.

Fred, Gunter and Mary set to clearing the ground with axes, spades and chopping hooks. Fred began slashing the bushes down and then lit a fire from old newspapers with some dry kindling. He piled the brushings on and when it was well ablaze he went back to cutting more pieces. Mary had to take the fresh cut gorse and pile it on the fire to keep it burning. Some she managed with the use of a pitchfork and the bigger pieces she dragged with her hands. The gorse was so prickly she wrapped pieces of hessian around her hands; despite this they still became very chapped and sore.

Gunter had the hard graft to do; he dug out the roots with a pick and a spade where necessary. Young saplings of ash and alder had got quite a hold in between the gorse bushes and these had not been disturbed for years. Little by little the field was cleared.

1941 opened with a surprise, a letter from Sam. It was addressed to Fred Tomas, The Willowmoor by Wellington. Fred opened it when he came in for breakfast with Mary.

"Surry about time" he sat down to read it. He chuckled "says here that this is the third letter he has sent. His mate does the writing for him and he thinks he may have got the name and address quite right this time, daft beggar". Dorothy sat down

"Well where is he?" Fred read on, mouthing the words, he did not answer for a while.

"Doesn't say but it sounds as though he is in good spirits and keeping well." He passed her the letter then when she had read it she passed it to Mary.

"Are you going to write back Dad?" she asked.

"Aye, maybe when I get some time, sounds as though he won't be in need us any more, at least not for a while." He had expected Sam to write how much he missed the farm but it was to the contrary. He was having a grand time his training had gone well and he was enjoying the food and free cigarettes. He expected to be in the thick of it somewhere soon but a censor's pen had been busy. Still the letter was well received and when the youngsters were told they were overjoyed.

"So when is he coming home?" asked Grace.

"He is not lass" said Fred "not until the war is over anyway."

Hannah started to cut out items from the newspapers where there was a reference to the army in action. It was so that when he came home she might have one for where he had been. Fred forgot to write and the letter found its way into Hannah's scrapbook.

Mr Jones organized the order in which the farms were to have their corn threshed He called around while Fred was busy after walking the fields and inspecting the full stackyard and barn he went to the house and told Dorothy to expect the threshing machine a week on Monday. "Good lord that is good news. A week on Monday you say, will it be Jack Munslow?"

"Yes it will and they will be bringing the threshing box on the Saturday and then set it up to start work on the Monday morning."

Fred came into the kitchen a short while after Mr Jones left and took a piece of sunlight soap to go and wash his hands under the pump on the back yard.

"What did he want?" he asked excitedly.

"He said he was very pleased with the way you have cleared the gorse off the field by the Hatch. He reckons that you should have a good crop of potatoes up there especially if you could spread a bit of muck before you plough it."

"Surry I don't know about spreading muck that field is a bit steep to get the cart up, still we can give it a try." He was just about to leave when she said "In that case we had better be ready for him and clear a bit of space over the next week". Dorothy was concerned "are you sure we are not over stretching ourselves the war is getting far more serious now".

"No matter what happens we still have to carry on lass and at the moment we are doing better than ever".

"I'll agree with you but who have you organized to help, they will have to be told you know."

"I've the word of Joe Evans, he and his lad said they should be able to come along. We can give them a hand in return some day they are finding it hard going on the Wrekin Farm."

"Give him a hand Fred Thomas; I think that you have enough to do here as it is without running to give help to others. Oh lord, let's hope everything goes all right. Who else have you asked?"

"I've had a word with Charlie Davis and he says he'll come. Of course I've asked Wilf and One-eyed Jack, he's always keen to earn a few extra bob."

One-eyed Jack's real name was Jack Latham. He stood over six feet tall and was as thin as a bean stick. He appeared to have seldom seen soap and water and always needed a shave. He got his nickname because he always wore a dirty looking cap at a precarious angle almost covering his left eye.

He lived with his sister and brother at Cluddely and between them they farmed about twenty acres. Dorothy had first met him at the market and he could talk the leg off an iron pot. Never short of a tale to tell he would lean on his home-made walking stick chain smoking Woodbines and ramble on to anyone with time to listen. He was hard to get away from but he was always willing to help out for a good meal and a few shillings to buy his cigarettes.

"That sounds all well and fine but what help will I have because I suppose they will have to be fed?" she asked indignantly. Fred could see an argument coming so he picked his words carefully.

"Well we'll have to give them a bit of grub Dot, can't expect them to come here and not to be fed. Keep the girls off school to do the running about for you it's a shame it's not Lizzy's day off".

"Well what do they expect in the way of a meal? I am not going to the trouble of cooking for that lot."

"They reckon once they start the machinery up they'll not stop it for any length of time. A bay a day they reckon they can get through so they will have their work cut out, there will be no time for them to go home and eat. Something quick is all that you need to give them."

"Well that's going to be two days they will be here at least with our two bays. As if I haven't got enough to do." She swept up some crumbs from the table into her hand and threw them out on to the back yard for the hens. Fred went and got his wash.

Fred and Gunter prepared a base in the stackyard for the straw to be stacked. They laid down large branches first then smaller ones all saved from the autumn hedge cutting.

Fred asked permission for Gunter to stay all day on the Saturday. He normally only worked until one o'clock but Fred wanted him to help with the milking to leave Dorothy and Mary free. Dorothy complained about having to feed him some dinner, Fred was not impressed.

"He's a good worker and he might as well stay and help me with the milking, no point in you coming out to do it. Mary's doing her best but hasn't got the hang of it like you. I can find him plenty to do," he said.

On Saturday morning Fred and Mary were up early and had done most of the feeding and the cleaning up by the time Gunter arrived.

They set to the milking while Mary went off to finish feeding.

"Don't forget those calves in the loose box Mary"

"No Dad, but what time will they be here, Beccy hasn't finished the eggs yet."

"Don't worry about the others lass. I want them out sweeping before we start."

When they were done they went for breakfast. Gunter took his tea and sandwich off to the farmyard out of the way.

"Have you swept that yard?" asked Dorothy as they went into breakfast, "we can't afford precious corn to be wasted in the muck".

"Next job. What's say Rebecca and Grace lend a hand, we can't afford waste."

The two girls had thought they were to have a quiet day.

"Yes Dad" they said, Mary smiled to herself.

"Granary to be swept as well," Mary added.

"So it had better be".

No sooner was breakfast over than Fred was back outside again with the girls in tow. They had only just swept the yard when they heard the sound of a tractor.

Dorothy had been watching from the kitchen window not wanting to miss out on the day's events. She saw the tractor pulling the threshing box slow down outside the farm gate.

"Here they come," she shouted "get round to the buildings and tell your father Grace, just in case he hasn't seen them".

"But I thought I had to scrub these chairs."

"Don't go answering me back now, you get yourself outside, there are gates to be opened. They don't want to be here all day, once they are set up they finish work for the weekend. Their time costs money."

Grace ran out but she need not have bothered, Fred had heard the engine and sent Mary down to the gate. She decided to stay and watch it was much better than scrubbing chairs and listening to her mother moaning on. The driver of the tractor waited till Mary was well out of the way then turned in, the threshing machine looked enormous. Mary shut the gate and walked behind, the driver took it steady, farm tracks had a habit of being very uneven sometimes dangerous. He stopped just on the yard, stood up out of his seat and bellowed to Fred "where do you want her set up Gaffer?"

Fred ran across "Between those two brick bays do you reckon?" he asked, not having worked threshing corn before. He needn't have worried. "Right you are, piece of cake, mind your backs now." The tractor was a Field Marshall and looked quite new. Fred moved the girls to the cowshed out of harms way with Gunter. He noticed two little faces at an upstairs window, Helen and Hannah were not going to miss out either! As the threshing machine was maneuvered into place a well worn green Morris van came bouncing onto the yard. The driver, who was dressed in overalls covered with oil and grease stains, got out of the van.

"Morning Gaffer" he shouted to Fred. "Thought we were never going to find you. Called at that café down the road and they told us where to come." He looked around, "You sure are out of the way here. How do you manage if the winter is a bad one? Just look at the hills" he said pointing to the fields behind the stackyard then, before Fred could speak, he set off to where the tractor was.

"We have to get a move on Gaffer, we want to have this machine set up and be on our way, things to do there's a war on you know."

It was two o'clock in the afternoon before they were happy with everything.

Fred and Gunter were lugging water from the back yard.

"Finished now Gaffer. Got her all fixed up ready to start eight o'clock sharp Monday morning." Fred left Gunter and went out to see what they had done. As they walked across the yard the man said "Do you feel safe having a Gerry around the place?"

"Can't do without him I'm afraid, they took my hired hand to fight" Fred replied.

"Well you shouldn't be doing all that lugging of water by hand; I suppose you're still milking by hand as well eh?"

"Afraid so" answered Fred.

"Well for a few bob I could fix you up with a very nice little pump a bit of pipe and you could stop all that water lugging lark."

"Aye it would be good but I would buy a new one if I had the money can't trust second hand."

"Rubbish owd lad, I have just the thing for you, petrol, not thirsty. Some pipe and a good big tank that I just happen to have lying around, maybe a trade? You would need coupons or somebody in the know if you get my drift."

Fred did and the idea appealed to him. There was an old well in the stackyard just behind the loose box with a stone cover and a cast iron pipe protruding from it.

"I've an old well round the back of the stackyard that has never been used."

"I'll take a quick look. By the way I'm Bob and my mate in the van is Norm, we work for Jack Munslow." They went to the stackyard and Bob dragged one of stone covers aside then he dropped stone down.

"Piece of cake. A couple of quid for the pump and we could be talking poultry here, maybe a ewe a bit later on, shame how they disappear, sort of fall down wells they do."

Fred grinned "Aye accidents happen round this time of year".

The two men left and Fred took a good look at the threshing box and the Field Marshall tractor, what a magnificent set-up it seemed. Perhaps he would have a tractor some day but he could not afford such a thing as yet. A motor car must come first and he may need the coupons for a pump but he was not going to get his hopes up.

Later when Mary brought the cows into the yard for evening milking their ears twitched and raised their heads, they stopped and shuffled nervously. They refused to pass the oily stinking monstrosity; they only knew the smell of the paraffin lamps and had never encountered anything that smelt so strong before.

Mary was stumped, they were going nowhere, and she shut the gate behind them.

"Close that cowshed door" Fred shouted pointing to the bottom shed. "Don't you let them go in there or all hell will be let loose." He need not have worried a calm brown cow stepped forward and calmly led the others the long way round the yard to the top door and to their places. She was the current favourite with Fred; there was always an 'Old Brown Cow'.

By Sunday evening everyone was so excited they had all looked over the machinery.

"You can all get to bed early tonight," said Dorothy at teatime. "A right early start we will need in the morning, four or five extra men to be fed besides all of you. I've used up two weeks meat coupons. We will have to fill them up with plenty of potatoes and carrots so you are with me Grace and Hannah."

"What about Mary and Rebecca?" Grace wanted to know.

"They will be outside working to clear the chaff away and you can look after Helen as well." Lizzy smiled and annoyed Grace even more by saying "Shame I am at the Glen both days they have a party on Tuesday night that can't be put off, there will be more for you to do Grace."

Everyone was up at the crack of dawn and Helen got in everybody's way. When Gunter arrived milking was almost finished. By half past seven the cows were milked and turned out into the field, they had stayed in all night. It would be several months until they were turned out at night. The morning was cold and there had been an overnight frost. Dorothy was worried that the help might not turn up but Fred did not let it concern him he had too much on his mind. Lizzy was glad to get off to the Forest Glen and leave them to it.

As soon as the dairy was done and the churns put on the milk stand at the gate ready for collection, they had breakfast. It was a hurried affair, a dish of bread and milk and some bacon sandwiched between thick rounds of bread. The wireless was kept switched off.

"No news is good news" said Fred "it stays off all day, if anyone asks it is broke, got that girls?"

They all nodded "Yes Dad".

Dorothy glanced through the window. "Oh, here's One-eyed Jack coming now". She saw the tall gaunt figure walking the track to the farm.

"“There'll be no smoking for him for a while" Fred said, "We'll not have the bay go up in smoke".

"Let's hope the others turn up" said Dorothy.

Fred washed and shaved while the girls got on with their tasks. Rebecca, Grace and Hannah fed the hens and the pigs and then collected the eggs, which they would clean and pack later. The helpers arrived, all except Wilf and everyone was milling around in the farmyard. Dorothy had Fred take them a pot of tea. Just after 8.15 the green Morris van turned in at the back gate just as Wilf put in an appearance.

By 8.30 all was ready; the men were in their places.

One-eyed Jack and Joe Evans were to work in the brick bay, passing the stooks of corn to Charlie Davis and Joe's son Mort who had very sharp knives enabling them to cut the twine quickly. Jack Latham and Wilf were to take the straw and stack it with Gunter's help. Fred himself would see to the sacks of grain and Bob was to keep the machinery working and help out whenever an extra pair of hands was needed.

Mary and Rebecca were to use the garden rakes to clear the waste chaff from underneath the box.

Bob started the tractor and engaged the drive, the flat drive belts started to move and the threshing box came to life. The big wheel began to turn as the slipping belts began to grip, soon the machinery was all functioning fine. The girls were amazed watching the wheels and belts turning and the clatter and din of it all. Everyone moved closer to make a start. Mary and Rebecca went to their places shown by Fred. The noise was deafening now that the feeder flaps were moving up and down. Bash flap, bash flap,

As the first stooks of corn were fed to it the rhythm altered slightly. Fred stood by the four sacks he had secured ready to collect the grain. Bash, flap bash flap went the machine as it took the golden corn down inside, he pulled the sacks to make sure they were secure, about the fourth time so far! Jack and

Joe were casting the stooks by hand as they were at the same level as Charlie and Mort.

More went into the feed hole then "here it comes" Fred's face lit up with joy as grain fell from the pipe into the first sack. He let the grain filter through his fingers. Here was the fruit of long days of labour. Things had changed forever, no turning back.

Hannah had been watching from upstairs she ran down to the kitchen.

"Can we go and watch what is happening outside?" she asked.

"You're not going out around that yard. Machines like that are far too dangerous and the men can't do with kids running about, they have enough to do as it is" Dorothy warned her.

"I will go with her," said Grace "come on Hannah". She started to make for the back door.

"Stop right there you are not going outside. Grace you start peeling the potatoes and see that you peel them as thinly as you can, I don't want you cutting half of the potato away. Hannah, take Helen in the other room, I've lit a fire in there to warm it up a bit. You stay there and keep her from under my feet unless I call you" she got a large enamel pot and put it on the table.

"Fill that" she said to Grace then she went into the larder and fetched another pot to put the carrots in.

"Oh lord why it is always the same when there is something interesting happening?" said Grace.

"You can stop that moaning young lady and get on with that peeling if you know what is good for you."

The kitchen was a hive of activity for the rest of the morning. The girls were kept too busy to argue; when they went outside they could hear the din of the threshing machine.

Pump more water, fetch more logs, fill that coal bucket again, what about the eggs, and take this to the pig. Get and clean this mess up.

At last there was a job that they had been waiting for "take these jugs of tea and cups to the men Grace, Hannah fetch the big white cloth from the other room". Grace grinned and set off. Hannah stamped off into the front room and came back with a cloth. It was too small.

"Where's that big cloth?" Dorothy wanted to know "go and fetch it. Look in that bottom drawer, bring the right one".

Hannah was furious, she stamped out of the kitchen she wanted to stamp on the cloth and shout and scream. She ran upstairs and looked out on the farmyard, she could see everyone working and there was Grace by the loose box door with a jug of tea.

"She has all the luck it is not fair" she moaned under her breath. She returned with the correct cloth. "Come on Helen fetch the salt and pepper from off the other table." Helen was four and a half and her mother was already giving her small jobs.

Grace returned and Dorothy sent her to give the peelings to the pig.

"I would much rather have gone to school" Grace whispered to Hannah as she passed.

"So would I but we have to do as Mam says."

At midday Dorothy wanted to know when to serve the dinner. "Hannah you go out and get your Dad, I want to know when to have dinner ready." Hannah was overjoyed and was out of the back door without her coat into the cold.

She was soon back. "Dad says be ready in half an hour and they will be in." They set the table and when the meat was ready Dorothy fetched a large blue and white serving dish from the top shelf of the larder where it stayed unless required for a special occasion. She lifted the cooked meat from the oven and placed it on the serving dish, how good it smelt.

"They will be in soon for their dinner so let's be ready, you girls stay back, in fact go to the far room out of the way."

Ten minutes later Fred came in "Are you ready?" he asked.

"Yes if you are" he went back and soon all the men came round onto the yard except Gunter who had stayed stacking the corn not wanting to join the others, he knew that Bob did not like him being there.

"Half an hour we got" said Fred "left her just ticking over". He took the soap and a towel and went back outside. Mary and Rebecca came in and washed in the sink from a jug of water. When the men had washed they all crowded into the kitchen.

"What's on the news Missus?" asked One-eyed Jack.

"Don't know" said Fred "radio is broke at the moment".

"Ah well no news is good news I suppose" said Joe Evans.

"Exactly" Fred replied.

"All right, all right sit yourselves down," Dorothy ordered. They sat and she began to dish up the food. She spooned the hot food directly from the pots on the range on to the plates. She set one plate aside and when all the men were eating she said to Rebecca "you give Gunter this" and handed her a big dinner plate piled high with potatoes, carrots, meat and gravy. She set off towards the door.

"Don't tilt it like that," Dorothy yelled "there'll be no gravy left on it." She realized she had been a little on the loud side!

"Well it would have ended up on the floor" she said.

She served them fruit pie and rice pudding then a cup of hot tea. She sent Grace and Hannah to bring back the used cups from the morning break.

"We are hungry and we have to get back out" said Mary.

"You can have yours when the men have finished. There will be no chaff under the box until they have had it going for a bit."

When they were finished they rose as one and thanked Dorothy then went back to work.

"Now can we have ours?" asked Rebecca.

"Put them dirty dishes in the sink first and give the others a shout." They soon cleared the table.

"Come on then and get what's left" Dorothy started cutting more meat from the joint and putting it on clean plates. "Get your own potatoes and carrots."

When it was over Dorothy sat down and relaxed in Fred's chair.

"Thank the Lord for that. You two do the washing up," She said pointing at Grace and Hannah. Grace started to say something about the amount of dirty dishes, pots and pans but thought better of it.

"Let's get it done, I'll wash you dry," she said and started to sort the plates and cutlery, "We can go and see what's going on outside when this is done. We can also take Helen to have a look"

Dorothy overheard, "Don't you go too near them moving belts or that'll be the end of you. You're Dad can't be watching what you are doing, he has got far too much to do he has". Thinking their Mother had dozed off to sleep. Hannah was startled and almost dropped a plate.

"Look what you are doing girl, don't you go breaking those plates they cost money to replace."

By four o'clock the daylight was starting to fade and it would soon be dark, the men were coming to the bottom of the first bay. It was much harder feeding the box having to throw the heavy stooks up on to it.

"Any rats in it?" called Bob, "we could do with some sport!"

"Not likely" Fred replied from the front end of the machine.

"I reckon there'll be a few, we are getting near bottom and we had best finish it. We can thresh the other one tomorrow. I'll slow everything down for a little while." Sure enough as they came to the last three layers of sheaves of corn, things started to move. "Bloody hell, where's me stick?" shouted One-eyed Jack.

"There are rats sure enough" shouted Joe and got a pitchfork he skewered a rat as it rose from the straw. He put it against the wall and crushed it with his boot then let it drop.

"What's going on?" asked Fred, the machine had almost stopped.

"Get ye sticks ready" shouted Bob.

"Rats" said Charlie to Fred as he dropped to the ground; he went in taking a shovel with him, Mort stayed aloft. They threw up the stooks one at a time and several rats appeared which were quickly killed, only a layer to go.

"Get them wenches out of the way" shouted Bob. The girls were all there but they ran back as the excitement grew. All the men except Mort were now in the bottom of the brick barn. As sheaf after sheaf was lifted, rats began to run in all directions. The men went after them, sticks, pitchforks, boots and the spade striking down on the evil brown creatures scattering in all directions. The shouting of the men, the clouting of the sticks and pitchforks against the brick walls and the squealing of the terrified rats brought Jingo into the fray, he caught those trying to escape into the stackyard.

Fifty one, fifty two three four and fifty five the men counted as they laid the dead rats side by side at the end of it all. "Thought you got no rats, Gaffer?"

"Surry I would not have believed it had I not seen it myself. All those rats eating the corn."

"Afraid so Gaffer, they're always around, the little buggers. Only takes a bit of grain and they breed, oh boy can them devils breed."

"Think there'll be any in the other bay tomorrow?"

"We'll wait and see Gaffer. Good for a bit of fun Eh, don't you think?"

"We'll get her set up for the morning before we go. We've got a couple of lanterns with us. It's oats again right? We'll see to it now you go and get them cows sorted they are waiting to be milked."

Fred was tired and exhausted that night, he had carried all the one hundred weight sacks to the granary that day. It had been no easy task and he just wanted to lay his weary body down for some rest.

Tomorrow was another day and would be just as hectic. Not all the hundredweight bags of oats would have to be carried up the stone steps to the granary. He would have to stack some of them in the cart shed underneath, there would be too many for the granary alone.

Next morning Fred and Mary were up at five o'clock and started milking early. They had almost finished and Gunter would arrive soon, they would get a quick breakfast before the men would arrive. Fred went up to the granary to fetch some feed for the cattle; he looked at the bags of oats neatly stacked one in front of the other.

"Eeh Surry" he said aloud not realising that he was talking to himself, "just think of it, the first grain to be grown on this bank." Voices interrupted his thoughts.

"'Where are you Gaffer?" the van had arrived early. Fred stepped outside.

"Up here taking a look" Bob came up the granary steps. "By the look of them bags, by the end of today you should have enough oats to make porridge for half the country."

"Aye," replied Fred "at last I feel we are doing a bit more to help feed the folk". He turned his back on the sacks and went back down the worn stone steps to the yard. Bob followed "I have something for you in the van" he said "thought I would get here early". They went to the van and inside there was a huge galvanized tank and lengths of pipe. "There's a pump under there as well if you want it. Yours for a couple of quid and a bit of livestock".

Fred thought for a moment "I've no way to set it up Bob otherwise it would be grand". "You don't have to worry about that. Let's get it out of sight before the others arrive and I will see you all right trust me you can't lose."

"Aye all right then you can come and have a bite to eat."

They unloaded and went to the kitchen; Dorothy was not happy but put on a brave face. Afterwards the two men went back to the farmyard Gunter was busy so the two men sat and smoked, it would not be long before the others arrived. Fred was very fond of his briar pipe which he had bought when he first started smoking. The bowl could be removed for cleaning and he made sure it was safe putting it in one of the airspaces in the cowshed wall. Bob outlined his idea for the water pump and Fred was keen to go ahead with the deal. It would cost some poultry now and a couple of lambs later in the year. When the others arrived he was the boss in charge and proud of it.

"Right men let's see what we can produce today."

Bob started the tractor and the threshing machine came to life again. They set to work on the second bay, each man carried out the same role as the day before. Mary and Rebecca joined them and helped as before. Fred kept track of progress,

The stack of straw was getting bigger and full sacks of grain soon had to go in the cart shed. Dorothy fed them as the day before and the radio was said to still be broken. At four o'clock the men were nearing the bottom of the second bay of oats. "Do you want us to carry on and finish tonight Gaffer or come back tomorrow? It will take another hour yet to get the rest through."

"Can you finish tonight? I'd be glad if you did, save the others coming back tomorrow."

"Just as you wish." He looked at the cows lined up by the gate waiting to be milked. "You will be milking those cows of yours at nine o'clock tonight."

"They'll have to wait a bit" chuckled Fred, taking no notice of the mooing the cows were making. He did not want the cows to come in until the machine had stopped. He decided to have just Rebecca on the chaff as there would not be a lot more now. He looked around; Hannah and Grace were stood watching.

"Mary, go now and start feeding. Tell your Mam we'll be late finishing; ask her to mix the calf milk for you and get those two helping. It's going dark soon and we'll need the lamps for the milking."

"But what about the rats, we want to see them catch the rats. That's why Hannah and Grace are here."

"If there are any more rats here, which I doubt, it will be no place for you. Now get off with you". Reluctantly Mary, Grace and Hannah left and went to the quiet of the backyard.

"It's not fair" Grace complained, "Rebecca is still there".

Fred had been wrong there were more rats and in the frenzy and the daylight fading several escaped. When the dust had settled there were eighty four corpses.

"Surry" exclaimed Fred "where have the beggars come from and what use are those bloody cats?"

"Reckon we deserve a bonus Gaffer," Bob said as the two men stood and looked at the heap of dead rats.

"I'm sure you do." The last few stooks were thrown in and the last sack hauled away. The tractor was switched off and everyone relaxed, they walked out onto the yard and lit their cigarettes and pipes. Bob offered Gunter a cigarette. "There you go Kraut, have one of theses, you have earned it." Fred went and fetched some money which he handed to all the helpers so they could get on their way.

Bob came across as they left "We have got another four farms to go as yet, it'll take us a day to move and set her up again. I will be back with Norm tomorrow and we will get it moved".

"Well, you have done a good job here today; this is the first grain to be grown on this side of the Wrekin."

"Should be proud then Gaffer, it can't have been easy working on those fields. Anyway we will see you tomorrow morning". He went to his van and set off.

Fred went and looked at the stacks; he took a handful of straw. Oat straw was quite soft and often used as a substitute for hay during the winter months. "Things are looking up" he said to himself. Not all the oats would be sold. Fred would keep some back and take it to be milled when he needed it for the horses or as feed. Now that would be good, rubbing shoulders with the other cereal farmers. He still had it in mind that he would try and buy a motor car, it would all depend on the results of this two days work. It would have to be a second hand car. Fred knew that he would not be able to afford a new one and anyway there were none being made because of the war. It made more sense to him to buy a motor car rather than a tractor as he had the horses, it was time he needed and time he lost plodding into town fetching and carrying. He would also need the petrol for the pump if that ever happened but then Bob seemed fair enough, only time would tell. He decided that it was the last time for a while the cats would get any milk at the dairy. There were some rats out there that needed to be got rid of. Maybe if they were a bit hungrier the cats might do their job. It was turned nine o'clock that night before all the work was finished and Fred was able to sit in his chair and take his last smoke of the day. Dorothy was tired and irritable. "Come on Fred Thomas don't go sitting there all night puffing at that pipe, time we were in bed."

"Sit you still Dot, only just finished we have." She decided to stay awhile.

"What yield do you think you have got?" she asked him.

"Oh average I reckon, about one and a half tons to the acre but who'd have thought there was all those rats chewing away at it. I'll be glad when the sacks have gone otherwise the little beggars will be chewing holes in the bags."

"Never mind them. Are you going to sell all of it?"

"No we will keep a bit back for feeding. We will count up in the next day or so, work things out then you will be able to write to Turners and tell them they can come and fetch it. These subsidies and the set prices are going to see us all right."

"Well let's hope it carries on, the war could turn it on its head but I daresay the cheque should be a pretty good one, do you reckon?"

"Aye" agreed Fred, every bone in his body was aching and he pondered whether a tractor may be the best idea after all.

"I reckon Dot, if that wheat we have sown does well, we could be able to afford one of those tractors."

"Just you hold your horses a bit. It's a motor car needed here is it not, and a few things for the house."

"Aye just thinking out loud, the horses can manage we have done well so far. I've been thinking about that, if we ploughed another twenty acres think of the subsidy we'd get, that would be forty pounds".

Dorothy looked at the fire; it had burnt low and was giving no heat. The room was getting cold.

"You have been lucky with the weather, it is not as cold as I expected. Still bank this up well, I'm going to bed and by the look of you, you had better come or you will be asleep in that chair."

Fred joined Dorothy in bed half an hour later.

As he lay there too tired to sleep he thought to himself. "I will use some of that oat money, we really need a car, Dot deserves something better she is older now.

Over the following days the weather turned bad. Fred checked on his grain at regular intervals. The girls found it was great fun playing on the sacks in the granary, jumping on them felt good, they sounded just like the bean bags they played with at school. Hannah asked if they could have some bean bags made on the sewing machine and filled with the grain. Dorothy told her she had better things to do and Fred said that the grain was far too important. If he had seen how much she jumped on the sacks in the following days he may well have changed his mind!

Fred forgot all about Bob, he had so many things to do occupy his mind then one morning Bob's green Morris van came into the farmyard. Fred was in the dairy when Bob found him. "Morning Gaffer, that bloody dog of yours is a sneaky bugger, kept his distance all round the farmyard and bit me overalls as I got to the side of the house." Fred looked; Bob's overalls had a tear in the leg.

"Sorry but he's like that, gets you when you least expect it. What brings you here?" Bob looked over his shoulder.

"Is that stuff still here?"

"Aye of course, it's where we put it." Bob's face brightened.

"Grand well if you're agreeable, I can fix it up for you."

"Most agreeable."

"Well if you put that bloody dog away I will see what needs to be done while you finish here." Despite his shifty manner Fred felt he could trust him.

"I'll tell the Missus to rustle up a brew for you."

"Aye but don't say too much just yet let's make it a surprise."

Bob had everything worked out when Fred found him in the stackyard. He was by the old well again and the cover was off. He had been rummaging in the pile of old farm implements in the corner,

"Is the Gerry here still?" he asked.

"Yes you walked past him earlier."

"Good well you need him to dig holes here and here to set a base for the pump, there is a good bit of oak over there, I've pulled it out already. Come with me I want to go inside but I don't trust you farmers not to have a bull or such like waiting for me."

They went round and through the cowshed to the loose box.

"I want to set up the tank up there in the roof trusses" said Bob "I will put the pipes in myself when you have done it. Now how are we fixed on the little deal we mentioned?"

Over the next week Fred and Gunter helped Bob set up the tank and base for the pump. Fred banged iron cleats into the wall to hold the pipes where Bob had marked with chalk. Dorothy was in no mood to be approached and did not care what was going on anyway. Mary was fascinated and so were the other girls whenever they went to see what was happening.

Finally Bob was ready to try it out; he produced a steel tin and poured out some petrol into the tank on the side of the faded green engine. He took a small starting handle and with a couple of swings soon had it ticking over.

"What happens now?" said Mary standing out of the way.

"We stop it and prime the pump" said Bob and he snatched the lead off the spark plug. "Only way to stop it I am afraid, can give you a fair kick so be warned." He took his stillsons and removed the top of the pump housing.

"Fill the chambers with water" he said "and we will be ready to go." He lit a cigarette while Fred fetched a bucket of water off the back yard. With the pump primed he started the engine again, it soon changed pitch slightly.

"It's working" said Bob and rubbed his hands together. "Let's go inside." The tank was sat up on oak beams resting between a roof truss and the end wall; they could hear the water running into it.

"When it is full you will see the water running out of the pipe I have stuck through the airspace up there" said Bob "that's when you stop the engine". Fred was so impressed he was lost for words. Mary went and fetched Rebecca, Grace and Hannah. They rushed out before Dorothy had time to complain.

"Now ladies and gentlemen!" said Bob, "you have heard the water arriving in the tank now witness this marvel of modern engineering". He led them back into the top cowshed to where a tap was fastened to the wall the thick iron pipe led from the tank in the loose box.

"Before your very eyes I will amaze you with a feat of magic." Hannah's eyes went wide, she liked magic, and she read about it in storybooks. Bob turned the tap, there was a long sigh and wheeze followed by a series of coughs, the girls moved back a pace.

Then water cascaded out, it was wonderful, it was so unlike the hand pump it did not stop.

"Surry Bob what a sight" Fred was quite lost for words.

"I thought you would be impressed, welcome to the modern world. This will save you some time with all this stock."

The engine ran until water cascaded from the overflow and Bob pulled the lead off.

"Now to business" he said. The following week Fred gave him three pounds. It was more than he had asked for but the subsidies were in and Fred felt generous, there had never been running water before and the time and effort it saved was incredible.

Dorothy had been difficult at first she could not see why the farmyard should have running water before the house. She argued that with the baby on the way she needed a tap more than Fred did. She soon realized how much effort was saved and was quite happy to let Fred keep the other half of the bargain. Bob came and took away some poultry and later a couple of lambs.

The petrol was a problem but Bob could arrange that easily for a payment in kind.

"Get a car Gaffer" he said to Fred on one of his visits. "I can get you extra coupons if you want."

Fred's mind was made up.

CHAPTER 4

A break in the clouds

By March Dorothy was certain she was pregnant again. It was a bolt from the blue she would be thirty eight this year and she was very unhappy. After another week her displeasure turned to anger and all the family were on the receiving end. Nothing was right or good enough for her and if they said anything she would bite their heads off with a quick retort. Helen would be five in June and would be starting school at the beginning of September. Dorothy thought it would be better to let her stay at home until she was six years old; she was small and thin for her age. Nobody would notice.

It suited Dorothy to have her at home, it was surprising what a five year old could do, she was ideal for fetching and carrying and running errands. She was the youngest. Dorothy would be alone as Mary was outside all day and Lizzy at the Forest Glen.

"Oh God, why did I have to be pregnant again?" she sighed to herself. They hardly ever made love nowadays; Fred was always too tired after a long day's hard work. When this had happened she had no idea, it must have been just that once at Christmas but she could not remember much about it. She had been able to afford a bottle of whisky and sherry. Lloyds the grocer had an allowance in and gave her the chance to buy, as she was a good customer. On Christmas day she and Fred made the most of it, it had been a very good day and evening. There was nothing she could do about it now though, a child was on the way and that was that. She would just have to cope. Besides the baby could be the boy she still longed for. She had never wanted such a large family and felt it unfair that she got pregnant so easily. The doctor had been of little support to her.

"It's what the Lord sends you. I see others with bigger families than you; thirteen or fourteen and some women give birth to more." He gave her no sympathy whatsoever.

"But I'm thirty eight; I can't be having another at this age!"

"It will be due at the end of August or beginning of September. Women older than you are still having babies. Healthy ones at that, it gets like shelling peas after a while it seems." It was an attempt at humour which failed.

"Just like a man to say something like that," Dorothy said to herself.

She made an appointment for a further examination in two weeks time and left to find Fred.

She had not told him why she had been to see the doctor it was not customary to discuss those sort of things. She waited until they were well on their way back. As they rode up the Ercall she gave him the news. He was taken aback "Good lord Dot how on earth can this be?"

"Well it isn't an act of God and I am not pleased about it myself. This had better be the last one for us and God willing it will be."

He fell into a stunned silence, how had she come to be pregnant again? The prospect of another girl and the depression that would follow, how would he cope?

They rode along in silence, Dorothy got her paper out and read for a while but it began to rain.

"I can't even read the paper in peace. What a day, haven't I got enough to cope with?

I am too old for nappies again, this can't be right and there is a war on."

"We'll manage" he said to comfort her. "The girls are all much older now and it just might be a lad this time."

"It had better be Fred Thomas, I have enough to feed and clean for. There is not much of a future to look forward to."

"Now lass dunna say that, we are doing so well now despite the war." She sat quiet for a while putting the baby out of her mind. The rain got harder and Fred pulled the piece of old tarpaulin from behind him and they unfolded it and huddled down to keep dry.

"Did you get those batteries for the wireless?" she asked

"Aye lass" He said and thought of the motor cars he had seen at Pearce's garage. He looked across to see the water dripping off Dorothy's hat, Perhaps it was time to think of a little more comfort. Neither of them mentioned the baby again until after the examination two weeks later. She simply confirmed what she had told him before. The baby was due August or September. Fred found it easy to keep busy and not to concern himself with the problems the baby could bring, he was happy for it not to be mentioned at all.

When the weather was right the muck was shifted onto the fields. This year there was so much to plough and there was still so much stone and rock in the ground.

The new fields were very stony and the plough brought lots of it to the surface including some very large pieces which Fred was able to remove with Gunter and Mary's help. He then had all the girls help out with clearing the smaller stones which could block the pipes of the seed drill. Stone picking was a job that the girls detested, it was such hard work. Filling buckets with stone and carrying them and tipping them in the hedgerow. When Rebecca, Grace and Hannah came from school they would change into old clothes then go straight to the field and begin work. Taking a bucket each they walked across the field picking up the largest of the stones. Grace continually complained but it was of little use, they knew that they dared not disobey their Father. Fred had never laid a finger on any of his daughters and rarely raised his voice or shouted at them but the girls knew by the tone in his voice that he meant what he said and that they must obey him. Sometimes Fred would take the horse and cart and they would spend the whole day picking stones. When they were at the table Fred told them how much easier it was getting to prepare the ground and next year would be better again. Grace was unconvinced "By better it means less big ones and more small ones I expect, either way we won't get a break."

"Well Dad says that we may be seeing something for our efforts very soon." Said Hannah "He wouldn't say what though"

"Well it won't be any money or some nice clothes" said Grace cynically.

Fred took the required samples of Oats to Turner's mill; he also took two sacks to be rolled for feeding the horses. He would have to wait his turn so he went into town to sort out the batteries for the radio. He tied up the mare where she could rest without being in any ones way. He picked up the two wet batteries from the floor of the trap and made his way to Pearces Garage, there were two charged ones to be picked up and he needed a new dry one. He walked into the yard and headed for the workshop then he noticed a yellow and black Wolseley over on the far side. It looked abandoned. He found the charge hand and handed him the two batteries.

"Thank you Sir. Got two to come back I see," he looked at the labels tied to the metal carrying handles.

What's that car doing?" Fred asked him.

"Oh that one came in yesterday, owner died I believe, his Missus can't drive, take a look if you want, it is a Wolseley."

Fred walked over to have a look at the car. "You are a real beauty" he said looking over it, he liked it a lot. He went back to the garage.

"Is it for sale?" he asked.

"I don't know, have to see the boss, but he's gone for his dinner. He will be back shortly if you can wait?"

"Yes of course, I have to wait for my corn to be milled anyway." He sat on one of the empty oil drums in the yard and smoked his pipe. Ten minutes later Mr Pearce the owner drove in and got out of his car. Fred went across to speak to him.

Mr Pearce looked at him "Can I help you?" he said.

"Yes I am interested in that car over there I hear it may be for sale" Fred replied.

"That depends. The Wolseley is a good car you know, one of the best and it will not be cheap".

"Well it is just what I need right at this moment. Would you consider selling it to me?"

"That depends if you can afford it".

"I reckon so, done well on the subsidies and I have just taken some oat samples to Turners to be graded. I should get a good price for the lot."

Mr Pearce was interested, he knew the subsidies were being paid and that farmers were becoming wealthier, however they did not normally come looking for cars always tractors.

"I see. Let me show you over it and see if it is what you want then we can go to my office and talk about costs. I've one or two customers who will be disappointed if they hear I had this model in and let it go without giving them a chance." The two men discussed the car. Mr Pearce knew Fred was good for the money and a price of ninety two pounds was settled on.

"I will just have a word with the bank before I write you a cheque" said Fred.

"Yes I think that would be wise of you. Come back to me afterwards".

They shook hands on the deal and Fred went to the Bank to ask for help until the cheque for the oats was paid to him. He asked a clerk if he could see the Manager

"If you can wait a few minutes I'm sure Mr Simmons will see you Mr Thomas, please take a seat". Ten minutes later Fred was shown into the manager's office, he sat opposite the manager's desk. Despite the huge amount of money he felt quite relaxed. He was always at ease discussing money matters with Mr Simmons. He had no sweeteners to offer such as a brace of pheasants or a bottle of spirits so he told his story of Dorothy being pregnant again, the acres now growing corn and the time he would lose when the baby arrived.

Mr Simmons was an educated man, shrewd and particular. A man who did not drink in public and he did not smoke, hands clean and well manicured. He knew Fred's finances were good and he was working hard as were all the farmers to support the war effort. Fred told him how he planned to buy a car.

"Are you sure you wouldn't be better off with a tractor?" he asked. "After all it is you that carries the burden of all the work. If this war does not come to an end very soon you will have a lot more to do. The Germans are really giving us a hammering with their U-boats, so little is getting through."

"Aye may be so but I can cope and I've proved that over the last year my horses are fine for now. I even get my own oats rolled now saving on feed stuff and we have straw and running water."

"Well, Mr Thomas, you are a good customer and I know that you and your wife have quite a family to rear. You have had your ups and downs and you are working very hard, very hard indeed. I still think a tractor would be more appropriate. After all, the more cereal crops that you can grow the more money you will be paid."

"Yes but the car will give me time which I don't have at the moment" Fred said "the Missus will need to be run to hospital and I will be on my own when the little one arrives. She is getting on and she feels the cold so much more. The Wolseley would be perfect for the job, keep her warm and dry. I have thought about it and I can't take a pregnant woman shopping on a tractor".

"A Wolseley did you say? Not black and yellow by any chance?"

"Yes, actually!"

"I know that car. I would like to buy it myself" said Mr Simmons "that is a good price you are being offered" Fred felt as though he had lost his chance.

"You know for where you live that car would be ideal, it would have no problem with the banks and it would take your family with no problem. I will telephone Mr Pearce and have a word with him myself if you would be so kind as to wait outside for a moment."

Less than ten minutes later Fred was back in the office and Mr Simmons had two cups of tea brought in.

"I say yes, you go ahead and buy the car. I have spoken to Mr Pearce and he will make sure it is serviceable for you."

"Why thank you" said Fred "the Missus will be so pleased".

"Maybe so but you really should have a tractor, there is going to be more pressure on you farmers as time goes on."

"Aye but with the cereal I have already sown and the root crops a tractor may be along sooner than we think" said Fred getting ahead of himself.

"Yes, well one step at a time, I'll put up the money and charge you a small interest fee only for the time you need it, let's hope that sample of oats impresses the buyers, not that they are going to refuse to buy. There's a war on and a country to be fed."

Fred thanked Mr Simmons and returned to the garage. Mr Pearce was all smiles.

"You had better take delivery very quickly. What about Saturday, could you fix it up for then?"

"Oh I think so, but I will have to apply for petrol coupons you know, can't run this on oats and water, four wheels it's got not legs," Fred said laughing.

"I can help you there, if you let me have your cheque I will help you fill in the forms."

Fred agreed to return with the cheque on Saturday and they shook hands to finalize the deal. Fred got his batteries and returned to brewery yard, Kit the mare was still where he had left her, and he patted her on the neck.

"You going to have it a bit easier lass, you are" he said. He was sure the horse understood every word he said.

"We are going to get a motor car. You've worked hard you have." He gave the horse a drink of water from the tap in the yard "let's get back and see what they reckon to those oats." He was in luck the oats were fine and would be collected in the following week, a cheque would follow. As Fred made his way back home he was overjoyed. Then a thought struck him, in all the excitement he had forgotten one thing.

"What have I done? Oh Lord, I have just bought a car and I have never driven apart from an old lorry in the Great War and I crashed that!" He pondered the problem for a while as he plodded alongside the Ercall, then he said out loud to Kit "no matter I can soon learn then you can take a rest. It can't be that difficult if you look at some of the daft sods behind a wheel." A couple walking along the path just inside the wood looked at him and wondered who he was talking to.

"Our Gordon got up here in his lorry and he is nothing special" he chuckled remembering his brother in laws face as they had driven up this road eight years before.

When he arrived home he told Dorothy the result on the grain, she was pleased.

"How about we look around for a car now lass?" he said. She looked at him "I don't know as we can afford to, we will have to see how much they cost" she was having second thoughts even though it was the one thing she thought would set them apart like her father driving around in his Rover.

On Thursday they went to town for the shopping. Fred tied up in the Brewery yard.

"I'll go and get a battery for the wireless" he said.

He did go to the garage but to see Mr Pierce. He gave him the cheque and had another look over the car.

"The missus does not know I've bought it as yet. I'll bring her along in a while" Fred said.

He was just leaving when Dorothy came by. She was not looking very pleased. She had already been back to the brewery yard and put some of the shopping in the float. She looked at him and he was looking extremely pleased with himself.

"What are you grinning about, is me hat crooked, you have been in the pub haven't you? Left me to carry the shopping."

"Nay woman," he said, "and your hat is all right. Come with me I want you to look at this motor car." He led the way back to the garage and the Wolseley.

"What do you think of that?"

"What do I think" Dorothy's face was expressionless, "not a lot, it's half yellow."

"But does the colour matter? The other half is black."

"You can't have a yellow car. When we can afford one it will have to be a black one or a navy or maroon." "Oh dear," thought Fred "I never thought about the colour".

Mr Pearce came up behind her.

"Well, what do you think of the car Mrs Thomas?"

"I don't really know?" Dorothy stammered.

"Your husband seems very keen to buy it so take a look inside. As I have already explained to him I will have to have a quick decision. A good second hand car is snapped up so quickly I have at least three other gentlemen waiting for something like this and as you know there's not a cat in hell's chance of getting a new one until after this damned war is over. They are now making aeroplanes". He opened the door

"Take a seat madam" she did as she was told.

"Oh it is lovely" the brown leather upholstery felt so comfortable, the warmth of the sun on the windscreen accentuated the smell of the interior. She felt like a lady for a few moments, if only they could afford it, would the colour matter? She got out quickly as her thoughts faced facts.

"Well, do you like her?" Fred asked.

"Of course Fred Thomas it is splendid."

"In that case it's ours. You sit yourself back in that front seat for a few more minutes and have a good look at her."

"What do you mean have you agreed to buy it?"

"Is it still all right to take delivery on Saturday Mr Thomas?"

"What did he say Fred Thomas?"

"Saturday would be grand," Fred was smiling "It's bought and paid for lass" he loved those moments when she was lost for words.

"I've been to the bank and it's all right" he said to her.

Mr Pearce smiled he had often seen Fred coming in to the garage on a Thursday to collect his wireless batteries. Mr Simmons call had convinced him Fred was a safe bet and that he was a worthy cause. Mr Simmons had told him that he farmed the old Bromley place and they had needed a car. In fact Mr Pearce had sold the Bromley's their Morris. He liked the way Fred always had a smile and was pleasant to the young lad he employed. A lad just left school but not yet old enough to be called up to fight. He took Fred aside while Dorothy came to terms with the car.

"Come about 11 o'clock and you can take it away."

"That could be a problem, see I have not driven anything since the last war."

"Ah in that case I will take you for a run in it first and you can try it out where there is not much traffic about.

"Thank you very much, that would be very good of you," They shook hands again. "Good day to you."

"Let us get on our way Dot and you can think on how much better it will be this time next week." He helped her out of the car and they went and finished the shopping together. Then they loaded up and set off for home.

As they headed up the Wrekin Road she asked him "So have you really bought it?"

"Aye, I have that. Just think you'll be able to come shopping just like a lady" he said and grinned at her.

To think that Fred had actually gone ahead and done it without consulting her, she was shocked. She should be angry, even furious with him. She could not think of any smart remark or cutting statement instead all she managed was "a lady indeed!" Then she thought "Have you got the wireless batteries or did you forget them in your excitement of buying a car".

"Nope I didn't forget."

"So how have you paid for this new motorcar?"

"It is sorted, I have seen Mr Simmons and it was him that swung it for me. He will let the cheque go through and we can give him some back when the cheque for the oats is paid to us."

"I hope you know what you are doing Fred Thomas". Oh the thought of riding in that car instead of this horse and trap. "Yes," she thought, "it would be grand". A good many years she had sat looking at the tail end of the black mare in front of them.

"Dot don't you worry. It will be grand you will see".

She knew that he was right. She had had known that ever since leaving the garage.

The rest of the way home was travelled in silence, each enjoying their own thoughts. On the backyard Fred unloaded the shopping before he took Kit around into the yard.

"All being well, that was your last pull up them banks with the shopping, you've been a good girl," he said to her, slapping her rump as he turned her out into the field.

Fred then went back into the kitchen where Dorothy was sat at the table with Mary and Helen.

"So, coming up in the world are we not" he said and winked to Dorothy. Mary looked puzzled.

"You tell her Dot" he said,

"We have a car; your Father has bought it today."

"Lordy, a car? A real car?" Mary was shocked, "what colour is it?"

"That's right, a motor car it is black and yellow and a Wolseley," said Fred.

"A wasp" said Helen "that's black and yellow".

"No the car is" he said. "I want your Mam to have things a bit easier from now on."

"And about time too, I reckon it will make a big difference to us especially with another little one coming. But how are you going to fetch it back here on Saturday?"

"I have given that some thought, I'll walk it."

"Walk it, how come?"

"If I walk to collect it then I will have to drive it back."

"But you can't drive."

"Well I was thinking it'll be a case of drive that car back here or walk back and I don't fancy walking both ways."

"Can I come with you Dad?" Mary asked.

"No lass I don't want any distractions."

That evening when everyone knew of the car Fred was bombarded with questions. The girls followed him around they couldn't wait for Saturday. Fred checked out the garage alongside the house, it was full of coal sticks, logs and bits of farm implements. He showed Dorothy and suggested the girls clear it on Saturday.

On Saturday Fred set off for town right after breakfast. As soon as the eggs were in Dorothy rounded on the girls. "Now then, we'll have that garage cleaned up, come on all of you" she said as she led them round to the front of the garage and flung open the doors. "Shovel all that coal up tidy, bag up those sticks; stack those few logs in rows along the side there." Mary, Rebecca, Grace and Hannah set to with a vengeance. This new car to them was the most exciting thing to have happened since the wireless set had been bought, and they could hardly wait. An hour later the garage had been put tidy, the earth floor had been swept so many times and the dust had just about settled. They made their way back to the kitchen where Dorothy was sat in Fred's chair reading.

"Good lord look at the state you are in" they were all grey from the dust. Hannah coughed and dust fell from her hair.

"We are finished Mam, come and take a look" said Mary. Dorothy got up "stay where you are, don't come any further in. I will get the kettle on you deserve a drink."

She put the kettle over the flame and got her coat. The girls went outside and she followed them keeping her distance as they were so dirty a grey cloud of dust could be seen surrounding them.

She stood well back as they opened the doors it was wonderful what they had done it was eight years since the floor was last seen, she was very pleased with their work.

"Brush off the worst before you come back in. I'll do you a drink of coffee as a treat, it is expensive but you have earned it. You can give yourselves a good scrub in the dairy later as you will not be going near the car in that state."

After brushing off as much as they could they sat down for their coffee which tasted so good after all the coal dust and cobwebs. Dorothy went and put the tin bath just inside the dairy and when they were ready she put plenty of warm water from the cooler into it and fetched a bar of sunlight soap and some of the rougher towels, she knew a lot of the dirt would be rubbed off rather than washed off. One by one the three girls washed themselves sitting in the bath they used the measuring cup to pour the water over their heads then dried themselves off and dressed in clean clothes. When they were all back in kitchen Dorothy brushed their hair. Looking down the drive she said "I wonder how your father is getting on?" She was concerned knowing that he had not driven a car before.

"Can we go outside and wait for him?" Rebecca asked.

"I suppose so but don't get in the dust." The girls were soon back outside; they waited by the garage watching the edge of the wood in the distance for a yellow and black car. "Here it comes" shouted Hannah with excitement.

"Run and open the gate" said Mary, Grace was off like a whippet. As it pulled up at the gate Helen was disappointed, she had expected to see a car with black and yellow stripes. Grace swung the gate open and the car came through slowly. None of the girls could wait, they ran to meet it keeping to the grass then they turned and skipped alongside till it pulled up in front of the garage. Dorothy's face appeared momentarily at the window.

Fred sat in the car with the engine running it had been quite a daunting trip but now he was home he could relax. The girls were bouncing up and down with excitement; he needed just a moment before he faced their chatter.

Dorothy came up just as he switched it off; she opened the driver's door and looked in. "Sitting there like a lord himself you are" she said. "We were getting worried."

"I feel like one" he said grinning from ear to ear. "Just taking me time, didn't want any mishaps" he grinned.

Mary opened the passenger door and Grace, Hannah and Helen scrambled into the back. Fred started the engine "listen to that, it hasn't missed a beat" he said. Dorothy looked around the car again,

She walked round to the passenger side all the girls were now in.

"Now come on you lot, get out," Dorothy ordered. "Let's get your Dad a cup of tea and something to eat." Fred got out and joined Dorothy; all except Grace had got out.

"Watch them doors when you shut them. Chop your fingers off they will" said Fred. "You can get out as well Grace. Sitting there like a little duchess, there's work to be done to pay for this car" Dorothy added. Grace still sat there, she did feel like a duchess very grand sat in the back of the car.

"All we need now is a chauffeur and to the ends of the earth he could drive us" she giggled to herself.

"Get out Grace," Dorothy shouted. "She really fancies herself that one does" she said to Fred. Grace got out and Mary shut the door carefully and they all set off for the house. Hannah walked alongside Fred; she did not like her mother shouting.

"When can we go for a ride?" asked Rebecca.

"Just you wait a minute young madam. One step at a time, your Dad's only just got through the door". She turned to Fred "How many petrol coupons are we going to be allowed I wonder?"

"Mr Pearce says he has filled her up for the time being. I think we will be all right though because we're Farmers. He reckons we have to go to the post office and fill a form out then we should get the coupons through the post," he replied.

"We can't take it very far until then. We would look right fools if we ran out of petrol and could not get back here, especially if we were on our way home with the shopping."

"Oh don't worry Mr Pearce said I could do about one hundred miles with the amount that he has put in the tank. Anyway it has got a gauge to tell you how much you have left."

"One hundred miles?" Grace piped up. "That would take us to the seaside."

"Talk sense girl, we are not going to the seaside. I reckon if the work is finished early tomorrow night your Dad might take us all for a ride. What do you say Fred?"

"Aye that would be grand."

"The garage is all cleaned up Dad, when are you going to put the car inside?" Mary wanted to know.

"In a minute, when I've changed into my old togs."

"You are not getting in that car in your dirty clothes Fred Thomas. It has only just come here and already you want it to smell like the rest of the farm". Fred reluctantly went back outside and drove the car into the garage he closed the doors behind it.

By the time he had returned to the kitchen he had decided he would not drive out tomorrow, why wait?

"Let's go tonight" he said "if we all chip in we should be done in no time."

"Hurray" squealed Rebecca, Hannah clapped her hands. The evening milking and feeding was finished in record time. As soon as everyone was out of their working clothes Fred reversed the car out of the garage then got out and waited while Grace opened the gate to the road then ran back and clambered in with her sisters. There was not enough room for all four of them so Helen had to sit on Mary's knee. He made sure they were safely in then got back in the car, Dorothy was wearing her hat and had difficulty getting settled. Fred waited patiently with the engine running.

"Well what are you waiting for?" said Dorothy.

"Aye right let us go then" Fred said and put the car into gear. He let the clutch up carefully because of the extra weight and they drove back into the garage! Nobody said a word, Fred pulled and pushed the gear stick until he found reverse then they went back out of the garage turning the steering wheel frantically as they went. He stopped again on the grass they were now pointing towards the road.

"Watch the duck pond" said Dorothy.

Fred found first gear and they bumped onto the rough surface of the drive, he stayed in that gear until he was through the gate then he stopped and went to get out to shut the gate then changed his mind and put the handbrake on.

"Oh Lordy" said Mary in the back.

"Shut up" said Dorothy.

"Where are we going Mam?" asked Rebecca.

"Shut up and wait and see" Dorothy snapped. Fred got in again and they set off cautiously down the road. After some time, due to Fred holding the car back by staying in a low gear, they arrived at the Forest Glen. Fred pulled up on the car park next to the pavilion to see if Lizzy wanted to come with them.

"That was good wasn't it girls?" said Dorothy.

"Yes Mam" they replied together.

Lizzy came out with Percy Podmore and went to the passenger door while Percy went over to talk to Fred who wound his window down.

"What a wonderful difference this is going to make to you and your family," Percy said. He looked the car over and said it was in fine condition. He could see all the girls in the back. "I hope it has good springs and brakes" he thought to himself.

"Taking it for a spin are you?" he asked Fred.

"Aye this way we will find out how good it is for getting up the banks."

Lizzy looked in and saw her sisters crammed on the back seat Dorothy wound her window down and asked if she was coming for a ride. Lizzy looked again and decided she was not going to try and get in there. She had ridden in Percy's car on occasions and she still remembered Granddad Wainwright's Rover.

"No thank you I will be making my own way back later, it's easier as I have my bike."

"If you're in before we get back you can see to the fastening up of the hens and ducks then" said Dorothy.

Fred looked across "Are you coming lass?" he said.

"No thanks Dad" she said "I had better be getting back".

"We'll be off then. We can go round the back I reckon. See how she goes."

As they pulled away Percy thought of all the times he had seen them passing in the horse and trap sat together with old blankets and hessian sacks covering their shoulders and knees to keep out the wet and cold. This would be much better for them.

They drove on along the bottom of the Wrekin, through Uppington and around to Garmston then on to

Eaton Constantine. Fred could have gone up Spout Lane to Little Wenlock but instead he carried on down the narrow lanes to Leighton where he pulled up outside the Kinnersley Arms.

The girls had not said a word, it was such fun sitting in the back, and the car had seemed to go so fast at times. They looked out. "Why have we stopped?" asked Mary. Fred turned around "How about a bottle of pop?" he asked. The girls in the back couldn't believe their ears.

"Yes please" they chorused.

"How about a nice drop of stout for you Dot, what say?"

"All right then," she agreed. Fred got out of the car and went into the pub. She wondered how he was going to pay then decided not to worry. She turned to the girls and said "All of you get out; you can sit around that wooden table over there if you want". They scrambled out with a certain amount of pushing and shoving, they had never been to a pub before. They climbed onto the rough wooden benches. Five minutes later Fred was back carrying a round tray with all the drinks. Dorothy got out and walked over to the table, what a treat this was.

"You know Dot, having a car is going to make life a bit better for us, I'm enjoying this, we will do it again." She had to admit to herself that it was very pleasant to sit here and relax; they seemed so far from home though.

"Don't you go getting ideas too grand just yet, Fred Thomas? What if we can't get back, have you thought of that, it's been all down hill pretty well." He grinned and took a drink of his beer. "Dunna worry she'll be fine. Aye fine indeed" he took out his pipe and relaxed. The girls chattering did not bother him at all. When they had all finished Fred returned the empty glasses and bottles back to the bar. Everyone was in the car he took a detour and went to have a look what was at the back of the pub. The ground fell steeply down to a big brook. He was wondering if it went down to the Severn when he remembered them sitting waiting to go. "Another day" he thought.

"Get a move on" Dorothy scolded when he got back in. "We have to get back soon or it will be dark and past their bedtime."

"We are all right" said Hannah.

"What do you know?" snapped Dorothy, "come along Fred let's get going". Fred started the engine and moved away from the pub. He followed the road towards Ironbridge. After a while they could see the Buildwas power station, the girls had only seen the chimneys of it from the top of the Wrekin. When they reached it he stopped the car so they could get out and have a closer look. They were fascinated; it was so huge they had not seen anything like this before. The six tall chimneys looked as if they went all the way to the sky. Dorothy was getting anxious.

"Don't worry Dot. Just relax a bit. It'll do them good."

"There is still a lot of work to be done tomorrow, just don't forget that."

Fred thought it best to say no more. He got out and persuaded the girls to get back in the car. He told them "We have to climb Jiggers Bank and if we don't get moving you could end up walking home". That sounded bad and the girls were quickly seated in the car again. Fred drove into Coalbrookdale and turned left where they began to climb, on the left was the huge iron works.

"Is this Jiggers Bank" asked Hannah worried that the car was going slower.

"Just the start lass," he drove on ever higher, then changing down another gear he said

"This is it. Let's see if she will climb up here. I hope so or you will all have to get out and push". There was a sharp intake of breath.

"Have to push this nice new car?"

"You sit tight and hold your breath" he said. The road rose steeply in front of them and the car soon slowed again. Fred went down to first gear.

"Come on old girl, come on" he muttered, this was the first time the girls had seen Jiggers Bank, not a whisper came from them.

The engine seemed to be groaning as they neared the top then suddenly it picked up and they seemed to shoot forward onto the top.

"We've done it" said Fred relieved, "that is one steep bank, and I was worried there for a moment".

Everyone was talking at once; it was bedlam for a short while. Then when everyone had got their breath back Mary said "Doesn't the Wrekin look funny from here?"

"It looks a very long way away Fred Thomas, we have the Malthouse Bank to climb yet" Dorothy said concerned. "This car will get up there I know it" he said grinning and they flew down to Horsehay.

"Are we going back now Dad?" asked Hannah.

"Yes we turn off here by the pub." There was a burst of laughter from Mary and Rebecca. "What's that?" Mary asked. They were laughing at the painted board hanging outside the pub which depicted a woman in Victorian dress trying to scrub a little black boy white in a bath of soap suds.

"Keep going Dad, don't go home yet, there's more to see" she said. He stopped the car "That is the 'All Labour In Vain' he said. "What I will do is take you down to Wellington and back up the Ercall."

"Think about the petrol" Dorothy reminded him. "You can't turn this out into a field to feed itself." Fred took no notice, he pulled off again he was enjoying the ride out, and he hadn't been around the Wrekin since selling the motorbike. On they went down the Dawley Road to Wellington where he turned left onto the A5 known as Watling Street at that particular place.

"There's the pop works" he said pointing to O.D Murphy & Sons. "That's where they made the pop you just had."

It was such a big building. "I'll bet they have thousands of bottles of pop in there" said Grace. "Millions" said Hannah, only knowing it was more than a thousand.

"No Millions and Millions" said Grace again.

"A lot" said Fred chuckling at his daughters arguing.

Turning off at the Ercall the rest of the journey was familiar and they had no problem getting up the banks.

Back home the girls tumbled and scrambled out of the car and ran in to tell Lizzy all about the ride. Lizzy was sat at the table, the kettle was boiled and the teapot was waiting. The girls all began talking at once it was only when Dorothy came in and passed her coat and hat to Lizzy to hang up that they paused for breath.

"Is the poultry fastened up for the night?" she asked Lizzy

"Yes Mam."

"Right you young ones. Get a drink then off to bed with you." The tea was made and Lizzy heard all about the big adventure but she was too tired to be bothered she had not gone. In fact she was quite glad, "Imagine being pressed into the back of the car with this lot of chatterboxes" she thought to herself.

When Fred had put the car away he came in, sat down and lit his pipe feeling quite contented with life. This was more like it. He had often dreamt of what it would be like to own a car, now it was a reality.

With the arrival of warmer weather Fred and Dorothy often drove to the top of the Willowmoor Bank and parked to walk the fields together, usually with Helen and Hannah trailing behind them.

Oh how good the new spring wheat looked after a shower of rain.

"Growing nicely" Fred said as they walked along the edge to the wood. "Better put a few snares down the rabbits are eating everything in sight" he continued.

The corn was patchy where the young shoots had been eaten and the grass was also very short next to the fence. They began to go into town twice a week. Dorothy would make some excuse that there was something or other needed, it saved her from having to do all the shopping on a Thursday. Saturday mornings after milking and breakfast Fred would drive her to town. She liked people she knew to see that they could now afford a car. She met folk she knew from market. The war was always the biggest topic of conversation. They would be glad when it was all over and they could get back to doing the trade they once used to do.

She made friends with an old lady who lived in Wrekin Road and liked to go and visit her. On these occasions Fred would leave her in town to do her shopping and return home to carry on, he would then return later to pick her up. It only took ten minutes to get into town. Dorothy enjoyed these times; the war meant no market stall so it was a break for her. It was a break for the girls as well. Saturdays became much more enjoyable once the scrubbing was done; it gave them more time to do things for themselves.

When Mr Jones paid them a visit, he walked with Fred and was most impressed by what he saw. They sat on the hedge bank by the Limekilns and looked out over the farm and fields. "Well you certainly turned this place round" Mr Jones said.

"Aye good incentives though, despite the war" Fred replied. Mr Jones looked up into the sky, all was clear. "There's a lot more aircraft about these days" he said. "You never know if it is going to be a German raider, one followed the railway line through here the other week."

"We tend to be out of it here" said Fred "unless they drop in like last year". Mr Jones chuckled; it wasn't supposed to be funny.

"Do you think you can keep up the pace?" asked Mr Jones seriously.

"Aye, Gunter's a great help and of course there's our Mary."

When does she leave school?"

"Next year, she will be fourteen then" said Fred.

"In that case I advise she stay and work here on the farm, otherwise she may have to work in a factory. Register her as a land girl when she leaves school."

"Aye sounds good to me, the others all help out as well." They sat quiet for a while and Fred lit his pipe.

"I was puzzled when you bought a car, it seemed out of place for the situation we are in, most farmers want a tractor and yet you have done grand."

"Aye I knew it would stir up folk but I managed these fields with the horses and hard graft and I can do it again. We have another little one on the way now I can't be cut off anymore from the outside world, we get no deliveries now and the time I save let's me get on here."

"I understand now, next you will be getting a telephone."

"Lord no, my missus can talk enough as it is. No it will be a tractor."

Back at the farm Dorothy brought them a cup of tea, she was quite sociable.

"Ever since we got the car she has been a changed woman" said Fred.

"Well let us hope it is a boy this time for you. You wouldn't think there was a war on would you." He looked around, it was a lazy day and all was quiet, none of the windows were taped.

"Not worried about the bombers then" he said.

"Who is going to drop bombs up here?" Fred said and chuckled.

"True, I will be on my way." Mr Jones waved goodbye to Mary and Dorothy as he went back to his car. He liked Fred; he recognized the hard work that had been put into the farm. Perhaps they deserve a car he thought to himself as he drove off to his next appointment.

Dorothy wrote to her Mother telling her of the new car and how grand it was. She did not mention being pregnant again in her letter preferring to stick with the good news as she knew her mother would not approve. It was the end of June before she put in a letter that she was to have another baby in September. She knew that her mother would not be pleased that she had left it so long before telling her.

"I can't believe it" Sarah Wainwright said to her husband when she read Dorothy's letter. "You would think that they would avoid such things now that they are getting older, they surely ought to have more sense. I have to admit that I am more than a bit annoyed to say the least. How old is that youngest of theirs she must be five years old now? You would have thought that the pair of them would have been more careful. Are you listening to me Bill?"

"Yes dear, I can hear you but I suppose it's this longing Dorothy has for getting the son she has always wanted. You certainly saw to it that we had no more family." He said begrudgingly to himself. "Threatening to sleep in a separate room" he thought to himself. "I would have been the laughing stock of the neighborhood if it got out that Bill Wainwright, squire of the Manor was not sleeping with his Missus in case more kids came along. Still must not grumble, Dorothy and Jane did their share when they were here and the lads will inherit it all" he thought. Sarah left him alone and went about her housework, she said no more about the new baby to Bill but she had an idea in her head and it would not go away. After several days she could contain herself no longer.

"I've been thinking for some time now Bill, what would you say if I were to offer one of Dorothy's girls a home here. Now that Jane has left I miss having her around to give me a hand. I could do with someone to do some of the little jobs for me. This house is so big and we are not getting any younger." Bill lowered his paper "What woman? Where has this sprung from?" he said loudly.

"Well I think we could really do with a bit of extra help. I was thinking about young Rebecca. She seems to be a real lively child. Put your paper down for a minute" Bill put his paper down. He looked quite angry.

"It seems to me that you have already worked this out and that I will have very little to say in the matter. So you had better see what you could do about it". He rose from his chair "Where's my walking stick. Now where have you put it?"

"I have not put your stick anywhere but I suppose I will have to go and see where you have left it. My goodness you do need someone to run about after you". She turned on her heels and headed down the passage towards the back kitchens. Bill sat back down. She just might have a point; he too had missed having his daughter around. She had always been his favourite and had fetched and carried for him.

"Here is your stick; it was where you had left it. I suppose you have forgotten that you had to wash and shave this morning and you did not need to use it at that time."

The gout in his legs was getting more and more trying for him and he found that to be able to put a little of his weight on the stick was quite a comfort. He also felt much more secure negotiating the cobblestones around the stock yard and farm buildings. It was handy to put his weight against it when he wanted to shoot a pheasant or have a shot at any dogs he caught sheep worrying.

Dorothy received a letter back telling her they would be coming to visit on the first Sunday in July despite the petrol rationing. Dorothy was looking forward to seeing them as it was two years since their last visit. Although her pregnancy was causing her to feel very tired, the house needed to be given extra cleaning. She persuaded Fred to take her to a sale, which were quite popular. Money was scarce but not for Fred and Dorothy. They had more crops sown and despite the back breaking effort, Dorothy had been out in all weathers with Fred and Mary, the others had also worked hard when not at school. They decided to put something into the house as a reward for all the effort. A beautiful light oak sideboard was bought for the front room. It had a gilded mirror and Dorothy began to fill the cupboards of it with better china and cutlery. They bought some pieces of carpet which were better than what they had to brighten up the place and Dorothy sewed some curtains from material she bought using money from the egg payments.

All the family was looking forward to the grandparents visit. Fred was keen to show off the car and the fields now they had been ploughed and were producing crops. Dorothy knew that her mother would be pleased with the way that she had improved the house.

On the day of the visit, the girls waited patiently for Granddad's Rover to come into sight, they were all washed and tidy. They knew that Grandma would have some little things for each of them.

It was Rebecca who spotted them first and ran to open the gate. Grandma would always bring over useful presents, most often it was clothes for the girls. She would say that they had been too small for Jane, or odd things she had found rummaging about on second hand stalls. Dorothy however noticed that virtually all the clothes had not been worn. This trip was no exception.

"To help you out a bit Dorothy" her mother said. The price tag could still be seen on a pair of socks.

If the weather was fine Dorothy and her mother often took the girls for a walk while the men talked. Their favourite walk was to the Half way house. Where they would sit and drink tea and talk while the girls played after having had a treat of pop and crisps. They let the girls go as far as the Point to look out over Wellington, or sometimes further up the hill but not all the way to the top that was too far now.

As Dorothy was pregnant again there was no such walk this time. The girls were told to behave themselves while

Mother and Grandma took their tea in the front room. The girls grumbled they had to stay clean.

When they were seated, Dorothy poured out the tea into her best cups. These were not china, just ordinary crockery which she had purchased at one of the house sales. They were white with a maroon and gold pattern made by J. Friar & Sons of Staffordshire and looked very good against the best white tablecloth; that too only came out on special occasions.

"How are you coping?" Sarah asked her daughter. She could see that Dorothy looked very tired.

"The best we can, we are coping much better with the farm now."

"I can see you are. You know Dorothy, Fred seems to be making a go of things, your father and me never thought you would make ends meet and manage this place like you have. The girls have been such a help to you."

"They have to earn their keep, pity they had not been born lads".

"You should be very proud of them just the same. Perhaps this one that you are expecting will be the boy you have always longed for."

"I wish it would be so. Lord I'm due a break."

They chatted for a while then Sarah said "Incidentally Dorothy, now that Jane has married and left, I miss having her around the house; you know how cantankerous your father can be. I was wondering if you would agree to let Rebecca come and stay with me for the summer holidays. Then perhaps, well we could talk again another time. If she wanted to stay perhaps you would agree to let her live with us."

"What do you mean live with you? That you want her to stay for good? But we need her here."

Sarah had sown the seed and Dorothy had reacted as she expected. "Well give it some thought both of you. We will probably make it worth your while, I'm absolutely sure of that. We would give her the best you know, she would want for nothing."

"We'd better think it over; I'll see what Fred says." Dorothy was thinking what a good idea it was. Letting Rebecca go to live with her Mother would be one less child for her to keep and clothe.

Fred took Bill to the top of the Willowmoor Bank in his car to show off the fields of wheat that were doing so well. "What a difference this new fertilizer and a covering in basic slag makes" Fred remarked to the older man. Bill leant on his stick and looked around, he was quite impressed.

"The Ministry have said that we can have a covering of lime next and that should kill a few of the wire worms and such" Fred continued.

"All done with the horses" Bill said looking at Fred's work. "What you need is a tractor here, it may not suit some of these banks but it would save a lot of work."

"We can't think about one of them just yet, only just bought the car and Dot's so pleased with it besides the horses are fit and strong."

"She is quite right too, no joke sitting in a trap in the winter months."

Fred was quite amazed at the older man agreeing with what they had done.

"Fred you were lucky to get that Wolseley. It is very difficult to buy one now unless you are in the right place at the right time. It's taking this country all its time to fight this war not one bit of spare metal to make cars. Perhaps you ought to think about getting a tractor next year".

"We will have to see what this wheat yield is like" said Fred. "It will depend if we can get the subsidy to do some more ploughing anyway."

"Oh I think that you can get that all right. If not you ask Dorothy to write to me and I will have a word in the right quarters."

Fred could not believe his ears, his father-in-law offering to help!

He must be getting soft in his old age. So amicable despite the gout in his legs getting worse.

Fred and Bill talked at length about the subsidies and the benefits to those that took them. "Be in mind Fred that the subsidies are a double edged sword. If you don't meet the required targets or fall out of favour with the ministry you could lose it all. I know of tenant farmers being turned out and replaced if they don't come up to scratch."

Later, after they had eaten, the old couple left. The girls had managed to stay on best behavior and Granddad gave each of them a silver sixpence. Grandma was smiling warmly at Dorothy as she left.

The family watched them drive away and Dorothy took the money from the girls.

"Now get changed and get some work done" she told them.

As soon as they had gone she told Fred about her Mother wishing to give Rebecca a home.

"So that's it. I wondered why the old man was so pleasant and giving a bit of encouragement instead of finding fault and criticizing everything he saw" Fred replied.

"What do you mean?"

"Well the old devil was pleasant today, even suggested we get a tractor next year. He had nothing to grumble about. I'll give it some thought."

Dorothy said no more until later in the evening when little ears were tucked up in bed.

"Well what do you think about the idea of letting Beccy go to live with them?"

"I'm not sure, we can't go giving the kids away just like that. Beccy is a good one. I like her sharp and quick thinking, have a try at anything she will."

"What if we give it a try, she can always come home if she wants to and besides they can afford to give her more than we can." She made it sound so good. "I don't like to say it but it's taking us all our time to feed and clothe what we've got and there's another one on the way."

Fred could see she had made her mind up. It did not matter so much to him as there was so much work on now, one less to feed and clothe would not affect him.

"What do you think? Should I write and tell them she can go for a fortnight and see how things go from there?" Dorothy went on, craftily putting the onus on Fred to make it look as if it was his decision.

"All right, write and tell them they can have her for a couple of week's holiday, and then we can see how things go."

Dorothy was relieved, she did not want to mention how her Mother had said they would make it worth their while one day. It just might look as if they had been bribed.

"Yes I'll do that, they break up in a few weeks for the summer holidays. I will tell Mother to come and fetch Beccy then. They can keep her for a couple of weeks and then if she wants to stay a bit longer we can sort something out."

Two weeks later Mary met the postman at the gate as she was driving the cows across the road to the field. She took the letters from him; he was always pleased to pass the morning post to anyone who was available. It saved him having to open gates and drive to the farmhouse especially if there was only one letter to be delivered. Mary saw one of the letters was from Grandma so she took it to Dorothy as soon as she got back.

"A letter from Grandma" said Mary "I can tell by her hand writing". Dorothy knew that Mary would not go from the kitchen until she had some idea why her Grandma had written so soon after her visiting.

"Not coming again is she?" Mary asked, thinking about all the extra fuss and cleaning. "Yes Grandma says they will be coming over next weekend. She's says that she would like Beccy to stay with her for a couple of weeks as they are all on holiday, to do a bit of running about for her."

"Beccy going to stay for two weeks" Mary said in amazement.

"Yes, she says that they will not stay long, your Granddad has so much work to do at the Manor. This means that I will have to buy one or two things for Beccy she will need a new coat for a start."

"A new coat! Just to go there for two weeks."

"Yes I think so. Your Grandma will want to take her shopping with her on Wednesdays". Dorothy did not give any hint to Mary that Rebecca might not be coming back. Later she fetched Rebecca into the kitchen and told her that Grandma and Granddad wanted her to stay with them for two weeks holiday and that they were coming to collect her, Dorothy said nothing about her staying for good. "I will have to buy you a few new clothes" she said. Rebecca was pleased.

She told the others she was going and that she was having a new frock, coat and shoes.

"It's not fair" Grace complained to Mary, "Beccy having all those new clothes just to go for a holiday at Grandma's".

"We could all do with a coat each" Mary replied "but Mam says there are not enough

clothing coupons for all of us to have something at the same time. So it doesn't look as if you are likely to get anything".

"It's just not fair."

"You can moan all you like."

"One day I'm going to be well dressed, I am going to be beautiful."

"You're hoping, what are you going to do, marry a prince?"

"You never know."

"And pigs might fly."

On the Sunday Sarah and Bill came to collect Rebecca in the morning. They had a cup of tea and a piece of cake in the kitchen then made their excuses to leave as soon as they finished. Rebecca was dressed and waiting for them. She looked very smart wearing her new coat as she sat in the back of the car. Sarah finished saying her goodbyes. "We will take good care of her" she re-assured Dorothy as she gently kissed her daughter on the cheek and got into the passenger seat. Dorothy, Fred and the girls stood and waved away until the car had gone from sight. The school term was due to start in September and as the date approached, Hannah was beginning to miss Rebecca so much she started to ask questions.

"When's Beccy coming home, school starts soon?" she asked her Mother.

"I don't know" Dorothy dismissed the constant questions.

"But she has to go to school."

Eventually Dorothy said "perhaps your Grandma will let her go to school there".

She knew that Rebecca would not be coming back to start school. Her mother had written to her saying how Rebecca had settled down well and that she was such a little treasure to have around, even her father enjoyed her company.

"Go to school there, where?"

"Cheswardine."

"She can't do that" Hannah argued, "She has to go to school with us".

"We will wait and see your Grandma has no one to keep her company."

Hannah told Grace what might happen.

"Why Beccy? Why not me?"

"Because you're not old enough."

"Oh yes I am."

"I wouldn't like to live with old Grumble Guts Granddad." Said Grace

"Be better than here. She'll always have nice new clothes to wear. It's not fair."

"Don't you go letting Mam hear you say that?"

"Well it's not fair."

When the girls started the new term Dorothy made it quite clear Rebecca would be staying at Cheswardine. There were some moans and long faces but they stopped asking questions. Dorothy was relieved; she had not noticed the absence of Rebecca enough to let it worry her. She had seen to it that Grace and Hannah had to do a little more work around the place.

Sarah did suggest to Bill that they take Rebecca to see her parents and her sisters just in case she was missing them.

"No damned petrol to run about for nothing" he replied. As far as he could see Rebecca did not seem to be homesick, if she was she had not said anything.

He was right. She was not the slightest bit homesick, she was so busy, there was so much going on. Grandma kept her so busy when she was not at school.

Her two uncles Arthur and Harry who worked the farm were always teasing her. "Fetch this, take that, Little Miss." 'Granny's little helper' they called her. Granddad liked having her about the place. She was so quick and lively compared to how his daughter Jane had been.

"Fetch me boots lass" he would say and she would run and bring the boots back immediately.

"Where's me hat?"

"Here it is Granddad" she would have it ready knowing that would be his next question. She had quickly learned the order of his dress before he went outside. Bill liked having her around the house. He was kept busy with the Manor and with the war effort so they saw little of him during the day.

Rebecca did most of the jobs she had done at the Willowmoor Farm. She would pick up the windfall apples from the orchard and lay them on trays in the larder for Grandma. Carry the potatoes from the buildings to the kitchen. Any jobs that saved Grandma's legs were no trouble to Rebecca. A close relationship developed between the older woman and the ginger headed girl.

At first Rebecca was missed by her sisters. There was now more work for each of them to do and Hannah especially missed her company. They were pleased to get a letter saying how she was happy and that she had settled in. Dorothy did not show any interest in the letter she was heavy with her pregnancy and grew more and more tired. Now that she was older she found it much harder going, she ached more and was always out of breath. The harvest was good and Fred had to bring in some land girls to help. Mary was quite shocked at some of the things they told her. Wilf was busy on his own ground and so was Joe Evans but folks from the village offered help. Fred fetched some of them in the car. It was hoped that the harvest would be in before Dorothy had to go into the nursing home.

The threat of invasion by German troops had lifted. The German planes still bombed at night but during the day there was the reassuring sight of the familiar British and American aircraft in the skies. Fred began to dream of owning a tractor, turn it on and away you go, load up the trailer switch it off and leave it. He had ideas of clearing the two side fields under the Wrekin to plant potatoes.

Dorothy had ideas she told him that she intended to rear more poultry making an early start in the New Year. All she needed now was to get the pregnancy over with. When she went into labour she knew from experience that it would not be long. "Get the car I want to go now" she told Fred as the pains gripped her. She had waited a while before sending Helen to find him. She was booked in at a nursing home in Wellington and Fred quickly drove her down in the car.

"This looks more homely and very smart," she said as they walked to the door and rang the bell. It was answered by a very friendly looking woman who was the matron.

"Come on in dear and I will show you to your room. You are on the ground floor until after baby is born and then I will have you moved upstairs to your own room to rest." The thought of having her own room, Dorothy smiled despite the contractions coming at very close intervals.

Matron could see that this baby would soon have to be delivered and showed Dorothy to a quiet room containing just one bed and other equipment. Everything was very clean and sparkling, white sheets were turned back on the bed. An antique table stood in the corner of the room and a vase filled with fresh flowers. Dorothy looked out from the window, there was a well kept garden and it looked as if it was from here that the flowers had been gathered.

"You get yourself undressed and quietly into bed I will be back in a minute with Sister, and we will have a look at you"

Matron looked at Fred with concern as she saw him to the door.

"By the look of your wife she will have the baby tonight you telephone in the morning and see if there is any news."

"Perhaps you would be good enough to ring this number and they will send a message to me. You see we have not got a telephone of our own." Fred handed her a piece of paper that Dorothy had written the number of the Forest Glen on.

"Yes I will do that if there is any news, and I am sure that there is going to be."

The next morning Fred had everyone up early it was the new term. Lizzy helped out by making the sandwiches and preparing the bread and milk for breakfast before she went off to work.

Later while Mary and Gunter finished the milking. Fred started some breakfast and cleared the dishes away. He was turning the eggs in the frying pan when a voice made him jump

"Morning Gaffer, have I got news for you" Fred turned around and saw the postman standing in the doorway.

"It's a lad this time" he announced. Fred dropped the knife he was holding "A lad! Good lord" he said a huge grin on his face, a son and heir at last. "Surry I don't believe it. The missus will be pleased."

"The Podmores at the Glen asked me to pass the message on."

"Thank you kindly, that's good news. I'll go and see her tonight."

"Guessed it would be. Take the new car Eh?"

"Aye, yes" Fed said half listening. At last a son he thought, perhaps she will be a contented woman now. The postman could see Fred was lost for words so he said goodbye and left.

Fred put the pan aside and ran round to tell Mary and Gunter he wanted everyone to know he had a son at last. After breakfast he went down to the Forest Glen and phoned his mother.

"We have a son" he told her simply.

There was silence for a moment then his mother spoke clearly choked.

"I am so pleased for you son, I cannot tell you how happy I am for you" the phone went quiet and then Kathleen came on.

"Mam's overjoyed but she is bawling her eyes out at the moment" she said. "She has not been well lately but this is brilliant news. I will let Rose and Isabel know."

Fred felt the warmth in her voice he too became emotional, he said goodbye and hung up.

He pulled himself together and went to leave but Margaret stopped him.

"You have to have a glass of sherry with us" she said "Percy and I want to congratulate you. Elizabeth can join us as well."

She led him to the middle kitchen where Percy joined them with a very embarrassed Lizzy. Fred felt better. He was the focus of attention and he did not mind one bit.

"Have you any idea of what you are going to call him?" Fred asked Dorothy that evening when he visited her and saw how pleased she looked. "I thought William Charles."

"Aye, that'll be grand." Fred looked at his new son with pride. The baby was lying in the cradle at the bottom of the bed. Dorothy was so happy. Fred had never seen her looking so pleased.

"Now we've really got something to look forward to."

"Aye we have that, a son and heir." He looked around the private room Dorothy occupied. This was much better for her. Flowers were arranged on a polished table, smart curtains hung at the window, the floor was carpeted. Yes very smart, worth paying for. The girls were back from school and Mary had told them the news.

"A baby brother" Grace had exclaimed, "What do we want a brother for?"

Hannah and Grace had so many questions when Fred arrived

"Your Mam will have to rest for a while when I fetch her home so you will still have to do a bit extra."

The girls faces dropped "Do a bit extra?" Grace complained quietly so her father did not hear her "are we not doing enough as it is. I certainly don't want to look after a baby."

"Oh Lordy" said Hannah "it's going to mean more work for us all I suppose".

Fred took no notice of the girl's response; he was so pleased to have a son and to see Dorothy so happy.

Dorothy enjoyed her stay in the nursing home. She was able to bath every day if she wished. To be able to turn the taps and see the bath fill with water was a pleasure that she did not have at home. Dorothy would lie and relax in the warm water and enjoy the sweet smelling soap that the Matron provided. This was luxury to her and she made the most of it. It felt so good, much better than having to fill the galvanized bath with buckets of water from the boiler after the children were in bed just to be able to keep herself clean

Fred collected Dorothy and their new son home from the nursing home the following weekend. Dorothy wanted a new pram for William but with the war there were no new ones to be bought, so she settled for a second hand one that was in very good condition. Dorothy fussed and cooed over the new baby and would not leave him. Mary and Fred had to do the shopping for the first few weeks after she was back home, she would not trust anyone with the care of her son not even Lizzy when she was there.

"Rock that pram. Don't you pick him up you might hurt him. Do this, do that." William was not allowed to whimper never mind have a good cry.

Dorothy went with Fred in the car to Ironbridge to register William, she nursed him on her knee all the way there and back, and she idolized the baby.

Grace came in from school and saw Dorothy sat in Fred's chair breast feeding William and she was quite upset about what she had seen. She could not believe her eyes so she quickly ran upstairs and changed into her old clothes and went outside to find Mary. She ran into Hannah on the corner of the buildings.

"Mam's letting William suck at her like the calves suck the cows," she told Hannah.

"You don't think there is really milk in there do you? It looked horrible."

"I don't know" replied Hannah "but I know what you mean, I saw it the other day. We will have to ask Mary, she will know".

"Mary will know what?" said Mary, coming up behind them.

"William is sucking at Mam's chest" Grace said, "There is not milk in there is there?"

"Of course there is. She is feeding him, just like the cows and the sheep feed their babies."

"Oh Lordy "said Hannah. "We never knew you had to do that when you had a baby. Having to change him all the time is bad enough those nappies smell awful and that bucket she soaks them in."

"All that washing he makes means more for us to do" said Grace.

"Yes, we are having to fetch more and more logs to keep the boiler fire burning" Hannah added.

"I hate having to turn that mangle" said Grace. "Mam used to do all the washing when Lizzy was at home. Now she's doing it three times a week. I certainly am not going to have any babies if this is what it is like" she moaned.

"Stop moaning the pair of you. We will all have babies when we are old enough. William is here now and we have got to help look after him, Mam does not do the shouting like she used to. She is happy now that she has him to look after."

"Trust her to take Mam's side. I'm fed up with all the fuss William has caused. I heard Mam telling Lizzy she was going to have a party when she has him christened."

"Perhaps I can have a new frock for it" Grace smiled at the thought of new clothes.

"You will be lucky" Hannah laughed. "I don't think so and if you do I will want one and so will Helen."

Dorothy arranged for the christening to be held on the last Sunday of October. Fred asked what the hurry was.

"Can't leave it too late, I don't want him dressed in thin clothes if the weather turns cold. He would catch his death."

"Well what about godparents?" he asked her.

"Oh yes I have thought of asking those two brothers of mine and our Jane can be the Godmother."

"Will we put on a bit of a do, do you reckon?"

"I've already thought about that. I've asked Lizzy to see if she can get a cake made for me. I know that food is rationed but they have those big cakes for the weddings so there must be a bit of fruit about, she will let me know today. You will have to spare a drop of cream from off the milk so that we can make a bit extra butter." She looked at him smiling.

"I don't know about that Dot, you know that the Ministry have threatened that they are going to test the milk to see if we are pinching the cream off it and if they catch us they will take our licence away."

"Oh get on with you Fred Thomas, its only gossip that you have been listening to. I reckon they are in much need of the milk to take away our licence; they will not miss one or two little jugs of cream. If they do they will just give us a warning, if it is our first offence."

Fred was just happy to agree with whatever arrangements she wanted. It was so good to see her happy.

"Do you think the godparents are a bit one sided don't you think that someone on the Thomas's side ought to be asked?" Fred was thinking about how hurt his sisters would be if they found out about the party and had not been invited. They had very little to do with Fred's family other than Kathleen and his Mother.

Dorothy still held a grudge against Henry since he had made no effort over the years to repay the hundred pounds he borrowed. There was only the occasional letter concerning a birth or death.

"We could, but there is only Kathleen we hear from and I don't think she will want to come, she has her own to look after." She could see Fred was not happy with her response. "Tell you what I will do, I will write to her first and then if they can't come I will write to my Mother."

A week later Kathleen wrote saying that they would not be able to come to the christening. They had the baby to look after; her husband Colin was in the home guard and was on duty when not at work and also Frances was unwell.

"There I told you they would not come" said Dorothy, Fred was disappointed.

Her mother wrote saying that her two brothers would be godparents and how she was looking forward to seeing her new grandson. Rebecca would be coming as well; it would give her a chance to see her sisters again, as well as her new brother.

Dorothy wrote invitation notes; she posted several to their neighbours Joe Evans and his wife, also One-eyed Jack, his sister and brother. She was a bit reluctant to ask the last three but Fred pointed out that One-eyed Jack did give a hand with the threshing of the corn and always had time to be sociable.

She gave the invitation for the Wilkins to Mary, to take up the fields.

Mary took Grace and Helen with her, they stopped at the spring for a drink, and the bucket was there as usual. Joyce had seen them coming and opened the door as soon as Mary knocked it. Mary jumped then handed over the note.

"So your Mother is having a christening party."

"Oh yes Mrs Wilkins" replied Mary. "It's for William."

"Mam's having a fancy cake made for it" Grace said sullenly.

"We will all get a piece though" added Helen.

"Oh indeed, I am sure that is going to be wonderful. It is so difficult to have a party cake with all the food rationing."

"Mrs Podmore at the Glen is making it" Helen piped up.

Joyce said no more, instead, while they waited, she wrote her response saying that she and her husband would be delighted to share their joy of having a son and heir.

When she handed it back she gave each of them a liquorice blackjack and one for Hannah then sent them on their way.

"I wanted an orange" said Helen "Hannah likes them too".

"Not while there is a war on, eat your blackjack and be grateful."

Joyce watched them go, "So scruffy" she thought to herself.

She shared the misgivings she had with Wilf later that evening. "I can see that boy being spoilt something rotten, Mrs Thomas gave no party to little Helen in fact she did not care tuppence for the child, and I don't see that she cares for any of them now. I suppose she now has what she always wanted and that is a son."

"I can't see what they want all those kids for" Wilf replied. "The future is so uncertain god only knows what is around the corner."

"Yes well it is human nature I suppose" she said ruefully.

Fred had put away a pig the year before. He had left it off the returns, he would just say it had died if anyone queried.

Also he had a patch of ground dug to look like a grave just in case.

It had been killed, salted and hidden in the cellar. If an inspection was asked for by the ministry a candle was to be taken down so as to reduce the light. The cellar was very dark and they would go no further than the bottom of the steps.

The flitches of bacon and the hams were laid out on an old brick settle behind rows of old steins and bottles so that they could be quickly covered up if need be. It would look as if a pile of old hessian sacks had been thrown in the corner out of the way.

Joe Timmins and Wilf would not say a word they had taken their own reward.

As the day approached Dorothy skimmed off a little cream to have with the tinned fruit she had got from the grocer. That was another deal agreed on involving a cockerel getting killed by the dog and some eggs getting broken.

"Now you be careful how much you take" Fred had warned her, "you know that they check the milk nowadays, and they will stop our licence to supply milk just like that. You know that we still need the milk cheque to pay the rent."

"I will be very careful, I would not let that happen you know that Fred. I think we dare to take a little over a few days." Dorothy did not want Fred to think that she would put a party before keeping the milk licence.

Dorothy had boiled a ham in the big enamel pot and it was put in the cellar to go cold along with jellies and blancmanges, home-made butter and the cream.

The cake Margaret Podmore made had white icing and was decorated with pale blue flowers. Williams's name had also been written on it in blue. It was placed on the front room table and covered with a clean white cloth.

The girls had not seen a cake like this before. Dorothy threatened all of them that they would not live to see the Christening if they dared to pick at the icing. The front room was polished and the best china and cutlery cleaned ready.

The day of William's christening was a huge success, the opposite to that of the other children. Aunts, uncles and grandparents came. Dorothy had managed the food really well considering the rationing.

It was the first time the girls had seen Rebecca since she had been driven away at the beginning of August. Grace and Hannah wanted to know all about what it was like living at the Manor. She told them of her new school at Cheswardine and the new friends she had made. Grace noticed that she wore a new coat and her shoes were girls' shoes not like their boys' black brogue lace ups. Grace was quite jealous of Rebecca she complained bitterly to Hannah.

"She uses that coat Mam bought her just for going to Sunday school. Two coats she has now." Hannah was also annoyed, she had pleaded with Dorothy for proper girls' shoes for the big day the response was as always. "You have to walk that bank every day. Girls shoes won't last five minutes, you have got to have some good strong ones and anyway they are better for your feet."

Their Grandmother had been using all their clothing coupons to buy things for Rebecca telling her

"Your Granddad and me don't need new clothes like you do" she had said "We have stopped growing now." She was delighted to have new clothes and asked no questions.

Granddad decided that he would stay and have a rest while the family and friends went to the church service. He considered that he had been to enough christenings to last him his lifetime. Mary was asked to stay behind and keep him company. "Why me" Mary grumbled, "why not Grace and in any case Lizzy is here".

"You are the one who he can talk to the best," said Dorothy "because you work outside. There is so much that you can talk about. Lizzy will have enough to do and if he falls asleep you can give her a hand." That was the end of the matter.

Lizzy had reluctantly been given the afternoon off from work but only because it was late in the year. She had been offered the choice of working late to make up for the lost time or take fewer wages. Lizzy decided to work late. Now she wished she had stayed at work, there would have been less to do. She had to keep the fires well made up; the kettle and the enamel pot were to be boiling for making tea when everyone got back from the church. The boiler had also been lit so there would be hot water to do the washing up when everyone had gone.

She had to put the food out and lay out the cutlery, giving it an extra polish at the same time.

All the best china was to be used from the front room cupboards. "It will take me all afternoon" she thought to herself.

Grace, Hannah and Helen wore new dresses made by Dorothy on the sewing machine. She managed to buy some red and white gingham from the sewing shop in town; it was all Miss Wally could offer. Grace had protested when she saw the material.

"You know that I hate red."

"You will have to put up with it young lady, this is the only material I could get. It is this or go in what you have got." Grace knew that was the end of the argument.

Dorothy had saved herself quite a bit of money and clothing coupons making the dresses herself. She did not let on to anyone that she had passed some clothing coupons to Margaret Podmore as a little bribe for making the christening cake. She had wanted a better material something more expensive looking but on the day the girls looked fine. Grace still complained that she did not look as smart as Rebecca in her nice coat. Dorothy told her that she could not afford a new coat for each of them. They would wear what they had or do without. Their coats were too short and the new dresses would show and look silly. All three chose not to wear a coat to go to the church service despite the weather looking as if it might rain. The red and white dresses did not look too bad on Grace and Helen they had dark brown hair but it did nothing for Hannah whose hair was still a very golden colour. What they did not know was that Rebecca's new clothes had been especially bought for her to show everyone that she was being well looked after and also so that Rebecca herself would see her sisters less well off and therefore not want to return to the Willowmoor farm. Sarah did not want to lose such a grand little worker. Rebecca was so clean and tidy, so obedient and polite. She was such a godsend to them running and fetching for them and Bill had taken a real shine to her.

At the church Hannah watched the Rev Barnfield christen William and when she started to shiver with cold she concentrated on the figure of Christ in white robes looking down at them from above the alter. She was so glad when it was all over and they were allowed to go out into the fresh air. The air was warmer outside than it had been inside as there was no heating whatsoever in the church. The girls played hide and seek around the yew trees in the church yard until the rest of the family and friends came out of church where they had been talking to each other whilst waiting for the vicar to fill in the Christening certificate.

Hannah was surprised again when Rebecca did not come and climb into the Wolseley with the rest of them; instead she kept close to Grandma and went with her to Granddad's car where Uncle Harry was waiting to drive them back. Hannah felt the bond they had as sisters with Rebecca in the past was now gone.

Most of the conversation at the party table was about the war.

"I will shoot any bloody stranger that steps foot on my place" Bill Wainwright told them loudly. "There will be no surrender to the Germans. I'll shoot the lot of us I will before I let them take us prisoners." On this everyone else respected his opinion and agreed. Bill liked to be the centre of attention, he considered the bombing of the cities at length, and the evacuees were seen as a burden by him. They all felt the RAF had done the most to protect them forgetting the navy and the merchantmen.

Bill was quite an authority on the movements of the war however misguided. He continued "The Americans have not declared war on anyone as yet but I can see them getting more and more involved. Thank God they let us have lease lend or we would not be able to continue, I say they will join us eventually. 'The Times' say that Germany is running short of oil whereas if we can get the tankers across the seas we will be all right. We have the convoys you know."

The rest of the party muttered words of encouragement, they would not dare to disagree with what he said, well not to his face.

Wilf had sat listening, he had to say something "I believe we should beware of the Japanese they are allied to the Germans, there is a great danger out there".

The room was silent.

"Yes well there is North Africa first" said Bill not knowing anything of the Japanese.

"Let us cut the cake" announced Dorothy and everyone agreed.

A toast was made for William's health. Each of the grown ups drinking a glass of sherry, where Dorothy had got it from, no one asked. The girls made a toast too with a cup of Dorothy's home-made lemonade. They had been on best behaviour and at last they were all allowed to leave the room and go to the kitchen, including Mary and Lizzy. Dorothy had made it clear that all the feeding and fastening up of the poultry could wait until after the visitors had left. Listening to the grown ups talk of the war had really scared the girls, they did not want the Germans to take them prisoners but it sounded much worse to have their Dad shoot them.

"Will they kill us all?" Hannah asked Mary.

"I don't know and I am as scared as you are so, shut up and don't talk any more about it. Let's get some of this washing up done. Come on Lizzy I will wash and you dry, the rest of you can sit and keep quiet with whatever you like." Lizzy sat in her father's rocking chair she looked very pale. All the talk about the Germans coming had terrified her.

Rebecca sat with them but did not like what she saw of her old home, she had got used to being the only child at her Grandparents. She did not like the constant bickering between her sisters. All the mud around the place and the mud that could be walked in on shoes, Grandma would not allow that.

She looked at the clothes they wore and decided that she was going to stay with her grandparents.

When it came time to say goodbye she reassured her Mother that she was happy living with her Grandparents.

"Of course Mam" she said, "Grandma needs me I have so many jobs to do, I do go to Sunday school at Cheswardine church and I am being ever so good for Granddad".

"That's good," Dorothy said smiling. She did not want to have Rebecca back anyway, now that she had William she had no interest in the girls and one less to feed and clothe was a blessing in disguise.

Joyce Wilkins had kept out of the way all day. She had watched the way Dorothy had idolized the baby throughout the afternoon and noticed in contrast what a poor little thing Helen was becoming. She considered her too thin for her age and it seemed that the others did not share much with her; Grace and Hannah were close, as were Lizzy and Mary. An idea struck her, she could encourage Helen to come and see her. Yes, that's what she would do. It was obvious she was just tolerated for the jobs she did around the place. She would need a friend; she had been the baby of the family for five years and should be at school. William was the favorite and she was clearly not wanted. That evening when Wilf had finished outside she said "You know it will be interesting to see what happens to that family of girls, quite a few weddings to attend in the future".

"I reckon that boy will want for nothing" said Wilf. "He'll do no good if they spoil him too much." He was not that keen to talk, he had found Bill Wainwright tedious and too brash. He knew he must acknowledge she was trying to make conversation with him or she would get annoyed and go to bed before she had put his supper in front of him and she would not speak to him for several days. He continued "Well thank God I've not got that lot to keep. Mind you they have given one away to the grandparents".

"I expect they are really proud of their family even if they do not show it" she said.

"Fiddle sticks" said Wilf. "All those two have done is crave for the lust of life. They should be ashamed of themselves."

"It could simply be that they have been trying for a son and heir." He was not listening.

"How many have they had now?" He paused for a moment. "Six girls and one boy that is seven in all."

"I think Lizzy earns her keep and so does Mary. Those girls seemed to do most of the work today" said Joyce.

"I'll grant you that. Mary works so hard outside. But I wonder if they are going to stop at seven or add even more to the number? Disgraceful, so many mouths to feed."

"Life's just not fair" Joyce thought. What a selfish man she had married. It had been his wish not to have children. She had married him and promised to obey him. He would never know how much she had longed for a family of her own, for him to make love with her. She had given up years ago trying to reason with him, it only made things worse. She was afraid that he might lose his temper and harm her.

She had loved him when they first married but he had denied her what was considered the most important part of a marriage for two people to make love and have a child of their own. Was that not every woman's dream? Wilf had been adamant right from the start that there would be no children. Joyce however had not believed him thinking that he would soon change his mind once he was lying next to her in bed. He would not be able to resist her. What a let down it had been for her after they married and she found out that he had no intention of making love to her. She remained a virgin and he celibate, he took no risks and was quite happy to stay that way and she could not change him. She decided life was just not fair, not fair at all. She thought back, she had no family as such. An only child, her parents both died when she was a small girl, she had been grudgingly given a home by a spinster aunt. She had been an exceptional scholar and had taken a good job in bookkeeping. She was bowled over when Wilf had asked her to go for walks on a Sunday afternoon. They walked the paths of the Ercall; and sometimes they walked up the Wrekin leaving his pony and trap tied safely in the rough car park at the Forest Glen. Wilf would often take her hand as they walked. Sometimes when parting he gave her a hug and a kiss on the cheek. Her Aunt had already laid down the rules of courtship saying that a respectable man would go no further until after marriage. Wilf eventually asked her to be his wife. He had convinced her that he loved her. She saw how isolated his farm was, his old Mother had died and left it to him. They married in the Methodist Chapel in Wellington, the only guests were her aged aunt and a couple of friends she had made through her work. What she did not know was that all he wanted her for was to be his housekeeper and to work alongside him as he saw fit. She was astounded when she moved in to find that he would only take her to town shopping once a month. He did the majority on the Monday when he went to the cattle market. "I can't afford to keep you just to do house work" he told her soon after they were married "you must work with me." She was expected to feed him and help with milking, harvesting and the vegetable garden.

There were times when she thought of running away. Where could she go? She had promised for better for worse, and until death parted them. Worse was when she found that he had no interest whatsoever in her physically. He always insisted that she went up to bed before he did. By the time he retired she was undressed and wearing a long flannelette nightgown and often already asleep from exhaustion, he had never seen her naked. He was the first to rise in the mornings and went from the bedroom in his nightshirt to the living room below where he dressed in clothes he had left there the previous evening. Joyce was afraid that if she went downstairs as he dressed himself before he lit the fire and made the first pot of tea of the day he might lose his temper and really do her some harm. After a while she began blaming herself. Thinking she was not beautiful enough for a man to want her despite the fact he was prepared to sleep with her. She came to the conclusion that Wilf only shared a bed so that he could be warmer in the winter months than he would be if he slept on his own. She had to accept life for what it was, she could never reveal her longing to have a man take her in his arms and make love to her. She always became depressed when she heard of new arrivals and more so when they were at the farm below. If Dorothy only knew how jealous she was of her family she might look after them a bit better.

She had plenty of time to consider her plight, she would count what few blessings she had and feel a little better. After all was said and done, she did have a roof over her head and most of the time she was her own mistress. Thank goodness she enjoyed cooking. She went out of her way to make mouth watering cakes and meat pies for 'her Wilf' as she referred to him.

Joyce had little to disturb her high on the hill overlooking the Willowmoor farm. She had her garden and indoors her cooking and embroidery. After the christening was over she would sit for hours at her window and wonder how little Helen was doing down there. She thought of Dorothy with Fred and the children then of herself and Wilf. Why could she not have just a small part of what Dorothy had? Life seemed so cruel.

CHAPTER 5

Unwelcome visitors

As the nights drew in the family sat around in the kitchen and listened to the radio more often. Fred paid more attention to the news now, he was deeply concerned for Sam, and there had been no word for some time now. The war appeared to be grinding along in North Africa and Russia and apart from the air attacks there was little to worry him on the home front. It came as a great shock when the news broke at the beginning of December that Japan had attacked the Americans at Pearl Harbour.

"Where did that come from?" he said to Dorothy.

"It was on earlier in the day; do you think it is important?"

"Good lord yes. It means the Americans will be fighting them, where that leaves us I don't know."

The girls said nothing. Later Hannah asked Grace where Japan was and they decided to take a look on the globe at school the following day.

Their interest soon faded, the war with Rommel was much more interesting.

Gunter had settled in well and despite his status he worked hard with Fred. In his spare time he liked to sit with the girls. He taught them how to plait string and make string sandals. He could make things from all sorts, he cut up tin cans and shaped them into flowers, he would carve figures and animals from pieces of wood. The girls got on with him really well, they even began to learn some of the German language but Dorothy soon put a stop to that. One day he handed Hannah a little aeroplane made of Perspex, he had carved from a piece that had been brought back as a souvenir from the crash site under the Cuckoos Cup. It was after the harvest was in that Gunter took a fancy to one of the village girls who cycled past the farm every day to work. His leaving time often coincided with her returning home from Wellington. He was seen talking to her and rumours quickly spread to the village, her father wanted it to stop and threatened to report Gunter. She had begged her father not to and changed her job to work in Coalbrookdale which lay in the opposite direction to which she had been going. She knew Gunter was honest and that it would cause him to lose his job at the farm. Her father did not pursue the issue.

It was getting near to Christmas, only a week to go before the girls would break up for two weeks holiday from school. It was early evening and all the girls were busy around the table except Lizzy who would be late as there was a dinner dance on at the Forest Glen. The lamp was turned up to get the most light. Mary was busy knitting a pair of socks and was quite pleased with her ability to master the use of four knitting needles instead of two. Lizzy had bought them with the money she earned at the Forest Glen.

The wool that Mary was using was tough navy blue wool, which had been allocated to be used for knitting socks for the forces. Dorothy had obtained some from the Army and Navy stores. She was told that the wool could also be for knitting items for the land army girls. Dorothy said Mary was a land girl so she was entitled to her share of wool. Grace was working on a spare piece of cotton sheeting her mother had found in a drawer and had grudgingly given her to make into a tray cloth, saying that it would have made a good patch for a sheet. Grace was good at embroidery and spent hours doing intricate flowers with what silks were available. Thank goodness Dorothy had the sense of mind to buy little things like needles and silks when she saw them at the house sales. She knew they would come in useful with so many girls in the house.

Hannah was trying to knit a pair of mittens from some wool unravelled from an old jersey. Helen was sat on her Dad's knee practically asleep; he was rocking gently to and fro happily drawing on his pipe enjoying the tobacco. He had to ration the amount he smoked nowadays. One ounce had to last him a week or until Dorothy could buy him another ounce and that would depend on when the shops had some in. Margaret managed to get him a little bit through the quota of cigarettes and tobacco, which she was allowed. The family was settled down for the evening, satisfied with their days work and glad to get out of the cold and frosty air. Dorothy was sat by the range she had put William to bed in his wooden cot in her bedroom and he was fast asleep. There was music on the wireless which was quite soothing. The girls were sat at the table chattering quietly, they were excited because Christmas was not far away and they were looking forward to some treats.

"There will not be much for you lot to get excited about this year," said Dorothy picking up on what the girls was saying.

There was just nothing much in the shops as far as treats were concerned. A new points system for rationing had been introduced and although it did not affect them much Dorothy was reluctant to use up the coupons. Bread tea and sugar were her biggest concerns, the rest of the commodities they would make do. There was an advantage having Lizzy at the Glen Margaret Podmore had let drop that she was always on the lookout for extra eggs, cracked of course to help out with her catering.

Dorothy had stopped in for a chat and an agreement was reached. Lizzy noticed her mother often called in on shopping days and sometimes her dad on his way to market.

A good crop of wheat and oats was stacked in the brick barns waiting for the threshing machine. Fred was thinking about buying a tractor to make the work easier but as yet had not voiced his thoughts to Dorothy. That could wait until after the corn had been threshed in the New Year.

"Are all those pens shut up tight? It's too close to Christmas to be losing any of my poultry to the fox or even a thief. Good time of year to go thieving I hear."

The word had got round that poultry was being taken for selling on the black market.

"Every bird will be wanted. We can start plucking tomorrow." The girls stopped what they were doing.

"Oh no" said Grace, lowering her head.

"You lot have no need to look like that" Dorothy said. "Fred Thomas are you listening to me? I said I hope them pens are fastened up properly." She picked up the poker and gave the fire a good poke to let the air flow around the logs burning brightly. There was now very little coal to be bought and what was available was fetched from town with the horse and cart, they could no longer get it delivered. The coal was rationed and they had to take what they could get. Dorothy was never satisfied "How am I supposed to manage on that fiddling bit of coal?" she would grumble.

"Perhaps I had better go and make sure" Fred answered, knowing that there would be no peace until he had checked the pens for the night. He knocked the ash from his pipe onto the fire and putting it in the brass ashtray he rose and put Helen to sit in his chair until he came back. Then on with his coat, cap and heavy boots. If a fox took Dorothy's prize birds, because a pen door had not been fastened properly he would not hear the last of it for quite a long time. Certainly she would start by not speaking to the girls for a week or more, unless it was to give orders and that would mean it would not be a very happy Christmas for any of them. Hannah dropped her knitting onto the table.

"Can I come with you Dad?" she asked.

"Aye wrap yourself up warm lass." He handed down her old coat and pixy hood from off the pegs behind the back door. Then he picked up one of the oil lanterns, from by the sink and going to the range he took a slip of paper and lit it from the fire.

Out into the cold night air they went, Fred keeping the lantern close to his side. Not that it gave out a great deal of light, half of it was covered with brown paper to prevent it showing too much light at nights in case there were enemy planes about.

The night air was sharp and the sky was clear of cloud. The moon cast ghostly shadows as Fred and Hannah checked that the duck and fowl pens were secure for the night. There was going to be a sharp frost tonight. Behind them searchlights pierced the sky over Wellington but Fred was too busy to notice them He was looking for any openings in the pen doors that a hungry fox might use as he looked for a tasty supper. The dog would not hear a fox about whereas if a poacher was around the dog would hear the pen doors being opened and the poultry being disturbed. They moved slowly the poor light from the paraffin lantern hampered Fred. The civil defence leaflets had told them that they must not allow naked lights to be used after dark putting not only themselves at risk but also their neighbours. "What neighbours" thought Fred as he fumbled about. He stopped and held the oil light closer to the wooden door of a fowl pen; he could see that it was not closed properly.

"I need to put a prop against this" he muttered. "Let's see if we can find a bit of wood to do the job. There should be something over there." He swung the lantern to give some light on some bits of wood that were left lying around. There were always bits and pieces of wood put to one side, usually left propped up in a corner of a building to keep dry. They always came in useful.

"Fetch me one of those lass, I'll stay here and keep an eye on this door in case we disturb the hens, they don't like folks poking about after dark." At that he kicked the door tight in the frame where it had been sticking out. "Crafty beggars foxes are and cunning too. That's why folks refer to a fox as the sly one."

With the light of the moon and what little light the lantern gave, Hannah could see the pieces of old wood not more than a few yards away; she fetched a stout board two feet long. It was part of an old fowl pen that had rotted and fallen to bits.

"See that's where he would have got in," Fred told her as he wedged the piece of wood she had found for him firmly under the fastener of the door. Hannah looked at the door, which was now tightly closed.

"Can't let the old devil take the hens or the ducks. It's Christmas in a week and your Mam will not be very pleased if there are no birds to sell."

"What about the geese?" asked Hannah? "Won't the fox take one of them? If he does; Mam will be just as mad."

"He will not try to take a goose because they make such a noise and he might not get away with one."

"But they are not fastened up like the hens and ducks."

"They're all right in that end pig sty he would have to jump the wall to get at them."

"What would you do if he comes for the geese though?" Hannah insisted with her questions.

"If I hear a commotion I'll be out with the gun double quick and he knows I would have a shot at him. There are plenty of rabbits about but he does not have to work so hard if he can take the odd hen or two. They can be lazy as well as sly."

They finished checking the last pen and turned to head back. The night air seemed colder so Fred pulled the collar of his jacket closer around his throat then pushed his free hand deep into the pocket of his well-worn jacket.

"Ooh look at the searchlights" Hannah exclaimed as they returned towards the house. She was watching the beams moving slowly from left to right and back again across the night sky over Wellington. Fred turned and looked towards the town in the distance, the lights lit up the sky.

"They must be expecting Gerry over tonight."

"Will the Germans drop bombs on us and kill us all?"

"I don't think so lass, anyway it's getting cold out here, best thing is to get inside. It's the cities they are after like Birmingham and Liverpool, the bigger targets that is where they can cause the most damage, docks, factories and the like. They want to bomb the factories to stop them working. If one lands here it will be a mistake, nothing to be gained dropping their bombs here. A few sheep perhaps and if they hit the camp down the road they'll only kill their own.

"What about Gunter?" Hannah asked "they mustn't kill him we need him to do the work".

"If a bomb is dropped on the camp it would kill the lot."

The searchlights piercing the night sky over the town were fascinating to watch and Fred forgot about the warmth of the kitchen. As they stood there they heard the drone of aircraft in the distance.

Fred put the lantern under the front flap of his jacket to hide the light.

"Those are German," he said quietly and listened intently.

The noise of the engines was a distinctive drone, different from any of the British aircraft which they heard in the daytime passing overhead. There was going to be a sleepless night for a good many.

"They're definitely Gerry planes" Fred hissed. "We might have to spend the night in the cellar." The cellar had been prepared by piling soil against the rusty barred little window, which had previously given a little daylight, to make sure that no lamplight could be seen from the outside. Fred covered the soil with clods of grass. One would have to look very hard to recognise that there had been a window there at all. It also made it less likely for nosy folk to see what was down there.

"Let's hope the Anti aircraft guns spot them and shoot them down before they get to us" Hannah said trembling not from the cold but from the thought of the Germans dropping bombs on them all and killing every one of them. "They have got big guns at Wellington haven't they Dad? Come on it is cold out here" she started to move. She felt more secure the nearer to the cellar door she was.

"Aye we had better; your Mam will be getting worried. We've been out here a while."

As he turned to walk back to the house the back door opened.

"Come in this house now" Dorothy screeched, her voice echoing in the cold night air. "Standing out there in the cold is not going to do you two any good." She stood silhouetted in the lamplight.

"Mam there's German planes out here," shouted Hannah.

"Close that door Dot we're coming in" Fred ordered.

They went into the kitchen; Fred blew out the lantern and put it on the floor. He kicked off his boots and hung their coats his cap and Hannah's pixy hood on the hooks behind the back door alongside all the other old coats and hats.

Hannah couldn't wait to tell them all about the lights and the enemy planes droning over and that they had seemed to be coming towards them. Probably heading for Liverpool.

"Can we go and have a look?" asked Grace.

"Certainly not" Dorothy snapped. "There will be none of you going out through that door tonight. Oh my goodness William is asleep up there," she pointed to the ceiling. "I wonder if I had better fetch him down here to be a bit safer. Then if we are hit we will all go together."

"Dad says they could drop their bombs anywhere at all even on the camp down the road then we would not have Gunter to help with the work."

"Oh lord I hope not" Mary looked up, from her knitting, "we need him".

Fred went over to the fire, which was still burning brightly. The logs he and Gunter had sawn gave out a considerable amount of heat. He held his cold hands towards the burning flames.

"It would be a bad job if their bombs were to hit the railway line. They say that the Gerries fly along the railway lines looking for something to bomb or shoot at. If they can stop the trains running they know it will cause havoc, nuisance bombing some call it."

"Dad there was a Junkers seen flying along the line in the daylight according to Danny's Dad" piped up Hannah.

"Is that right? You hear some stuff you do." She was not to be stopped.

"They could have spies and have found out about that place at Donnington. They will be looking to bomb all sorts of places if our fighters don't stop them."

"What a load of rubbish you talk" Grace said to her. "That Danny Probin is a liar."

"No she is right" said Fred. "I don't know how true it is but they reckon that it is an ammunition depot so they could well be after it." He looked at the heavy curtains covering the window. "Pull that curtain across that window a bit better Dot. Don't let any light get out if we can help it. The Gerries could still be overhead."

"Curse them Gerries," she got up from her chair and pulled at the makeshift curtains.

"I would not disturb the little lad as yet" he said.

"I suppose you want me to blow the lamp out and manage with a candle" Dorothy said sarcastically.

"Aye perhaps it would be as well. We can sit and listen to the wireless a bit before we turn in. that is if there is nought passing over us otherwise we had better go into the cellar."

"I'm not spending the night in the cellar Fred Thomas. This kitchen is cold enough. No I am not sitting down there for the night. If I am to be killed, it will be in my own bed, Germans or no Germans." She took the blue and white enamel candlestick holder from the kitchen windowsill. The candle in it had already burnt half way down.

"There's not much here. I'll have to see if I can get a few more candles from Walter Davies's on Thursday. Have any of you got any more candles about the house? This is no good on its own," she said looking around the table where the girls were seated.

No one replied.

"I suppose I'll have to ferret around myself then."

She picked up the newspaper she had been reading, tore a strip off the edge of it and then twisting it deftly in her fingers to make a spill. She lit it from the fire and lit the wick of the candle, quickly tossing the remainder of the spill on to the fire as it was burning towards her fingertips. She blew out the flame of the brass oil lamp on the table, plunging the kitchen into darkness making it impossible for the Mary and Grace to continue with their work.

Scowling in the flickering candlelight she took it to the pantry to see if there were any unused candles in there that she might have missed. Finding none she placed the candleholder in the middle of the table and returned to her chair.

"Just you wait till Thursday I'll have a word with that manager. They reckon they have not got this and not got that, but I know different. It's wheels within wheels and it's who you are that matters. Those shopkeepers, they keep stuff under the counter and only let it go to those prepared to pay a bit extra or throw in a sweetener. It is to those that they sell the best of their goods to. It is not for the likes of us." Fred sat back and relaxed in his chair taking his tobacco tin and filling his pipe. He tore a piece off the newspaper Dorothy had been reading earlier. She did not try to read again as the candle did not give off enough light.

"I'm fed up with having to manage like this" she said.

Fred proceeded to make a spill to light his pipe with. It annoyed her that he did not tear the paper with care down the outside margin. Instead he just tore at it without thinking he was spoiling what was probably an interesting article. He decided to wait for half an hour until half past seven and enjoy his smoke; it might be the last he would be able to have before morning. He had a thought, "While you are in the shop for candles can you ask for a box of matches lass?"

If the Germans did drop any bombs and the family had to go into the cellar there was no fire burning down there from which to light his pipe. He was only allowed a few matches to use outside. Matches were only used to light the fire in the mornings and the rest of the day paper spills were made from newspaper. Sometimes the girls would make some ready for use by carefully folding strips of newspaper between their fingers and then putting them in a jam jar on the mantelshelf.

Fred decided he would go back outside in a while and see if he could hear any aircraft about. If there was nothing to be heard they could then turn the wireless back on and listen to it for a while. The civil defence leaflets that had been issued had a warning about using wireless sets. It was said that wireless sets gave out radio signals and that in certain areas the Germans might be able to pick them up. They would then make easy targets for their bombs.

"Well let's hope they don't drop any bombs here tonight, I want to sleep in peace in my bed tonight," said Mary sleepily.

"Jean Pardow at school says her aunt lives near Wrexham, and they all go and lie in a ditch when they hear the German planes coming near them. She says there are a lot of factories at Wrexham and the Germans would be happy if they could stop them working."

"We are not spending the night in the ditch, nor are we going to spend it in the garden shed as I have heard that some villagers do" Dorothy reassured Mary very firmly. "The cellar will do for us. The roof of that is strong enough. Fred go outside now and see if you can hear anything, if they were coming our way they should be overhead by now and if they are not this lot can get to bed."

"I don't expect that they will come this way" Fred said, he was in no hurry to have to put his feet back into his cold boots again.

"Best make sure though so best be on your way," she said. Fred got his coat and cap and made his way back outside.

"Mam were you able to get any ointment for my chilblains when you went into town last week?" Mary asked her.

"Here try this" Dorothy said reaching for a yellow tube off the mantel shelf. She hesitated a moment to make sure she had the right tube of ointment, the light from the candle was not very good. Dorothy often put tubes of different ointments on the mantel shelf to stop them from solidifying. It was warmer there than it was on the shelf in the back larder where she kept most of the medicines.

"There's no peace in this house. Can't sit down for five minutes before one or the other of you want something," she grumbled as she passed it across the kitchen table to Mary, practically throwing it at her.

Poor Mary, how she suffered, her heels and toes felt as if they had been thrashed with a bundle of nettles. They were red raw and were so very painful. Some days she had great difficulty in walking, but there was no sympathy to be had from anyone. There was so much work to be done. She could not understand why her Father had refused to take up the offer of another German prisoner to help them; they could certainly have done with one.

"Can I have some as well?" Helen's little voice enquired.

"Why do you want some? Mam got it for me" snapped Mary.

"My feet hurt too."

"You can't have any. I'll bet you're lying."

"Now give over you two" Dorothy interrupted, practically shouting as she rose from her chair once again.

"Come here with you," taking hold of Helen she sat her on the edge of the kitchen table causing the light from the candle to flicker. She needed to be able to see what she was complaining about.

"Let's have a look at your feet." Sure enough Helen's feet were covered in the tell tale red patches of chilblains.

"No peace. How come you've got chilblains at your age?" Dorothy complained as she rubbed some of the cream on Helen's feet.

"It's because my feet are always cold. That's why."

"Well keep your socks on in bed" Dorothy pulled Helen's socks back onto her feet.

"If Helen can wear her socks in bed, so can we" Grace piped up.

"Oh shut up the lot of you. Time you were all in bed" Dorothy said gesturing towards the ceiling.

"It's only eight o'clock" Grace complained.

"You be quiet and get to bed" was the reply.

"But we've broken up for holidays."

"There'll be no holidays for you this Christmas. There are all those cockerels and ducks to be plucked, and that's besides the geese. The Glen wants all we can supply for the dinners they are catering for. I wonder what time it will be when Lizzy comes up that road tonight. It will be early morning again I shouldn't wonder. If we have any spare birds after Margaret Podmore has had hers the butcher is waiting to grab them. Every bird we can spare is badly wanted. There are some poor devils will get very little this Christmas."

Fred returned from outside.

"All seems quiet enough out there, there's no more planes about now. They must have made off towards Liverpool they reckon the poor beggars are taking a pounding. Wilf Wilkins says we are safe enough here a plane can't fly low enough to do any harm because of the Wrekin."

"How much longer will the war go on?" Grace wanted to know.

"How do I know, let's hope it will come to end in the New Year" Dorothy interrupted not to be left out of a conversation.

"We've been at war for over two years now, I wonder where Sam is, and if he is still alive."

Being reminded of Sam was enough for Dorothy. Both she and Fred had missed having him working for them. The fact they had not heard from him and did not know where he was made things much worse.

"Now come on the lot of you get to bed."

"I'm off" Mary said, taking the tube of ointment and a jug of warm water from the range. She needed to wash her feet before applying the cream. She would wash her face first of course. She stopped and looked at the solitary candle on the table.

"How am I supposed to see where I'm going?"

"You can light the lantern and take that" Dorothy said now getting to the end of her tether. Mary picked up the lantern removed the glass and lit the wick with a piece of newspaper from the fire stepping carefully between her parent's feet on the hearth.

"Just mind what you are doing with that," Dorothy shouted as the burning piece of paper came too near her hair for her liking.

Mary said nothing not wanting to start a row.

After lighting the lantern Mary extinguished the piece of paper by dropping it in the water which had been left in the bowl in the sink. She did not dare go back to the fire in the grate.

"The rest of you can get up the stairs with that light," said Dorothy "I want you to start killing the geese tomorrow,"

The girls rose together that was not good news.

Dorothy continued "It will stay cold for another few days which will be good for us. I don't want them birds going green on me or I will never sell them."

"Is that right?" asked Fred absorbed in his own thoughts.

"Well the forecast on the six o'clock, news said it would stay cold and I hope they have got it right. The birds will keep better" Dorothy replied.

"Oh. Lord" complained Grace, "feathers and more feathers."

"Guts and more guts" 'Hannah replied, "I hate it" as they too went towards the stairs. Grace took Helen by the hand and followed Mary who had given the tube of ointment to Grace to carry for her; she placed the light at the top of the stairs. The reflection would light both the rooms enough for them to find their nighties, undress, wash and get into bed. Fred would blow it out when he came up to bed.

"I'm not going to stay and work here after I leave school" Grace said still worried about the German planes flying so close. She did not feel like going to sleep so she started a conversation with Hannah. "What are you going to do when you leave school?"

"I don't know. What do you want to do?" Hannah replied sleepily.

"I don't know yet, but I'm not staying here" aid Grace.

"You had better not let our Mam hear you say that. She is expecting us all to stay and work really hard. She wishes we had been boys and expects us to work as such. After all she has only got William."

"Dear little Willy" said Grace "he has everything, must not even be given cause to whimper. It is going to be a long time before he grows up."

"Don't let Mam catch you calling him Willy. You know what she said when he was christened. We are to call him William and that she was not going to have his name shortened. Anyway I want to be a schoolteacher."

"You're not clever enough." replied Hannah.

"I can try, I'm good at arithmetic."

"Oh are you and I'm good at English."

"Let's get to sleep" said Grace now getting tired of Hannah always trying to get the last word.

"If we've got to do plucking tomorrow, how I hate plucking the geese, it's like plucking them twice, all that down to get off, they're far worse than the cockerels and ducks. My fingers are already sore from plucking that pheasant we had for dinner today."

"That won't get you out of plucking geese tomorrow."

The next day as soon as the breakfast dishes were washed up and cleared away they set to killing and dressing the geese. Two at a time they were beheaded and taken for plucking. With all the mud and wet around the farm, at this time of year loose feathers clung to wet and mucky wellingtons so there was a constant trail of feathers from the garage to the kitchen and the dairy. If it happened to be windy the mess was incredible, the smell carried around the house, a wet sickly smell. Dorothy was always mindful of the feathers. "See that you bag all of those feathers, don't let 'them blow away, there's always a buyer for them." Fred and Mary cut holly and tied it into bundles which Fred took into town and sold it to a shopkeeper. Dorothy sold her surplus poultry to the butcher and bought small treats for the girls. She made a real effort to provide a happy Christmas for all the family. She cooked a goose and made a fruit pudding and a cake with her small allowance of dried fruit. Margaret Podmore did send her a mincemeat pie and some extra chocolate using some of her own sweet coupons in exchange for some of Dorothy's clothing coupons. Fred and Dorothy were looking forward to the New Year. 1941 had been a very bad year for many but not the Thomas family. All the hard work had paid off. Looking back over the year Fred found it hard to believe he had come so far so fast and now he had a son and heir as well.

"Surry things aren't doing too badly lass" he said as he made the most of his bit of baccy.

"Don't see how you can say that Fred Thomas, try feeding this lot on what they allow us."

"Ah well there's no pleasing some folk" he thought.

The weather stayed just above freezing until the New Year. One-eyed Jack came round to see Fred. He liked nothing better than telling folk what he thought.

"Well. I thought all this war business would be over by now," said Jack as he leant on his stick. It was a bitter morning. He drew heavily on his cigarette and continued "the Gerries have worked out they are not going to walk over us like them others."

"Well it's definitely not over yet Jack lad, if anything it's a bloody sight worse," said Fred and he stopped shovelling cow muck into the heavy cart. The ground was frozen and ideal for getting on with such work.

"Aye. Well you would say that seeing how you have your wireless fixed now and you sit there listening to all that stuff of fighting and bombing. They wants you to think that so as they can keep us short of stuff."

Fred could tell Jack was settling into a long discussion. He couldn't help himself; he had to rise to the bait.

"Jack we dunna sit in front of the wireless set we haven't the time but they have news bulletins and the war is bigger now than the Great War. This is a world war, Japan and America are fighting each other now, the Gerries have declared war on the Americans, this is serious, haven't you seen the spitfires from Atcham?"

"They tell you that but how do you know?" Propaganda they call it. Look around, this is what counts, not what folks get up to in far off places, them spitfires are just show so we think it matters."

"I know that, but you don't see me fretting. I get stuck in and do my work; we are doing our bit as much as any around here."

"Yes, you have to otherwise they chuck you out. But why do they send our lads to Africa I ask you, what is it to do with us?"

Fred realised Jack was not listening to his side of things, he simply wanted an excuse to ramble away. He thought of fetching Hannah out, now she would be good for him to talk to.

"You ought to talk to our Hannah; she reads up on theses things and keeps bits out of the papers. She was only telling me the other day how the Germans are fighting on different fronts now. We can wear them down that way."

Jack looked at him blankly for a moment and then said, "I ain't got time to stand around talking to your daughter. I want to know when you are threshing."

"Right, well I will be letting you know pretty soon but it will be mid February by the looks of it."

Jack hung around for a while hoping for a cup of tea which he eventually got when Mary shouted Fred to come in, as there was a pot ready.

Jack sat down and was passed a cup. He looked around "Where's the sugar?" he asked.

"Back in the cupboard" said Dorothy "There is little to be had these days, eight ounces a week each we get, as you know."

"Can't drink tea without a bit of sugar, need it to keep me going I do."

She fetched the sugar and put a spoonful in his tea. "That's your lot for now we have enough trouble in this house over sugar as it is." She glanced at Fred. He looked out of the window not getting drawn into the sugar debate again. With rationing Dorothy had cut back on the use of sugar in their drinks and the cooking. Each year since then she had bottled the fruit from the orchard without sugar and stored it away as usual. There had been no problems until she served up a damson pie made using unsweetened fruit. It was so sour; the whole family was not at all happy about this and started complaining. Dorothy had rounded on them.

"Well I have run out of the sweetened stuff now this is all I can do with rationing being what it is.

If you want sugar on your pie you will have to give it up somewhere else". The matter was dropped but the girls were very unhappy. The only preserved fruit bearable was apple; the custard was so bland too there were many arguments over who was having the most sugar. Hannah decided to forego sugar in her tea and asked her mother if she would weigh the eight ounces that she was entitled to and then she would keep it in a jam jar and only she would use it. Dorothy thought this to be quite a good idea so she decided to do this for all the family. They could each have their own ration but they had to give her a little for jam making. It was amazing how good the system worked Dorothy kept Fred's and William's and her own in the cupboard of the sideboard so that it was kept under lock and key. The girls were threatened what would happen to any one of them that dared to take any from the cupboard. From that day on Hannah and Grace did not take sugar in their tea again.

Dorothy did not mind Jack but he had a habit of outstaying his welcome when he started spouting off about the war. She had had enough only the week before when Wilf Wilkins had sat at that table bemoaning the fall of Singapore to the Japanese. He had been full of opinions. Dorothy cared little for what was happening so far away. It was the worry of the Germans across the channel and the damage they were wreaking on the cities. She knew through the letters from Fred's mother that the threat of invasion was only too real, softening us up she had considered. The Americans could deal with the Japanese, what British colonies did she did not care.

"Haven't you got anything better to do than sit around talking?" she said to him after his second cup. Fred and Mary had gone back outside.

Eventually he set off after stopping Fred again.

The New Year had started badly for Dorothy, again she had not sent Helen to school with her older sisters so that she could help out around the house and run errands for her. During the previous term nothing had been said but one week into this year's new term she received a letter.

Mary had not meant to blurt it out about Helen being at home. Mary had not attended school that often but one wet and miserable week when there was not a lot of work to be done on the farm she went in for several days. On the second day there was needlework for the girls and art for the boys Miss Evans had no materials for sewing due to the war to teach the girls with. She would have liked to teach them how to make pinafores, nightgowns or even tray cloths. She had told them to bring something from home to do if they could. Mary along with some of the other girls had brought in knitting. The majority of the class were to make patterns on the back of old wallpaper using paint and half a raw potato. They cut designs in the flat face of the potato then dipped that side into the paint and pressed it on the paper. The older boys were able to use pieces of linoleum gouging out the pattern with sharp tools. It was amazing what parents were able to provide the school with. Miss Evans made use of any clean paper and any other materials that she could get her hands on.

When the class had settled down to the work, Miss Evans watched as Mary showed her ability to work using four knitting needles to make socks and gloves.

"Well I see you have learned something even though we rarely see you," said Miss Evans praising Mary.

"Thank you Miss, I have knitted Mittens for Helen already." Miss Evans thought for a moment

"I don't know Helen do I. How old is she?"

"Five Miss" too late she realised her mistake.

"She is not in Mrs Hayward's class is she? When is her birthday?"

"No Miss, June I think."

"Don't you think she should be coming to school with the rest of you? Not that you turn up very often but we tolerate it because of the help you are giving to help get us through this dreadful war. Besides you finish school this year anyway." Mary thought it best to say nothing. Miss Evans was thinking.

"I will write you a note for you to take to your mother. See me after school." She was interrupted by one of the boys.

"Miss. Billy has stuck a moustache on my face pattern and says it looks like Hitler. What do you think?"

"Yes, very good Tom. Where was I?" She lowered her voice "Mary I would not like to have to report this to the authorities if indeed a child who is nearly six years old has not started school as yet". Mary collected the letter later in the day. Miss Evans had spoken to Mrs Hayward who in turn had asked Hannah about Helen.

"Mam needs her to run errands and get eggs and get wood and tidy and watch William and..."

"Yes, I get the idea" interrupted Mrs Hayward.

Mary had dreaded going home that day with the letter. She tucked it under the elastic of her knicker leg until she had changed into her working clothes. When she went back downstairs she put the letter on the table.

"A note from school for you Mam" she said and then made her escape out through the door to find her Dad and explain what had happened. She knew that he was the only one who could calm her mother down when she let off steam. It was not her fault that the school did not know about Helen.

Dorothy made a big issue of it about how she would have to buy new shoes for Helen as well as a new coat. It would mean using up the clothing coupons so the others had better look after what they had got. She did not want the Education Officer calling to see her, so Helen started the following week. Mrs Hayward was very pleased to see her and made quite a fuss of the latecomer.

Dorothy sent a letter saying that Helen was small for her age and that she had been such a sickly child and that was the reason that she had felt that it was best to keep the child at home during the winter months. Miss Evans and Mrs Hayward had to smile when they read the letter.

"That Mrs Thomas could make a silk purse from a sow's ear without a doubt" said Miss Evans.

Dorothy despised having to keep a constant eye on things and fetch her own coal and logs in. She sat and read more or listened to the wireless. She was concerned that the Germans might spring a surprise attack as the Japanese had done against the Americans. One night before they retired, Fred made light of the news of the Germans being pushed back in Russia. She looked at him seriously and said "I dread the Germans coming across the Channel. It's been a while since the battle of Britain they could be ready to have another go at us.

"Nay lass we have nothing to worry about, it's just talk."

She was not convinced. "Oh Fred what ever should we do? Do you think there is a let up because they are coming" He could see the tears in Dorothy's eyes.

"Don't worry too much about it Dot you are reading too much into these broadcasts. If they did come across the water it's the south that they would take first, London and such. Do you see them dropping bombs round here?" We are not worth the effort. Now come on let's get to bed and some rest. I could do with some". Fred knocked the remainder of the ash from his pipe into the dying embers of the fire and put the empty pipe in the brass ashtray where he normally put it. He would not like to think that he had started a house fire by not extinguishing his pipe properly. He rose from his chair and picked up the lamp from the table.

"I suppose that you are right. It's the kids that I worry about; I would not like to see you shoot them. Come on let's get some sleep if we can there is going to be another sharp frost tonight. I will be glad when this snow that is hanging about melts and it gets a bit warmer".

"Dot I have said before that I will not let the Gerries take us alive. I reckon that they have taken on more than they have bargained for. They took on the Russians last time round but they did not beat them, I reckon they were glad then to lose the Eastern front. They are finding it tough going from what the radio is saying, getting stretched out too far, all the better for us I reckon. It's these winters that will beat them."

"I know I have heard it myself but every day they come over here they may not be able to keep them out forever."

"Aye well we must not worry there is so much to do this year with the farm, and all, that they are going to have to get on with. We can only keep producing more grain and livestock."

With that Dorothy gave no more thought about the Germans and went to bed

Next morning the postman handed Dorothy three letters; she instantly recognised her mother's hand writing on one them. Another had the Turners corn merchants' logo, which would be the bill for feed. The third had OHMS stamped along the top of it. "More forms, whatever next?" she thought.

She decided to read her mother's letter first so she poured herself a cup of well stewed tea and sat in Fred's chair. She was still worried that her mother might want them to have Rebecca back. Despite losing a pair of helping hands she found that she gave little thought to her daughter. It was one less mouth to feed and one less to clothe. She opened the letter; it was clear in the first sentence that Rebecca was not coming back. She relaxed and read on. Her mother wrote how Rebecca was settled in her new school, she had new friends and enjoyed helping around the house. She referred to her as a 'little godsend' and how much she and Bill enjoyed her company. "Well they are welcome to her," Dorothy said to herself "one less from under my feet" she looked across at the shiny black pram in the corner where William slept, she wondered if she should go and check on him.

She finished the letter there was nothing much of further interest, local gossip, the German planes flying overhead, how everyone feared being bombed. However the last line was to tell her that Rebecca's ID card was now changed, she officially lived at the Manor. "Well that makes it permanent," she said with a smile.

Dorothy's thoughts turned to the other letters. "Let's see how much the corn is then," she said and tore open the envelope. "Not too bad", she had a good idea of their bank balance. The milk cheque was due any day now. It was hand to mouth but the last year had been very good, all the stock being sold at guaranteed prices, no standing around at a market stall. Sheep, lambs, pigs, calves and bullocks. A good wool cheque and then the oats, wheat and potatoes, yes this bill did not worry her at all.

She left the letter with OHMS stamped on the front and went to brew a fresh cup of tea; the fire was in need of a bit of coal as well. She soon completely forgot about it with William waking and the breakfast to get ready. When Fred came in for breakfast she mentioned the corn bill then remembered the third letter, she went and fetched it to the table and sat down with her cup of tea while Fred was eating.

"Good lord, what next?" she said "just you have a read at this".

Fred looked at the letter in her hand he was not that interested.

"What's it about lass is it Sam?"

"No not at all it's about evacuees, here you read it," she said as she waved it in front of him.

"What's this all about then?" More questions I suppose", he read in silence.

"That can't be right!" he exclaimed, "They must have the wrong address". The letter was informing them that a woman from the Welfare Office in Shrewsbury would be calling soon with the intention of them taking in evacuees.

"It is about us taking in evacuees" Dorothy spluttered. "Evacuees indeed whatever next?"

"I know lass I can see what it says" he looked at it again.

"Well they are not coming here, that is for sure. Can you imagine it, of all the cheek! They are not coming here!" she stated very firmly.

"This can't be right we have a house full all ready. But according to this we don't have much choice. I think the best thing is to let her come and then she will see this place is not suitable." He handed the letter back to her.

"What do you think has made them pick on us?" she asked. "They evacuated back when the war started but we were never involved and they all went back anyway as I heard".

"Maybe it's all the bombing going on. The cities are taking a hammering perhaps it's that."

"But why us?" The postman lets on if others are getting the same as us and he said nothing. Could it be because Sam and Rebecca have gone since the last one?"

"Surry lass I don't know, steady down a bit. Let us see her first and then perhaps there will be no need for you to be worried".

"But with the spare room upstairs, the far room where the girls play and the parlour where my incubator is, they could make us take in some more folk. We have never dealt with strangers. Fred what are we to do?" They will tell me to put the incubator outside and then that will take more paraffin oil to keep it at the right temperature during the nights."

"For goodness sake Dot, calm down, there is nothing here that says we are going to have actual folk moving in." Dorothy scowled at him and pushed her hair from her face, the thought of strangers using the stairs made her really angry

"Alright she can come if she must but I will have a thing or two to say to her whoever she is. Evacuees indeed, they will not be using my stairs."

Fred ate his breakfast and made a quick getaway, he was not happy with the idea of evacuees moving in but he wanted to find out more before passing judgement.

Mary had been on her way to the dairy when she heard her mother's raised voice. She went to the wooden shutter that let the steam out from the boiler in the kitchen. She could hear clearly what was being said.

"Evacuees coming here!" she thought to herself, "whatever next". She listened for a moment then went on to the dairy she did not want to be caught eaves dropping. When her father came out she tagged along with him hoping he would say something but as usual he kept his thoughts to himself. He was very preoccupied so she asked "everything all right Dad?" You seem very quiet."

"Aye lass. Things to do must get on and fetch some bracken to save on the straw."

Gunter had brought Kit to the cowshed for Fred to carry the bags back for him. It was time for Mary and Gunter to have breakfast so she turned and headed back towards the kitchen. She would wait and talk to Lizzy without mentioning it to her sisters. She had begun to resent her younger sisters, they were able to go to school and learn, and they would likely do better than her. She had little future other than farm work. It did not matter that she would soon be registered as a land girl, the name so often praised on the wireless and in the papers. "Keeping the Country Going" they said. Well it was backbreaking work from morning till night. Never away from the farm, little praise or thanks from her Father and none at all from her Mother. It really annoyed her when her younger sisters arrived back from school chattering away nine to the dozen of this and that, who said what and to who. They ought to get on with helping rather than talking, she often thought. She did like having their help though, Hannah could be good company and Helen was funny. She went about her tasks then went inside and found her breakfast ready for her; Gunter's was on a tray.

Fred had said that it was not fair to expect him to work so hard all day on one meal at dinnertime and the bit of bread and cheese he brought with him. Dorothy had agreed she considered that it would do no harm to give him a bit of breakfast, he was such a good worker he deserved it.

Mary took his tray out to the dairy where he was washing his hands. The weather was very cold so he took it and began to eat immediately.

Back inside she took off her outdoor clothes and sat down to the usual plate of fried eggs, bacon and fried bread. She was most surprised when Dorothy sat down and told her of the impending visit and the possibility of evacuees turning up. Her parents did not normally share information with the girls. Mary felt quite pleased, she decided she would not tell the younger girls however, let them find out in due course.

That night as Lizzy folded her clothes and placed them on the wooden chair by the bed ready for morning Mary told her.

"Mam told you that? I don't believe you, she only tells us when something is decided and then to all of us."

"I know she must be getting soft. She will not have any here if she can help it though".

"I wonder what evacuees they would send us."

"Well I don't really know. Kids from the big towns she says, those that are getting bombed out last year there have been a lot of places flattened. Safer here in the country I suppose."

"Well I hope Mam tells them where to go, they are not having this room we had enough of sharing with all the others, now we've got this room for the two of us we are going to keep it that way".

"The woman is coming to see how many spare rooms we've got so they will go in the spare bedroom or downstairs. You should have heard her going on how she was not going to shift her incubator out of the parlour."

"So, shall we tell the others?" We could tell them that the evacuees are to go in the far room where they play." They both laughed as the candlelight flickered around the bedroom.

"Let's wait and see, I'm tired, I will have more cows to milk tomorrow as it is Sunday and there is no Gunter to help."

"You are not the only one that has got to work on a Sunday," said Lizzy "Mrs Podmore wants more spring cleaning done. It is cold riding down there on my bike and dangerous with the ice. At least I don't have to stop to pick flowers for her when the weather is like this." The next week the snow fell and life became even more difficult. Lizzy could not get to work and the younger girls stayed off school. They helped with clearing snow and tending the stock. The tap in the cowshed was a god send; the heat from the animals stopped it from freezing. Not having to struggle with buckets on the snow and ice from off the backyard saved so much time and effort. The roads were soon cleared and Lizzy was pleased to walk to work. The milk and eggs got away as usual and the bank was cleared. The girls were soon back at school Dorothy was not going to risk keeping them at home to help out. The old ritual of burning bracken around the hand pump was only necessary when it was really cold as it and the motorised pump in the stackyard were wrapped in sacking and had wooden boxes packed with hay put around them.

Dorothy put down the book she was reading. The kitchen felt cold, the fire had gone very low and almost burnt out. The wind still blew from the north and outside the air was bitterly cold, it looked as if it would remain so all day. She shivered and rose to get some life back into the fire. She put some thin dry sticks with small pieces of coal on to it to get it burning quickly. The dry sticks were to start the fire first thing in the morning but that did not matter to Dorothy at the moment. The girls would have to bring some more in and put them in the bottom oven of the range for Fred to use in the morning. Once the sticks started burning Dorothy quickly added a little coal and more wood, coal was precious so she put some small logs to keep it going. She would be glad when the wind blew from the south again and the days became warmer. She checked on William, he was sleeping soundly in his pram after having had his dinnertime feed, the girls were at school. She glanced through the window towards the road and saw a little Morris Eight at the gate. A woman got out and opened the gate. "Who on earth is this?" she thought as the woman closed the gate and began walking towards the house. She was carrying some papers in one hand and a small handbag in her other. Dorothy realised who it was.

"I bet it's the woman from the welfare. Blast of all the times to come round." The sink was full of crockery waiting to be washed up. She quickly picked up the full enamel bowl and put it in the larder out of sight. She replaced it with an empty one then ran to the dresser and took out a piece of rag. She damped it in warm water from the pot on the grate then wiped William's sticky face. The child stirred and wrinkled his face as she cleaned him. "God this was bad timing" She ran back to the dresser and grabbed a clean sheet to place over him. This time he began waving his arms he was about to start crying even though not fully awake. She pushed the pram into the front room and hoped that he would go back to sleep. She returned to the kitchen and wiped her own face with the wet cloth just as the woman came onto the back yard. She threw the cloth behind the curtain that hung in front of the copper boiler.

"Why is that dog never around to see folk off when you want it?"

There was a knock at the door. She quickly combed her hair back from her face then took a clean flowered apron from the kitchen drawer and put it on, not noticing in her hurry that she was still wearing her dirty one. She went to the back door, took a deep breath and opened it.

The woman was looking down the yard and the hens were around her feet nosing around for crumbs. She turned as Dorothy opened the door, she wore plain clothes, a brown suit, brogue shoes, her hair was very neatly cut short and she wore a small brimmed felt hat.

"Mrs Thomas?" she said.

"Yes, I saw you coming up the drive. I guess you are from the Welfare Office. You had better come in." Dorothy stepped aside and the woman walked in, the hens following close behind. Dorothy had to push them back out with her foot to close the door.

"My name is Miss Shore and I take it you have been notified of my visit?"

"I have indeed. To talk about having strangers in the house, is that right?"

"Quite right, I am here to see how many spare rooms you might have."

"Sit yourself down" Dorothy said pointing to a kitchen chair at the back of the table. "I expect you can drink a cup of tea" she turned to the range and lifted the top plate with the iron hook.

"Well I suppose I could," said Miss Shore. She unbuttoned her coat and sat down, it did not seem that warm where she was sitting.

The fire was burning brightly; Dorothy gave it a good poke and placed the kettle over the flames. "Always a good idea to set off on the right foot" she thought as she went to get the cups.

Miss Shore looked around in dismay. The floor was dirty in places where shoes had trod in and out and needed a good scrub especially in the corners. In one corner she saw a bucket of soiled nappies and there were boots and all sorts behind the door. There were newspapers and magazines all over the place. She could see a pile of them behind the rocking chair; they should have been given up to the collection centre.

"What a dingy room, when was the last time the windows were cleaned and why had they not been taped up as instructed in the civil defence warnings?" She thought to herself.

Dorothy was standing opposite her and Miss Shore realised she should say something.

"Well the reason I am here is simple, the cities are still taking quite a pounding although not as bad as the last twelve months. People have been moved out before, some abroad, but as you may know the loss of those children on their way to Canada was a terrible thing to happen. No more children will leave these shores." Dorothy said nothing so she continued "We intend to place children in safe accommodation such as you have here away from the bombing."

"Oh!" said Dorothy in dismay. Miss Shore pressed on.

"It will be necessary for me to see how many rooms you have in the house and how many you actually use".

"Right. In that case I suppose I had better show you round while the kettle boils." She went to the door leading from the kitchen. "Come this way". Miss Shore followed not sure if she should leave her coat or at least wipe her feet. Dorothy would have preferred not to co-operate but she knew she must. In the letter it was made clear they would be breaking the law if they did not.

They went into the front room where William was asleep in his new pram. Miss Shore looked around the room and glanced at the sleeping child. "What a cold room it is to put a sleeping child in" she thought.

"This is the front room" said Dorothy and made no effort to go further.

"Well, may I see the others?" There are more than this surely" said Miss Shore.

"Yes, there's the little one at the bottom of the stairs and the big one leading off this one."

"Mrs Thomas as our correspondence stated, you have to show me all the rooms you have." She could see her presence was resented.

"Well it's like this" Dorothy said assertively, "I'll not have anyone using the upstairs rooms. I've only four and I need the use of them for us. You do know I have seven children".

"Six I believe" said Miss Shore, "one has been re-registered." The icy stare told her to not press the matter. "Well we will stick to downstairs; can I see the other rooms please?"

"Come on then, but there is nothing for you to see".

Miss Shore followed Dorothy past the bottom of the stairs and noticed that the stair carpet was like new. "Not that hard up" she thought to herself. Dorothy opened the door to the parlour.

"Very small" she said as she stepped inside. "What is that smell?" They had moved the incubator outside into a small fowl pen. Fred had persuaded her to show willing as it did not look good hatching chicks in the house. Dorothy did not answer; she stood by the door a look of defiance on her face.

"Still at least two children could sleep in here. Now let me see the other one".

"Nosy beggar" thought Dorothy to herself but led the way to the far room.

"Now this is a better sized room, we could put two single or one double bed in here easily".

"Two beds; how many of these people are you expecting us to have?" Dorothy sounded alarmed.

"I was simply speaking out loud we may have a couple from Liverpool and two children for you. I will make out the paperwork and you will be notified of any decision in the next two weeks. Now I think I can manage that cup of tea you so kindly offered. I can fill the forms in while I am here".

Back in the kitchen Dorothy made the tea she gave Miss Shore one of her best cups to impress.

While the forms were being filled in Miss Shore re-emphasised the need to evacuate people from the cities.

"We must save as many of the people as we can and your help is going to be so much appreciated," she said.

"Oh I expect it is we do hear so much on the wireless about the terrible things happening in the cities" Dorothy answered glibly. She was not happy at the thought of four strangers in the house.

Miss Shore finished filling in the forms and drank her tea then stood up to go. Dorothy went to the door and opened it; a hen stepped smartly in. As Miss Shore stepped outside Dorothy booted the bird back out and followed.

"I suppose you could use half a dozen eggs to take with you?"

"Oh yes please" Miss Shore's face lit up.

"Promise you'll say nothing, we're not supposed to you know".

"Well you are giving are you not?"

"Of course, can't sell them. We'd be fined for that".

Dorothy disappeared back inside and came back with six good sized brown eggs in an old paper bag.

"There you are, nothing like a nice boiled egg for your tea."

"Thank you so much. I am sure if you take in evacuees they are going to enjoy their stay here."

It was as much as Dorothy could do to control her temper.

"What happens if they don't?"

"Oh we will find somewhere else; they may have to return to the cities." Miss Shore added.

"By the way I assume you have plenty of spare sheets and blankets and that you can put a double bed in each of those rooms, a couple of chairs and a few bits and pieces to make it as homely as you can for them". Dorothy was dumbstruck.

"No I have not got any spare blankets. I need all I've got. They will have to bring their own," she said sharply.

"That is not very considerate of you. The evacuees we have in mind have nothing. They are lucky to be alive and have lost everything in the raids." Dorothy realised how bad her comment seemed.

"Well we can not afford to buy stuff it costs money you know."

"You will receive help for taking them in. I need people like you to co- operate, this war is taking a terrible toll on those less fortunate than yourselves."

"Well I suppose if we get a bit of help we could maybe pick up a few bits and pieces."

"Oh thank you so much, it makes my job so much easier and as for the blankets I will have to see if we can get a few from the army stores. Goodbye, I will be in touch", Miss Shore walked across the yard careful to avoid the hens and their droppings. When she got back to her little Morris Eight she put the eggs gently on the back seat out of sight.

"That Mrs Thomas could have spared at least a dozen eggs. Mean woman, all those hens flapping about. The trouble with people like her is that they do not know that they are born. Probably making a lot more than a few eggs on the side while all we have are our meagre rations. Still it will be good to have a fresh egg for my tea and that is the equivalent of my six months ration." She thought to herself.

She drove off towards Wellington, glad she had this job. It was much better than having to work in a factory, despite difficult farmer's wives. She also felt glad she was not in the land army, "Imagine having to work at a farm like that. How could they live in such a mess?"

Hannah's natural golden curls had long gone from her mothers' constant attention with the kitchen scissors. "Got to keep it short or you'll have a head full of bugs and nits." She was told when it came to the weekly combing with the fine tooth comb dipped in paraffin oil and the subsequent wash with the smelly black medicated soap. The smell was terrible and the girls hated it but they knew what happened to children if the Nit Nurse found lice in their hair. They were given green cards to take home to their parents and the lice had to be gone before the next visit in four weeks time. If they were badly infected they were given brown cards which meant they had to attend the clinic at Dawley where their hair would be shaven off, several children were sent to the clinic. The whole class saw the cards handed out. When they returned to school they looked as if they had been scalped. A month later Grace and Hannah were given green cards, there was a very slight trace of lice in their hair.

"The Indians are going to get you the next time the Nit Nurse comes." Danny Probin teased Hannah. "Shut up or I'll shake my head by you and you will get them as well" she said and Danny moved away quickly.

Back at home Dorothy doused their hair with paraffin oil and left it to soak in.

"Now let's see if anything can live in that" she said. "A good scrubbing with the soap will be next."

"Do we have to have that horrible soap again?" said Grace

"Indeed you do, coming back here with bugs in your hair, whatever next?"

The next day followed with a thorough scrubbing with the stinking black soap. "Probably got them off those Bailey boys," Said Dorothy "they are probably lousy with them."

A few days later the letter Dorothy had been dreading arrived. She read it as soon as the postman left. It said there were to be four evacuees assigned to them, two adults and two children. She was not happy despite the possibilities of being paid for putting them up.

When Fred came in for breakfast she did not wait for him to take his cap off.

"You will never believe it, we have got to provide beds for them folk that are coming and they could be here in about three weeks time. Oh that woman, she knew I did not want them here."

"What are you going on about, the evacuees?"

"Of course, here read it yourself." Fred read the letter. They would have to put up a married couple by the name of Winter and two children named Sybil and John Lucas.

"I thought it would just be children," he said.

"So did I, we would have put them with ours and it would have not been a problem".

"This means we have to set up the rooms proper."

"Which rooms?" he asked.

"Far room and the parlour, they will have to have furniture."

"We had better have a look what sales are on" Dorothy went to the table behind Fred's chair and started sorting through a pile of out of date papers and magazines. "Where's last week's paper?"

"I have not got time to go to furniture sales Dot".

"Well in that case I suppose it will have to be me as usual and I suppose that I will have to go on the bike. That is if you can't find the time to take me. It is no good Fred I will have to learn to drive that car myself." Fred's jaw dropped.

"But not many women can drive cars Dot, it's so dangerous now there are getting so many cars on the roads. I would not like to think of you getting hurt." Dorothy was about to argue when Mary walked through the door.

"They are sending us evacuees after all," Dorothy said.

"Really how many?" And where are they to stay?" She did not want anyone else in the bedroom she shared with Lizzy. Fred gave her the letter. Dorothy returned to the table.

"Look here is a sale in Wellington. If I went to see what I could get, you and Mary could take the horse and trap and fetch it the next day. We can't argue with them Fred Thomas. We have got to do as we are told and I don't like it any more than you do." He said nothing but thought at least she was going to co-operate and not be awkward. They did not want any trouble with the authorities.

Dorothy went back to fixing breakfast, Gunter would be sitting in the dairy, and soon she would send Mary out with a mug of tea for him.

When the day of the sale came around Dorothy kept all three girls from school.

Hannah and Grace were to take care of William. Helen was kept from school because Dorothy said that a five year old child should not walk that distance on her own. To make her point she told them "And you never know where German spies might be hiding. They could be hiding in any of these woods around here".

"Why would the spies want to talk to Helen and not all of us?" asked Hannah.

"It's not safe is what I meant" said Dorothy realising her mistake.

"Oh Lordy, will they kill us then?" said Grace.

"Look just stay here and get some work done, you are all safe to walk to school together. Hannah do not go blabbing to the teachers about spies".

"Oh we know who the spies are Mam, the boys keep an eye on them, especially that Mr Pitchford who goes in the woods to see Mrs Simms when her husband is at work" Dorothy had to laugh so the postman was not making it up after all.

"We always keep a sharp lookout Mam" Hannah went on but Dorothy put a stop to it.

"Your Dad can't spare Mary to come in to do the cleaning so you lot can make a start".

She gave strict orders to them on what work she wanted done while she was away.

"But that is our play room" said Grace "why do they have to go in there?" Dorothy rounded on her.

"You have nothing to moan about; I had to move the incubator out. I've now got to go pathering outside every hour to keep an eye on it."

After a final check on William she got dressed up against the cold, took her gas mask and went to find Fred.

"I have left them cleaning, I want you to set a fire in those rooms, damp from floor to ceiling they are. It will need to be dry before those strangers come".

"Aye well we will see to that, at least the weather is not too bad, we are going to get the muck up onto the Slang today all being well."

"I am only buying what I think they need no extras. Blankets indeed, they will have to bring their own. Take a years clothing coupons to buy them and that is if you could find any that are for sale."

For the girls it was work and more work. Grace continually moaned about the fact that they had to put up with these strangers coming to live in the house.

"Can't they go to bigger farms?" she protested as she carried an armful of logs to the fire in the far room. "It's not just us," said Mary as she helped her, she had taken a break to help with the fires,

"Anyway Mam will be getting paid to have them here."

"So we get to do the work, it is never fair is it?" moaned Grace.

"Nothing is in this place" agreed Mary. "We just have to get on with it."

Dorothy considered that she was more or less ready after a few days. She had all the furniture fetched by Fred despite his misgivings about getting it all back in one piece. He and Mary found the journey so slow after the car, there was more crockery and linen despite her previous statements. The incubator was put in a shed and despite being away from the house it worked fine. Dorothy was soon hatching as many chicks, ducklings and goslings as she could. They were fetching a good price and with the lower ground around the farm being wet the ducks and geese were able to feed themselves during the day. They were only fed a little corn to entice them inside at night so that they could be fastened up in case a fox came for them.

CHAPTER6

Life away from the city

Mary was warming her hands at the range when she glanced through the kitchen window. It was a fine afternoon and she could see a large black car coming up the drive from the front gate and a man following on foot. Her Mother was doing some farm accounts in the front room.

"Mam" she called out "it looks as if those folks from the town are here. A big black car has just turned in at the gate".

"Go and meet them" Dorothy shouted back "I had better tidy myself up a bit, keep them talking if you can". Mary heard her mother going up the stairs so she went outside and around the garage to meet the strangers. The car had turned and was stopped under the Bannut tree, the driver was getting out.

"Afternoon Miss, is this the Willowmoor farm?" he said to Mary. He was a tall cheery sort of chap.

"Err yes" said Mary. He went to the boot and started unloading suitcases. The man on foot reached them; he looked at Mary in her shabby working clothes and Wellington boots.

He was in his late thirties or early forties, quite tall and slim. He wore a trilby hat, which he touched with his finger

"Morning, so this is the right place!" he said to the driver who had the suitcases out and was piling on army blankets placing them carefully to keep them as clean as possible.

"It is. And a far cry from what you have left behind no doubt."

The tall man went to the back passenger door and opened it. A woman and two children, a boy and a girl got out of the car and looked around them in trepidation and alarm. 'The children were not very big. "About Hannah's age" thought Mary. The girl, whose hair was the colour of ginger, took one look at Mary and did not like what she saw.

"There you are mate, that's the lot, got to be off. Just make sure the door is shut will you," said the driver opening his door. "I've got more to pick up at the station. You enjoy the country you will be safer here by what you have been telling me. I'm glad I'm not living in the city". He looked around "Not another house in sight" he thought to himself. "The best of British luck, what a God forsaken place to live". He got in and drove off down the drive opening and closing the gate as he left.

Mary looked at the small group standing there each with their gas mask, their cases and blankets on the ground behind them. The two children were huddled up to the woman who had an arm on each of their shoulders. It was a warm day the girl was wearing a pink and white dress underneath a pale blue coat trimmed with a dark velvet collar. Very thin soled button bar shoes and white socks. The boy was wearing grey trousers to his knees and a green jumper. He carried some sort of coat or jacket over his arm. His black shoes were well polished.

Mary looked at them and thought that those shoes would be of no use to run about on a farm.

"Hello. I am Mary," she said to them. "Come and meet my Mam, you can leave your cases there for now, but I would bring those blankets, the hens are about and might make a mess on them". The man picked up the blankets giving some to the woman to carry.

"We are the children's Aunt and Uncle" he said. "My name is Ken Winter".

"Best if you speak to me Mam" she turned and they started to follow her. They could see she was wearing an old frock a size too small for her and an old dirty coat, her hair was wild and unkempt. They could see her clothes were covered in dried mud and manure. The cleanest part of her was the bottom half of her boots where she had washed them under the tap in the cowshed earlier.

Alongside the garage they went, the Aunt's high heeled shoes sinking into the path causing her to walk with great difficulty. Around the back of the dairy onto the back yard, several hens ran from the pigsty to see if there was any food to be had. At the sight of them the girl screamed and ran to her Aunt who stood rooted to the spot.

"My God, these are live chickens".

Mary turned around "yes of course", she replied. "Hens really, the cocks are down the yard". "Wait till they see the geese" she thought "that would cause them to run!" "Come on they won't hurt you," she said. The little group was not convinced.

"Shoo, go away now" said the Aunt "do something Ken!"

"Just ignore them and walk on" he said.

They carried on, looking in disgust at the muck under their feet.

"This is terrible, there is muck everywhere," said the boy.

Mary led them to the back door where she scuffled her feet on some old sacking that served as a doormat, they tried to do the same but only made their shoes dirtier than before. Mary opened the door.

"Come on in. Keep the hens out though" she went in and they followed, she shut the door behind them, they looked even more concerned standing there.

Dorothy stepped forward from by the range.

"How do you do and what are your names?"

Ken Winter offered his hand, which Dorothy shook with hesitancy.

"I'm Kenneth Winter, just call me Ken and this is my wife Imogen, I call her Ginny for short.

"What a funny name" thought Dorothy but refrained from making any comment.

"These two are my niece and nephew Sybil and John Lucas. Come and say hello" Ken reached for Sybil's hand but she stood stock still behind her Aunt.

"All in good time" he said. Dorothy looked from one to the other. They did not know what to make of this rough looking woman in a tweed skirt and woollen jumper partly covered by a reasonably clean flowered cotton pinafore.

"Well I am Mrs Thomas and you have met Mary. Sit yourselves down and have a cup of tea." Then she noticed the blankets they were carrying.

"On second thoughts let's take them blankets through to your room and bring the rest of your stuff in. You don't want the hens climbing all over it. When you have finished come and have a cup of tea". The little troupe followed Dorothy through; she showed them the parlour then took them to the far room, which she had prepared for them.

"Come back to the kitchen when you're ready" she said, and then she turned and left them while she went back to boil the kettle. Ken and Imogen put the blankets on the double bed in the corner of the room.

Imogen and the two children sat on the bed alongside the blankets and looked around in dismay.

"Oh dear" she said aloud. A good fire was burning in the fireplace but the room still smelt musty. The wallpaper looked as if it had not been changed for years.

"Ken I don't think these windows have been opened for years."

"I think you are right, it definitely smells a bit damp. There probably hasn't been much in the way of heat in here." He looked around; there was a table, with an assortment of crockery, and cutlery on it. Four chairs, a cupboard and a good-sized chest of drawers made up the rest of the furniture. There was a large bowl and a jug with a towel alongside. A couple of old fashioned pictures on the walls and an oval mirror hung over the mantel shelf. The best thing in the room was the fireplace, which was of black iron with a hearth and surround of Victorian green tiles. Ken could see it had not seen much use. Dorothy only lit it to dry washing or when it was too cold for the girls to play outside and she did not want them under her feet.

"You stay here dear with the children" Ken told his wife. "I will fetch the rest of our things."

He came back with the rest of the luggage and saw the complete bewilderment on his wife's face.

"Come on dear, you will feel better when your had a cup of tea, come to the kitchen with me now. Mrs. Thomas says the kettle has boiled "Imogen rose and with the two children they went through to the kitchen. There were cups and saucers on the table.

"Sit yourselves down and have a drink" Dorothy poured out the tea putting extra milk in the ones for the children. She went to the back door, opened it and shouted to Mary who was wheeling William around in his pram to keep him quiet. "Mary, go and give your Dad a shout and you might as well have a drink now that I've made a pot full." Mary put the brake on the pram and then ran off to fetch Fred.

Dorothy sat down and looked at Imogen. The woman was much smaller than her, blonde hair and blue eyes about ten years younger. It was obvious by her small white hands she had not been used to doing any rough work and as for her shoes, well? What earthly good were they going to be to walk around a farm? They would be ruined by the time she had walked to the road and that paint and powder on her face. "Well whatever next, well I suppose that they do come from the town," she thought to herself. Imogen had only a slight covering of make up, just some face cream dusted with powder and a touch of lipstick. She had wanted to give a good impression for the sake of her husband but now she could see that she need not have bothered. She looked at Dorothy from the other side of the table and thought what an attractive woman she could look if her hair was cut shorter and she wore a touch of make-up. She had such beautiful dark hair and what a difference it would make. But on second thoughts as she looked around her Imogen felt what an absolute waste of time that would be, if this were how she lived.

"Have you brought some stronger shoes Mrs Winter?" Dorothy asked.

"Oh yes, I can see I will only be able to wear these that I have on for shopping when we are in the town."

Dorothy was puzzled by the woman's accent; she had a little of the Liverpudlian accent but Dorothy felt that she seemed to be a foreigner of some sort, she turned to Ken.

"Are you from Liverpool then?" asked Dorothy.

"Yes, but we have little left there now, our house and everything was destroyed".

"So do you all live together?"

"No we had been staying at my sister's house in Birkenhead but that got hit as well so she has stayed while we left with the youngsters here". He picked up his cup and drank. He was forty four years old a quiet, well-travelled man. He made a point of saying little. "To listen is to learn" he would say.

It was true their house had been flattened, Ken had not been there and Imogen had been at his sisters, he was often away for days at a time.

Dorothy wanted to ask more questions but she felt awkward which surprised her, after all it was her house and they were strangers. She thought for a while. "What can it be like to see everything destroyed? All that you own just gone." She felt some sympathy for them.

"Would you like a piece of cake with that? It is good Farmhouse cake."

"Yes please" they said they were quite hungry. Dorothy went to the pantry and brought out a cake.

"So what is your line of work Mr Winter?" she asked.

"Public sector, administration, that kind of thing". He did not elaborate nor did he need to, Dorothy had already pigeon holed him as a pen pusher. That suited him fine as his line of work was far more clandestine. Dorothy handed out a piece of cake to each of them then took a look outside to check that William was still in view.

"Do you like your cake children?" Dorothy asked when she returned to the table.

"Fine thank you" said John. Sybil had only taken a small bite of the heavy cake she thought it tasted odd and left it on the plate. The tea was different too; it smelt odd, sort of sickly. There was an awkward silence as they sat each with their own thoughts. "And how old are you two little ones?" asked Dorothy. "John is eight and Sybil is ten" said Ken.

"Have you been on a farm before at all?" she asked.

"No" said Imogen and the two children shook their heads.

"Well we have quite a lot of ground here, all the fields you can see are ours".

"You have no neighbours?" asked Ken.

"Oh yes, there is a cottage over the back, one on the hill and another off in the woods. Not neighbours as you folk might see them."

"No we lived in a street, there were people all around us" said Ken, "so what are these hills?"

She told them of the area, what they might expect from the weather and of the town and village. Imogen and the children were dismayed. Maybe the risk of staying in Liverpool was better than staying here in this wilderness, miles from anywhere. Ken listened politely then added "Little chance of being bombed here then or anything else happening".

Ken was not here by accident; the situation was perfect. Secluded but close enough to a town with a railway. It was better for them to be away from Liverpool and the bombs. His work took him away for days and sometimes weeks. Here

Imogen would be safe. The back door opened and Mary came in.

"Dad's on his way" she said and went to pour him a cup of tea. They watched her aware of her grubby appearance and dirty hands.

"So how many of you are there?" asked Ken?

"There's Fred and myself, Mary here, Lizzy the eldest who is at work, three at school and baby William outside..." Fred coming into the kitchen interrupted her.

"How do you do" Fred's cheerful voice echoed around the kitchen. He took off his cap showing his disheveled blond hair. Ken Winter stood up; he glanced at Fred's ragged old jacket and knees of his breeches shining with cow manure. He still had on his boots and oh the smell! "Hello Mr. Thomas, my name is Ken Winter and this is my wife Imogen, nephew John and niece Sybil". They shook hands; Ken Winter took a deep breath. Fred's grip was stronger than he had expected, he looked down at the callused hand, and it was like a piece of tree bark, rough with ground in dirt and grime. They studied each other for a moment. Fred's face was rosy red and weather beaten whereas Ken was pale and drawn through worry and lack of sleep.

"Look as if you need a bit of fresh country air. From Liverpool aren't you?" He took his jacket off and hung it on the back door. "Err, yes that's right", Ken was unsure of what to say so he sat down again next to his wife.

Fred collected his cup from the table and went to his usual chair by the range where he put it down. He reached to the mantle shelf took one of Bromley's blue invoices, tore a piece off it and folded it, then took out his pipe, refilled it and lit it from the fire. Once he knew the tobacco was well lit he sat back and relaxed. Mary brought the pram in and stayed by the sink, she did not join them at the table. She was studying the strangers from a safe distance. Fred puffed on his pipe then took a drink from his cup; he then turned back to the evacuees.

"Well pleased to meet you all are you going to like living in the country?" there was a stony silence.

"That is very difficult to anticipate" said Ken. "It seems such a long way from the town you appear to be so isolated."

"We don't think it too far from anywhere, do we lass?" There's ways and means to get around. We have the car these days but we can't use it as much as we would like to with the petrol rationed".

"Yes, we have the horses and there are always bicycles if you can get hold of one" said Dorothy.

Fred could see the dismay in the faces of the little group on the other side the table and decided to change the subject.

"Have you seen cows being milked?" He asked smiling. Imogen and the children shook their heads. Dorothy turned to Mary "Take Gunter some tea and bring William in on your way back".

"Who is Gunter?" Ken Winter asked slowly.

"Oh he is a German prisoner from the camp and works for us, they have to do a bit of work to earn their keep" she said. Imogen went as white as a sheet.

"They! What do you mean?" Ken said. "You have Germans here?" his fists were clenched, he was clearly angry. Fred and Dorothy had grown used to Gunter being around, they looked at each other.

"I am sorry" stammered Ken recovering his composure, he took his wife's hand and patted it as if reassuring her, "so you have Germans here how many are there?"

"Just the one. Dunna worry old lad he is no trouble."

"Of course not" said Ken "we have not come into contact with them before so it is quite a shock."

Looking at Imogen Winter and the two children brought memories flooding back to Fred of the refugees that he had seen in France during the last war. The look of loss and despair was plain to see. He realized they had no future to speak of, what must they be thinking? He decided to change the subject once again. "Have you looked around yet?" That hill out there is the Wrekin and from the top the views are fantastic. You must go up sometime, there is a house up there and they have ponies that you can ride."

"I don't think we have seen so much countryside as we have since we got off the train, have we children?" Ken said to John and Sybil.

"No Uncle Ken" said John "there are no people or houses out here, when can we go home?" Dorothy looked at them and put her teacup down.

"Why you have only just got here. Grace, Hannah and Helen will be here from school in a while and they can show you around."

"Yes, I am sure they would love to see the animals" neither of the children responded.

Dorothy and Fred smiled and relaxed, no one spoke, the only noise came from the fire and the clock softly ticking, nobody wanted to be the first to speak. Eventually Fred stood up and put his cup on the table.

"Well, I've got to go and get on with the work before my bit of help goes back to camp. Stay awhile and have another cup of tea. Later on when you have changed out of them smart clothes you can come and have a look around. Mary here and the others will be pleased to show you around and take you to see the cows." He got up and went to the backdoor where he put on his jacket and cap then he went outside and Mary followed. There were several barks from Jingo who had wandered around and sat outside waiting.

Dorothy looked in on the baby then sat back down and poured out some more tea.

For a while they said little, the Winters felt uncomfortable sat there.

"Do you follow the war on the radio?" asked Ken.

"Oh yes we would be lost without it." She did not want to switch it on so went back to describing the farm.

Where is the WC please?" asked Imogen.

"The what?" said Dorothy?

"The toilet or bathroom please, we may need to go later."

"Oh, the lavvy, it's down the yard past the pigs. If you get to the pear tree you've gone too far." The group was stunned. It was too much for Imogen, Ken could tell, he decided they should go to their room.

"It has been quite an upheaval today I think we need time to settle in, so we shall go to our room if you don't mind" Imogen and the children rose as one.

"By all means" said Dorothy, "You go ahead". They went off to the far room and shut the door.

"My god this place is filthy said Imogen. "They just walk in and out without a care in the world; did you see the state of the floor?"

"Yes dear but this is not the town you know and anyway this room is not bad if we kick off our shoes before coming in we should be all right." The children were too glum to say anything they sat on the bed and stared at the window. He looked again at the basin and jug; he had seen no water taps in the kitchen so that was their lot.

"You all get some rest I will go and find out some more about this place while I can."

"Find where the WC is while you are out, that tea was not such a good idea" said Imogen with little enthusiasm.

Ken rose and left the room; he took his gas mask and went through the kitchen and outside without stopping to chat with Dorothy who was too busy stuffing something disgusting into a large saucepan.

Once outside he turned right and wandered through to the farmyard, he looked around and was surprised at the size of the place. "God look at all that muck and mud, and it is only April what will it be like in the winter, glory only knows" he thought. The concrete apron was freshly swept and the buildings seemed huge. The smell from the piles of manure was strong. His attention was drawn to movement within the cowshed on his left. As he stepped forward a man emerged and without a glance set off across the yard. "That must be the German" thought Ken as he watched him go. There was further movement inside so he stepped into the dimly lit building.

It was musty, there were no cows but he could hear something from the next section. He walked through the opening between sections and could see a huge bull in the end stall. It was darker in here; the only light was from the air holes built into the wall. Fred was doling out hay in the troughs. Ken looked around and realized there were no lights. It suddenly dawned on him, he had known something was missing the moment he stepped into the house - there was no electricity!

"Good lord" he sighed, "Ginny is not going to like this, no electricity or running water. Perhaps the city wasn't so bad after all despite the bombs".

Fred stepped out from the stall still with hay in his arms.

"Taking a look around eh Mr Winter?"

"The name's Ken. Yes, I have been sat down most of the day and it does not do me any good."

"Well if you like to walk this is the place for you."

"So I see. Mr Thomas, how far away from here is this German camp."

"Just down the road, not far away but you have nothing to fear."

"Was that Gunter that just left here?"

"Aye, he is a grand worker, quite a surprise really. They called up my farmhand a while ago and we couldn't cope so along he came, He doesn't come in the house and goes back to the camp every night. There's quite a few of them working around here. Don't suppose you see them in the city."

"No we don't!" said Ken, surprised at Fred's relaxed attitude to Gunter.

"Well, don't let it concern you. There have been no problems with any of them. It was the prisoners that drained my fields so we could get corn planted, it all goes to the war effort you know. Dot was scared at the prospect of them being here, she thought we'd all be murdered in our beds."

"They are still German though and it is somewhat of a surprise to see them up close. We are used to being on the receiving end back in Liverpool".

Fred threw the last of the hay to the bull. "Well from what I hear we are giving them a pasting as well now we have the Lancaster. Supposed to change it around as I hear."

"There is that" said Ken. The Lancaster was being hailed as the greatest bomber in the world capable of turning the tide in the air war against Germany.

"Hopefully our lads giving them a taste of their own medicine may bring a stop to this bombing."

"Quite" said Ken. He was less concerned about the bombing now they had made the move but his mind was on the fact that they were coming into contact with actual Germans. He had good cause to be concerned on two counts. First there was Imogen, she hated the Germans, not just for the bombing of the cities but because she was Dutch and had lived in Rotterdam. The city had been smashed by the Blitzkrieg in 1940, her family and friends were still there. Secondly it was extremely unlikely but he or his name could be recognized by this Gunter and jeopardize his true work. Fred went past him into the first shed, Gunter had brought more hay and was about to leave to get more when he noticed Ken in the shadows. He looked for a moment then simply turned and went on his way.

"Does he speak English?" asked Ken, staring after him.

"He is learning a bit from me and the kids. He understands more than he speaks" Fred said puzzled by his interest in Gunter.

"Does he bother you?"

"No not really, just curious you know how it is!"

Fred could understand the children being here but was a little curious about the adults. Surely they should be working in factories or some where, they were clearly out of place here on the farm.

"You are not part of the war effort then?" He said "Not been called up to the home guard or helping out with the air raids?"

"No, No I have not" said Ken taken by surprise. "I am not much use to them. I was injured in the Great War, not fit for much these days. I took a load of shrapnel in my legs and managed to get gassed into the bargain. Lets me down you see, cannot run or do much lifting cannot stand too long either".

Fred looked grim and shook his head sadly. "I was in that. Oh aye I got myself gassed in France serving a battery when they hit us with the bloody stuff. What were you, Infantry?"

"No a spotter for the guns, forward observation at Ypres."

"That is a name that will never be forgotten," said Fred "I was at the Somme. Let's step outside into the fresh air. Do you smoke?" he said reaching for his tobacco tin.

"Yes" said Ken taking a silver cigarette case from his jacket pocket.

"You won't be in need of that here I reckon" Fred said indicating the gas mask.

"Force of habit" said Ken.

Fred passed him a milking stool with his free hand; they went outside and sat down.

Ken looked at Fred. He had a new respect for this blond haired farmer. They smoked in silence; Ken relaxed as the peace and quiet settled over him. After a while they heard the sound of a plane overhead it was a lazy sound, Fred did not look up. Ken watched it with interest. "Trainer" he said. "How did we get into this mess?" Fred said "They said there would never be another after the big one".

"Yes it seems so far away at the moment though sitting here."

They talked over their memories for a while Gunter came and went. Without being told he prepared for milking. Mary hurried passed and mumbled something. Eventually Ken said "I had better get back inside see how things are. You must understand we had electricity hot and cold water and a bathroom."

"Aye we are a bit behind here, I have heard of city life from me Mam she lives in Dudley."

"I don't know if we can cope with such an extreme change. Ginny and the children you know".

"Aye well let's give it a go, the girls will be back in a moment, you will like them."

Dorothy meanwhile had finished what she was doing and was fussing over William when a thought crossed her mind; she rose and went through to the far room where she tapped sharply on the door. Imogen called out "Yes?" Dorothy entered.

"Have you brought any food with you or made arrangements for your tea?"

"Why no we have left everything" Imogen stammered. "The Welfare said that we were to be housed on a farm and that there would be plenty of food".

"Well they got it wrong as I've enough to do feeding this lot" said Dorothy sharply. "You've to provide your own food and you will have to cook it in here." Imogen was lost for words.

She looked at the fireplace, how was she expected to cook on that; she had used a gas cooker back in Liverpool. Someone from the Victorian age might be able to cook on it but it was just a fireplace to her and there were four of them to feed.

"I do not know where to start Mrs Thomas, we have nothing like this back in Liverpool, is there not a stove we can use?"

Dorothy looked at the two silent children sat on the bed and softened a little "I am sure you will manage, you have ration books don't you and I am sure your husband can fix up something for cooking on. Perhaps Fred can help him out." She had no intention of letting them join the family for their meals. She noticed the bags still unpacked. "What are you going to do about money and work if you have not thought of food?" she asked.

"We have to go to Wellington, tomorrow I do not know what will happen yet."

"Well you are responsible for seeing to the two young ones, I have enough with my own."

"I know, we will take them with us but I will talk to my husband and see what he has to say. Is there a bus to town as his legs give him trouble?"

"No there is nothing like that, anyway I have work to do the girls will be home soon."

She left the room and Imogen sat silent.

"Are you all right Aunt?" asked Sybil.

"Not really."

Ken walked down the yard and found the toilet, how he was going to explain this to Imogen and the children. He walked back to the house and entered without knocking.

Dorothy was sitting at the table.

"Mr Winter, your wife tells me you have brought no food with you and have no arrangements."

"Well no" he said taken aback "the priority has been to get us away from Liverpool; the last few days have been very difficult".

"Well as I have told her I have to look after my own you will need to get your own food. We are rationed the same as every one else. The only thing we get a bit extra of is the milk and a few eggs maybe a cockerel now and then."

"I see," said Ken "I will see what we can do. I don't suppose you have a telephone?"

"No" she replied. "What I can do is get you fixed up for tonight. I'll give you a loaf and some eggs to tide you over until tomorrow. You can cook over the fire in your room for now." At that she turned and went into the larder, "take these in for a start" she said emerging with eight eggs on a dinner plate in one hand and a packet of butter in the other; she had a loaf of bread under her arm.

"There you are come back in a few minutes and I will have something else for you, you can have some milk as soon as they milk the cows."

"Right" he said "thank you" and went through to the front room.

He found Imogen sitting on the bed with her arms around the children. He put the provisions on the table and looked at his wife, "I have some food to tide us over and there is more to follow including fresh milk". She looked at him "We cannot stay here I can't, I won't." Tears filled her eyes and ran down her face causing the powder on her face to smudge.

"Now dear, calm yourself, it could be worse." He went to sit beside her and John moved out of the way. "We are away from the bombing, you must never forget how close we came to being killed the other night" he said putting his arm around her shoulder.

"How much worse, look at this place it is impossible."

"Look" he said firmly "there are many worse off than us. There is no electricity here, no hot water, no taps and the toilet is a hole in a piece of wood but we are alive and in one piece. We have to thank our lucky stars. We will make do, it is not impossible, let us see what can be done to boil some eggs on that thing" he said pointing to the fire grate, "Boiled egg with bread and butter how's that sound?"

"I'm hungry now" piped up John.

"We have some biscuits your mother gave to us when we left for the station this morning. You can have those until we sort something out. You get on and find them Ginny; you may as well start to unpack while you are at it."

Sybil found the paper bag with the biscuits and Imogen shared them out.

"Climb on to the bed and take a look through the window" said Ken. "See all those fields, we will be able to go for walks, no traffic, you can learn all about country life ready for when we do go back home. That's if there is a home to go back to, those bombs wiped out the entire street next to ours only two nights ago. Oh this damned war." He looked so despairingly at his wife. "Let us find some older clothes to wear and then we can make up the beds we can sort out our other room later."

The children seemed satisfied for the time being. They were gazing outside.

"I can see some girls out there" said Sybil.

Ken went to the window while Imogen began unpacking their possessions. She separated the least important clothes she could find and put them on a chair, but even these seemed too good compared with what she had seen Mary wearing.

"I think the girls are home from school" said Ken as he returned to the middle of the room. He looked at the clothes "We will go into town tomorrow and see what we can find that would be more suitable. At least we have our clothing coupons and ration books with us."

"We will have to walk, there is no bus, what am I supposed to walk in, Ken?"

She picked up the shoes she had arrived in "Just look at my best shoes, ruined, ruined, they are.

What can we wear on our feet with all this muck and mud around?" she sobbed. She sounded pitiful.

Ken said "Come on John and Sybil take your good clothes off and get into these here" he looked at the bewildered children, "Come on and help yourselves a little and give me a hand. Tomorrow we will go into town, and then I am sure you will feel much happier".

"But its miles away and what of those woods" Imogen protested.

"I'm sure there is nothing in those woods only trees." He was beginning to lose patience with his wife. "Mr Thomas will assure you there is no danger in the woods."

He turned his attention to the brightly burning fire and thought how best they could cook over it. "If I could put some strong metal over it to form a grid it would make it safe to use small pots and pans, a sort of shelf that would be much better. I'm sure Fred will help out with some bits and pieces of wire."

"Come on" he said. "Let's go and see if we can find some wire and maybe see how they get the milk from the cows." He picked up the large jug "We will also need some water for boiling the eggs and a saucepan."

"You go" said Imogen, the thought of seeing cows terrified her. The hens around the back door had been enough for the time being. "I'll try and make up the beds while you are gone."

"Come on Sybil and John let's go."

"I need the toilet" said John.

"Me too" said Sybil "but I do not want to go by pigs."

"Come on then" he said "We can look at the animals. Nothing is going to hurt you."

They put on their shoes on and then picked up their gas masks.

"You will not need them, so leave them here" said Ken and he took them by the hand.

"I'm scared" protested Sybil, holding back and not wanting to leave her Aunt.

"Oh come on, you're safe with me."

"I want my mum" She whimpered like a puppy.

"I know you do, but your mum can't go to work and look after you. We have tried to explain to you that all the mums not only yours are working very hard in the factories making arms to help stop this awful war. Some of the mothers are working very hard in the docks helping to paint the ships so that they can get them sailing as quickly as possible. Come on now let's get out of your aunt's way. She has to get a bed ready for you two as well as try and get something for us to eat".

John did however seem more eager than his sister to have a look around and to get out of this smelly room and went eagerly toward the door. Ken knocked on the door to the kitchen before entering. They were surprised to see three girls sat around the table drinking milky tea, Dorothy turned from the sink.

"Ah there you are Mr Winter, and with the youngsters. These are my daughters Grace, Hannah and Helen" she said. "Say hello girls to Mr Winter John and Susan that is their names is it?"

"Sybil" muttered Sybil.

"Hello" chorused the girls.

"I've put you a small kettle and a saucepan there on the table along with some more bits and pieces you can borrow." "Thank you" he said "we will need water, do we use this jug?"

"Yes" she replied "or one of the buckets if you prefer". She paused and looked around "I suppose you will want to have a cup of tea" she took two teacups from the cupboard then fetched the tea caddy from the mantle shelf and spooned some tea out. Then she did the same with some sugar. "I will find you a little teapot".

"They can use my little one" said Hannah.

"That is a bit too small" said Dorothy smiling. "I can't spare much; the rations don't go very far. See how you get on."

The girls stared at John and Sybil.

"Have you come from Liverpool today?" asked Grace.

"Yes" said Ken, the two children looked scared to death.

"Have you got nits?" asked Hannah.

"No!" said John.

"My friend at school says kids from Liverpool are crawling with them."

"Shut up this instant" snapped Dorothy "sorry Mr Winter I don't know where she gets it from". Hannah was grinning and swinging her feet.

"I don't like it here; I want to go home now." Sybil grizzled.

"I'm afraid you will have to get used to it for a little while. It probably will only be for a very short time, and then you can go back home," Dorothy said.

"You can't and that is that" said Ken.

"Well you can't" Hannah chimed in.

"I think we will head outside" said Ken "I need to find Mr Thomas".

"Going to have a look outside, that's good, the girls will show you around, come on now Grace and Hannah," she said to the girls, "you can do that, and then get your jobs done later".

"Can I go?" said Helen.

"No there is work to do in here."

Grace and Hannah got down from the table, they had on their working clothes, which were extremely shabby they put on Wellington boots and led the way outside.

"I want the toilet" said Sybil.

"Where is the toilet please?" asked Ken. Hannah looked at Grace.

"The lavvy?" said Grace.

"I suppose so," he said.

"Follow me," said Hannah and opening the back door she skipped off down the yard the others followed. The hens always on the lookout for food were around their feet immediately.

Sybil was frightened and kept close in to Ken "Keep them away Uncle Ken" she squealed "Why are there so many of them?"

"Where do you think eggs come from?" said Grace "there is a war on and everyone wants them".

John walked boldly forward and ignored them. He set off after Hannah and was catching up when he jumped at the sound of the pigs snuffling in their pens. He hurried to where Hannah was waiting for them. "Here you are" said Hannah pushing the wooden door open. John's face dropped "This is a toilet?"

Ken stepped forward, the smell was awful, and it did not bother him as he accepted the fact that they were in the sticks but this was more primitive than he could have imagined.

It was some time before Sybil was convinced to sit on the wooden seat. John however went into the orchard. Ken studied the surroundings; the fields loomed over the farm. "So all these fields belong to the farm?" he asked.

Yes" said Hannah "so what is it like in Liverpool?" Ken told her of the city and where they had lived till the bombs took their house while Grace tried to convince Sybil it was all right to sit on the seat and that she would not fall through. Hannah listened politely; she had only ever seen Wellington and the surrounding area when she had been out in the car. "Can I come and see Liverpool when you go back?" she asked.

"If there is anything left" said John. Ken sighed, "That's true it is hard to imagine the destruction that goes on when you stand here and look at all this peace and quiet."

"Mam shouts a lot" Hannah said then remembered her chores and went off to get on with the feeding. A short while later the trio followed Grace around to the farmyard.

"Now you must not be afraid of, the cows" Grace said looking at Sybil. "They will not hurt you; they are all tied up with chains around their necks." Jingo the farm dog ran up as they came to the cowshed "Sit" commanded Grace "don't you go jumping up." The dog sat down, Grace took a quick glance inside and said "They are here".

They went inside and Jingo lay down by the cowshed door he knew better than to go inside. Cows were temperamental animals and Fred never allowed a dog near them when being milked.

Fred and Gunter were busy milking away, sat on the three-legged stools, caps turned back to front leaning their heads on the cow's belly in comfort. They held galvanized buckets between their knees and squirted the milk from the cow's udders. Strip, strop went the milk rhythmically as it hit the inside of the bucket. The group watched for a while, then when the cow gave no more Fred got up moved the bucket back and smiled with satisfaction.

"Well done old girl," he gave the cow a hard slap on the rump. "Earned her corn tonight she has." His bucket was three quarters full when he saw the little group watching him. He smiled

"That's good, come to see how it's done." He picked up his stool and walked to a bucket standing near the door where he poured the frothy milk into it.

"That's ready for the dairy now" he said "and I'll start another."

John and Sybil stood and watched. The smell of the cows plus the fresh dung in the gutter was too much for Ken Winter.

"I think I need a bit of fresh air," he said as he stepped outside and lit a cigarette. Mary came round the corner and went into the cowshed, returning with a bucket in each hand, each three-quarter full of milk, Sybil and John followed. The buckets looked heavy, she was carrying them away from her careful not to spill any.

"Where are you going?" he asked looking at Mary.

"The dairy to show what happens to the milk, I will show you" she answered "come with me". Ken was curious.

"Let me carry one of those buckets for you they look heavy". He took a bucket and a deep breath.

She led the way carefully round to the backyard and into the dairy, the little group followed her. They watched as she stood on a solid block of wood to reach the tank over the cooler and carefully poured the milk in. It then ran down from the tank cooling as it went and passed through the wadded sieve and into the churn.

"You have to do this every day?"

"Yes, we milk twice a day."

Hannah stuck her head round the door "Do you want to see the ducks?" she asked.

"Actually I am meant to be fixing up a way for us to cook" said Ken. "Do you think your father would mind if I looked around for some wire to make it a little bit safer to cook something to eat".

"I'm sure he won't mind" said Mary "we will go and ask him as soon as I've emptied the other bucket."

John and Sybil stayed close to Ken and they went back with Mary to the cowshed where she spoke to Fred and then led them to the cart shed. They picked their way through the mud of the yard trying to keep to the patches of clean concrete to avoid getting muck on their shoes.

Eventually Ken found what he was looking for and decided to head back. Again they bumped into Hannah who offered to take them and show them the various animals but Ken wanted to get in and try his idea for cooking.

"Maybe later then" Hannah said directly to Sybil who had looked away.

Ken led the children back to the house. The table was clear, no sign of the things Dorothy had put out, she was sat with William on her lap. "I had Helen take your things through" she said.

"Thank you, I will go and see how Ginny is getting on". He ordered the children to remove their shoes before going through to their room. He took his own shoes off and carried them through.

When they entered he was pleased to see Imogen had cheered up a bit. She looked up as they entered and gave a smile. "I've done the beds and look" she said pointing at the table "we have enough to make a meal and a cup of tea".

They put their muddy shoes on some packing paper by the door.

"I will have to clean them later" said Ken "God knows what it's like out there after rain, a nightmare I should imagine" he turned back to Imogen "well done, you are an angel it seems you do not need my help after all".

"Well I don't know how to boil those eggs over this" she said "I am used to the gas at home".

"Well look, I have found some wire to make that fire safe to put the saucepan or kettle on. Tomorrow we go into town and buy the sort of food we're used to and see if we can get a small paraffin cooking stove."

John and Sybil sat on the bed and watched as Ken fashioned a strong grid that sat over the flames. He was quite pleased with his efforts. "There put the eggs into the saucepan and cover them with water from the jug and boil them on the fire."

"But for how long?"

"I don't really know, about five minutes I should think will do".

"I thought we were going to have our meals prepared for us".

"They've got enough to do and there's no room around that table for four more. Let's manage tonight. Tomorrow we go into town, there are bound to be service men's canteens or we might just find a café, anyway we saw some tearooms just down the road".

Ken put four eggs into the saucepan, they still had muck on them but he did not want to draw attention to it.

"There were eggs in the orchard when I went earlier Uncle Ken, you could see them under a bush."

Ken poured water from the jug over the eggs and some into the kettle. "It is amazing," he said. "At home they are so precious yet here they are left around. Do you remember last month when young Irene was carrying eggs and a bomb went off?" Imogen laughed "That was not really funny it could have been worse than six smashed eggs".

"Shame her mother did not see it that way" he laughed.

He placed the saucepan and kettle on the grid which was firm. Sybil told her aunt of the toilet, the smell and the flies, there were pieces of paper on string and how the wind blew up through the hole.

"Oh well" said Imogen "I suppose I will have to go, will one of you come with me and keep those horrid chickens away?"

"I will" said John he got his shoes and Imogen put on an old pair of her own. They were not gone long and John was excited when they returned. "I shooed them away" he said "and stood guard, the animals are all being fed so it is a bit quieter."

Imogen said nothing, she was just glad to be indoors, it had been worse than she imagined. Soon the eggs were boiled and a pot of tea prepared. Imogen prepared the table and buttered some bread.

She poured some water into the bowl and they washed their hands, then they all sat down at the table.

Ken popped the eggs into egg cups and passed them round.

The eggs were steaming Sybil looked at hers.

"I don't want it" she said "it's horrible".

"Do not be silly," said Ken "we need to eat something it has been a long day." He cut the top off his with a knife, Imogen did the same but the two children sat there.

"Come on now, try you two" Imogen cut the top off John's egg and then Sybil's.

"It smells," said Sybil. "Why does everything smell around here?"

"It is fresh that is all. These are real farm eggs. Better than the powdered kind we get nowadays."

John began to eat his but Sybil slumped on the table "I do not want I, I want to go home".

Imogen took the egg from her took it out of its shell with her knife and spread it on the bread and butter.

"There you are, a nice sandwich, now eat it and drink your tea or you will be very hungry before morning."

"Do as you are told" Ken said sharply "this is our first night away from the bombs let us be thankful for that".

Sybil pulled a face but ate the sandwich and drank her tea.

"I expect Mrs Thomas will supply us with milk every day if we ask her, and of course some more of these eggs." She looked across at her husband enjoying the freshly boiled eggs. They ate silently.

"We have a few things to do if we are to live here" said Ken looking around the room. His thoughts turned to all they had lost "another new start" he thought. They had got out of Holland just in time. Imogen had never really settled in Liverpool and she would probably not settle here. Time will tell. His knowledge was crucial to the war effort and he had to get back to work as soon as possible.

The light was fading; it had been a fine day. Ken looked through the window. "It seems so calm out there" he said "I think I will go and talk to Fred later about transport".

"I will come with you" said John.

"There is none," Imogen said "we will have to walk".

"Yes but I would like to find out what the news is on the war, a radio is going to be a necessity".

Later he and John went through to the kitchen. They said hello to Dorothy and the girls and Ken said how nice the eggs were.

"I will put you some more for breakfast" she said.

They went out and found Fred who was in the dairy. John decided to go for a walk.

Fred smiled "You have a good look around lad" he said "you will bump into Hannah and Mary if you go round to the buildings. Mind the bull though."

Off he went and Ken smiled, Fred was washing down the equipment. "Are you finished now?" asked Ken.

"Pretty well" he replied "the girls finish off usually".

Ken wandered out onto the yard and smoked a cigarette. When he returned he asked Fred if there was a bus to town.

Fred told him how folk got around, horses, bicycle, walking, or some, a few like Fred, had motor cars.

Ken thought for a moment "A bicycle it will have to be. What news today from North Africa?"

"Dunna know haven't listened to the news today, Dot will know though. I listen to the evening broadcast after me tea. We haven't had the radio that long, still."

"We follow the war quite closely not just what is happening at home. John used to keep clippings and all sorts even had a world map."

"Sounds a bit like our Hannah, do you want to come through later and have a listen?"

"Yes please," said Ken.

"I'll send one of the girls to get you later then" said Fred.

"That would be good of you" said Ken and went back inside. He took the eggs that Dorothy had put ready.

Later in the evening, as it was going dark, Ken lit the paraffin lamp and set it on the table. The little group felt so far from home, they were all rather tired. "It's this country air," said Ken to Imogen who was rather glum.

"What have we come to?" she asked "it is so primitive".

They sat around quietly until Grace knocked on the door and invited them to come through to the kitchen. Ken and John went through and sat at the table to listen to the news.

Lizzy had returned from the Forest Glen and was introduced.

There was plenty of optimism, the Russians were doing well against the German onslaught in Africa, the Allies were going from strength to strength and at home it was said the drive was on to produce more than ever.

"That's us," said Fred "we are getting the muck out now and soon we will be ploughing and sowing again".

There was no news on the occupied countries, which were where Ken's concerns lay.

John spent some time talking to Hannah who showed him the pieces she had kept from the papers. Eventually he felt so tired that he went back to their room. Fred had Ken sit next to the range and they talked over issues from the broadcast. Ken gave Fred more insight into the day's events than he had realized.

"Surry there's so much we don't understand" said Fred "that is the trouble with always working".

"Quite so, maybe it is better not to know too much."

"What worries me," said Dorothy "is them Germans coming over and killing us all in our beds or making us prisoners".

Ken smiled thinly "There is little likelihood of that happening but you should spare a thought for all the poor souls under occupation right now".

Dorothy was tempted to complain about rationing but thought better of it.

They stayed talking for a while then Ken rose and returned to the far room.

The two children were ready for bed but refused to sleep on their own in the little room. It was decided that Imogen would sleep with Sybil and Ken with John. They retired early; the lack of anything to do was compounded by the poor lamplight.

That night Sybil woke several times screaming from nightmares, the animals had frightened her so much.

At the end of the evening Dorothy went to bed leaving Fred to bank up the fire. William was quiet, sleeping soundly in his cot. She lay back leaving the lamp lit on the bedside cabinet, the light danced on the walls and she felt the change in the house.

"Strangers in the house" she thought "oh how times have changed". She wondered about Imogen. She did not like her dressed all smart and foreign as well. "It's not my problem but those two little ones will need feeding up if they are going to walk up that bank every morning" she thought to herself. When Fred came in he saw her sat up in bed, "Is something wrong?" he asked.

"You know Fred," she said "I reckon that she is a foreigner".

"She is Dutch" Fred said wearily.

"You don't think that she could be German though. I won't share my kitchen sink with a German!"

"Don't fret, she is Dutch, left her family behind, she hates the Germans more than we do."

"We don't know much about them do we? They arrived here all unprepared like they were going on holiday."

"Don't judge them too harshly lass; they have been through a lot with getting out of Holland by the skin of their teeth only to end up being bombed in Liverpool."

Dorothy whispered "What did you say? They come from Holland but that's where the Germans are!"

"I will tell you what Ken told me this afternoon but let me get into bed first." He undressed to his shirt then got in. He told her all that Ken had told him in the afternoon. Dorothy understood the reaction to the mention of Gunter.

"I think we ought to help them out a bit more" she said, "The little ones look like they are half starved".

"Aye that's the spirit lass, I reckon I can run them down to town in the car tomorrow save on the chaps legs."

"Don't you get carried away Fred Thomas, we don't get petrol for nothing what about shopping the day after?"

"It's the least I can do so I will hear no more about it" he said "now I need to sleep so blow out the lamp and get some rest yourself". She sat for a while pondering "There is no more to be said really" she thought "see what tomorrow brings if it is rain they will regret turning up in those stupid shoes". She turned the wick down and blew out the flame, Fred was already breathing deeply.

The morning dawned fine and Fred was up early, he had just lit the fire when he was surprised by Ken Winter coming through the back door, he was wearing a large overcoat and his trilby hat. Ken saw his surprise "Couldn't sleep, believe it or not, It has been too quiet, so I thought I would take a walk outside".

"There will be a pot of tea soon" said Fred "you are welcome to join us, Mary will be down soon then Lizzy."

"Thank you" said Ken. "You are up early it is not even light."

"Always up this time milking has to be done early then we have the rest of the day, we will be shifting muck later on with the horses, young en's might want to see." He filled the kettle from the bucket by the sink.

"Maybe" said Ken "I was just outside, it is so peaceful. Seems a far cry from the city there is always some noise, you get noise from the docks and hooters from the factories but here there is nothing".

"Oh you can hear the trains when it is cold, they sound as though they are just in the woods yonder."

"Do you get the water from the pump out there?" asked Ken.

"Yes it's off a tap in the buildings, just not got round to the house more complicated you know. I suppose it's the same with electricity as well probably.

"Yes Ginny finds it difficult to come to terms with. As you know we blokes just get used to things being bad."

"Aye well take off your coat and sit down" said Fred sitting at the table "the kettle won't take long".

As soon as Ken was sat Fred told him of his decision to take them down to Wellington in the car.

"That would be most kind," said Ken. "It is a good day for a walk but the distance would be a problem for me that is the one reason I was out now, seeing how my legs feel, not too bad actually".

"Well I can run you down after milking and leave Gunter loading the muck."

Ken said nothing but having the German here with just the womenfolk was a concern.

"Have you a gun?"

"Of course and if you are worried about Gunter he is no trouble. Anyway you want to see Dot shoot, we keep the gun where she can get it quick if needs be. Next time I go shooting come with me if you want."

"Yes fine" said Ken "I must sort out with my people what work, I have to do. I may have to be away some of the time but it sounds as though you are well prepared here."

"Dot fears the Gerry's will invade any moment, drop from the skies."

"They have bigger fish to fry at the moment; the Americans coming into the war may have tipped things in our favour." He stopped there it was not wise to talk too much, he did not know how much Fred spoke to Gunter, best wait a while.

When Dorothy came down and the girls began to stir Ken went back outside, he was in no hurry to wake Sybil and Imogen.

It was when the girls left for school and the bedlam had subsided that he went and woke Imogen and the children. He then boiled water for a pot of tea. Sybil was very tired and complained as she dressed. They washed in the china bowl and added towels to the list of things they would need.

After Fred had eaten his breakfast he set Gunter to loading the muck cart and then fetched the car out of the garage, Ken was impressed.

"She is a beauty" he said looking it over and clean, that was a surprise!

"The girls gave it a wash," said Fred reading his mind "and cleaned inside, must have known we were having visitors".

Imogen brought the children out saying Good morning" to Dorothy on the way.

They all got in and in minutes were in Wellington. As Ken got out he said to Fred "Don't worry about us we will get back under our own steam".

"Right you are" said Fred and set off back to the farm.

Ken watched him go and then turned to Imogen and the children "Right let's start by finding ourselves a good sized meal and then I have important work to do."

They arrived back at the farm quite late and were driven up in a large black car. When Dorothy saw it she knew it was not one of the taxis. The driver helped them unload; there were all sorts of packages and boxes. Imogen was wearing trousers as was Sybil; they looked a different group than the day before.

When they came onto the back yard she opened the door for them. "Thank you" each said as they marched through. Helen opened the next door and they went to their room then Ken and John returned for more. It took two more trips before everything was inside. Hannah had seen them carrying their shopping across the back yard "They must have a lot of money" she told Mary. "I wonder what his job is, Mam said he is a pencil pusher but Dad says there is more to him than meets the eye. Perhaps he is a spy, that Mrs Winter is foreign. Mrs Hayward told me not to talk daft though and next week she expects us to have the boy and girl with us when we come to school. Who told the school Mam wouldn't have." "Don't know but Mrs Hayward knew their names as well. I don't think they are spies then do you?"

"No I suppose not but it would be good if they were then we could sneak in and catch them red handed and get a medal and see the King who would give it to us."

"Time you sorted the hens out" said Mary and went back to her work.

Back in their room everyone was unpacking. Ken was unpacking a radio.

"This will bring us back into the world" he said smiling everyone was happy except Sybil; she simply wanted to go home. After finding a meal at a working men's canteen they had all gone to the Welfare office in Walker Street where they sat with a clerk and gave all their details. Afterwards Ken gave Imogen some money and all their coupons.

"I have to speak to some people on the telephone" he said "so I will be a while. Try to get as much on our list as possible we will collect it when we leave" she nodded.

"Why are you not coming with us Uncle Ken?" asked Sybil anxiously.

"I have important calls to make; we will meet up here in two hours time."

He made his call. As expected arrangements had been made to ensure that he could begin work as soon as possible. He was to take the train each day from Wellington and a rail warrant was waiting for him at the ticket office. He read out a list of new requirements and agreed to be outside the station at three o'clock. He then went to find a stove.

When they met up again Ken was pleased and so was Imogen. At first she had found the townsfolk suspicious of her accent but when she told them their plight she had received all the help she needed. Her first priority had been footwear and clothes and she had bought her first ever pair of Wellington boots.

Ken left them again and went to the station where he met an officer in civilian clothes standing by a large car. "Afternoon Sir" he said and they got in.

"Got what you asked for except the bicycle. Captain Evans asked if you want a basket on it and if you have cycle clips already?"

"Very funny, have you seen where we have been put, when they said safe from the bombing they did not say how safe? We are up the side of a bloody mountain!"

"Best place to be Sir, every town is a target and this place is no different" to add effect he craned forward and looked at the sky. "There is an ordnance depot just down the road."

"How about a telephone?"

"Captain said don't be silly, just settle down and take things easy for a while. Nothing much happening at the moment, anyway the big stuff is being dealt with down south. I have some homework for you" he pulled out an envelope from the parcel shelf under the steering wheel "forms to fill in, expenses and the like".

"I feel a bit out of it here, there must be more to do."

"Well you won't be going back over for a while; the occupation is well established now so stick to the paperwork."

Ken was not happy but he knew there was little he could do. He had been into Holland several times gathering information but now Britain was on her own the bombers ranging at will it seemed. His job would be deciphering the reports for tit bits and translating documents. He knew he was not well, he could see that every time he shaved, the gaunt look, he looked worn out.

He put the envelope in his pocket.

"When can I get the bicycle?" he asked.

"Tomorrow, when you said it needed good brakes we decided to not give you the spare we use for fetching odds and sods from the village."

"Good well I will walk down tomorrow but I want it here for me when I return."

"Fair enough, now do you want a basket and clips, the Captain said there will be a pump and a repair outfit as standard."

"Yes go on and a sprung seat. Now let's get back to today. I will go and finish the shopping then we will meet you here in say one and a half hours then you can take us back."

"Beats working for a living, I will take a walk and get something to eat then."

Ken told Imogen that he had a taxi for them and they began taking items down to the station. The children had books and sweets and were quite content to stay with the parcels while Ken and Imogen fetched more. When the driver returned they loaded everything aboard. Imogen was suspicious as to how a wireless set was already on the back seat under a coat but knew better than ask.

Once Ken had the stove working he went to find Fred, he needed to run his aerial outside. As he stepped into the kitchen Dorothy was preparing a meal.

"Are you all right for your tea Mr Winters?" she asked.

"Yes thank you but if I could purchase some eggs it would help."

"Oh right, well I could see my way to letting you have a few as long as it doesn't get out. I used to run a successful Market stall before the war you know."

"Good you know all the ropes then. Ginny will come and see you about shops and the like in a while, she is busy right now."

He went outside and found Fred.

"Heard you had a good day" said Fred "the girls reckon you have bought half of Wellington".

"A few necessities" said Ken "which is why I am here I need to rig up an aerial for our wireless".

"Surry that was quick, I thought they were scarce."

"Not if you ask the right questions but that is another story." Fred got the ladder and they soon had a wire run to a tree in the garden.

Ken asked to borrow an old bucket as well "I will get another soon but I forgot today, not on my list. It is to empty the chamber pots" he said embarrassed. "That's all right Mary will dig one out for you. Come through later after the kids are in bed and we will have a chat" said Fred.

Ken thought a moment then said, "Yes that would be good. I have some paperwork to do first as I begin work again tomorrow."

"What doing? You have only just got here."

"Apparently there is a great need for a man like me in the administrative departments at Wolverhampton."

"How will you get to and from town?" asked Fred.

"They will help me get a bicycle, so it seems."

"That leaves the Missus here all day, what will she do when the children go to the school?"

"Maybe she will find a job in town, you never know."

Fred had work to do and needed to get on, he was pleased for Ken he seemed a lot happier than yesterday. He went back to his work and Ken returned to try out the radio.

After a meal cooked part on the stove and part over the fire they all relaxed, Ken to his paperwork, the others to books bought in town. Later when Imogen went to speak to Dorothy she found her busy with William. "None of your own Mrs Winter?" asked Dorothy.

"No never the time, I shall just go down the yard" she said not caring for babies, she decided to speak with her in the morning and ventured out casting an eye round for the hens. When she came back in she retired to read her book.

After completing his forms and relaxing for a while Ken went through to sit with Fred and the family.

The next day Ken took a leisurely walk to town, it took a long time and he had no intention of repeating it twice a day. His legs and feet ached and he felt exhausted. He was pleased to find his bicycle waiting at the station.

When he got home Imogen told him she and the children had walked to the school and they would start next week they would need sandwiches and she had been to the shop.

"All seems fine" she said "I am told the ration books are good and that we can buy there. A man asked me if I wanted to buy a bicycle but I did not know what to say."

"Say yes," said Ken "you will find it a lot easier as I have today".

"What about money?" she asked concerned.

"How much did he want?"

"He said one pound would be all right and that it was a proper ladies bike."

"I will give you some ten bob notes, it is quite a lot but tomorrow I really think you should go back and get a bike, trust me. Just do not show the money around and if anyone asks, say it is the last of our savings."

Imogen was pleased, she would go, and she knew a good bike when she saw one coming from Holland it was natural. Anyway what on earth was she going to do with herself all day? With John and Sybil at school she did not want to stay cooped up in their room. Sybil would not leave the room she said she was too frightened of the animals. She rarely had a full night's sleep and was losing weight but John enjoyed being out. He went out and found Hannah and helped her with the feeding and counting. On the day they started school at Little Wenlock they set off before the Thomas girls. Imogen took her bicycle, pushing it as she walked alongside the two children. She gave Sybil a ride when her legs grew tired of walking. The day went badly for Sybil and John the other children picked on them because of their accents. Grace and Hannah joined them at playtime but Sybil was so depressing they left her with John and went to play with their friends. At the end of school Grace said to John "Come on we will all walk together".

"We cannot, we must wait for our Aunt. Sybil will not go without her."

"Please yourself" said Grace and she, Hannah and Helen went without them.

"What is wrong with them?" asked Helen "they never come out they just stay in their room".

"John is all right it's just that they miss their Mam."

"I wouldn't miss ours" said Grace "I would have a holiday".

"But you would miss us" said Hannah "and that's their problem too, all their friends are in Liverpool and they think with all the bombing they may never see them again. I think it is scary." They saw Imogen cycling towards them.

"She is all right after all," said Hannah.

"You have gone soft" said Grace.

"John told me how her family is trapped. The Germans live in her country now."

Imogen stopped by them "Where are John and Sybil?" she asked.

"They wanted to wait for you" said Grace.

"Oh dear" sighed Imogen and set off to the village.

That night Sybil was worse than ever so Imogen spoke to Ken. "It is better they are here than back home" he said "the bombing continues. I will talk to her and John". After their meal he sat down with the two children and they talked. He managed to convince Sybil to try and make an effort. The next day they went to school and at playtime they were joined by Hannah and Helen. Danny Probin joined them; he wanted to know all about the bombing of Liverpool and was keen to listen. Sybil talked with him for a while but became depressed. She missed her mother so much and withdrew into herself. After several days they began walking to and from school with Grace, Hannah and Helen, this pleased Imogen she stopped worrying about them and that left her free to concentrate on their washing and welfare. She agreed with Dorothy that she could use the sink at certain times and also when she could wash clothes and use the mangle.

Imogen used her bike to go into town to do their shopping and Ken cycled to and from Wellington every day. After a week Ken realized he was looking better, he was sleeping better and his legs felt stronger. He commented such to Imogen who laughed.

"I have noticed and have you noticed you hardly cough these days?"

"Well you should talk, you have more colour in your cheeks these days and that is not make up."

The children too were looking healthier although Sybil still was not gaining weight.

Ken wrote to his sister and told her of the problems with Sybil but it was considered too dangerous for her to return. In turn Imogen wrote to Miss Shore from the welfare that had been responsible for relocating them, she had a big workload but nevertheless paid them a visit and talked to Sybil. It was decided that despite her unhappiness she would remain on the farm. If by the winter months there were no improvement then they would have no choice but to send both her and John back to Liverpool. Dorothy soon found it a problem the extra people in the house. There was the washing to be dried; she could not use the far room so had to use the front room. She asked Fred to arrange with Ken for them to buy their own coal and collect their own sticks but as it turned out the girls always picked a few extra for them.

One Saturday afternoon Ken walked through the kitchen on his way outside. Dorothy had several dead rabbits on the table. "How is the girl?" she asked not looking up.

"Coping" he said and he watched amazed how quickly she dealt with each rabbit. She had a razor sharp knife with which she cut its belly open then she pulled out the innards and threw them into an old milk churn she had put at the end of the table. She then chopped the feet off and with a few strokes of the knife to help it over the head she had stripped the skin clean away.

"There you go, one skinned rabbit" she said, "the guts go to the pigs".

"Do you leave the head on?" he asked he had eaten rabbit before but always with the head removed.

"Oh yes, the girls often argue as to whose turn it is to have the head. We all enjoy eating the rabbit's brain, very good for you, you know."

"Have they been shot?" he asked.

"Oh no snared, we can't waste cartridges on them. Would you like one? I am sure the children would enjoy it."

"Yes please" he said glad for some extra meat. There were definite advantages to being out here in the country.

She had a half-grown rabbit. Not big enough for a family meal she picked it up...

"I will skin this one for you. If you like you can roast it in the oven after I've done ours tomorrow, make a nice Sunday dinner that will." She skinned it and then cut a piece of hazel stick she had taken from the hedge. "This will do as a skewer you may as well sit down you can watch me do the stuffing when the others are ready. Would your wife prefer to prepare it?" she asked.

"No I doubt it very much" he said "I have cooked them up years ago in the army, so if you don't mind I would like to see how you do it round here."

She stuffed the belly with breadcrumbs mixed with chopped onion and sage from the garden. Then taking the wooden skewer she joined the two sides of the belly together by threading it in and out of skin leaving it in place. She put small pieces of home cured bacon onto the belly and looked up.

"There I am sure the children will enjoy that but don't go telling folk about this or we will all get in trouble."

"Certainly not" said Ken knowing when he was on to a good thing.

The next day when Ken brought the cooked rabbit through everyone was pleased but at the end of the meal none of them could face eating the brains. "I will take it to the pigs later" he said "but we do not want to offend so we ate all of it right!" They all agreed. From then on Fred always set an extra snare and Ken often accompanied him when he went to check on them. It was on one of those trips that Fred warned Ken to watch out for the gamekeeper.

"Might not take kindly to a city dweller like you," said Fred half laughing.

"Not always lived in the city, Fred," he said "you know we learned a different way of living back in France, not pleasant at times some of the things we did."

"Aye you are right there, and as he found out a while ago, you can't always judge a book by its cover". Fred then told him of the gamekeepers meeting with the men from the town. Ken thought it was funny and agreed to watch out for him.

With the warmer weather Ken and Imogen took the children walking as much as possible. They usually walked through the Hazelhurst wood or up the Wrekin. They were often accompanied by one or more of the girls as they collected sticks for the fires. At the weekends if they were going up the Wrekin, Grace, Hannah and Helen would tag along as they knew Ken would pay for them to go on the swing boats or ride on the ponies at the cottage. Despite keeping themselves to themselves Sybil and John began to enjoy the warmer days. Occasionally they joined the girls at play around the farm, careful to keep away from where the animals were. They picked flowers for their room putting them in jam jars on the windowsills. One day Helen was showing them how to squeeze the flowers on the foxgloves to make a popping sound.

"We call these poppies because of the noise they make" Helen said. John popped several then Mary saw him handling the flowers. "They are poisonous stupid" she said to him "and you should know better Helen". Sybil was mortified and did not touch a flower for weeks. The next time was a sunny day when she and John joined the girls in the field by the house to make daisy chains. Imogen was very pleased to see Sybil happy when she returned with her necklace bracelets and a little headband all made of strung together daisies. Ken went away for a while during June. He simply told everyone it was official business. Imogen was worried and when the large black car had driven him away she felt some of her frailty return. It was quite a surprise to her when Sybil and John took control of fetching and carrying for her, they helped tidy and kept her spirits up till Ken returned. They seemed happy to be helping. It was shortly afterwards that Ken, John and Sybil accompanied the girls to see the gamekeeper's cottage. It was all barricaded with barbed wire to the height of six feet or more. "Is it to keep someone in or out?" he asked darkly and walked on quickly. While they were up there the girls checked the fences along the top fields and then went down into the Limekilns to show them the caves and old workings where the lime had been excavated years before. Hannah and Helen went delving into the holes making scary noises. Sybil was terrified of the dark cavities and screamed when Grace took her by the hand and tried to lead her into one of them. She had nightmares for a week! Hannah was the same age as Sybil and complained to John that his sister was a sissy. "I bet you would be scared of the places we go into back home" he said.

"Like what?" she said, "the bogey man lives in the woods here and we are not scared of him".

"Well we have him at home and he lives in the cellars where people have died and we go in them even though we are not supposed to."

"Dead people?" said Hannah.

"Ghosts" said John. "When we go home nothing will scare us because we know where all the bad things are and we will be with Mum again and if Sybil is scared Mum makes it go away."

"When you go home can I come with you then?" asked Hannah "will you ask you're Mam?"

"I doubt it," said John "but when we see her again I will ask".

John and Hannah spent time together following the progress of the war through the radio broadcasts. There was much more activity in the air now as Atcham base had been handed over to the Americans. Different aircraft appeared in the sky over the Wrekin. It was the Americans training and they had new planes that had never been seen before. One such plane stood out above all others, its shape was so unique, twin booms with an engine on each and a short fuselage between the booms, and it was fantastic to see. Danny Probin told Hannah it was the new Lightening, the P38. Known to the Germans as the forked devil. The sound of one climbing steeply with its twin Alison engines on full power was incredible to hear. The familiar sound of the spitfires and hurricanes seemed lazy in comparison. Dorothy wrote to her Mother saying how American aircraft was flying over the Wrekin every day. The sight of the planes and the stories going around town of the Americans confidence that Hitler would soon be beaten made her feel more secure. She asked if her Father still believed the Germans would invade as their propaganda suggested and if he would still carry out his threat to shoot them all and then himself. She remembered how the men of the family had boasted at William's christening what they would do but if it came to it, how many of them would have the guts to shoot their entire families. Fred never talked of such a thing now. He said he was too busy to go worrying about what would happen.

Her Mother's reply dismayed her; she wrote that her father was still adamant that any invasion and he would shoot them all. He had not changed his mind. He always had his shotgun close to hand in case the worst happened she said. It did nothing to cheer Dorothy up. She told Fred her Father's attitude and he was sympathetic.

"I know what he is thinking lass it is still a worry but think of our William and the girls. Lord knows we don't want anything to happen to them. There are many good folk prepared to put up a fight to protect this country we even have the home guard."

He was not overly confident despite his words. The British army was not doing well in North Africa and the Americans were committed to fighting the Japanese, they could still desert them. The fact was he still thought that he would choose to shoot the entire family and then himself if the Germans did overrun the country.

Fred and Dorothy had heard nothing from Sam. They could only assume that he was somewhere overseas and hope that one day he would come back safely.

John became quite interested in farm life, particularly the ploughing and sowing. When harvest time arrived he helped out stacking the stooks. Ken was away again and Imogen stayed indoors looking after Sybil who had a cold.

When Ken returned he seemed more optimistic and spent more of his free time outside talking with Fred but never when Gunter was around.

The news broadcasts were more promising with Americans now operating from Britain, the Russians holding the German tide in the east and a huge advance in the air war against Germany. Ken told Fred it was believed the Germans had over stretched themselves and were going to come unstuck. The first American air raid on Germany took place in August.

At the end of September the raids on Britain were declining. Ken said it was the drain Russia was placing on the German air force. As the nights drew in and the air became damper Sybil's health deteriorated. She began to lose weight again, developed a bad cough and the nightmares returned. To make matters worse the gander defending his harem of geese attacked her.

Imogen wrote and told Miss Shore the situation and Ken wrote to his sister. They felt sure that she would be really poorly if something was not done before the winter. Miss Shore paid another visit and agreed that it would be best to return them to Liverpool and their Mother. Imogen was relieved the responsibility was too great for her. She told Dorothy of the decision to return them to Liverpool.

"I still don't like to think of them being killed with the bombs."

"The risk is a lot less according to the letter we received, our old area seems to be left alone now so it is best for everyone" she said.

"Not for me" thought Dorothy "I will only get paid for one room now".

"You and your husband are staying though?" she asked.

"Oh yes, I think I might get a job in town, we have nothing to return to."

Miss Shore made the arrangements and the two children were to return in October, the chance of air raids would be even less with the bad weather approaching.

On the day they left Sybil would not speak to anyone, John was pleased to be going home to his friends but was sad also to leave the farm and Hannah, they had become good friends. Fred took Ken with them to the station despite there being a ban on driving unless essential business. Fred jokingly commented "It's your fault if we get stopped; this petrol wasn't part of the ration."

"Trust me you will not have a problem if we get stopped," said Ken with a smile.

Ken accompanied the children to Liverpool and stayed over for the night he returned the following day.

He joined Imogen in their room but it seemed horribly empty and lifeless.

"I really fear for their lives, poor souls, their mother was not at all happy but at least she understands that we have done our very best."

"Are you sure?" said Imogen "because I was sure if she stayed here we just might lose her".

"Well the place has taken a pounding but everyone has rallied around and it felt good. I think they are in the right place after all." She had to agree with her husband.

After the children had gone back to Liverpool, Imogen did not want to spend her days on the farm as, there was very little to do and with autumn setting in the leaves were falling and the ground was wet. It was no longer enjoyable to walk the woods especially alone.

She cycled to town eager to find some sort of employment. After several trips she found office work at the post Office in Walker Street. She would begin work after Ken but her finishing time coincided quite well with his return to the station. So each evening they went for a meal together at the servicemen's canteen before cycling home. They were fitter and happier than they had been for a long time. The ruggedness of the trip to and from town did not bother them at all.

CHAPTER 7

Too close for comfort

At the end of October the battle of El Alamein began. There had been no word from Sam for months and Fred suggested that he might be there. The family listened to every broadcast. Hannah joined Imogen one evening when Ken was away and told her all about Sam as they sat listening to their radio. Imogen liked to talk to Hannah; she told her how she and Ken had met when he worked in Holland before the war and his work in the petro-chemical industry.

"So he isn't a spy then?" asked Hannah. Imogen laughed "No but his work is very important. Petrol and oil are essential otherwise the ships, tanks and aeroplanes would not work. He must not tell what he knows and you must not say anything either."

"I won't say anything," said Hannah "at school we are told not to speak to strangers and I never do."

"Good, he tells us it is very important. And now he is away again for some days but I will not worry."

"Where does he go?" asked Hannah.

"He has to plan things for us to win the war and sometimes he must meet with important people. We must not ask questions and soon he will be back."

"Is he in Africa?" Hannah persisted.

"No dear, it is a long way away and he will be home soon."

Hannah was disappointed there was nothing to tell Helen and Grace now, only that Mr Winter was important.

They listened to the news from Africa which was all good, Rommel was taking a beating.

When Ken was away Imogen still took her evening meal in town and occasionally she was propositioned. She simply ignored the remarks with a shrug but was careful not to be followed as she made her way home. She had no fear of the countryside but the town now made her nervous.

Ken returned as the news broke Rommel was beaten, Montgomery was victorious. As he entered the kitchen Fred looked up "What of the news Ken? Are we out of the woods now?"

"Not yet" he said excitedly "but things are certainly looking good".

"It doesn't make it any better for us does it?" said Dorothy.

"Oh yes it does Mrs Thomas, it certainly does. The thing to watch is Russia now and particularly Stalingrad. After being beaten at Moscow Hitler could be losing his grip."

He smiled, nodded and set off to the far room.

Fred looked at Dorothy and the children looked at him.

"He is right," said Fred "we heard it on the wireless".

Later that evening Fred was in a good mood, he trusted Ken's statements and they were always borne out in the news.

"Dot I reckon that our lodgers are coping really well after the start they made. He knows what he is on about does Ken."

"Well I don't like her doing her washing on a Sunday afternoon."

"Don't grumble, she has to do her bit of washing some time and you can't do with her at the sink when you want it."

"It's all right for you Fred Thomas. You can get off outside, nobody there to get under your feet. Washing on a Sunday I ask you!"

"We don't see that much of them".

"Thank goodness. What does he do that takes him away for days at a time?"

"Don't know Dot, there has to be a lot of secrecy nowadays is not right to question too much."

"Hardly fair to her but she seems to be a lot tougher than I gave her credit for".

"Aye she is a tough little biddy all right. Settled down well to country life."

The family was well used to aircraft flying over at night, they were careful to make sure no light could be seen. Even the pens and out buildings had sacking covering the windows and door openings for the dark winter evenings when the stock had to be checked.

The Germans still carried out bombing but nothing like the scale of the previous years. Everyone agreed it had been right for John and Sybil to return to Liverpool. Therefore it came as a great surprise in the early hours of the morning when there was a distant explosion. Fred, being a light sleeper, heard it as did several of the children.

"What in the hell was that" he said and sat bolt upright in bed. "That can't be the quarry at this time of night." Dorothy stirred "What's the matter?" she said. Fred was already out of bed and pulling on his trousers.

"Don't know lass, sounds as though something is going on out there."

He opened the window, there were searchlights beaming across the sky. He could hear a plane far away; it was cold so the sound carried well.

"I reckon that was bombs going off or anti aircraft fire, it was close."

"Close the window and come away then" she said urgently.

He stood listening for a moment. "There's nothing to be seen out here but I had better check on the stock". He made for the bedroom door to go downstairs.

"You are surely not going out there are you? You could be killed and if that is the case we are both going to go together."

"I can't hear any planes around now, they have gone. Stay in the warm I will not be long. I've got to go and see if the cows need calming down."

Dorothy was worried, "What time is it?" she asked.

"Never mind the time. I am not going to strike a match to find out. I will look when I get downstairs."

He felt his way to the bedroom door and out onto the landing.

"What was that noise Dad?" asked Grace from another room, "is it thunder?"

"No lass, go back to sleep, nothing to worry about, I am just going to check on the cows."

Then he went downstairs. Once in the kitchen he struck a match and lit a paraffin lantern then he checked the blackouts were in place. Dorothy came in half dressed and grabbed a coat off the back door.

"It's two o'clock in the morning" she complained.

Fred was not going to argue the time of day with her. He took a hurricane lantern and lit it.

"Get the fire going Dot we might be up a while" He put on his boots jacket and a large coat. As he put his cap on he took a look around the kitchen "A cup of tea might be a good idea" he said and ventured outside shielding the lamp under his coat.

It was cold and he could hear noise in the distance from the town. He went into the first cowshed and pulled the sacking down over the door before uncovering the lamp. The cows were all standing shuffling softly in their stalls, as he moved along the line several bellowed and pulled at the chains fastened around their necks.

"Steady now, steady now" he said as he took a bowl and filled it with corn then passed between them patting each one in turn and giving them a little to eat. He did the same in the next section then returned to the door to go to the far cowshed. As he shut the large wooden door he heard the familiar drone of German planes again.

"Bugger off" he said out loud. There was an explosion in the distance followed by a second and then he felt a tremor through the ground. "Bloody hell, that was close" he kept the lamp well hidden. Should he go to the house or back to the cowshed, he was rooted to the spot. Jingo came running out, barking at the noise.

"That's near to the Glen," he said out loud. "Let's hope the next does not hit us". The planes were heading away into the distance and then there was silence again.

"Thank God for that" he said to the dog. "They are going."

He made his way back to the house, Dorothy was standing just inside the door and he very nearly knocked her over.

"What's happening? Fred should we get out?"

"Nay lass they have gone over now" his voice trembled a little. He looked at the range the fire was not lit. "Let's get the fire going and have a drink of tea. I need to get back to the cows."

They quickly got the fire lit and the kettle in place. Fred was impatient "I will go outside and have a listen, I'll be back in a few minutes" he said.

"Don't you go back out there leaving me here" she said alarmed at the thought.

"Don't worry" he said and went outside leaving her pacing up and down. He stood on the backyard listening but there were no aircraft about so he went back in.

"It is all quiet but the cows are restless" he said. They poured some tea and sat down not speaking, they both kept looking at the windows as if expecting something to happen. It took some time for them both to calm down. Eventually Fred returned to the cowshed to keep his cows company.

At 6:30 Mary came into the kitchen, Dorothy was frying bacon and eggs. "Someone's been up early" she said seeing a good fire burning in the grate, "where's Dad?"

"Out with the cows, he has been up since two o'clock he has. He just won't come in.

"Why ever not?"

"Them damned Germans have dropped bombs on us last night, too close for my liking. I don't know how they have missed killing the lot of us. Scared me to death it did."

"Is that what the noise was? We woke up but nobody said anything so we went back to sleep."

"You're lucky to be alive; your Dad was out there when it happened."

She put a thick slice of bread on to a dinner plate then placed the bacon and eggs on it covering it with a second slice of bread

"Here you can take this and a jug of tea out to him and see what he is doing."

Mary put on her coat and went out to the buildings. She found Fred sat on a milking stool in the bottom cow shed.

"Here Dad, I brought you a jug of tea and a bite to eat. Are you all right?"

"Aye grand lass. Has your Mam told you of the goings on during the night?" He raised the jug and took a drink.

"She has but where did the bombs fall and what damage has been done?"

"Don't rightly know all I do know is that it scared the living daylights out of us. A bloody good job these cows were fastened up. Probably scared the sheep as well, God only knows where they may be."

"Never bothered us" said Mary "was it really that bad?"

"Felt like it lass, it came as a bit of a shock. Mind I've been through much worse in the past. I think I'll make a start on the milking soon just in case Gunter does not come up today."

Dorothy saw Gunter when he came up the drive. She went out onto the backyard.

"What has been going on down there?" she demanded "what were the explosions?"

He told her that three bombs had gone off. One had fallen in a field near to the Forest Glen, one close to the POW camp and the last had wrecked part of a farm.

"Get round and tell the Gaffer what you told me" she said and went back inside to get the girls moving, they still had their jobs to do before they went off to school.

Gunter told Fred about the bombs.

"Bloody hell that is One-eyed Jack's place, are there any police or such there?"

"No Boss" said Gunter "not when I came past, I did not stop to look."

Fred decided there and then he would go down to see if Jack was all right.

"Let's finish this milking fast, I am going down to see if they need any help" he shouted across the yard for Mary until he got a response, then he went inside to carry on. When Mary found him he told her to go and arrange some more sandwiches, he would not have time for a proper breakfast.

As soon as he was finished he went in got his sandwich and then set off in the car not stopping to shave.

As he pulled up in the lane to Jack's farm he could see there was damage done to the outbuildings but the house looked all right.

"What a bloody mess" he said to himself. He walked into the yard expecting to see police or somebody but there was no one around. The grain shed adjoining the cowshed was destroyed creating a huge gap, the cowshed itself was missing part of the roof and the end wall had collapsed into the remains of the shed. Timber and rubble lay everywhere, he looked around, the house looked deserted and all the windows were smashed. He walked towards the cowshed where he saw

Jack sat amidst the rubble on a roof truss with his back towards Fred.

"Surry you have a mess on your hands owd lad" he said, Jack did not respond.

Fred picked his way through the rubble.

"What are you doing sat here. Are you all right?" Jack still did not respond. Fred had seen men in this state so many times during the Great War. "Jack, it's me Fred."

Jack turned around there were tears running down his face. His boots were still unlaced and his stick was lying by the side of him. His uncombed hair was peeking from under his cap. "Look what they gone and bloody done," said Jack.

"Where's Alice and Doug" shouted Fred.

"What?" Said Jack then realising what Fred had said he looked at the house. "Nobody killed, but look at it." He took the woodbine from his mouth and indicated the damaged buildings. Fred could see through the wrecked building there were no cows in the cowshed.

"Where are your cows? Have you milked yet?" he asked Jack.

Jack rubbed the sleeve of his old jacket across his eyes; he looked up at Fred and then back at the cowshed "What am I going to do?" he sobbed.

"Come on now man, pull yourself together, you have got work to do now where are the cows?"

"Out there, I had to turn them loose and let them go or they would have killed themselves pulling on their chains".

"Well come now Jack, let's round them up, sitting here like a little lad isn't going to put the place to rights, I reckon that you are lucky to see the light of day."

Jack got to his feet, stumbled and sat back down. Fred helped him back up and eventually got him to a clear space on the yard, he seemed to be getting to grips with the situation.

"How are we going to milk cows in there?" Jack said and pointed to the damaged cowshed.

Fred went inside, the wall at the one end was gone and there were a lot of cracks but half of the building still looked usable. He thought of Alice and Doug.

Back on the yard he sent Jack to round up the cattle while he went to the house. He went to the back door, it was undone so he knocked twice and stepped inside. Alice was sat at the table; her Brother Doug was trying to comfort her.

"Come on Doug, you've got to milk your cows," Fred said. Alice looked up, seeing Fred she started to cry loudly.

"You all right are you Missus?" Fred asked looking around the kitchen. The windows had blown in but 'Oh my goodness' he thought, what a mess! The place was filthy to start with. Dorothy did not go out of her way to do house work but her kitchen was fit for a king compared to this.

There was no fire burning in the range so he set to the task.

"Let's get some warmth in here and then you can get a pot of tea on the go."

Alice sobbed louder; she was in her forties and a spinster, caring only for herself and her two brothers.

"Come on now and calm down a bit" said Fred lighting the fire. "You can take care of this can't you Alice? Make a good pot of tea," She nodded still upset, "I'll try". Fred looked around it was a pigsty but apart from the window there was no damage at all.

"Now why don't you come with me Doug lad" Fred beckoned with his finger. "Let's give Jack a hand getting the cows in" he said and went to the door.

"Get your gear on man. We'll be back for a drink when you have made it Alice" and he stepped outside.

He waited on the yard till Doug caught up. "I will go with you to check out the cowshed, Alice is best left to get on with the tea and I hope Jack will be back with the cows soon." They entered the cowshed, which was much lighter than usual due to the missing wall!

Doug looked at the cracks and was reluctant to enter.

"Don't you bother about them" Fred told him "what's left of the roof is not going to fall in just yet, that far end looks pretty safe to me."

"What are we going to do? Look at it, we can't afford this."

Fred had no patience with Doug's moaning.

"Pick up the pieces and rebuild I shouldn't wonder."

"But we don't have any spare money."

He knew that the three of them had little acreage, only half a dozen cows and as a result very little money.

"What are you worrying about money for? I reckon you are lucky to be alive. I am sure that you can patch things up a bit and when things have calmed down I think I could be right by saying the Government will help with any major repairs.

Doug seemed to cheer up with the thought of compensation.

As they were looking around a cow appeared in the doorway. It stood quite still then looked right then left as though checking all was clear. Satisfied she walked forward and took up her place.

"Well Jack's found them so come on get them tethered and fed." Doug set to the task in hand and Fred made his way outside. Jack was following the cows into the yard.

"Good man Jack. Doug is in there setting up. I am going to have a look where the bomb fell."

"It is a bloody big hole and no mistake" said Jack.

Fred left them to get on while he went to have a look where the bomb had fallen. It had left a huge crater at the back of the farm buildings. A few yards to the north and it would have been far more serious flattening the rest of the buildings and possibly the farmhouse.

"Aye surry" Fred said to himself "they are lucky to be alive". He looked around. Bombs fell on Britain every day but it was a different matter when it was on your own doorstep. He made his way back to the kitchen; Alice had now pulled herself together a little, the fire burned merrily and she had made a pot of tea.

"The milking is underway" said Fred "I am sure they will feel better for a brew. I'll give them a shout" Alice did not answer she was a nervous woman.

"Well pour some out for them Alice. Have any of you had any breakfast her look told him no.

"I'll give them a shout then and you get that frying pan out and cook some bacon and eggs for them" she looked at him blankly.

Fred knew she had no cooking skills. It was well known locally that bread, cheese and pickles were the peak of her culinary skills, she left it to Doug and Jack to do the cooking.

"Come on Alice it won't hurt you to fry something up" Fred said knowing it would divert her attention from the situation. She went into the larder and came back with a basin containing what looked like pig's lard and a plate with some bacon on it. She put them on the cluttered table and rummaged around under the kitchen sink. She found the frying pan still with fat and burnt remains in it. "It's where Doug puts it" she said and went to the range where she lifted the plate and left it to heat.

Fred went back to the cowshed; Doug and Jack were busy with the milking. He was about to ask where their young stock was but thought better of it, one thing at a time.

He looked at the missing end of the shed, it was cloudy outside could rain soon.

"Alice is cooking breakfast. Have you got a tarpaulin for the end there, a fair bit of roof has gone" Jack looked up.

"Breakfast?" He looked surprised then remembered "aye we got one of sorts".

"Well you might want to get it now before you go in, it looks like rain."

Fred waited until Jack was finished then followed him outside and off to one of the sheds. In the back they found a green tarpaulin sheet lying against the wall. "That's the best we have got Fred, not very good but it might keep the worst of the rain out until we can get things fixed up a bit".

"Now you are talking. Got any ladders?" Fred asked.

"Only got the one big one up in the barn."

They carried the sheet back to the cowshed then fetched the wooden ladder. Fred surveyed the damage while Jack lit a cigarette. Fred decided Jack or Doug could do the climbing as the ladder did not look very safe at all.

"You and Doug ought to go and get some tea and food inside you. Now are you missing any stock?"

"I dunna know where me heifers are but they can wait. Will you come and have a cuppa with us? We can see to things out here afterwards."

"No I will go and see where they are and bring them back nearer the buildings. Then when you come out we can put that sheet over the roof and weight the corners down with some of these loose bricks."

"No Fred, that can wait I want you to come in with us. It would be better for our Alice."

Fred guessed that he did not want to go into the house in case his sister had not pulled herself together.

"OK I will just have a quick one with you then we will have to get a move on I must get back up that road and see how things are at our place."

Back in the kitchen the table was set after a fashion including a place for Fred. There was a plate with large chunks of dry bread and little else.

"Where's the tea Alice?" asked Jack.

"On the cupboard" she said. "I have bacon and plenty of eggs ready, so get a plate each."

Doug and Jack wasted no time. "They must be really hungry" thought Fred. He did not fancy eating anything so he got himself a cup of tea and sat down on one of the greasy wooden chairs.

Fred drank his tea quickly it tasted awful. He put down his cup and stood up.

"You lads take your time; I will make start sheeting up." He went to the door "Thanks for the tea Alice, be seeing you soon".

Jack was soon out to help him.

"How's Alice doing?" asked Fred.

"She is a bit better, done her good getting some breakfast for us. What are we going to do about the mess?" Fred despaired, "Clean it up to start with and if you've anything about you you'll get off to Pearce's building yard tomorrow, sand, cement and some glass for the windows is what you need.

I reckon that if you clean these bricks, mix some mortar and put them back where they came from you can soon make this place reasonably safe yourselves."

"Sounds easy for you to say, I am no bricklayer."

"Well get on to your landowner but I doubt you will get them to do much while we have a war to fight. Perhaps they will build you a new shed when it is over."

"Maybe Fred, maybe but it looks such a mess right now."

"You have got to give these things a try Jack, but for now let's get it sheeted up." Together they got the sheet in place weighting the corners down with bricks tied with twine.

When they had finished Fred took one last look around.

"Right Jack, I will say Cheerio to you for now. You get something sorted out soon. I think I just might call at the Glen on my way back to see how they fared. I'll bet this sure rattled their cups and saucers". He chuckled at the thought of all that crockery dancing on the tables and shelves.

"Aye" Jack chuckled, sharing the joke.

Fred went to the car and got in he was pleased that he had been able to help out. The tarpaulin sheet hanging over the damaged cowshed roof would not keep much rain out but at least it was something. All in all they were lucky to be alive. He backed the car up the lane and drove back to where the third bomb had fallen. He had seen thousands of craters, many bigger than this one, but being so close to home it left him quite shaken. He walked back to the car and leant against the wing for a while, soil and debris was scattered over a wide area.

"Aye surry" he said out loud, "I'll bet the Podmores are glad this one did not drop on top of them".

He drove on to the Forest Glen, parked and made his way round the back, the function room was mostly glass in a metal framework but there were no broken panes to be seen. Margaret Podmore opened the door.

"Oh it is you Mr Thomas, come in won't you" she seemed upset "take a seat at the table". She did not mention his muddy boots. He removed his dirty cap and stepped in; his blond hair was streaked with grey and shone in the light from the glass roof. He looked up and again saw no sign of any broken panes. "Got away with it then" he said. Margaret sat down and started to weep. Fred felt uncomfortable, it took him quite by surprise the bombs had really frightened her.

"Oh Fred they could have killed the lot of us" she sobbed. This was the first time that she had called him by his Christian name. He sat down not sure what to say. Thankfully Lizzy came into the kitchen. She saw how upset Mrs Podmore was again and went to the stove.

"It looks as if you two need a cup of tea" she said placing the large aluminum kettle over the heat.

"Are you all right Dad?" she asked "is anything wrong at home?"

"Nay lass. I have just been helping out old Jack at his place, one landed right by them. Did a bit of damage."

"Oh dear" she said and went off to the middle kitchen. Margaret sat in silence. When Lizzy returned with cups, saucers and milk she asked, "Have any of them been injured?"

"Just a good shaking although it has scared Alice out of her wits, not that it took a lot of doing, poor soul. They have just got to pull themselves together now." Margaret blew into her handkerchief and looked at Fred, and then he realized what he had said. She smiled before he could say anything.

"You are quite right Fred that is what my Percy said to me after the explosions. I must make an effort and get on with things." She turned to Lizzy who was waiting for the kettle to boil.

"Thank you. Bring some cake and plates please. Would you like a piece Fred?"

"Yes please" He said thinking it might get rid of the taste of Alice's tea. Lizzy went to fetch some fruitcake and jam. Margaret cheered up and they talked of the night's scare. No one had been out from the town. Percy was late back; he had said he would report the matter. Lizzy made the tea and when it had brewed she poured out two cups and put them in front of them both.

"Join us, Elizabeth" Margaret said and she pulled up a stool.

"We must get on with preparing for tonight's booking soon or Percy will want to know what we have been doing and I can't tell him that I have been a cry baby all morning, which would never do."

She spread some jam on slices of cake and handed them around. It was delicious and soon the drama was forgotten. Fred listened as Lizzy and Margaret told him of the dinner dances they held, of the American flyers and other military personnel that gathered there. When he left Fred felt refreshed, it always felt strange stepping out into the fresh air after being in the Pavilion as it was sometimes called. "Like waking from a dream" he thought. He set off home what a morning this had turned out to be.

Even though he did not offer to help out with any of the farm work Fred had taken a liking to Ken.

Sometimes they would go out together checking on the snares set to catch rabbits. It was on one of their walks that Ken hinted at the importance of his work.

"If anything happens to me I will need you to help my Ginny. I know she is safe here but my work is likely to put me in great danger."

"How is that?" asked Fred "are you worried about these nuisance raids?" It was well known for lone German aircraft to speed across the country hitting individual targets, a Junkers 88 had appeared following the railway line outside Wellington.

"No, that is of no concern. My work takes me much further a field and you can trust me to say that the war may be turning."

"I am glad to hear that. I can believe what you say, the last letter from me Mam was quite cheerful and it's what we are hearing on the wireless as well, is it not?"

"Yes, well I will have to go away again soon and each time the danger increases. I want you to take a letter for me. It is for Ginny's eyes only should anything unfortunate happen to me. You must promise to keep it safe."

Fred looked at the envelope Ken was holding out in the moonlight.

"Surry! I don't know, this sounds serious."

"Fred, it is and I do not sit in an office moving papers around. No one must know my work, which is why I have not worked with you. I cannot risk Gunter or anyone knowing me or what I do." Fred was speechless; he took the envelope and looked over the fields.

"This war is far away from here not like when we were in the trenches; it is someone else's war this time. I just want to get through it with my family in one piece."

"I know" said Ken "so do I but I have a chance to help free the people under German occupation, the same people who treated me as family, helped us when we first married. Ginny's parents. Just take the letter you will never have to open it trust me I know about these things".

"Let us get back to these snares" said Fred "I will look after this but don't go doing anything stupid".

"I have no intention of taking risks," said Ken.

The matter was never spoken of again Fred put the letter safe and told no one.

As Christmas neared Dorothy let the entire surplus poultry go to the butcher, some of the birds were hardly worth plucking but they went nonetheless. A good size bird was kept back for Christmas day and a smaller bird was given to Ken and Imogen. The girls were allowed to put up their paper decorations and Fred brought some holly in on Christmas Eve. On Christmas Day Dorothy put the Winters bird to roast in the oven with theirs. In the afternoon after their meal everyone relaxed. Dorothy had managed to get one or two extras for Christmas but not much at all. She handed each of the girls several presents, all clothes, there were also clothes from the grandparents. Joyce Wilkins had sent them some sweets. Later Hannah went through to see Imogen and Ken in the far room. Candles, set in a beautiful display on the table lit the room. Hannah sat down, the room seemed cosy and pleasant to her after the kitchen. There was a faint smell of flowers; Ken and Imogen were listening to music. When the piece ended Imogen asked her to fetch her sisters through for their presents. They all crowded in and Imogen handed each a neatly wrapped present. When opened each of the girls had a book and some sweets. There was some chocolate for William. Mary took it to Dorothy who put it away for later. In the evening Ken joined Fred in the front room where the fire was burning merrily. Dorothy was in the kitchen and Hannah was sat with Imogen hearing of Christmas in Holland and of Saint Nicholas. Ken passed Fred a bottle of beer "Let's share a drink and wish our forces a quiet night" he said.

"I will certainly agree there" said Fred taking the bottle. "It's the lads at sea I feel sorry for tonight, the weather doesn't let up."

"I don't suppose the Germans in Russia are having too good a time of it then" said Ken and chuckled to himself.

"Them bombs dropping down at Cluddely were a bit of a shock" said Fred "Sort of brought the war closer. Too close for One-eyed Jack" he added with a chuckle

They talked a while enjoying a smoke and the beer until they were joined by Dorothy. William was teething and she was tired of the grizzling.

She sat down and Ken offered her a beer, she declined, she was too tired it had been a long day.

"I don't know which is the worse the war or looking after snivelling wet children" she said.

"Surry lass look on the bright side; Ken here started the year with a house and a future and has lost the lot."

"I suppose so" she said "it gets so damp and wet around here it's good that your niece and nephew went home".

Ken smiled and took a drink "We have had a card from them. They are doing much better now. Their Father should be with them right now".

"I thought he was away fighting," said Dorothy.

"So did I" said Fred.

"He was but he was injured. Got shot up when laying mines over the Dutch coast. He is home now though."

"Well that is really good news. I wish we knew how Sam was doing though. Poor owd lad could be anywhere right now. He would love to see how the girls have grown up."

"Well here is to old friends" said Ken and tapped his bottle against Fred's.

"To old friends" said Fred. Dorothy smiled "How about toasting the end of this war?"

"Quite" said Ken "to the end of the war".

That night everyone slept peacefully. Hannah said a little prayer for Sam before she went to sleep.

CHAPTER 8

COUGHS AND CAMPFIRES

The New Year of 1943 came in bitterly cold, the icy roads made cycling risky in the mornings. Ken and Imogen did not mind the cold, wrapping up well before they set out for work. They would set off together and it was one morning down the Ercall that Imogen fell off her bike. Ken tried to dismount and he too fell heavily, the road surface was like a sheet of glass. They looked across at each other and burst out laughing neither was hurt but every time they tried to pick up their bicycles they fell down again. "This is ridiculous" said Ken as he crawled to the edge of the road "we will walk in the wood from here on and we will have to be more careful of this black ice, we could have been hurt".

At this time the girls began the new school term, walking up the bank as usual. They found the wind so harsh they had to bow their heads and keep their scarves tight as they made their way to the village. The weather stayed bitterly cold for several weeks. When the weather warmed it brought snow.

The girls were kept off school; there was plenty for them to do, much to their disappointment.

They had to clear the paths and ensure the stock was well fed. Fred had reared a pair of welsh ewes that were constantly escaping, there was always the worry that they would be taken and butchered for the black market, so the fences had to be checked regularly. It was girl's job to check all the top fences along the limekilns and the banks. They took the sledge and made the most of it spending several hours on the bank.

After the snow the weather was mild and the girls returned to school. There were several empty seats and the word was that the missing children were very poorly. Soon Grace, Hannah and Helen became ill. Dorothy considered her parents usual weekly dose of Epsom salts dissolved in warm water cured most children's complaints but not this time. They were seen by Dr Williams and he diagnosed whooping cough. Hannah was worst, the wracking coughing fits made her physically sick. Soon Grace and Helen returned to school, they brought back the bad news one child from the village who was Hannah's age had died as a result of the illness. Hannah was making little progress and Dr Williams saw her again. She had to take a cough mixture, which tasted as obnoxious as it smelt, three times a day. Dorothy considered the cost too great and begrudged paying for it at the surgery. However she made sure Hannah took it using the child's death as a threat to get her to swallow the medicine. The disease made it difficult for her to breathe and her chest hurt so badly she could not sleep at night. Her chest was rubbed nightly with an embrocation to help her breathe but still night after night she would wake everyone with her coughing and retching. She was put in the little room under the stairs to allow her sisters to sleep. She would lie awake trying to hold back the coughing. It hurt so much she cried constantly from the pain. The coughing kept her awake so much during the night it left her tired and exhausted in the morning. Dorothy left her in bed to catch up on her sleep. It was quite beneficial as far as she was concerned as Hannah could help with the housework and then look after William who was quite a handful. Fetching and carrying for her, especially to bring the logs from the woodpile. As long as she was persistently coughing there was no hurry to send her back to school so consequently Hannah missed all of the spring and summer terms.

At times Dorothy thought that Hannah was going to die. It was the silence after a bout of coughing that worried her, she dreaded going to her room in the morning in case the worst had happened.

Fred never spoke of Hannah's illness but he was gravely concerned.

Dr Williams said that was all that they could do was hope that she would get better when the warmer weather arrived. He said she should get as much fresh air as possible and it was this that made matters worse for Dorothy, she had to dry washing in the house and as a result the air was constantly damp.

Fred tried to make sure that she was outside as much as possible, whether keeping him company or working with Mary. He would find her little jobs to do but he was happy enough for her to sit outside and read or watch the aircraft that flew in ever greater numbers around the Wrekin. During the threshing she stayed out of the way, watching from an upstairs window, the yield was better than before; it would make a good profit.

Danny Probin called in one weekend at the beginning of March looking for Hannah He turned up with an old bicycle, coming through to the farmyard rather than going to the house. He would not say where he had acquired it from when Hannah asked. Just that he could only use it for a week or two. It was quite small, a proper girls bike, ideal for Hannah to have a go. They went down the drive and she practiced on the road. Fred came along to see how she was getting on. He walked up to Danny who was sat on the gate. Hannah was further away turning the bike around she had dismounted and was half lifting half dragging it around to return. She saw Fred and waved with one hand very quickly not wanting to fall over.

"Watch me Dad" she shouted. Fred leant over the gate.

"How's the war going Danny lad?" he asked.

"I think the Americans will blast the Germans away Mr Thomas. My Dad says you should see the guns on the Thunderbolts that are flying around here, 50 calibre and eight of them.

"Surry you know your stuff. How are things down on the camp anyway?"

"There are loads of them crashing, they practice flying low, call it hedge hopping they do."

"So I've heard"

"They fly down the main roads at the cars. My Dad says he has seen them do it. Practicing strafing he said but everyone knows they do it to scare the car drivers."

"Serves them right if they crash, doing daft stuff like that." Said Fred "He made a mental note to watch out when driving on the A5

Hannah rode the bike by standing on the pedals, the seat was too high. Her battered old coat was in danger of catching in the chain but Fred was unconcerned. She charged up to the gate putting her foot down to stop and wobbled dangerously.

"What do you think Dad? I can ride it, can't I?"

"Aye lass that you can."

"One day I will have a bike of my own just like Lizzy's, only a different colour."

"When is Hannah coming back to school Mr Thomas?" asked Danny.

"When she gets rid of this whooping cough."

"I am much better now Dad" piped up Hannah.

"But when you get indoors it starts again so it may be a while."

Hannah knew not to argue. It was true, she did not cough much during the day but it was at night she suffered. After Fred had returned to his work she carried on practicing. That night she asked Lizzy if she could borrow her bike.

"Not on your life, I paid for that myself and I don't want anyone touching it." Later Hannah told Helen "I don't care, one day I will have my own bike and it will be better than hers you'll see."

The threshing had gone well earlier in the year and the cheques were paid into the bank, Dorothy was very pleased. The war was not going badly for them at all. Everything they produced was being paid for. The government offered incentives to improve output and everything no matter how good or bad had a price. There was money coming in from all directions wool, meat, cereal, potatoes, Swedes even lodging money for Ken and Imogen and what was more Lizzy paid her own way.

Dorothy still complained that she was losing money not having her market stall. It was one evening when she was moaning about having to darn socks and the coal not being as good as it used to be that Fred asked his standard question "But am we all right?"

"What! Of course, but we can not sit back now. God only knows what is around the corner."

"Well I dunna think the Gerry's are going to invade now lass. The tide has turned with the Americans here; it is just a matter of time before we take the fight over there."

"I still worry that we are not safe," she said.

"I am sure we are and what's more I reckon it is time to get a tractor."

"What on earth do you mean Fred Thomas, a tractor?" She was stunned.

"Well we could do more. I've been thinking, I could clear the fields at the top of the slang, get 'taters in there." She looked at him as he lit his pipe.

"What has brought this on?" she asked.

He puffed on the pipe and rocked back and forth while she waited patiently.

"There's never been a better chance," he said. "I know I can talk to our Mr Jones and he will back us up. There are more tractors out there now than ever before and I can say that a tractor will guarantee the farm carries on producing." She did not answer, instead she got up filled the kettle and set it on the range to boil. Then she pulled a chair up to the range and sat down again.

"That's a grand plan" she said. "Have you any idea of the cost, because what happens if this war does go bad?"

"In that case us owing money to the bank is not going to be top of anybody's list now is it?"

Dorothy sat down; she had to admit Fred had a very good point.

"You have it all worked out don't you?"

He grinned "Aye I reckon so. Now I am going to see Mr Simmons first chance I get. But it will probably be down to our Mr Jones to give the nod at the end of the day" she could only agree with him, the prospect of having a tractor was very appealing. She was worried that his health might not hold out, a kick from a cow or an accident could leave them in serious trouble, it was through his toil they had managed to get this far.

"I have to agree with you but it is going to cost. Have you any idea how much?"

"Not yet but I will find out."

She made them a drink and they talked for a while not mentioning the tractor again. Every now and again they would hear Hannah coughing.

As soon as he could Fred went to J.C. Bromley the Agricultural Engineers in Wellington to see about a tractor. He wanted information about which make of tractor would be the best to buy before making his mind up. He asked to see the manager, the same pleasant, middle aged man who recognized him from when he bought the shearing machine.

"Looking to buy a tractor" Fred stated simply.

"How big is your farm?" the manager asked.

"One hundred and four acres" said Fred proudly. "Some of it is bringing in corn now." The manager nodded, "Doing all right with the subsidies I'll warrant. There are a few like you out there now. The problem is there are no tractors available either new or second hand." He waved his arm around the yard for effect. "The banks are keen to help out these days; farming has never been so profitable." Fred was not put off and asked about some of the different makes, Field Marshal, Fordson, International and Alice Chalmers.

“All good tractors” said the manager “problem is if there were any to buy you would have to get agreement from the agriculture committee and even then you would only get what is available.” Fred was surprised “Surry I was hoping to get one before ploughing started; now I have made up my mind”.

“Sorry it’s not that easy. With your acreage you should certainly qualify so you need to get moving. I will give you the forms which have to be completed to make an application, take them home and fill them in then bring them back to me and I will see what can be done for you. I will give you some prices that you can take to your bank”. When Dorothy saw the forms she was unimpressed.

“Whatever next Fred Thomas?” Dorothy said when Fred gave her the forms to read and fill in.

“Did he say how long it will take to get a tractor after we have filled this lot in?”

“No idea, it depends on a lot of things. I suggest that you get cracking and fill them in pretty quick though, I’m off to the bank on Thursday.”

Fred went to see Mr Simmons who looked over the accounts and was quite pleased. He could see no problem the way things were. Fred had worked hard but it would be down to the agricultural committee as tractors were in short supply. Dorothy wrote to Mr Jones for Fred asking for his help in getting a tractor. Mr Jones called in on his way home one evening during milking. Neither Fred nor Dorothy had mentioned anything to the girls. Mary was left to take over while Fred and Mr Jones walked the fields. Grace and Hannah saw them walk up the slang.

“What’s going on?” asked Hannah.

“I have no idea but you can bet it will mean more work for us” Grace replied.

Mr Jones agreed with Fred, he was acutely aware how much the farm depended on Fred's health and for that matter the two horses. Fred would be put forward as a priority for 'mechanization' as he called it. After Mr Jones had gone Fred returned to finish the milking.

"What did he want?" asked Mary, more used to sharing in the running of the farm these days.

"Can't say lass" he said simply and went back to work. Mary was annoyed; she knew the others would pester her later on. She asked him several times later but he was not saying anything. The visit was soon forgotten and Fred set to ploughing with the horses as usual. Each night he came in worn out from manhandling the plough, he sat and wondered how long it would be before he had a tractor. It was those times when he thought a tractor might have been a better idea than the car.

The cough was very reluctant to leave Hannah. Fred took her with him whenever he could. He would make little cushions of hay and place them on the shafts of the hay turner. Hannah would sit and ride around the field with him until the job was finished. She would ride on the horse's backs going to and from the fields. Grace did not consider it fair that both she and Helen had to attend school and Hannah didn't. She would argue that if Hannah was fit enough to ride around the field most of the day she was fit enough to go with them to school.

Over Easter Fred and Dorothy were contacted by a member of the YMCA. Each year summer camps were run for children from the ravaged cities. Fred was requested to give over an area of ground for a camp in the summer holidays. He was unhappy about the idea of city kids running loose on his land

and made it clear to Dorothy over breakfast as soon as Mary had returned to her work.

"Let's not be too hasty, they will want milk from us, we can't be expected to have them here for nothing. It might be worth our while" she said.

"Not if they go running all over me fields and breaking down the fences, can't be doing with it."

"Why not talk to Mr Jones?" she suggested "make out it could hold us back, but still show willing,"

Fred was surprised. After all the fuss she had made when the evacuees came the previous year. He thought a moment. "Aye you might have a point lass. I could ask him if there is any sign of a tractor."

"We could put them on the rough fields under the Wrekin out of the way," she said "they couldn't cause much trouble up there".

Mr Jones came around and went with Fred to see the unused fields under the Wrekin.

"You can't put them on here" said Mr Jones "it is a bloody mess" there was little in the way of clear ground, brambles, gorse and shrub were well established.

"Been this way since we got here," said Fred "that was ten years ago".

"I know it is but you can clear some space in here surely."

"It will be hard going and we haven't really got the time. What it needs is a tractor but I don't suppose there are any available?"

"Probably at the bottom of the Atlantic the way things are going out there" he walked around the field and then crossed over to the other it was not as bad but still unsuitable.

After some debate it was agreed that Fred would clear part of each field for tents and they would use an area in-between for a fire and merry making. Mr Jones would use the clearance of the fields as an excuse to push for a tractor.

The camp was agreed, the situation was well suited in that it was secluded and unlikely to be targeted by German raiders, and not that any came around the area due to the strong American presence.

Children from Birmingham would arrive by bus at the beginning of the summer break then after a week they would return and more would arrive this was to last for six week. There was to be another camp at Church Stretton. They would have their own food but Fred would supply the milk, he would be paid compensation for the shortfall on his milk cheque.

In June Fred took Mary and Hannah to begin clearing some of the ground.

"Why are we doing this?" asked Hannah.

"As far as I can make out we are going to have lots of kids coming from Birmingham. The army is going to put up tents for them here but you have got to keep it a secret and not tell anyone. Not even any of your friends at school."

"How many are there coming and why can't we tell anyone?" Hannah asked.

"I don't know, bus loads they said and you can't say anything at school in case the Germans find out and drop bombs on them. They could kill them all."

"Who will tell the Germans?"

"I don't know, Mam says there are German spies everywhere."

"What does she mean German spies everywhere?" Hannah had stopped working and was leaning on her fork. "Kids are not really coming by the bus load are they?"

"Yes to stay in tents. Why are you always so inquisitive?"

"What do you mean by that big word inquisitive?"

"Nosy if you must know" Hannah pondered this for a while.

"What does a spy look like?" she asked.

"I don't know, the same as everyone else I would think, they don't grow horns and have long tails silly. All you have to do is keep your mouth shut when strangers are around or we will all be in trouble with the government."

"Oh I will but busloads of kids coming here. Oh Lordy. Will we see any of them?"

"I expect so; they won't exactly be miles away. Wait until they turn up, that is the only way to find out."

That satisfied Hannah's curiosity for the time being and the girls got on with their work.

At the beginning of July army Lorries arrived at the farm to drop off tents and equipment. Fred had them pile the stuff under the Bannut tree by the kitchen window.

During the following week a team of men arrived and took the equipment up to the fields under the Wrekin. Hannah was still off school because of the whooping cough. As it was the last week of term, Dorothy decided there was no point in her going in. She wanted to go and watch the men work but Dorothy rounded on her and sent her to tidy the bedrooms. Hannah couldn't wait for her sisters to arrive back from school.

When Grace and Helen walked down the bank they could see the top of tents. Once in the kitchen Hannah told them what had been happening. She wanted to go and look it was so exciting, the tents must be massive.

After a quick cup of tea and a change of clothes, Hannah and Grace sneaked down the back lane across the road and up the field. There were two tents bigger than any they had ever seen set upon the ground cleared of brambles and gorse.

They looked around; there was no one to be seen. Trenches had been dug for drainage into the ditches so they had to be careful. They peeped into the tents; one had tables already set up. After a while they returned to tell Mary and Helen what they had seen. Mary told them the tents were called marquees and one of them was to be used as sleeping quarters the other with the tables was probably for eating in. The campsite was soon prepared, as well as the two marquees there were tents for cooking and others set aside as toilets.

The last Saturday in July was to be the start of summer camp for the city children. The weather was fine. Early in the morning army Lorries turned up bringing cooking equipment and bedding. Fred came out of the granary; he was concerned about the amount of vehicle tracks across the fields. Before the fields were drained three years ago, they would not have got up there.

At midday five busses loaded with children arrived at the back gate. Fred ran to greet them

And told the driver of the first bus they would not be able to take the vehicles up the fields, as they would get bogged down. He pointed out the best place to unload was across the road where the track to the Wrekin farm began. He stood and watched as each bus was unloaded in turn. There were several organisers and they took control, blowing whistles. They soon had the excited chattering children lined up in tidy rows. Fred was unhappy, this lot could cause no end of trouble, and some of the boys were scruffy and reminded him of the lads from the village. One of the organisers called for attention then after a short lecture on behavior he set off towards the campsite, the noisy children followed in single file. One of the organisers came across to Fred and told him the plans for the following week and what they would require from the farm.

Fred returned to the farmyard where Mary, Hannah and Grace were watching from the Granary steps.

"Well they are here" Fred said to them.

"Oh my goodness" exclaimed Grace, "just look at them".

"You would think they had never seen green fields the noise they are making," said Mary.

"I reckon you are right" said Fred. "I don't think that they have ever been in the country before. It will do them good to get some of this Wrekin air in their lungs."

Later in the morning an army lorry arrived and drove up the field bringing food in metal containers. The army would supply their needs except milk and what eggs Dorothy could provide. There were several large piles of timber. Permission had been given by the Earl of Powys for wood from dead and dying trees to be gathered for the campfires. Later the lorry came down from the field and up the drive to the house. Two soldiers took away a churn of milk and some eggs.

Dorothy was quick to send the girls out to search all the out of the way places for any eggs they might have missed.

"Will we be able to go and have a look at them?" Hannah wanted to know.

"I wouldn't think so, Mam won't let us, and she never seems satisfied these days."

Each day the air was vibrant with the noise of the campsite. The city children played games on the field, walked in the woods and up the Wrekin. They went up to the Halfway house and rode on the ponies and swing boats.

Dorothy was looking out of the kitchen window; she could see the children playing a game of rounders.

"They're having a good time up there. I hope that they don't go breaking any fences down."

That's my worry," said Fred "we will have to check everywhere before we put the sheep back on those fields otherwise they will be getting out."

On the Wednesday morning when collecting eggs one of the organisers asked Dorothy if the girls would like to come over on Friday evening.

"Whatever for?" she asked.

"To sit by the campfire and join in the singsong. They would be very welcome."

Dorothy was reluctant to agree but Hannah overheard.

"Can we Mam? We will be very good, please?"

"I suppose so," she said sharply "just go and find something to do".

"We will be only too pleased to have them, the more the merrier. They should come across about six o'clock."

Dorothy decided that Helen, Hannah and Grace could go along to the campfire providing Mary went with them. Grace was reluctant, "They come from the towns," she moaned. "We won't fit in at all."

"Does it matter?" said Helen, "I've heard them singing it would be nice to join in."

"Well you had better not start coughing from the wood smoke Hannah or Mam will moan for days" said Grace.

On Friday evening the girls had all their jobs done in record time. They washed themselves in the dairy before changing into clean dresses and socks.

When they were ready, Mary, Hannah and Helen made their way to the campsite.

They were very apprehensive; there was quite a gathering around the fire, which had just been lit.

One of the organisers saw them and ushered them towards the group around the fire.

"Make some room you lot" he said and put them to sit on a log amongst a group of girls of Hannah's age. Mary sat between Hannah and Helen. The Birmingham girls were so talkative, they told the girls of life in Birmingham, the damage caused by the bombing, the food shortages and how different it was being in the countryside. Hannah was able to tell them all about the aircraft that flew over them and the crash site on the Wrekin.

The fire began to burn merrily, it was a grand sight but the girls could not believe their eyes to see so much wood being burnt.

"This is great" whispered Hannah to Mary.

"I just wish they wouldn't talk so much, you can't get a word in edgeways" she whispered back.

Helen was too busy.

There were hot sausages passed around with hot potatoes and squares of bread.

After they had eaten, one of the supervisors brought out a guitar and another piano accordion.

They began to play and everyone sang along to familiar songs such as Clementine, Coming around the Mountain, Yankee Doodle and John Browns Body. There were many more, some the girls had never heard of but they quickly picked up the words and joined in.

There was a special camp song specially prepared for the event, the tune was 'Bless em all' but the words were new to the girls. How they laughed when they first heard it and soon they were able to join in. The words of the ditty were:-

"They say there's a party just leaving from Brum
Bound for the Willowmoor Farm
Packed up with cases, kitbags and junk

Here at the campsite they are all going to bunk
And we're saying Hello to 'em all.
The long and the short and the tall.
That's why there's a shrieking
This side of the Wrekin.
So cheer up and welcome them all".

On the Saturday morning the busses returned with a new group of children who were unloaded and marched up the field. Those leaving came down singing their camp song, they were happy and cheerful and some were carrying sticks as souvenirs. They were loaded onto the buses and soon they were gone.

Helen and Hannah watched them go.

"Let's hope we can still go up there on Friday night" said Hannah.

"I like the potatoes out of the fire best" said Helen "they taste so good".

"Better than our Mam's" Hannah replied.

The routine was the same as the previous week and the girls went up on the Friday night.

After the singsong had finished Mary, Hannah and Helen made their way home. As they neared the road they saw three boys in the bottom field.

"What are you doing here Danny Probin?" Hannah asked.

"Just having a look, do you think that we could join in?"

"It's finished for tonight and the next one will be next Friday night, so no."

"Will you get us in?" said one of the boys.

"They might let you in if you ask but I doubt it. Where's that rusty old bike of yours?"

"Hidden in the wood" he replied.

"You get back to the village before your Mam misses you" said Mary.

"She does not bother where we are as long as we are out of the house."

The following week the boys turned up and asked if they could join in. Much to Hannah's surprise they were welcomed in. They were sat amongst a group of boys and Danny sat there like a nervous kitten. Gone was all his bravado as he was now out numbered. Eventually he relaxed and joined in. They came down each Friday night for the duration of the camp.

In one group was a boy called Bernie, about fourteen years old, he was keen to help and came over each day to fetch the eggs and milk. He asked Fred questions about life on the farm and was polite.

On the last day Fred asked him if he had enjoyed his stay in the country.

"I sure have, I wish I could come back, it's great here."

"Surely you want to get back home" Fred said to him.

"Not really there's not a lot back there, I would like to come back and stay here."

"Perhaps you can one day. You only have to bring a tent. Wait until next summer holidays and then you can stay for a few weeks."

"I will take you up on that," Bernie said.

Autumn term started and Hannah joined Grace and Helen insisting she was fit enough despite still waking in the night coughing. As they walked up the bank they could see activity at the summer camp it would be two more weeks before they had all gone. The school Doctor checked all children at the beginning of term. He agreed that she could attend full time despite the obvious problems with her chest. She still had her medicine and as long as she did not disrupt lessons with her coughing, she could get back to her schoolwork. Everyone was glad to see her back.

"How long are you stopping this time?" asked Danny?

"All the time I can" said Hannah "I have to catch up with everyone."

"That won't take long, have you got a bike yet?"

"No but one day I will. That is why I must work hard, I want to go to a posh school and be a nurse and I will need a bike then."

Danny changed the subject. "There are lots more soldiers around here now. Have you heard how busy the rifle range is?"

The range was situated on the Wellington side of the Wrekin and the noise could clearly be heard at the farm.

"Of course" said Hannah.

"Well they have sentries on the top and big red warning flags. We have been up there a lot during the holidays, seen some of the pilots from Atcham. But the sentries are foreigners, not ours."

"What do you mean, Americans?"

"Don't know. They wouldn't talk to us. How about coming up for a walk this weekend see if you can tell?"

"Me Mam wouldn't let me. The cough could get worse and anyway she always finds stuff for us to do."

"Well you could come with us to get some cases sometime off the range we go down through the burnt cottage." Years before, alongside a track that led up to the Half way house and emerging on the point overlooking Wellington, there had been a second dwelling which had burnt down and the area retained the name. Danny and the other boys often went to the range when everything was quiet and collected any empty cartridge cases or clips they could find. Again Hannah said no, she would like to go just to see what it was like but knew she would never get away with it. They talked of the war until it was time for lessons. Danny was quite sensible compared to lots of the other boys who spent most of their time playing war. A usual game went along the lines of:-

"Rat tat tat tat, you're dead."

"No I'm not you missed."

"Rat tat tat tat tat. Now you're dead."

"No I am not."

"Bang, now you are dead!"

"Bang, bang you only wounded me you're dead again."

Often someone ended up tied to the railings as a prisoner. If Miss Evans caught anyone tying children to the railings they got the ruler across the knuckles.

Nothing had changed as Hannah could see and she soon caught up with the work her classmates were doing.

With Hannah back at school Dorothy found it hard coping with William who was two years old and difficult at the best of times. Fred felt really sorry for Dorothy, after just one week without Hannah's help during the day she looked worn out. William was such a handful and Hannah's coughing still kept her awake at night. He persuaded her to have a couple of hours of well-earned rest on the Sunday afternoon. She was reluctant at first but Mary agreed to look after William and she gave in. So from then on Mary was left to keep an eye on things and have the tea ready for when they stirred in time for Fred to start the milking.

The last group of children left the campsite and the churns were returned to Fred, then the army came. On the Sunday the girls were sent to collect blackberries if there were any ready.

Taking an oblong wicker basket and two jam jars they headed over the road and up to the deserted campsite. When they got there the area was completely cleared, the grass was flattened in all directions.

"I wonder if we will see any of them again" Hannah asked Grace as they looked at the blackened patch where the fire had been. They missed the Friday night campfire and singsong.

"I wouldn't think so unless they come back next year" she replied.

Looking around there was little to put in their basket so they decided they would have to go further a field.

"We've got to fill this basket with blackberries, it's no use going back to the house unless we do, you know what Mam's like."

"If you don't pick the blackberries, you must not expect me to buy you any new clothes for the winter" Hannah said mimicking her mother.

"Yes well she sells them doesn't she; to the Forest Glen" said Grace "I want some new shoes, proper girl's shoes. I'm fed up with wearing boys shoes."

"So why don't we get them if we get her the money with the blackberries?"

"Mam says they last longer than girl's shoes which are too flimsy, that's what she will say, it's not the cost, I hate them. I will be twelve at the end of next month, I'm going to see Mrs Podmore and ask if I can get some work at the Forest Glen. I can start next Easter. Then I will have my own money and I will buy the sort of clothes I want not what Mam gets for us" continued Grace.

Hannah was surprised but she knew Grace was unhappy and that she wanted her own money.

"What will Mam say?" she said.

"I don't care, I'm going to have things other girls have."

"Well I'm going to see if I can take the Eleven Plus exam and go to the Grammar school."

"Ooh what a clever little clogs you are."

"Well why not? Miss Lewis says that I can try."

"And if you pass which school will you go to?"

"Oh Coalbrookdale or the Girls High School at Wellington."

"Wellington will be much better but remember you've got to pass first."

"And we had better get some blackberries or we will be for it." They carried on picking the fruit, each with thoughts of their own. "One day I want to be a school teacher," Hannah was thinking.

Grace had no idea of what she intended to do except to get away from the farm. She wanted smart clothes, dresses with bows and ribbons and proper ladies shoes. The girls tried their best to look as neat and tidy as they could, Christmas usually brought new clothes otherwise everything was handed down. They looked after their own hair but as it was cut short for school there was little they could do apart from curl it with home-made curlers fashioned from the strips of metal wire that had been used to tie straw bales. They still had to wash with paraffin on a Saturday to prevent nits. How they envied other girls at school with their tidy clothes and shoes.

After half an hour they had little to show for their searching.

They decided to go to the lime kiln woods where they felt sure there were plenty of blackberries just inside the wood.

"Are you sure?" said Hannah "what about the gamekeeper?"

"Which is worse him or our Mam? You know she will get the nut stick to us if we take this measly handful of blackberries back."

They went back through the farmyard and up the bank. Soon they were doing quite nicely; they found one or two good briar bushes laden with blackberries.

"This is more like it" said Grace "let's go in a bit deeper we can be finished sooner that way".

The basket was nearly full when a voice rang out "What do you two scallywags think you are doing stealing the blackberries from here?" It was the sinister voice of William Hollis.

"Be off with you before I set my dogs on you. If I say the word they will tear you to pieces." He turned and a black Labrador came forward from behind him.

"Growl Ben, growl" he said and the dog showed his teeth stepping towards the two girls.

"Heel boy, heel" and the dog returned to his side he stepped forward onto the small path where the girls were. Grace put their basket behind her so he could not kick it.

"We are not doing any harm, we were only picking a few blackberries" Grace said defiantly, still keeping an eye on the dog.

"A few blackberries indeed, I say what is to be taken from these woods not a cheeky little madam like you. Now be off with you, the only time you can pass through these woods is to collect those wretched sheep of your father's."

"We can't help it if they get out now and again" said Hannah "we check all the fences".

"Not well enough. They seem to like getting out and trespassing on your neighbours fields.

You are getting just like those townies, you think that you can trespass where you like, well I can see you wherever you go, and so don't you think that I can't. Be off with you and don't come back." The girls went to walk past him but he held out his stick.

"And when the hazelnuts are ready you can leave them alone as well. Do I make myself clear?"

"Yes" Said Grace bitterly. The Gamekeeper raised his stick and they hurried past.

"I will not tolerate any of you in these woods," he shouted after them "have I made myself clear?"

The girls wished they had not set foot in the wood.

"What a miserable man" Hannah whispered to Grace as they left the wood. She was stifling a cough

"It will be a long time before I go back in there," said Grace pointing back towards the wood. "He is a hateful horrid little man. He can keep his blackberries."

"Dad is on about clearing the slang all together, if he does we may have to."

"Oh Lordy I thought that after the hiding that he had been given we would have no problem ever again."

They made their way to the bramble bushes that grew in the hedges of the fields and collected a few more. "Mam will not be very pleased when she sees that these are all that we have picked, but if she grumbles we will blame it on that horrid gamekeeper."

On their return they told Dorothy of the goings on in the wood.

"What do you want to go messing in there for?" she said annoyed.

"What could we do? There's none up the slang," said Hannah.

"I'll have words with your Dad about this; now get out of my sight." At that she took the basket off to the larder.

"Blast that William Hollis" she said under her breath, he could be a problem. It was not the money she got from Margaret Podmore that mattered, it was the return gestures such as a nice pie, a cake or a few tasty leftovers from a function. Lizzy would bring back these treats in her basket. The slang would soon recover but if there were plenty up in the lime kiln woods it would be such a waste.

When Fred and Mary came in later she told Fred the problem.

"There's nothing we can do lass he is making it difficult for many around here."

She knew he was right. The crafty little man seemed to know whenever a farmer killed a pig in the neighbourhood and made the most of it.

", Well somebody should sort him out, there's a war on" said Mary.

"Aye, Joe Timmins would be first in line."

Joe was still called on to do a bit of slaughtering on the quiet. The ministry was not able to keep watch on all stock; animals did get sick and die. It was the excuse used if the records were checked and a pig, sheep or even a young bullock was missing.

William Hollis made it his business to follow Joe whenever he could. Keeping out of sight in the woods he was able to see if someone picked him up by car at the end of the quarry road or whether he went down to the New Works. If he was sure Joe had been to a killing he would make a friendly visit to the farm on the same day. It often resulted in him having a basin of pure pig lard or such like. He had paid Fred a visit after one of his pigs had been butchered, probably hearing the last squeal of the pig while watching from the bank. Everyone knew he would keep his mouth shut with a bit of bribery.

"Can't we play him at his own game?" said Dorothy.

"How do you mean lass?"

"Well he never goes short, he hands out pheasants to certain people so that he has favours done for him in return. The manager of the Johnson Estates might like to know about it."

"You are right lass but we are stuck with it, he takes off the land as we do. He is at odds with everyone but I think it is resentment at the end of the day." He was right, the gamekeeper saw everyone as doing better than him. He was quick to put the fear of God into anyone walking into his woods but he was good at his job, it was known the care he put into rearing the pheasants and the lengths he went to deter poachers. The rationing had brought more folk out from the town poaching at night. They took milk from cows in the early hours, root crops when available and any game possible. Without the gamekeeper there would have been far less in the way of rabbits, pigeons or milk at the Hatch.

CHAPTER 9

Broken fences

Several weeks later on a warm Saturday morning Dorothy announced at breakfast "You three can go and pick some blackberries this afternoon. They want all they can get at the Glen".

"I'm going as well" Helen piped up not wanting to stay behind watching over William for her Mother.

"You can all go. I need as many as I can get."

After dinner Mary took the two oblong wicker baskets out of the larder. She put four empty jam jars in the one basket for collecting the berries. They set off together, careful at the road because despite the lack of cars due to rationing, there were more Lorries and jeeps hurtling about. Up the big field they went to the slang and the rough ground where the summer camp had been. The brambles had recovered and there was an abundance of fruit.

The baskets were put safe on a clear piece of ground and then Mary smoothed a piece of old newspaper on the bottom of each.

"There you are, get your jars and let's see how quickly we can fill them" Mary ordered. She and Grace took two-pound size jars. Hannah and Helen took one-pound jars, which were easier for them to hold. The area was hidden from view and although people would walk long distances to pick anything to supplement their meagre rations, few visited that area. Dorothy had always told the girls to charge anyone found picking the fruit on their ground but the girls seldom did, they were very nervous of asking for money from strangers. Most town people walked to the Wrekin on a Sunday so there was no one around. They could hear the crackle of rifle fire in the distance, which was normal, but occasionally there seemed to be an echo from deeper in the Hazelhurst wood.

Helen was soon bored with picking the blackberries; she had eaten almost as many as there were in her jar. Suddenly there was the sound of shouting from further up the slope, too far away to be understood.

She sidled across to Grace who was doing very well.

"Who is shouting?" she asked.

"Don't pester me now, I don't want to get caught up on these briars it could be anyone." A whistle sounded a long way off.

"Who is that?" she asked again.

"For goodness sake, Helen" said Grace and carefully extracted herself from the bramble patch, her jar was almost full. As she turned to scold Helen for being a nuisance she glanced toward the Wrekin.

"There's something in the wood," she said alarmed. Mary and Hannah stopped picking and looked up. Grace was staring into the undergrowth.

"I hope it's not our cows," said Mary. "That's the last thing we need today."

There was a commotion deep in the wood and it sounded as if it was getting closer.

"Oh Lordy" said Hannah and went over to join Grace and Helen.

There was more noise as if several large things were moving through the woods towards them as well as to their left.

"It might be the ponies from the Half way house," said Grace.

It came as a complete surprise to them when a soldier in full camouflage dress burst into view, closely followed by several others and heading directly towards them. Helen squealed and ducked behind Grace. The lead soldier saw the girls and lost his momentum for a split second causing him to be hit in the back by the next soldier. He sprawled into the brambles cursing. Mary ran to join the others as the rest of the soldiers crashed through the brambles heading for the downward side of the rough ground. The girls crowded together and Mary pushed the baskets behind them out of the way. They watched terrified as more soldiers ran in from the wood most of them dropped behind the bigger bramble patches. Two slid to the ground six feet from where the girls stood rooted to the spot. One of the men with his face blackened and small branches sticking out in all directions looked up at the girls and whispered gruffly "Pretend we are not here." Then he lifted his rifle to his shoulder and aimed back up the Wrekin. The soldier who had fallen had finally extricated himself from the briars and was limping off after the others. The man who had spoken saw him, nudged his partner and they both laughed.

Hannah pulled at Mary's coat.

"Are they Germans" she whispered.

"Shut up, I don't know."

"They can't have our blackberries we've picked them," Helen said loudly.

The soldier turned back to them grinning "Don't worry about us we are not here to hurt you. We are Canadians come to fight the war for you, get on with picking your berries just like you have not seen us" he said. His voice was warm with a peculiar accent.

"He's got a funny voice," said Grace, "different to ours".

"That is because they are our allies from Canada. You know, the Commonwealth" Mary said.

"Oh that's all right then," said Grace. Mary bent down and picked up their jars.

"Now come on let's pick some more then we can get back to the house to tell Mam and Dad."

They couldn't concentrate as they picked the berries. More were squashed than were put in the jars.

The soldiers stayed where they were for several minutes without speaking. Nothing more happened and so they rose to leave. They turned to the girls, grinned and raised their fingers in the familiar V for victory salute.

"Goodbye girls" one of them said.

"We might bump into you again someday so take care," said the other. Then slowly they made their way after the others. Hannah returned the salute. "Well that was scary" she said, "Can we go home now?"

"I suppose so," said Mary. She looked in the basket there were not enough really, but they gave up anyway and made their way back to the farm.

As they came round the corner by the dairy they met Dorothy, heading down the yard.

"What are you doing back so soon?" she said looking them over. None of them was injured no tears no muddy clothes.

She looked in the baskets "That is not much use, what is it this time that gamekeeper again?"

"No Mam" said Mary "there's soldiers everywhere".

"What?" she shouted. "Where are they, what are they doing?" She was panicking and was all set to get the shotgun when Grace added "They are Canadian Mam; they said they are here to help us". Dorothy calmed down she knew there were maneuvers going on; Fred had mentioned it to her.

"Canadian are they, well what are they doing?"

"Running through the woods and over the rough ground. They scared us they did," said Hannah.

"You mustn't get talking to them," said Dorothy "otherwise they will be taking over the buildings next I shouldn't wonder. You could have spent another hour picking and filled both of those baskets, as it is you will have to go again tomorrow".

"But we have to go to Sunday school tomorrow" Grace said defiantly.

"Never you mind about Sunday school, there is a war on and the country has to be fed. Sort yourselves out. Today or tomorrow your choice, Margaret Podmore wants more than those few." The girls looked at each other, none of them wanted to return to the slang.

"We will go in the morning" said Grace and set off to put the baskets in the larder, maybe Dad would let them off if he heard the soldiers were running over the fields. As she put the baskets down Mary brought the jars in.

"I don't think the country is going to be fed on our blackberries do you?" said Grace.

"Not today anyway" said Mary and they went back outside.

Fred was not too pleased with the news that the Canadians were running around the woods.

There was far more activity in the area with troops using the Wrekin and surrounding areas for maneuvers. Trucks seemed to be everywhere when he and Dorothy went down town and a lot of them were driven by maniacs.

In July, the Allies had taken Sicily and at the beginning of September the Italian campaign had begun. Perhaps the Canadians were practicing ready to go out there, although Italy had surrendered, the Germans were putting up a terrific fight.

He spoke to Ken that evening as once again, it was all talk of the eighth army, New Zealand, Indian; Australian and American troops were mentioned but not Canadian.

Italy had been hailed as the soft underbelly of Europe, as Ken pointed out, the Germans were not going to give up easily, they were simply moving back towards Germany and would fight all the way.

Fred went back to the kitchen less happy. It was clear that the drive was on to defeat Germany with overwhelming odds, the Russians were doing just that on the eastern front. He was concerned for his livestock. If there were lots of soldiers there would be lots of damage. Several days later the trouble started when a mock battle broke out. Guns were going off and there were several loud bangs from thunder flashes. The cows nearby ran in all directions with tails raised and fear in their eyes. Fred was furious and decided to keep them closer to the farm but still they were scared as sudden outbursts of gunfire disturbed their peace. Fred was told there was nothing could be done, it was essential to the war effort that the practices continue taking into account all kinds of terrain.

Fred had to keep the bull fastened up during the day just in case any of the strangers came too close to him. Fred knew that Billy would turn very nasty if anyone upset his harem. He was let out at night to be with the cows. The girls were sent out everyday to check the fences particularly those where the sheep were grazing. The soldiers would often break the wire down and scatter the sheep. Before long the sheep would spot the broken fence and they were out. Sometimes they would wander as far as the golf course, which came up to the edge of Wilf's top field. It was usually Mary who had to search for them and herd them back. She took one of the other girls whenever they were at home, it was easier with two. The neighbours began complaining whenever she had to go and retrieve the sheep from their property. It was not her fault that the sheep or cattle trespassed on to their land. They had even taken to tying and even chaining the gates to prevent them being left open.

One Saturday morning Dorothy noticed that the back fields were empty of sheep. She went down to the walnut tree with William; there was no sign of them. Later when everyone came in for dinner she asked them all if they had seen the sheep that morning. No one had.

"Oh not again" said Mary. "It looks as if they have got out again."

"Well I reckon you'd better get up there and find them. You can leave what you were going to do this afternoon" said Dorothy.

"Aye lass we don't want to lose them" Fred added.

"All right, I will go after them as soon as we have had dinner, but I'm fed up with having to go looking for them. As long as the army keeps breaking the hedges down what chance have we got?"

"I will go with you if you if you like" said Hannah.

"Yes I could do with some help. We can go to the Hatch first and see if Mrs Wilkins has seen them, she does not miss much that goes on under her window. I just hope they have not been through her garden."

They dressed and each took a stick from behind the door, it helped when herding the sheep and also on the climb up the back fields. Dorothy checked that Hannah was wrapped up well she did not want her making her cough any worse. Down the backyard and over the gate they went. Mary stood in the field looking around the steep bank in front of her no sign of the sheep.

"Let's go to Miss Stewart's place first instead of the Hatch, that bailiff of hers can be a bad tempered fellow if they have got on to his land. He could have them in his stack yard" she said. The bailiff, known as Old Shankly, had threatened to lock the sheep up if they went there again and charge Fred for their keep. The two girls made their way up the bank to the top fields and as expected there was no sign of the sheep, they really had gone missing again. Beginning at the right hand side of the field they followed the hedge looking for the hole where the flock had got out. As they skirted the lime kiln wood they found a section of fence where the wire had pulled away from the post leaving a gap for the sheep to jump through. There was wool stuck to the bushes on the other side, a sure sign of their passage.

"This would happen today" said Mary "Gunter is not here tonight to help with the milking. They could be anywhere in there. Come on let's find them." They squeezed through the gap careful of the barbed wire. There were clear tracks on the ground leading to the right away from The Hatch. Eventually they came to the boundary with Miss Stewart's, there were hurdles most of the way. Mary was hoping the sheep had stayed in the wood but they came to a point where only a single strand of barbed wire stood in their way. The sheep had simply walked underneath. They climbed onto the iron hurdles and looked down the field, which was at least twenty acres in size; quite a distance away they could see the farm buildings. Along the bottom hedge was Miss Stewart's herd of black and white Friesian cattle.

"The cows are there" said Hannah pointing.

"So I see but come on let's go and find out if Bill Shankly has the sheep locked up" Mary said as she jumped down into the field, Hannah followed.

As they walked down the field the cows saw them and began moving around.

Hannah looked concerned and Mary looked at the cows.

"Don't worry about them. Stay close to me and you will be all right".

"But what if their bull is out?"

"I expect that they only let him loose at nights, like Dad does with ours. Can't have them loose with the soldiers running around we have been told."

"Dad says that the bull here is a bit of a terror" said Hannah, not so sure. Before Mary could reply they heard a loud snort. Coming from out of the middle of the herd towards them was the biggest bull they had ever seen. They went cold with fear then Mary turned and pushed Hannah,

"Run Hannah run" she shouted. They began to run, the bull was quite a way away but it was uphill and Hannah found it difficult to run in her Wellington boots. She could sense him getting closer and closer behind her and she could not keep up.

"Mary, Mary," she screamed "he's going to get me". Mary turned, the bull was gaining speed, she looked ahead they were not far from the fence.

"Keep running Hannah, come on we are nearly at the fence. Come on run as fast as you can."

Hannah was running as fast as she could then luckily as if distracted the bull came to a stop, he bellowed loudly and pawed the ground then started forward again. Mary had reached the hurdles and was scrambling through. Hannah now had a chance she had gained some distance from the bull. Mary reached for Hannah's hand when she got to the hurdles and she dragged her through into the wood. They were both terrified, they turned to see the bull only yards away from the fence he stopped again to bellow and paw the ground sending clods of turf into the air. He bent his great head down as if he was going to charge again. Then he straightened, bellowed and turned back towards the herd snorting as he went.

The two girls sat down on the ground to get their breath back. Hannah began to cough deep and painful, she began retching, and there was nothing Mary could do. The coughing fit lasted some time leaving Hannah shaking with tears in her eyes.

"Oh Lordy" she whispered when she could get enough breath to speak, "that was a close one. What a size that bull is. That's the last time I go near those cows".

"Same here I did not think we were going to make it. Are you all right?"

"I think so" she said. Then she looked at her knees. One was bleeding quite badly; she had been so scared that she had not felt a thing as Mary had dragged her through the rusty iron hurdle.

"Oh dear" she said "that hurts" the shock was wearing off.

Mary took a piece of rag from her coat pocket and tied it around Hannah's knee.

"Who would have thought that they would let a nasty devil like him loose in a field? Well we now know for future. Now we will have to go the long way round."

"Those sheep had better be there after all this" said Hannah. Mary stood up; the bull was back with the herd.

"Come on Hannah. Get up and see if you can walk properly, that knee looks bad." There was a bloodstain appearing on the cloth.

"I will get you a stick to lean on; you lost yours when the bull was chasing you." She searched around until she found a good sized stick.

"Well we have got to find those sheep or we will be in trouble. We can't go back without them."

Hannah tried the stick; it was fine so they set off together staying in the woods until they came to the path that led to the lane. Hannah limped along and they talked over their experience. Once on the lane it was not far to Miss Stewart's farm.

They went cautiously into the farmyard and up to the back door of the house. They were more composed when Mary knocked as loud as she could on the door. It was Bill Shankly who opened the door. He stood and looked down at Mary and Hannah.

"Come for your Father's wretched sheep have you?" he bellowed, causing both girls to step back from the open door. "I've got them in the stack yard, it is a good job that you have come for them or it would cost your father a tidy penny."

"It's not our fault they keep getting out, it's the soldiers they keep breaking the hedges and fences down" Mary said defensively.

"Oh, blame the army. Well they are not just running over your place. I suppose your Dad has no time to mend the fences after them." He reached behind the door for his coat.

"Come on and take them out of my sight. Dammed sheep I would not have them on the bank. They eat the grass so low the cows get nothing at all."

"But my Dad" Mary started to say.

"Never mind your Dad, just take these sheep and keep them in your own fields". As he pulled on his Wellington boots he noticed the blood soaked rag on Hannah's knee. Mary thought she saw some concern in his eyes. He looked away and took a stick then he closed the door and led the way to the stack yard. Hannah limped along. The girls said nothing they dare not tell him that they had gone down the field where the cattle were, he would have exploded. They were both lucky to be alive after their ordeal with the bull.

"You stand in the lane and stop them from making off towards the village," he said to Mary.

"You can come with me" he said to Hannah. She followed him into the stack yard and there were the sheep, the welsh ewes at the front just waiting to escape.

"Let's get them on the road I've got other work to do not mess about with sheep. I'll let your Dad off this time as Wilf Wilkins has already told me about the goings on down your way. Seems you are getting a lot of damage caused by these army maneuvers."

"They have trodden down the fence by the limekilns" Hannah said.

"Is that where you cut your knee?" asked Bill.

"Oh no I slipped on the lane and did this" lied Hannah.

"I see," said Bill knowing she was not telling the truth. "Well you need to keep these sheep in." He pulled back a corrugated tin sheet, which had been used as a barrier.

"Let us get this lot back where they belong, your sister is waiting. Stand over there and stop them heading for the fields."

He waded in amongst the sheep and urged them out. Several turned for the fields.

"Shoo, shoo" shouted Hannah waving her stick. They turned back and off towards the lane where Mary was waiting to turn them. Bill watched them go, clattering hooves on the hard surface.

"I hear this training will go on for some time. Lad's in the Quarry are scared to blast and Wilkins is having problems but these sheep are more of a nuisance now than ever to everyone."

"Yes we try our best Mr Shankly and thank you for catching them."

"Aye well be off and don't come into our fields the bull's out."

"Oh. Thank you for the warning" they said "We wouldn't think of it".

"Judging by the racket somebody did a bit earlier" he said with half a smile. "Be off with you."

Mary ran ahead of the sheep to stop them taking any more detours while Hannah followed behind keeping them moving. At The Hatch they followed the track along the limekilns wood to the broken fence. All the sheep skipped through and wandered off to graze. Mary and Hannah hitched up the wire but the post was rotten, they did the best they could and made their way back to the farm.

"How is your knee?" asked Mary.

"Really aching. Mr Shankly knew it was us I reckon."

"Well he never let on and neither must we it will be a secret."

"All right" sighed Hannah. It had been a rough day the bull had scared her quite badly. They found Fred and Mary told him of the fence. He said he would fix it in the morning when he had more time. Then he noticed the rag on Hannah's knee and sent her off to have it looked at while Mary helped get ready for milking. Inside the kitchen Hannah hung her coat up and took off her Wellington boots, her knee was throbbing and she was hoping for a cup of tea. Dorothy was sat in Fred's chair reading to William, she looked up as Hannah walked round the table.

"What on earth have you been doing? There's blood all down you shin."

"I fell over and cut my knee" Hannah lied.

"Where are the sheep?"

"Back in the field, the fence was down and I tripped up on the wire" Dorothy got up and went to the kitchen cupboard for the bottle of Johnson's oils used to soothe all cuts and grazes. The alternative was to use iodine but oh how it stung when applied to an open wound.

"Sit on the chair and get that rag off" she said.

Hannah sat down and pulled the rag off; it stung as it came away causing the wound to bleed again.

Dorothy put some water in a basin and with a clean piece of rag she bathed the wounds then poured on a few drops of the oil.

"Rub that in and for goodness sake pick your feet up and look where you are going or you will break your neck I shouldn't wonder" she said. Hannah's knees were sore for days but soon healed over. Neither she nor Mary said a word about their ordeal. They knew that if they mentioned it to anyone they would get in serious trouble for going into a strange field with cows gazing and not knowing where the bull was.

The following week Mary got another fright when she came face to face with two soldiers skulking by the big water trough down by the walnut tree.

"What are you doing?" she said.

"We are about to neutralize that command post," said one pointing at the farmhouse.

"Mam won't like that one bit; she is in the middle of doing the washing."

"Let's go" said the soldier and they leapt over the gate and charged up the backyard sending the hens, ducks and geese scattering in all directions.

"The dog is never around when needed" she said to herself.

Soldiers began turning up in the farm buildings during the day but Fred did not mind too much, it was better than having them running across the fields firing their guns. The vet's bills were soaring. Several cows had charged the fences in panic and got caught up in the barbed wire; they received some very bad cuts. Luckily none had fallen in the ditches but the stress caused several calves to arrive stillborn.

One morning Hannah and Grace found some soldiers hiding in the granary, they were practicing observation. The girls collected the corn they needed for feeding and fled to the kitchen to tell Fred. He laughed and sent them on their way. When he went for breakfast Dorothy was not impressed.

"Is it right what those girls are saying, that there are soldiers in the granary?"

"Aye I had a chat with them, nice lads they were."

"We'll find one in the lavvy next," she moaned "we will not be able to go there in peace".

"They have come to help us win this war and whatever it takes it will have been worth it if Hitler can be beaten" Fred replied.

Late October Fred received a letter with Bromley's blue heading on the top of the paper. He had been notified that he was eligible for a tractor earlier in the year but nothing more had been heard since.

Dorothy had opened the letter as soon as the postman had gone.

"I don't believe it" she said and went out to the cowshed to tell Fred.

"What's wrong now?" he asked, seeing the letter in Dorothy's hand.

She read the letter. It was to tell Fred that there was a tractor available if he was still able to finance it.

"Surry" he said, "what do you reckon lass?"

"Let's see when you come in for breakfast" she said not wanting to talk in front of Gunter.

When he went for breakfast she said he ought to get to town and see the bank manager as she thought they could do it. The harvest had been good, the wool cheque was in and despite the vet's bills, and they were doing all right. They planned on clearing the top fields under the Wrekin and with a tractor they would be able to get a bigger yield of potatoes.

He went straight to town and arranged things with Mr Simmons then went to Bromley's yard. On his return Dorothy was waiting with William on her lap.

"Well how did it go?" she asked, rising to get them a cup of tea.

"They will be delivering it next Saturday."

"What! Really, on Saturday."

"Yes, next Saturday. We had better see to it that the yard is swept clean and tidy before Bromley's bring it."

"Where are you going to put it?" she asked.

"In the cart shed. I suppose they will bring it on a wagon and then we can drive it in."

"You see that you leave the unloading to Bromley's men, we can't afford you to go and get hurt."

She poured them a cup of tea and sat down.

"How much is it going to cost us?"

"Wait and see Dot. You know that we will be able to get a lot more done. I've been thinking that we might even have a go at growing some sugar beet, there is a good subsidy paid for growing that".

"Sugar beet, oh Fred Thomas whatever next. I only hope that we will see as good a profit next year."

"We will, you will see lass." He went to get changed into his working clothes. Dorothy picked up the iron poker out of the fender and gave the fire a shaking up.

"I hope you are not letting these big ideas go to your head," she said to herself. When the fire was ablaze she added some pieces of wood and turned back to the table. She picked up William and sat him on a chair.

"You stay there," she said then she gave him a piece of bread coated in jam. When Fred returned he picked up William and set him on his lap as he drank his tea. He smiled and turned to Dorothy

"We've got to do all we can for young William we have," he said. "Perhaps one day we can buy our own place and have something for him to inherit".

"Oh yes, grand ideas I'm sure, and you could be right but I want some things in this house".

"But we are now getting a few good bits and pieces lass."

"Yes but I want a piano one day."

"Wouldn't you want electricity or water on tap?"

"Oh yes one day, but I would love to be able to play one again."

"Well you shall have one when this war is done. And I shall get us one of them machines to milk the cows save doing it by hand."

"Good lord is there no end to your big ideas Fred Thomas?"

"Well maybe when we get the tractor we can buy one of those saw benches from a sale."

He chuckled as he lit his pipe with a strip of newspaper, "There will be no more sawing logs by hand for us" Dorothy liked that idea.

"Well all this may come but for now there's work to be done Fred, now get on with you" she said.

Fred set William down and made his way outside, Mary was all questions but he was very pragmatic.

"Let's wait and see what turns up, I have seen the tractor and it is a beauty, should make life easier for all of us" Mary liked the sound of that.

On the Saturday morning Bromley's blue flat lorry with two men pulled into the farmyard. Fred and all the girls were eagerly waiting. They could see a blue and red Fordson tractor sitting proudly on the back. As it swung around the yard they could see a brand new double furrow plough. Fred had convinced Mr Simmons that it made sense in the current climate to buy as borrowing only led to problems. There were tree roots and hidden rocks to be considered and if he were to break a plough belonging to someone else it could turn out to be a costly business. Dorothy was watching from the front room window holding William in her arms.

"Just you look out there, Son that is just the start for you. One day we might be able to buy this farm for you. One never knows what the future will hold for us now. Oh yes there is so much that we can do and it's all for you my son". It took very little time for the tractor and plough to be unloaded.

There was a drum of fuel and the two men showed Fred how to maintain it and start it. There was a book for Fred to read which he passed to Mary, preferring to listen to the instructions. The tractor sat there running sweetly.

"There you are Gaffer; you will be able to get on with some work now. Not that I would like to use it on some of those fields up there" he said pointing to Fred's top fields.

"I'll take care" Fred answered. "Now let's hear more of what it can do." After a while the two men got into the lorry and drove out of the yard. Fred stood back and admired his purchase. What a magnificent set up it looked. The morning sunlight shone on the red and blue metal paintwork. The steel shell boards of the plough glistened with their newness. The girls were all excited; it was a fantastic machine to them.

Dorothy was waiting for him when he went in half an hour later.

"Do you reckon that you can handle that tractor, it looks a bit big to me and will you be safe with it"? She said.

"I reckon so; it will be more or less the same as driving a car."

"It will not be like a car when you come to plough those banks you know."

"True but it is a real beauty don't you think?"

"I guess so, but now you've got your new toy let's see if it will earn some money for us. It has certainly cost enough" she said.

"Surry lass, I reckon it will. That tractor is going to be the making of us." She was not convinced,

"What if the war comes to an end and the government stop paying the subsidies then what are we going to do?"

"We will cross that bridge when we come to it. The country still has to be fed and it is us farmers who will do it. When this war is over and our lads come back there will be even more for us to do."

He looked around "Dot put that kettle on" he lit his pipe, and sat down in his chair picking William up to sit on his knee.

She went to the range and gave the burning logs a good stir with the steel poker to get some heat under the kettle. She fetched some cups from the cupboard then sat down to wait for the kettle to boil.

"It looks a grand machine Fred Thomas. I will bring William out to have a look later before it gets put in the shed"

"Of course lass." As he spoke the door opened and the girls trooped in, they took off their coats and hoods and sat at the table.

"I suppose you lot want a drink as well," she said. They all said "yes" and Dorothy fetched more cups.

"There'll be no going near that tractor for any of you apart from Mary, so keep well away from it. Squash you to death it will."

"Dad can I have Kit?" piped up Hannah.

"What do you mean lass, can you have Kit?"

"Well she won't have to work anymore nor are you going to sell her?"

"Sell her! Nay, I will never sell her. I couldn't do that. Been a good one she has, I won't let her go" he mused.

Hannah had always longed for a pony of her own. Nothing came on the farm unless it earned its keep. There had been no pony for the girls to ride. Although Kit was not a streamlined pony Hannah wanted to be able to have rides on her.

"There'll still be jobs for a horse to do that a tractor can't do," said Dorothy. "Besides there's no time for horse riding, there will have to be a lot extra work to be done, that machine will have to be paid for and it will cost money to run it".

"But think of the work it will do" Hannah answered back.

"That is the reason that we have bought it and there will be plenty for you all to do".

That was that, Hannah knew better than to bring up the subject again.

"Well Fred Thomas, you aren't half coming up in the world" Dorothy said as she poured the tea. "You girls can tell your friends at school we have a tractor and plough now." She turned to Fred "Let's hope it does what you want".

"Oh aye, I'm sure of it we can get the rough ground cleared now and plough it in the spring. Make a few pennies a bit quicker," he said smiling. She passed his usual cup to him.

"Pennies! Pounds more like it, pounds it had better be Fred Thomas!" She looked at father and son and smiled with contentment. They were doing all right then her expression changed as she turned to the girls who were waiting for their drinks.

"And don't you get any ideas about playing near the tractor even when it is not working."

"But we don't play in the cart shed, Mam" said Grace.

"And you'd best not start then" she was not having them near the tractor and was hoping Fred would back her up but he was bouncing William and miles away in thought.

All afternoon Fred worked with the tractor, he went around the yard getting used to the heavy peddles and the throttle. It was not as easy as driving a car as he had to admit but he soon mastered it. Over the next weeks or so Fred's blue eyes sparkled, as they had not done before. The cart shed was now known as the tractor shed and was out of bounds. Fred fashioned up a hitch on one of the carts and with Gunter set off up to the rough ground under the Wrekin. They were able to make some inroads into the dense undergrowth the tractor being used to drag the young trees out with a chain. Then the weather turned very cold and he decided to let the sheep in there to eat what grass they could and he would resume clearing in the spring. The tractor had already proved its usefulness in the time saved getting to the field and the ease at which it could be applied to heavy work.

In November a cold snap arrived and the nights were getting frosty. It had gone dark early and was getting colder by the minute Fred came into the cowshed ready to start the milking Hannah was standing just inside the door looking worried.

"What's up lass" he said

"Dad, there is a cow missing" she said. He had just finished a hard day's graft with Gunter clearing some ground under the Wrekin with the tractor. They had stayed as late as they could and Gunter had now gone back to camp. This was the last thing he wanted to hear. There would be a severe frost this night.

"Which one is it?" he said and went along the line of cows tied up in their stalls," There are none hanging back calving at the moment. He went to the top shed with Hannah following. Mary was there and it was clear they were one short.

"Surry I hope that she is not in a ditch somewhere. The soldiers have broken the fences down all over the place." He set off back to the first shed and grabbed a lantern.

"Mary, you and Hannah take this lantern and go and look in those deep ditches around the bottom field you can start at the gorses under the Hatch. I will ask your Mam to come and give a start with the milking. She is not going to like that but the sooner we get these milked the better. We could be in for a long night tonight."

"Yes Dad, we'll get off now. We will run back if we find her"

"Good. I hope to God that she has not slipped down into one of those deep ditches, it will take us hours to get her out."

The girls set off with the lantern but it was not much use having one side covered with brown paper. The light from the moon was far more use. The frost was already forming; it was going to be a cold night. They made for the fields where the cattle had been grazing during the day and went to the uppermost point by the Hatch. Then they followed the rough high hedge down towards the bottom field; and then the deep ditch that went into the brook taking the water down to the reservoir by the Forest Glen. As they walked alongside the brook Hannah stopped

"What's that?" She said.

"What's what?" said Mary. "I can't hear anything, stand still a moment"

"There it is again" Said Hannah. This time Mary heard the familiar low bellow of the cow

"That's her. By the sound of it she is stuck, but where? Let's walk on and shine the light into the brook if we can."

The two girls walked a bit further they heard the cow again, they were getting nearer. There was a section of wire fencing down and when they got close they could make out the shape of the cow deep down in the brook.

"Oh Lordy, Dad is not going to like this, said Mary "

The cow was in one of the deepest parts of the brook. She was not struggling much as she was too deep in the mud and the water had built up against her on one side.

"Stupid cow, how did you come to slip in there?" Hannah said not venturing too close. Mary could see the cow was exhausted.

"Come on Hannah, let's get back and tell Dad. This is going to be a big job to dig her out of there." She said.

They rushed back to the farm and told their father they had found the cow but that she was lying in one of the deepest ditches... He was clearly annoyed

"But why has it took you so long to find her?" he asked.

Mary explained how they had started at the furthest point as he had said so as to be sure they checked everywhere.

"Oh Lord, "said Fred "it is already starting to freeze. It's going to be a tidy job for us without Gunter. Let's not waste time she is one of the younger ones but we don't know how long she has been stuck. Damn and blast the bloody army."

"What do you want us to do Dad?" asked Mary

"Go and get one of the horses in and harness her up with just a collar and chains then bring as many sacks from the granary as you can carry. Hannah you go and tell your Mam that we will need her to give us a hand. And bring the spare lantern we will need it. Tell her Grace can look after the little ones. Off you go and be quick about it." She set off to the house. When she returned Mary had the lantern and was harnessing the horse. Fred had found some tools and had gone to the granary for the sacks and to save waiting for Mary. When he returned to the yard Hannah asked

"Do I have to come? It is going colder every minute."

"Aye lass we will need you to hold the lights". He knew Lizzy would not be back till late, he needed her help.

"Oh Lordy" she said, and pulled the old socks over her hands, it could take hours. And it already felt so cold.

Dorothy came out wrapped up well "What are you hanging about for let's get going" They went down the fields to where the cow was stuck. At first they could not find her, the brook ran about six feet below the level of the field. The sides were clearly too steep to pull the cow out so Fred clambered down. He had to pray and hope that hypothermia had not set in otherwise her legs would be useless. Mary threw down the dry sacks and he put them over her back to try and keep her a little warmer. The cow struggled and it gave Fred the sign he needed.

"She is not too far gone, let's dig the bank out and get her out.

First they dug some ground away behind the cow so that the water could flow on its way. Dorothy and Mary said little as they worked digging away the sodden earth. It was heavy going Hannah tried to hold the lanterns high enough for them to see what they were doing especially for Fred while he dug around the cow careful not to injure her legs Dorothy and Mary dug away some of the bank to allow the cow to climb out once she was on her feet. Occasionally the cow struggled and once knocked Fred down in the freezing cold water.

"More light here lass I've lost me boot" he shouted the sound echoing in the woods. Mary laughed then so did Hannah and Dorothy.

Fred clambered out.

"Bring the horse up and let's get a chain on her" He could have used the tractor but he was not confident enough yet. He wrapped the chains around the cow's horns and Mary talked quietly to Kit. The horse walked forward and pulled very gently to give the cow a chance to rise to her feet without doing too much damage. Too hard and the cow could be injured and may have to be destroyed, the loss of a good milking cow was quite considerable

Fred dug in front of the cow as she moved forward struggling to get her legs free. Then suddenly she surged forward with the help from Kit and

Up the bank she went.

Hannah brought the lantern across and the cow was unchained. She was very subdued and needed milking. The tools were gathered up and they made their way back. Dorothy went straight to the kitchen and fetched a bucket of hot water to wash the mud from the cow's udder and to warm her up a bit. Fresh sacks were thrown over her and tied with string to keep her warm during the night. It was after midnight when the girls went off to bed after a good wash in the kitchen sink. After being milked Fred placed bundles of straw around and underneath her she seemed no worse for her ordeal. He was very pleased as he had not wanted a good milking cow to go for dog meat. This time they had been lucky it was a wider part of the brook. The ditches were a different story, cows had died in them. The lorry from Boons the knackers' yard in Oakengates had been needed with its special pulleys and winch to get the dead bodies out. Every few hours Fred got up and checked how she was. Next morning when the rest of the family got up he was smiling, the cow was fine. He was very pleased and thanked Dorothy and the girls for their help he could never have got her out on his own.

May and Hannah hoped that this was not going to be a regular occurrence. The fences were still being knocked down and with the darker evenings it was all too easy to miss a trapped cow.

As it was, the cold gave way to snow in December and as there were not many soldiers around the fences were staying secure. Fred put the sheep over on the rough ground up by the Slang. It was a surprise to Mary on one Sunday afternoon when she looked out of the small kitchen window to see sheep crowding by the fence at the top of the slang. She had got up from Fred's chair and put her knitting down to put the kettle on for when her parents came down from their afternoon rest.

"I don't believe it, those sheep look like ours. They are off the rough ground trying to get in the woods." It was quite a distance but she knew there would be no one else's sheep up there.

Hannah and Helen were with her in the kitchen. William now two was taking a nap and Grace was upstairs reading.

"Now this is one job that I could do without this afternoon, there is no peace to be had at all. Hannah you can keep an eye on the others and if they play up give Mam a shout?"

"Can't I come with you?" Hannah protested.

"No you have to look after Helen and William."

"I'll be all right. I've my jobs to do later but Grace can give me a hand" said Helen who was busy with a picture puzzle.

Mary looked back through the window it looked as if there were fewer sheep than before.

"Oh Lord I suppose that I had better go and fetch them before it gets dark".

"I can help" insisted Hannah.

"I can't take you or you will be coughing all through the night and then we will all hear about from Mam tomorrow morning."

"I promise to keep my head under the eiderdown if I cough in the night, I promise I will." Mary considered for a moment.

"All right get your coat and boots and be quick. Helen go and find Grace and tell her where we have gone and keep an eye on William, if he cries call Mam" she started to get ready.

Hannah soon had on her Wellington boots, coat, pixy hood and woollen mittens. They each picked up a hand made walking stick from by the back door and stepped outside. Mary gave a whistle and Jingo came from the garage where he had been sleeping. He spent a lot of time watching out for visitors especially the soldiers. He would run around barking when anyone turned up although never challenging directly and always keeping his distance.

The girls liked his company and they set off down the drive pulling their scarves tightly around their necks as they faced the North wind. Jingo following quietly behind them. They made their way across the road and up the fields towards the bottom of the hill; there were no sheep in sight. Mary was quite glad of Hannah's company although she never seemed to stop chattering. They had to stop every now and then so Hannah could cough that horrible croupy cough before getting her breath back.

"Mam will kill us if you are worse after me letting you come with me in this cold wind, there will be no peace for days" Mary said as she waited. At the edge of the wood there was a hole in the fence the sheep had gone through and onto the track that went all the way around the bottom of the hill.

"What Dad had to buy those two welsh ewes for I do not know, they are always leading the others to get out" said Mary wearily.

The girls followed and turned left. They slipped and slid their way on the snow covered muddy surface. They followed the sheep's footprints until they were directly below the cuckoo's cup looking up the slope they could see the sheep under the needles eye.

"Good lord what are they doing up there?" said Mary "you can't go up there with your cough; I will go on my own".

I will come with you I've come this far" said Hannah. Mary knew she would need her help

"All right but stay under the covers tonight". They started to climb steeply holding on to the netting wire fence that was there to separate the fir plantations. The snow from the branches fell into their faces and the uneven rocks beneath their feet caused the snow to slip into their boots melting and making their feet very wet. They stopped a few yards down from the sheep that were oblivious to them. Mary looked around. "Keep quiet now or they will hear us coming try not to cough. You go around that side with Jingo" she said pointing to the West of them. "Hold on tight to the heather so that you do not fall. It is a steep drop down that side. I will go this side of them and when we meet at the top we should be able to drive them back down." Hannah did as she was told and made her way along the slope then up with Jingo closely by her side. It was difficult but she was tough, her mittens were wet through and her knees were red and sore from creeping and holding on the wild heather. Out in the open the North wind blowing across the top of the hill took her breath away for a few moments, she was glad to see Mary coming to meet her she began to cough.

The sheep had been busy foraging for the scutch grass under the snow. At the noise they looked up startled. Mary waved for Hannah to move them down the hill.

The sheep turned when they saw Hannah and Jingo heading towards them and started downhill. Level with the Cuckoos cup Hannah stopped to cough and then, without knowing why, she shouted loudly "fairies and goblins take my cough away" Mary looked across at her.

"Be quiet Hannah there are no fairies or anything else like that up here" she said.

"I have read that there are fairies everywhere" shouted Hannah.

"Fairies and goblins take my cough away" she repeated. It felt good to shout out over the snow covered countryside, so high she could see for miles.

"Fairies and goblins take my cough away," she shouted for the third and last time then carried on down after the sheep, which were moving quickly now. The two girls were glad they had their walking sticks as they slivered and slid down the side of the hill. At the bottom the sheep headed off back the way they came and Mary was able to get ahead and turn them back into the field.

As soon as they were all back in their place Mary blocked up the hole with sticks and what loose branches she could find.

"Thank goodness for that" she said "we will make a better job tomorrow, now let us get home the light is almost gone".

Dorothy was very angry when they went into the kitchen and she saw how wet Hannah's feet were.

"You get those wet socks off young lady. None of us will have any sleep tonight; you will cough all night long. Just see if you don't". Despite being wet, Hannah's eyes shone with pleasure and her face was rosy red from being out in the cold wind. Next morning Hannah was up as usual and ready to go to school. As she sat with the others eating her bread and warm milk Grace said "You did not wake me up with your coughing last night." Dorothy heard her and stopped making up the sandwiches she turned to Hannah "We never heard you either," she said. "Me and your Dad had a good night's sleep. I was expecting to be awake all night with that cough of yours and I thought you would be in no fit state for school today."

"That's because the cough has gone" Hannah said brightly. "I told the fairies to take it away when we were on top of the Wrekin."

"Fairies indeed, whatever next will you have us believe" said Dorothy.

"It's true I know it is I feel so much better" said Hannah to all of them and it was amazing but her horrible cough had disappeared and was never heard again.

On Christmas Day, as Dorothy and Fred sat in the front room they reflected on the year.

"Perhaps there are fairies up there" said Dorothy. "I can't believe it but that child is completely different these days, there is no sign of the cough at all thank goodness."

Both Ken and Imogen Winter said the same as they sat by the fire in their room.

"I wonder if we should have taken Sybil up there, perhaps it would have done her good" said Ken.

In the occasional letter from his sister, Sibyl's health was always said to be a concern.

From that Christmas on the story was told of how Hannah's whooping cough had disappeared overnight. Dorothy told everyone she met and soon the story spread. For many years afterwards children with bad coughs or chest problems were walked to the top of the Wrekin and it seemed to work as they quickly recovered and were well again. The next time that Hannah went there she asked the fairies and goblins to send Sam home. Nothing had been heard of him for months. Fred never mentioned him but he feared the worst.

CHAPTER 10

Pastures new

The spring term of 1944 saw Hannah back to full health. She was keen to get to school and would walk ahead of Grace and Helen not waiting for them to catch up. Danny was keen to tell her all that he had seen and heard of the American flyers and the soldiers practicing in the woods and fields. He and his friends had been told off several times for wandering in the areas where they were carrying out exercises.

At the end of the first week back Miss Evans called Grace to her desk and handed her a letter.

"Here is an important letter for you to take to your parents. I would like a reply as quickly as possible. Please give it to your Mother as soon as you get home, they have the weekend to respond, and then bring their reply to me here on Monday morning."

When Grace met up with Hannah and Helen to walk home she showed them the letter making sure nobody was close enough to grab it.

"Looks important," said Hannah. "I'll bet it's to let me take the Eleven Plus exam this year."

"Well, I bet it's not," Grace said firmly as she put it in her pocket.

"It might be" Hannah argued "can you see inside it?"

"No. We will just have to wait and see. Let's get home quickly and give it to Mam that is the best way to find out."

"You are hoping. She won't tell us we, will have to ask Mary or Dad."

As soon as they arrived in the kitchen Grace handed the letter to her Mother who had William clutching at her skirt.

"A letter for you Mam, Miss Evans said that it was important."

"Now what can she be wanting. Not in trouble are you?" they shook their heads. "That school always wants something or other. Not more material for sewing class is it?" she opened the envelope. "Let's have a look what they want now."

She went and sat in Fred's chair picking up William in the process. The girls stood in anticipation, waiting to see what the letter was about. Dorothy was thoughtful then she looked up "Go and get changed you three" she said, giving nothing away.

Disappointed, they went upstairs, "Told you," said Hannah.

When they came back down to the kitchen there was a pot of tea made and Mary was leaning over the range getting a warm, the letter was on the table. Dorothy picked it up and put it on the mantle shelf, "we'll see what your Father has to say about this," she said.

"What does Miss Evans want?" Hannah asked.

Dorothy ignored her and began pouring the tea into the cups.

"Will she let me take the Eleven Plus?" Hannah persisted.

"We'll see."

That was enough to satisfy Hannah's curiosity but not Grace's.

She waited until Dorothy was busy with William then took the letter from the shelf and read it quickly while Helen kept look out. When she put it back she could hardly contain herself.

"Is it good news?" asked Helen.

"Oh I would say so. I must tell Hannah."

She went outside and found Hannah. They went into the stack yard to talk away from the sheds so they would not be overheard.

"You know that letter from Miss Evans? I've had a look at it."

"What does it say?"

"It says that if it's all right with Mam and Dad there's no reason why you can't have a go at the Eleven Plus exam and if you pass you would go to the High School for girls at Wellington."

"Oh good, I want to have a go at it and especially if I can go to the posh school."

"But that's not all" said Grace her eyes sparkling.

"Oh? Well what else does she say?"

"She says that the high school is also taking in twelve year olds and there is a chance for me to go there if I pass an interview with the Head Mistress."

"Does that mean that we could go together?"

"If you pass the exam and I pass the interview."

"I will, I will, you wait and see" said Hannah excitedly. Grace looked around, "Don't let on to anyone that I have seen the letter. Mam would give me a hiding if she knew I'd been peeping. We will just have to wait and see what they decide. The problem is that when it comes to making decisions like this, she is the boss."

Later that evening when the girls were in bed Dorothy gave the letter to Fred to read. "Surry that is good news, the two of them stand a chance of going to a better school. They will do us proud."

"Hold on Fred Thomas, the village school has been good enough so far. Lizzy is doing all right, earning now and only walking distance from home. Our Mary might have done it but for the war starting."

"You are right there Dot, but I reckon it will do no harm to let the two of them have a go at the exam and then they can go to the high school. I reckon this could be the right time to think ahead. This war is on the way to being won as I see it. Just look around."

Dorothy for once was not thinking of the war "It will be expensive if they go there. They have to have uniforms and goodness knows what".

Fred smiled "If they are accepted we can worry about the cost of it then".

"By what Miss Evans says in that letter she reckons they can do it. So it will be sooner than you think. Good lord they will need coats, new shoes and bicycles. We can't have them walking that distance." Despite her reservations Dorothy was pleased to think her daughters would be going to High School, it would be good to write and tell her Mother. Fred puffed on is pipe.

"Let's wait and see" he said. "They have got to pass those exams first."

"Yes you are right, I will reply and say that we want them to have a go then."

Fred nodded "That's the spirit, nothing ventured, and nothing gained."

She took the letter and returned it to the mantle shelf.

"They better not let us down."

"Wait and see" said Fred and carried on rocking in his chair and puffing on his pipe.

Over the weekend Dorothy wrote a note to Miss Evans giving permission for the girls try for the High School. Grace asked several times what the letter was about but got no reply. On Monday morning Dorothy gave Grace her reply sealed in a brown envelope. As the girls walked to school, Grace grumbled that if she had not looked at the letter she would still have no idea. "Why won't she tell us anything, we are not German spies?"

"Dad has been no better" said Hannah, "we normally get something out of him but he won't let on either".

Grace handed the note to Miss Evans as soon as she arrived.

"Thank you. I shall see you later now get along with you."

It was lunchtime when Miss Evans asked Grace to stay behind for a while. She had her mother's reply in her hand.

"As you may know, your parents have agreed to let you try for a place at Wellington Girls' School despite your age." Grace said nothing. Miss Evans re-read the note.

"It would be good if you and Hannah could make it; however, she must try very hard this term."

"Yes Miss," said Grace. Miss Evans then placed the note in the drawer of her desk. "You will be asked to go for an interview with Miss Bygott the Head Mistress. I will let you know nearer to the time." She looked Grace up and down. "On the day I suggest you wear your very best frock. You will do well to make a good impression." She did not know that Grace was wearing her best frock. Grace thought of the dress she was making in sewing class from green serge material. It was certainly not a colour she liked but it was all her Mother could get and then she had complained of the cost for weeks after. Grace was determined to do her best she had not been able to take the test the year before, the reason had been given as a shortage of teachers due to the war.

"I will do my very best Miss" she said "I want to do so much when I leave school, so I will do my very best".

"Good now be off and by the way clean your shoes more often."

Grace went to join the others; she had no intention of letting herself down.

As soon as the weather was dry enough Fred returned to the fields off the slang with Gunter. He wanted to clear as much as he could, spread some muck on it and then, if possible, plough in May for potatoes in September. They cut back the overhanging branches and boughs to get as much light as possible to the edges. The trailer was filled with any boughs that could be sawn for logs but all the brushwood, brambles and gorse was piled into heaps ready to be burnt. It was as they were taking a break that Ted Lockett the ditch cleaner came on the scene.

"You've been busy" he said, "Looks like you could use my services."

"Aye I reckon so" said Fred "they are in a bit of a state".

"I had a look the other day" said Ted "and I've seen worse". The two men looked over the ditches then sat for a while under the edge of the wood. The snap of gunfire could be heard in the distance.

"It is a lot quieter around here these days," said Fred "don't see so much of them Canadians".

"Oh they are still running around," said Ted "bloody nuisance they are. If I get 'Halt friend or foe' one more time I swear I'll swing for 'em." Fred laughed; he thought the sight of Ted Locket in his waterproofs would be questionable.

"They've probably never seen a ditch cleaner before" he said.

"That's as may be, you know what one daft sod said to me last month? He said where's your gas mask if you are a civilian? And I says, why, you got an awful bad ditch needs clearing have you?"

Fred chuckled "What did he say to that?"

"Said I was barmy and ought to speak English. So I told him to sod off back to where he came from."

"You dunna want to upset them, they might do just that and leave us to fight the Gerry's on our own."

"Never, they are spoiling for a fight. I reckon they can't wait to get stuck in. The Gerry's have had it, just a matter of time. Have you heard from young Sam lately?" Fred stopped laughing and his expression changed to one tinged with sadness.

"Nay, I think he's gone. It has been so long and he would have got word to us by now if he was all right." Ted realized he had touched a nerve, he stood up to go.

"Well Gaffer, I hope they haven't scared off the old woodpecker, he knocks out quite a racket, and it would make them think they were under fire. Now I'll be off, I'll sort your ditches out for you."

"That would be grand Ted," said Fred keen to get on with the clearing.

"Well always remember, the brook runs free, especially when I am about."

"I will that," said Fred and as Ted went on his way he went and helped Gunter finish the cutting and piling up. It was getting late so Fred decided not to start the fires until Saturday morning when they could be watched over during the day in case they got out of control and spread to the woods. The next day he harnessed up the horses and with Günter's help loaded the cart and began spreading muck. The horses were ideal, they would step forward on command allowing the muck to be dragged off the trailer and spread.

On the Saturday the fires were lit. Fred was still spreading the muck so on returning to the farm he told Mary to go back over and keep an eye on the burning while he got on with shifting more muck. Hannah spent most of her time with Mary and was quick to ask if she could go as well. Fred was quite happy for her to go but warned Mary not to let her get in the smoke too much and not to get covered in ash. He knew Dorothy would not mind, she had Helen to play with William and help out with the housework. He made sure that Hannah was well wrapped up against the cold then gave them a pitchfork each and sent them on their way.

As they walked down the drive to cross the road they could see the smoke drifting through the trees it was hanging over the whole side of the Wrekin.

There was little wind so the chances of burning down the Hazelhurst were remote.

"Dad worries too much" said Mary "I'll bet it is almost out, we will probably have to get it going again". They crossed the road and set off up the big field.

"There'll be no picking blackberries up here this year" Hannah said. "No, but Mam will still expect us to find and pick enough blackberries for Mrs Podmore at the Glen from somewhere" said Mary. "She will have us do the work so she can sell them, it is never fair."

They rounded the corner into the cleared field, it now seemed massive and they could see the farm buildings belonging to the Wrekin Cottage over the big hedge. The fires had burnt right down leaving circles of unburned brushwood around the smoking embers.

"Let's pile it up into one heap on that one over there" said Mary pointing to a fire that still had a healthy glow. They began collecting the brushwood from around the spent fires and piling it up, it soon blazed up and they continued to clear the dead fires, then they began collecting from further a field. They had wandered up to the hedge concentrating on their work when a voice boomed out "Looking for something?" They jumped with surprise, as they had not seen anyone about. Peering through the hedge they could just make out a large round figure standing in the next field.

"Oh it's you, Mr Watson" Mary said. There was no mistaking his bulk "We're clearing up for our Dad and making sure that the fires are all right".

"Quite right" Mr Watson said. "We would not want the wood catching fire; it would go right round the Wrekin."

"That's what Dad said Mr Watson," said Hannah. She too could make him out through the hedge.

"Well your Dad and his helper have been very busy, I just came to see how it is going" at that he moved away. Hannah looked at Mary and grinned, they always found his appearance funny. He had worked for Miss Birrell at the Half way house until she died, then he had taken over. They had often seen him when they had been up there.

"Let's get on," Mary said, frowning at Hannah.

Several minutes later they saw Mr Watson just inside the wood. He climbed awkwardly over the fence and walked over to the fire. Hannah could not help but laugh he was wearing a great coat with the collar turned up against the cold and a well-worn trilby hat. It was his great waxed moustache that stretched across his face from ear to ear that made Hannah giggle. At the fire he pushed the hat back off his face and adjusted the moustache between finger and thumb. He rubbed his hands together and held them out to the fire. "This is nice and warm" he said and looked around, "by gum your Father's going big now he's got that tractor, stopping at nothing. Does he intend to plough this ground?"

"Oh yes and then he is going to plant potatoes" Mary replied.

"Indeed, well there is room for a good sized crop and no doubt". Hannah was still stifling a laugh, Mary noticed and glared at her younger sister.

"Dad says it just needs a good spreading of muck first, and with King Edward seed

He reckons that he should have a good crop."

Mr Watson again looked around, "Well there should be less work for you soon and I've been thinking, do you think that your Mother would let you come and give us a hand in the tearooms this summer? My wife's got her hands full with the little ones".

Mary was speechless; she knew he and his wife Gwen had four children.

"But there can't be much to do with the war on can there?"

"Don't you believe it; the Americans come up in their jeeps and folk come from the town to watch the planes flying around, as well as the usual walkers. It is as busy as ever, there are some Yanks up there now."

"Well I have all my feeding to do and I bring the cows in for milking."

"I see, well we could do with your help mainly on a Sunday and Bank Holidays."

Mary thought for a moment "Well that would not be so bad, I'll have a word with me Mam, and I expect it will be OK."

"We would be much obliged if you would. Now don't let me stop you clearing up, I can see your sister needs something to do." Hannah blushed she had been staring at his moustache and did not realize that he had noticed. She skipped off to collect more stuff to burn.

Eventually Mr Watson said cheerio and went off towards the cottage.

"There's a turn up" said Mary. "What do you think of that? I could do with earning some money of my own."

"What will Mr Watson want you to do?" asked Hannah.

"Oh sell cups of tea or be a waitress for one of the tea rooms, that sort of thing."

"I wonder if I could come with you I want to earn some money too."

"No it was me he asked not you. Anyway it is about time I had some money, I'm fed up with having to ask our Mam for every half penny. I only get to take that old bike of hers down town when the weather is bad, otherwise they have me working all the time or looking after William."

"Well what about the work here?"

"There are enough of you, you heard him say it is only Sundays and Bank Holidays."

It's not fair" said Hannah sulkily.

"It is fair. Now don't you say a word, this is my chance, I will ask Dad later not Mam."

Fred was not much help; he said it was all right with him as long as she was back in time for the milking. It would be up to her Mother as someone had to look after the little ones while they had their nap. He wanted to keep the peace as much as possible. "Damn it" Mary said to Hannah later on. "I hardly go anywhere from one week to the next, all I do is work, work, work and what can I see, it's nothing but hills. If I can earn some money I could buy a decent second hand bike and then go to town now and then to buy things for myself."

She had to be careful choosing the right moment to ask her Mother. She waited until washing day when she was helping wring the clothes and it was almost at an end.

"Mam can I go to work at the half way House? It will only be Sundays when they are busy." Dorothy looked at her coldly "what about the work here, don't you think we are busy?"

"Yes well it is only Sundays and we don't do much, no one goes to Sunday school right now and Grace can look after the little ones."

"Got it all worked out haven't you? Well I am going to speak with your Dad before I say yes. Going off to give other folks a helping hand! I will hear no more of it now." The next hour dragged for Mary, she finally got away and stamped off to the buildings to get the feeding started. Much later in the afternoon Hannah joined her when she returned from school and had got changed, Mary was muttering to herself.

"Chunder, Chunder that's her every time, it's all right for her."

"All right for who?" Hannah interrupted. Mary looked up with a scowl on her face

"Our Mam, moan, moan, moan".

"Did you ask her about going to help out up the Wrekin, because she is in a stinking mood?"

"Yes and she won't give an answer."

"Guessed so, we had better keep out of her way for the rest of the day."

"Well I just don't understand why she has to be so mean. How often do I go down town? Or anywhere for that matter, dipping the sheep is the furthest I get; I'm putting my foot down over this."

"Really" said Hannah. "She won't have any of us getting one over on her, so you will just have to wait and see."

"Not any more, she goes swanking off to town in that motor car, expects me to have the housework done by the time she gets back, I have to look after William while you are at school. You know she never says thank you. He is just a spoilt brat."

"I know but he's Mother's only boy," said Hannah quietly.

"Never does anything wrong in her eyes. It won't be long before he's driving the tractor." Hannah started to laugh visualizing a three year old sat up on the tractor trying to drive it.

"You could be right Mary, you put your foot down and go and help up the Wrekin. We can manage."

"I will" she said, "just let her try and stop me. She won't dare get the nut stick to me".

Dorothy complained to Fred the first chance she got. He lit his pipe and listened while she gave her opinion on the matter; it was well known that Gwen Watson had started work as a kitchen girl at fourteen. She became pregnant and Eric married her to keep things quiet. Now they had four children but Dorothy said that they would be a bad influence on Mary who knew little outside the farm.

When she had finished, Fred simply said she should go if only to try it out. A few pennies of her own would do her good and there were plenty of folk walking up and down the hill. Despite the rationing, Eric had a catering license and still served breakfasts of ham and eggs. Little had changed after Miss Birrell died and he had taken over the tenancy. He was a creature of habit, he still did all the baking himself and the eggs were from the guinea fowl that still wandered around the cottage and roosted in the trees at night.

Fred told Mary she could go and that her Mother had agreed. She was overjoyed and could not wait to tell Hannah.

"Just one thing lass" he said "you watch your step up there. It gets busy with all the off duty soldiers I am told. They say the Yanks seem all right but have more money than sense and take advantage whenever they can."

"Oh Dad I can look after myself, I just want the chance to earn some money of my own."

"I know lass but you be very careful."

"Lucky you" said Hannah when Mary told her. "I would love to meet the pilots they must be very brave and handsome."

"That is not why I am going and you know it. When I have some money, I am taking Mother's old bike and going down town."

"So! What now? When do you start?"

"As soon as I can" said Mary and went off to get on with her work.

In March she walked across the fields and up the track to the cottage. Eric was pleased to see her and took her to meet Gwen and the children. It was agreed that she would help out the weekend before Easter to get an idea of the work involved. She hung around watching the people that came by. She could see her Father was right. Despite the weather not being that warm there were men in uniform some accompanied by local girls. The Americans stood out with their bright insignia and smart jackets. Eventually she went home promising to return before the Easter weekend. She did not mention she would be working on the Easter Monday to her parents, she would tell Fred Easter Sunday night while they were milking.

The next week Dorothy went with Grace to the Girls' High School. Grace looked very smart, she had washed and brushed her thick dark brown hair until it shone, then combed it back and secured it with a hair slide. She had on her green dress and new socks and shoes. They met Miss Bygott, who was quite impressed with Grace's appearance. Dorothy too was very smart, dressed in her best tweed; she spoke briefly to Miss Bygott before Grace was taken to a small office for her interview. After some time Grace came out and Dorothy went in. Miss Bygott told Dorothy that there was a place for Grace and if she wished she could start after the Easter break.

Grace was so excited she could hardly wait to tell her sisters. Lizzy and Mary were unimpressed but Hannah and Helen were pleased.

"I will try hard now" said Hannah "if you can go, so can I" she had her chance the following week. The exam took place on a Saturday morning and her Mother and Father accompanied her, Grace was left in charge of William. It was cold in the classroom but Hannah was comfortable and had no difficulty with the questions. Afterwards Fred and Dorothy were sitting in the car when Hannah came skipping through the gate, she was so cheerful they let her go with them down town to do the shopping.

At the beginning of the summer term, Grace was ready to start at the Wellington Girls' School. Dorothy had been very lucky to find the uniform but there were new shoes as well as gym kit, coat and satchel to be paid for. It all came to quite a price and Grace was constantly reminded of it. Dorothy moaned at Fred about the cost but the threshing had yielded their best ever cheque for the grain. The winter had not been a problem, the root crop had lasted well and they had done well with lambs. Fred had been thinking of new implements for the tractor but decided to keep quiet for now. He knew some of the horse drawn things could be converted and if anything happened to Kit or Bonny then that is what he would do. On her first day of the new term Grace set off to Wellington on the old bike. Despite enjoying herself at school she hated struggling with the bike and when she finally got home she began complaining to Dorothy, who listened for thirty seconds then told her, at length, what she thought. Later when Grace joined Hannah outside, she was very unhappy.

"Mam says that I can't have a new bike. I've got to go to school with that old sit up and beg thing of hers. Why can't I have one like Lizzy?"

"Because Lizzy has paid for hers with her own money" said Hannah.

"With all the work I do around here Mam should buy me one too. She goes on about having no money" they were joined by Mary.

"What are you complaining about I can't get away from here at all now you have taken the bike."

"I don't want it you can have it. I want a new one like Lizzy's."

"Fat chance" said Mary "you are lucky going to that fancy school while I am stuck here".

"You can go off at weekends if you like."

"You know I work now on Sundays and that only leaves Saturday afternoon."

"There you are, you can have the old thing on Saturday and you are welcome."

Mary was even more annoyed but decided to leave the matter. As it turned out, if she got ready for dinner time on a Saturday she could go into town for an hour or two and walk around the shops.

Two weeks later Hannah was given a letter and told she had passed the Eleven Plus exam and that she would be able to join Grace at the Girls High School in Wellington. She skipped out of the classroom to find Helen and bumped into Danny Probin he had been waiting for her.

"I can go to the posh school in Wellington now," she said happily.

"Why do you want to go there?" he asked, you could go to Coalbrookdale like some of us."

"I don't want to end up on the farm. I want to get a job being a nurse or something."

"Well what about me, I still want to be your friend; I thought we might go out to Atcham camp to see the Thunderbolts in the holidays." Hannah thought for a moment.

"It is a long way, too far to walk and I don't have a bike."

"I can get you a bike" he said "I could bring it down. You know we might see a crash, so many are crashing these days"

"I would like to" she said "anyway why don't you want to go with your brothers?"

"They are only interested in fighting and anyway wherever we go these days we get in trouble."

"What sort of trouble?"

"You know" he said raising his eyebrows. He cast a quick glance around "We found a tent in the woods the other day and got caught by some soldier as we were taking it down. They reported us, said we were a bloody nuisance and deserved a good hiding."

"Well what do you expect" said Hannah.

"It's not fair. Everybody thinks we are going to run off with something, last year we even got blamed for pinching turnips and Mr Johnson's dog."

"Dad says he lost quite a bit to people taking the potatoes and swedes last year" Hannah replied.

"Wasn't us" said Danny defensively.

"We keep coming across the soldiers as well. You can see where they have driven their armoured cars along the track and Dad says we are to run into the wood if one comes along. He says they are like madmen the way they drive the things." She paused for a moment, "It would be nice to get away for a while, I would like to see the Thunderbolts, there's Lightning's there too. I'd love to see one of those closes up, with its two engines."

"Well if you want to go it is too far to walk, you will have to get a bike that is safe, not like the one I brought down to your place last year for you to practice on."

"I will need a bike for going to Wellington with Grace but that won't be for a while yet."

"There you are! When you get your bike then we will go." Hannah liked the idea and agreed to see what she could do then she ran off to find Helen. Poor Helen this would mean her walking to school on her own in September. Back home she wasted no time in telling everyone including Gunter, who smiled and said "Well done."

Later when Ken and Imogen were home she went through to tell them her news. They were very pleased for her and congratulated her. "The journey will certainly keep you fit" said Ken, "and you will have to be careful in the winter."

"I know Lizzy has already told me how easy it is to crash on the ice."

Ken and Imogen turned to each other and laughed "We know all about that don't we dear?" he said. "Indeed!" Imogen replied and they both laughed loudly. Hannah laughed with them, it had been a good day, and all she needed now was a bicycle of her own.

After she had gone Imogen said to Ken "I am so pleased for those two girls, it will give them both a chance to mix and perhaps go on to bigger and better things".

"I agree with you Ginny, the school will be a bit of an eye opener for them but it is a long way for them to go each morning and night."

"I think they will cope they are quite tough, Hannah has recovered well from the whooping cough."

"That was strange" he said and they settled down in front of the fire.

That evening Hannah asked Dorothy if she would be having all the new things that Grace had been bought.

"I suppose so" was all the reply she got.

"A new uniform and socks and shoes and a satchel and pencils and hankies and…"

"That's enough" said Dorothy "we'll see closer to the time".

"And a new bike as well?" Hannah persisted.

"You won't be getting a new bike I can assure you. Not with the amount I am going to spend on all the other things."

"Can I have a new bike now then, when you sell the lambs?"

"No! Not even if we could afford one."

"What about when you sell the wool?"

"Didn't you hear what I just said, now get out of my sight and get something done." Hannah shuffled off outside and found Grace.

"What's the matter with you?" Grace asked, seeing Hannah so unhappy, "don't tell me you have been talking to Mam".

"Yes. She said I can't have a new bike."

"What did you expect, you will probably end up with a rusty old hurdle like that thing I use."

"Oh Lordy, I hope not, I will ask Danny Probin to find me one if I have too."

When the weather was suitable to start ploughing Fred went to the cart shed now called the tractor shed. He opened the door to the unique smell of fuel oil, straw, muck and mud. He tapped the fuel tank, it rang hollow so he picked up his fuel gauge a two foot stick and removed the fuel cap. As he thought, it was nearly empty. He had several five gallon drums of TVO in the stackyard and transferring the fuel was by means of a gallon can and a large funnel known as a tun dish. He half filled the tank and put the can and funnel out of harms way then he got into the seat and tried to start the engine. It turned over but would not start then he remembered he had to turn on a tap to give the engine petrol. He did so but still no luck, he was getting worried. Mary came into the shed.

"What's wrong Dad won't it start"

"Nay lass, I've filled her up but she dunna want to go." Mary looked the tractor over it was a majestic machine.

"Has it got any petrol in it?" She asked.

"Of course it……Ah, I never checked" He realized he had forgotten to make sure there was petrol for starting the engine. Ten minutes later after a gallon of petrol in the second fuel tank the engine fired. Mary was pleased as punch. Now that was one to tell her sisters.

When Fred was finally ready he hitched up the plough and set off to the fields. It was so easy, he whistled as he drove the tractor, the double furrow plough made light work of the usual fields. After all the fields were ploughed and ready he turned his attention to the rough ground under the Wrekin. He drove very slowly not wanting to damage tractor or plough and a lot of time was spent clearing the stones and rocks. Despite the delay with the rough ground it seemed no time at all and he had the ploughing done. He borrowed a disc harrow but then used the spike harrow normally pulled by the horses.

Once the ground was broken down all the sowing was done behind the horses. Wheat, oats and barley were sown. Despite only just starting at the new school, Grace was made to stay off and help with the sowing of potatoes on what had been the rough ground and a small patch of ground at the end of the top fields that had been cleared of gorse bushes and bracken. At the end of each days work when the tractor was switched off with the smell of fuel and oil strong in the air, Fred would light his pipe and stretch his limbs then pat the mudguard or engine cover.

"You're a beauty", he would say puffing away at his pipe before heading off to the house.

Because he was ploughing so much ground the sheep were now limited to stubble and the roughest ground which had not seen the plough as yet. When on the top fields they seemed to do their best to escape usually heading for the golf course where there was a good supply of fresh grass around the greens. With the warmer weather Helen, who would be eight in June, would join in the hunt. This pleased Joyce Wilkins, as they often stopped off to see if she had seen them go past. Joyce was a much kinder person towards the girls since William had arrived, especially towards Helen. She made them much more welcome whenever they called round with messages. She took to inviting them to sit around the table with her if they did not have to hurry back home, she actually enjoyed their chatter. Joyce would give the girls a glass of homemade lemonade or a cup of tea and she made cakes when the rations would allow. Joyce knew that her husband had noticed the girls were stopping by more often but she knew he would say nothing. He had refused to let her have her own child and she never forgave him. If he said anything Joyce would go into one of her moods and not speak to him for days on end and he hated that. The girls never seemed to have much in the way of decent clothes always wearing the same shabby dresses and cardigans handed down from one to the other. Poor little Helen was at the end of the line and never looked tidy. Joyce knew that their grandmothers sent presents but it was usually for the older girls. Dorothy did the same when she bought clothes with the coupons. Sometimes she bought second hand woollens which they unraveled for knitting but apart from mittens or gloves Helen would get nothing, just the cast offs.

Joyce bought a new dress for Helen's birthday the year before and had sent it down with Mary after stopping her in the field on her fence checking rounds. Dorothy had never sent a thank you but Helen was overjoyed and had said so the first chance she got. This year again Joyce bought a dress with clothing coupons as Helen's birthday was close and was delighted when a week before Helen's birthday she came to the door with Hannah to see if the sheep had gone over towards the greens.

"Do come in for a while children" she said "I have something for you".

There was Helen's parcel on the table. It was tied with a pretty bow. First Joyce handed Hannah some bags of sweets.

"These are to be shared amongst all of you" she said. "Thank you" said Hannah, pleased as punch. Joyce turned to the table where Helen was staring hard at the parcel.

"Well young lady, do you think that is yours?" Helen was too shy to answer.

"Well it is for your birthday but you must not open it till then."

"Oh thank you. Thank you very much Mrs Wilkins."

"Pick it up on your way back, but you ought to get on after those sheep, they went down the lane a while ago."

When they got home Dorothy was not impressed, she did not buy presents on birthdays.

"That woman thinks that I can't afford the child a new frock but I don't see the need to buy when we can get so many handed down," she complained to Fred.

"Can't see a problem lass, she looked nice in last year's dress."

"Well there is no point in my buying her a new frock when I know that woman is buying one." She just had to have the last word.

Grace was not impressed.

"Why do we never get presents on our birthdays? It makes me mad, I am going to get a job as soon as I can and buy my own things."

"Me too" said Hannah "but right now I want a bike to go to the new school on".

Later Hannah asked Mary why Joyce bought Helen a dress and not her.

She is Helen's Godmother" said Mary.

"Have we got a Godmother?" Hannah asked.

"Not that I know" of she replied gloomily.

"Can we get one before my birthday do you think?"

"Ask Mam, I think the answer will be no though" Hannah did not bother.

Ever since its arrival, the wireless set had sat on the table in the corner of the kitchen behind Fred's chair. Dorothy had placed an embroidered cloth under it and it was regularly polished. Because it ran on batteries its use was restricted to the evening, although Dorothy often put it on during the day when she was on her own. Every night when the news was broadcast the girls had to be silent so that their parents could concentrate. Hannah was always interested because she was following the fortunes of the British Army. At the end of May, Rome was set to fall to the Allies and big gains were being made in Burma. It was very pleasing as it had seemed only the Russians and Americans were getting anywhere.

It was a great surprise on 6th June when the news broke that the Allies had a foothold in Normandy. Fred was overjoyed, Dorothy was stunned, and "What does it mean? Where is Normandy?" she asked.

"Near France lass, little place not where you would expect, it is a fair way down."

"I will get my atlas" said Grace and rushed off upstairs, everyone else listened intently. After the news Dorothy put the kettle on as everyone began talking at once. The map was on the table.

"Surry this is a turn up" said Fred lighting his pipe "I thought we were coming up through Italy".

"This is wonderful." said Mary "I wonder if the Canadians are there?"

"Well it certainly has been quiet around here for a while" Fred replied.

"This will put a scare into Hitler and now the war will be over," Dorothy said.

"Let's not be hasty lass, this is a whole new start to things. It will be touch and go from now on, it is important to get inland. I only hope they have not got another Gallipoli."

"What is a Gallipoli Dad?" asked Grace.

"A very bad memory from the Great War" he replied.

The talk went on for sometime. Hannah was pleased to give her opinion and have everyone's attention.

The next morning Fred put the wireless on when he got up which was very unusual. When Mary came down he was listening intently, "I thought I was dreaming last night. The last war sort of ground to a halt, this is an invasion and it means we will be pushing to meet the Russians I reckon".

"How long will it take Dad?" she asked.

"It could take a very long time so there is not a lot of point getting excited just yet" and with that he turned the set off. "Better give them a chance to get inland a bit."

As the days passed Fred became anxious, it was the 12th June before the Allies had established a continuous front extending for sixty miles.

As the weeks progressed the news got better. Gunter asked Fred if he thought the war was ending.

"Not just yet, why do you ask?"

"I wish to go home, to my family in peace" he replied. Fred had never discussed Gunter's family, the less he knew the better he believed but he was curious. "Where are you from?" he asked.

"A town near Dresden, it is very beautiful and maybe soon the madness will end and I will be able to go back. I would like to go to work on a farm. To help my people, they will need farmers not soldiers."

At the end of June Fred was surprised to see Bernie, the lad from the previous year's summer camp, come walking into the cowshed.

"Surry lad what brings you back?" he said.

"Thought I would come back again. You said it would be all right."

"Aye, well there is nowhere for a camp now, got myself a tractor and it's all been ploughed up." He went to the door and looked out.

"How many of you are there?"

"Just me" Fred looked at him amazed.

"How did you get here?"

"On the train and then I walked. I have brought my own tent and some food, all I need is somewhere to put it up."

"There's plenty of room lad but what will you do with yourself? Are you sure there aren't others coming along later?"

"Just me I think. I was hoping I could work here to help out with my meals. I really like your eggs."

"Well I am going to be getting the hay in soon and I could do with a bit of help, but how long are you staying?"

"Don't know! A week but if there is work I might stay a bit longer."

"I'll have a word with the missus" Fred said and he went off to the house to see Dorothy. "Is he that skinny lad that used to fetch the milk? The one who was always asking questions?"

"Aye that's him. Seems keen enough and it would save us having to pay for help with the hay." At that she agreed, always happy to avoid spending. Fred went back to the farmyard where Bernie was sat on one of his milking stools seemingly quite at home.

"Well lad put up your tent in the field next to the house we can soon find some jobs for you."

"Thanks very much. Mr Thomas I want to do something different so any jobs you got I would be happy to help out."

Fred thought for a while. He had decided to carry on using the horses for haymaking because despite having the tractor the cutter could not be hitched up and anyway as Dorothy pointed out, fuel cost money and the horses were standing around doing nothing, so it made sense to save a few pennies on the fuel.

Fred decided Bernie could help out and gave him some small jobs. One job was walking the fields checking for holes or obstructions before haymaking. On the Monday Bernie joined Mary and they set off walking through the long grass.

"We won't have to do this if we use the tractor" said Mary making conversation.

"So why do you like it here, there is nothing but work for you. We all want to get away from the place."

"It is better than the city" he said. "There are so many people on top of you not like here. There is always rowing in our house and when you are outside there is always something going on, some problem or other. Here it is peaceful I feel free to walk where I want, no rows no squabbling." Mary laughed "Well wait till you meet the gamekeeper and an afternoon in the house with our Mam would change your tune".

He looked up at the sky "There does not seem to be a war going on out here, just a few planes flying around now and then. I like the hill, it is wonderful to sit up there and look around. I suppose if you live here everyday you get so as you do not notice it."

Mary looked up at the Wrekin "I suppose you are right, I work up there at the cottage on Sundays, it gets me away from here. But you have electricity and water from taps in Birmingham don't you?"

"Yes of course, why do you ask?"

"We don't. Nothing like that at all. Our granny lives in Dudley, she told us you have baths as well and toilets in the house."

"Only a tin one" he said "and we have an outside toilet down the garden. Your Gran must be posh".

"I didn't think so. I just thought it was all mod cons in the city" she said surprised.

"It is not though; some parts of the city are really bad. I like it here where it is so peaceful. I might stay for a while it is better than going back."

At the end of the day's work Dorothy gave him a meal to take to his tent and later on he joined in a game of catch on the back yard. Dorothy watched from the window.

"That skinny kid seems right at home out there, how did he do today?"

"All right, puts his back into it and doesn't mess about."

"Good, we will have to keep an eye on him with the girls though. There's no telling with these city lads."

The girls were keen to find out what it was like living in Birmingham, they had an idea from when Sybil and John had stayed in 1942. What Bernie told them painted a completely different picture. He told them of pieces of bodies lying in the streets after the German raids and how one night in a crowded shelter his Father, worn out from working in the factory, had turned over in his sleep and accidentally smothered his six month old baby daughter. The girls thought of how small Helen had been at that age. What a horrible thing to happen.

Sitting in the barn one evening, Bernie told them terrible stories of prison camps and the inhuman behavior of the Nazis over the Russians and the Jews. They did not know if he was telling the truth but it filled them with dread. He relished in stories of Japanese barbarity and cruelty beyond belief.

Everyone was familiar with tragedy it came over the radio every day. It all seemed so far away, almost unreal. Occasionally an incident stood out like the horror at the loss of HMS Hood with all but 3 out of a crew of 1400 men in one single explosion. Now Bernie was saying tens of thousands of ordinary people were dying in Russian cities and in camps. Such things as they were being told never crossed the girl's minds. Bernie said it was living out in the country where there was little to worry about. Back in Birmingham the bombing might begin at anytime.

That night Hannah couldn't sleep, she thought she knew all about the war, who was fighting who and where. Imogen had helped her with her geography of Europe when the bombing of the German cities had begun. Her maps showed the Pacific islands where the Japanese and Americans were fighting, Italy, Burma and now Brittany, Normandy and France.

Early in the morning she asked Grace "No one is that cruel are they? There are laws about keeping prisoners and every country has to obey them don't they?"

"How do you know? You read all that stuff and listen to the news but we don't know what is really happening, as Bernie says we live a quiet life here, there's no telling how nasty some folk can be. Imagine a country where the likes of Bill Shankly or the gamekeeper can say who lives or dies. All the Bailey boys would be gone for a start and probably us two for walking in the woods."

"Yes but Bernie says it is the Germans doing it to thousands of people. Gunter is so kind and gentle I don't believe it. People always make up stories to frighten us; it is what they do in a war."

"Yes but Bernie might be right. They might use people's skin to make lampshades" said Grace grinning, "you never know".

"That is so horrible. I do not want to be skinned alive to make a lampshade."

As soon as she was dressed, Hannah found Mary, she was always better to talk to.

"Don't worry; you have heard Monty on the radio hasn't you? Him and Churchill and Eisenhower will beat the Germans, they are on the run, just ask Mr Winter he always knows."

"Yes but the stuff Bernie is saying is about ordinary people just like us who haven't got guns or tanks, why would they want to kill so many?"

"Don't ask me, it may be true that Hitler is evil try not to let it bother you."

Hannah kept away from Bernie as she did not want to hear any more horror stories. Then Grace upset her by telling her that the Japanese cut off peoples head with a sword just for arguing back. She listened even more to the radio. Flying bombs were falling on London but otherwise the war was going well on every front, there was no talk of the atrocities Bernie mentioned, she went back to her clippings and map, she knew the allies were going to win and Sam would come home the hero.

Just after the hay was in the weather turned wet, Bernie said that he would like to stay a while longer so he was allowed to stay in the barn. Fred lent him some waterproof gear as he was keen to help outside. He walked the fields checking the fences and helped Mary fetch the cows in for milking. Fred let him have a go at milking and he proved to be quite good so he was allowed to milk the quiet ones. As the weeks progressed he was allowed into the kitchen to take his meals. The girls got used to him being around and they decided life on the farm was preferable to life in the big city if his stories were anything to go by.

CHAPTER 11

A do at the Glen

At the beginning of the summer holidays Fred was much happier, the Germans were being pushed back. Rommel, one of the greatest German generals, had been seriously injured by an attack from the air and the allies were pushing into France. Dorothy found a bicycle for Hannah; it was second hand and had belonged to a girl who had left to work in the city. It arrived in the boot of the Wolseley with the front wheel on the back seat.

Fred put the wheel back in as Hannah watched. It looked most peculiar, it was a girl's bike so had no crossbar, but the handlebars turned downwards and it had cable brakes. She had not seen one like this before. Later when she went to the kitchen, Grace asked her what she thought of her bike.

"Oh Lordy" she said. "It looks more like a boys' bike. How on earth am I supposed to ride it?"

"It's not as big as that thing I have to manage with" said Grace, a little too loudly.

"But I will be leaning right forward and I think if I put the brakes on hard, I will go straight over the top" Hannah replied. At this Dorothy turned on them "You had better learn to ride it" she ordered her. "That bike is the best that we can get and we have had the devil of a job to get it. You two had better appreciate things a bit more we are not made of money you know." The girls looked at each other it was better to say no more, once outside they would be able to moan as much as they wanted. Hannah went off and asked Bernie to test ride it on the road for her which he did.

"It is fine" he said "if you don't want it, I will have it."

"Oh no it is mine. Now I have to learn to ride it for when I start at the new school in September."

By now there had been several crashes involving the P47's from Atcham, tales of the recklessness of the pilots were commonplace. One had them flying so low they would knock the exhaust pipe off the tractors in the fields.

With more time because of the summer holidays, Danny Probin cycled out to Atcham to watch the aircraft landing and taking off. He had not forgotten that Hannah wanted to come along, so one Saturday he called in on his way. He came up the back drive into the farmyard and met Mary.

"What do you want?" she asked.

"Just passing, is Hannah here? I've got something for her" he said.

"Like what?" Mary said sharply.

"None of your business, it's a secret." Mary was annoyed but she knew Hannah was in the kitchen and she could see he was not going to go away.

"Stay here and don't touch anything, I will get her." Mary went straight in and told Hannah that Danny Probin wanted to see her.

"Don't you lot go encouraging him to come here" Dorothy said as Hannah got up from the table. She resented strangers coming anywhere near the house and she had no time at all for the local lads who were suspected of stealing from the fields and orchards.

"What do you want today?" Hannah asked Danny.

"Did you see the Starlings go over this morning? I am off to Atcham camp to see if they are there."

"I thought you said it's only a fighter base?" she said suspiciously.

"Yes, well, I thought you might like to come along."

"I would, and I have a bike of my own now but it would have to be tomorrow afternoon while Mam and Dad are taking a rest. Mam would kill me if she knew I was out that far."

"Well don't tell her, you do want to see the planes landing and taking off, I know that you do, you're a proper Amy Johnson."

"My Dad said that. He said I should get a job with the RAF spotting their planes for them, whatever that means."

"There you go what time tomorrow afternoon?"

"Early, right after dinner, don't come to the house and raise any suspicions, Mam has eyes like a weasel. I will get out with some excuse or other and meet you where the road goes into the wood. Now be off with you before you get me into trouble." She knew that she could not resist going with Danny to see the planes at Atcham.

Sunday afternoon, Mary was up the Wrekin. As soon as the washing up was done Hannah said she was off to practice on her bike. Grace would watch over William and Helen, so she went round to the garage and got her new bike. She walked down the rough drive to the front gate and out onto the road.

With her head down she set off and as she rode into the woods there was Danny waiting for her.

"Let's go" she said speeding past him. He soon caught up as she nervously held the brakes on going down the twisty road. They made their way to the A5 at Cluddely then past the Umbrella House, past the Bluebell Crossroads and the pub, there was little in the way of traffic, in fact most of the vehicles were military.

"There is nothing happening, I haven't seen or heard anything all the way down" said Hannah as they stood not far from the entrance to the camp. They could see the guards and felt that they ought to move away.

"Let's put our bikes out of sight and walk around for a bit" Hannah suggested. There was the sound of an engine running in the distance so they dumped their bikes in the hedgerow out of sight and walked around the perimeter fence. The planes were clearly visible and one had men working on its massive engine. It was a single seat plane but it was enormous.

"Oh Lordy, look how big that plane is. I never knew they were this size."

"That is what my Dad said; they are P47's, look at that engine, eighteen cylinders. They say it can have several shot off and still keep running." As he spoke there was the grumble of an engine starting in the distance. "Let's get closer" Hannah said and set off along the fence. A second engine fired up and a minute later they saw two Thunderbolts come rolling into view, they moved quickly towards the main runway.

Hannah clapped her hands together, this was so exciting.

Together the planes took off and headed away towards the Wrekin.

"Fantastic" she said.

"I told you so. Let's see what else is here." They walked around, there were lots of aircraft parked but nothing else was running.

"You see, there are big American planes here, my Dad said that there was."

Hannah was worried about the time "Come on let's get back or we will be in trouble". They walked steadily back to where the bikes were hidden. It was disappointing that nothing else was taking off but the two P47's returned roaring overhead before circling to land. Where they were standing they could see the pilots perched high in the fuselages as they taxied back. They were so pleased as they made their way home; talking over the sight of the taxiing planes it seemed no time at all before they were back at the Forest Glen. Hannah's legs were really aching whereas Danny did not seem to suffer in the slightest. After a rest they carried on and at the farm Hannah ran quickly up the track and put her bike in the garage, then she ran through the backyard and around to the farmyard where she bumped into Grace, who had seen Danny carry on up the Willowmoor Bank.

"Where the devil have you been with that Danny Probin?" she demanded.

"Just for a bike ride, I was trying to get used to those handlebars. Are Mam and Dad up?"

"Yes, but I don't think they noticed you were gone."

"That's good I'll get my feeding done then."

"Mam will be mad if she finds out that you have been off 'the bank' and with that Danny. You know that he is trouble wherever he goes."

"He is not as bad as you think we have seen the American planes taking off and landing."

"What not at the camp, surely not, that is miles away."

"Yes and I am not tired at all" she lied.

"I would not let Mam hear you say that if I was you, she will get the nut stick for sure. You know she can't stand the lads from the village."

"He's not that bad" said Hannah. She knew that he was a bit of a rogue and that her Mother would not approve of him setting foot on 'the bank' as she called the farm. "Did you know a cow chewed his trousers last week and he got a good hiding?"

"What on earth are you on about?"

"They go swimming over by Horsehay and he left his clothes in the field and a cow ate them but not too bad. He did not want his Mam to know he had been in the pool and he said he had fallen over. That is why he wanted to go this way today because he won't get into trouble with me around."

"You'll be the one in trouble if our Mam finds out, now come on get moving. I haven't been back long either."

There seemed more optimism in the air during the summer months everything was going well abroad and at home. The harvest went well and there was plenty of help available. In the skies there was intense activity as the Americans practiced their fighting skills, sometimes with tragic results. The radio broadcasts brought news of fresh gains in and around Normandy, Burma, the Pacific and the Eastern Front. Many folk were saying the war with Germany would be over by Christmas. Fred knew it would take time and was not one of them. He talked with Ken Winter whenever possible. He and Imogen were desperately worried, her family was in occupied Holland and it was rumoured that terrible things were happening. Ken was concerned that Holland would be abandoned in favour of taking Berlin before the Russians. He also knew of a threat from the revenge weapons that Hitler intended unleashing from the Dutch countryside.

Life around the Wrekin carried on getting better. For Fred the tractor had made a big difference and there was less damage being done through training maneuvers, so the livestock increased. Around the area there were many accidents claiming lives unnecessarily on the roads and in the air. The Americans at Atcham were suffering terrible losses as crashes were becoming more frequent. The threat of invasion was long gone but everyone feared for the lives of the servicemen fighting in Europe. The Podmores found they were much in demand to hold dinner dances, weddings and private functions. There were no shortages at the private functions, there was at least one a week during the summer with other events at the weekends. Lizzy found she very busy on these occasions but she was paid well for the extra hours. The function room was also the tearoom and could seat one hundred and fifty at tables. Work began setting out the tables and chairs as soon as it closed for afternoon tea.

Margaret had everything ready for when the doors were opened. There were curtains set all round the pavilion to act as a blackout and folk had to push them aside to enter. Lizzy would help with the setting up and then return to the kitchens until called upon to wait the tables. One such function was the Farmers Union dinner party mostly made up of local farmers and agricultural dealers. Neville Cotton had cycled from Wellington to look after the well stocked bar, there was no chance of him running out of beer or spirits. When it was time for the meal to begin, Percy carved the meat himself with a razor edged carving knife; he was a dab hand at the job. He placed an ample amount of meat on hot plates that had been kept ready in a special oven. There was lamb and beef, there had been no problem with the amount he needed, 'A word in the right ear' he smiled to himself as he carved. Lizzy was working as a waitress and was busy putting bowls of hot steaming potatoes, vegetables and gravy on the tables. The room was smoky and as it was a warm night the side doors were opened a little, while still keeping the light from shining out, the near miss was still on Margaret's mind. To serve a meal to a number as they had tonight and have it on the tables while it was still hot took a lot of discipline and co-ordination. Margaret checked the plates of meat before they went to the tables, they did not want any complaints at the end of the evening.

"This lamb is carving well tonight my dear" Percy said to his wife. "You have surpassed yourself yet again."

As the meal came to an end, Old Mr Podmore came through from the back; a few of the guests saw him and smiled. His toast "To all friends around the Wrekin" was famous around the area. There was an air of anticipation in the smoky atmosphere and then a sudden rush to the bar. The waitresses made sure that all the tables were cleared and when everyone was settled Old Mr Podmore stepped forward and called in a loud voice for order. Everyone turned towards him and he began:-

"To all friends around The Wrekin, and to His Most Royal Majesty,
The loyalty that he is seeking.
To Shropshire's Son's upon the sea,
On land and in the air,
There never were, nor never will,
Be finer, anywhere.

For they that never bowed the knee,

In bondage, to a foe,
Nor ever will, while they have breath,
To fight as best they know.

And may the Good Lord please rain down, upon our foes' bare shins,
As many Holy pebble-stones,
As they have committed sins.
In order that we'll know them,
By the way they cringe and crimp,
But more specially, so we'll know the buggers by their limp".

At the end there was a tremendous roar from the room and everyone clapped.

"I thank you all" said Old Mr Podmore, "I think we should take this moment to toast not only the King but all our gallant men and women of all nations who tonight are out there fighting to keep our freedom." The room was hushed, "We must remember the fallen and pray for their families." He paused "Ladies and Gentlemen. Please raise your glasses".

Percy went down the back stairs into the kitchen, trays and trays laden with dirty crockery spread around the floor and on every available space, the kitchen staff was working hard to clear them. The clatter of cutlery and plates as they were washed and dried was quite deafening, making conversation inaudible, each member of staff working away, knowing exactly which job they were responsible for. He helped by carrying the heavy piles of clean plates and stacking them on the shelves in the middle kitchen. Margaret was sorting the remainder of the food, preparing a light supper for the staff before they went home. He smiled to her "Very satisfactory, there will be a lot of drink downed tonight." She smiled back "Yes they were quick to get to the bar tonight. Mind you it was very stuffy in there, I am glad the doors were opened".

When everything was cleared away and surfaces cleaned down the staff sat around the table for some supper. As soon as they were finished, Percy took them home in his car.

Lizzy always stayed on to do the last bit of tidying up, not needing a lift home she could leave when she wanted. This was very convenient for Margaret, she would let her carry on until Percy came back and if all the work was finished in the kitchens she would then let her leave to cycle home. Margaret would then retire to her sitting room and a little later go to bed leaving Percy to take over the bar from Neville. He would not close before one o'clock in the morning.

Sometimes it would be after midnight when Lizzy set off home, she had nothing to fear as she pushed her bike up the banks through the woods in the darkness. She always carried something back on these occasions, a pastry usually. Although Margaret paid Dorothy for fruit and such, it didn't hurt to keep on her good side.

There was very little of the way home that she could ride her bike, it was mostly up hill. It was far easier to walk and she had no problem seeing in the dark, perhaps it was all the carrots they ate from the garden that Fred kept during the spring and summer. The last few years the garden had been well stocked and several other areas had been turned over for household vegetables.

When she got in she went straight to bed to rest her weary body. It would not be long before she had to be up again. Her only day off was Tuesday. Still she had earned her money, the night had been interesting and her Mam couldn't moan with the size of the pie in the pantry.

Bernie left at the end of August saying he might return someday.

Mary asked him how he could just up and go after settling in.

"It is the same way I came here" he said "I just do things like that. I will go home to see how things are and then I might move somewhere else".

"You can always come back here."

He grinned "I probably will, actually".

On the first day of the new school term Hannah was up very early and had all her jobs done in record time. Then she took a bowl of warm water to the bedroom and washed from head to toe. She dressed in her new school uniform and then went into her Mother's room so that she could see herself in the long mirror of the wardrobe. "My goodness" she said to herself. She felt so proud as she studied her reflection in the wardrobe mirror .The uniform consisted of navy blue tunic, pale blue blouse, white socks and new black shoes, boy's best shoes of course. Oh those shoes! How she wished she could have proper girl's shoes. She had tried complaining to her Mother but was told very firmly, "Those flimsy shoes that you want would be of no use at all. You need good strong shoes on your feet".

"But I will be riding my bike" she said.

"Not all the time. There are more banks to climb now. You've got to come up the Ercall and there's the banks past the Glen you'll see."

"Grace says I will soon get used to them like she has."

"Yes and she wears proper shoes as well, so that is the end of it" Dorothy said firmly.

Hannah checked her pocket for her hanky; luckily Grace had learned all the things a new girl was expected to do. She had told Hannah that a piece of old rag for a hanky or socks as mittens would not do. Dorothy had made it quite clear that there was no money spare for hankies, gloves or scarves. Hannah had loaned Lizzy's needles and a pattern then using wool unraveled from old jumpers she had managed to knit a reasonable pair of mittens and a warm scarf for the cold weather.

She had made several hankies on the sewing machine with Dorothy's help, cutting pieces of worn out sheets into squares and then hemming the edges all round.

Her hankies were unmistakable as each had a little flower embroidered in the corner just as she had been taught at school by Mrs Hayward.

After breakfast they checked their satchels one more time. Hannah's was canvas, whereas Grace's was leather and had cost quite a lot. Each of them had to take gym shoes for wearing in school, outdoor shoes were not allowed past the cloakroom. They were tied to the satchels and then they put on their mackintoshes that had been bought to keep them dry and their school hats. Outside the weather was fine, they went to the garage and got their bikes, they were not far behind the Winters. At the road they got on their bikes and adjusted their bags. Grace waited till Hannah was ready then said "I don't want you behind me if your brakes fail. You can ride in front." They set off, having, the bag on her back and the shoes swinging around made Hannah nervous at first but she soon got used to it and the journey was exhilarating. As soon as their bikes were parked in the bike shed, Grace took Hannah for a walk around the playground and pointed out the tennis and net-ball courts. Hannah was very impressed, the school was massive. Hannah was also amazed with the school building it was so big, much bigger than she had imagined. They had arrived early and there were not many other girls around but then Hannah noticed that every girl she saw had the same dark blue hat as Grace whereas hers was dark grey. Grace noticed too "take yours off for now" she said. "There will be others wearing your sort eventually."

Dorothy had been unable to get the correct colour hat as none were available when she got around to it. She settled for a grey hat the right style and sewed the school band to it. They carried on walking around. More girls began to arrive and two came over to join Grace. "So, is this your sister?" one of the girls asked.

"Yes, her name is Hannah" she turned to her sister "Say hello to Emily and Joan they are my friends".

Hannah mumbled hello and they laughed.

"The cat has got her tongue" said Joan. "You watch by dinner time she will be running around with the rest of the new ones." Hannah did not answer, she was looking around, the schoolyard was so busy, all the girls looked the same in their uniforms but many had long hair with pretty ribbons tying it back. Her hair was quite short, 'practical' as her Mother called it. She could see now why Grace made such a fuss over wanting her hair cut properly and a ribbon. Eventually the school doors opened, the bell rang and the girls were ushered in by the teachers. One of them stopped Hannah "Where is your hat?" she asked. Hannah took it from her coat pocket and looked at the floor as if it was about to open and swallow her up.

"Why is it the wrong colour? It is not even blue."

"There isn't any left Miss, because of the war Miss" Hannah replied without looking up.

"Alright it will have to do. You are not the only one today." Hannah followed the other girls to the cloakroom where everyone had a coat hook. She hung up her coat and changed out of her outdoor shoes putting them in the bag and hanging it up. She stood up and looked around to get her bearings; she was worried how she would remember where hers was at home time. The day began with assembly and prayers and then there was a lecture for all the first years. Hannah felt so proud sat at the front. The first day was wonderful and after eventually finding her coat and shoes she joined Grace for the journey home.

They rode side by side as there was no worry of other traffic the roads were all but deserted. All the way home Hannah chattered, barely pausing for breath. Grace listened patiently, passing comment occasionally. After the first week Hannah settled into her timetable well, she thoroughly enjoyed going to school and was beginning to plan for her future. The wet batteries for the wireless had always been recharged on a Thursday and Saturday when Dorothy and Fred went down town, now the girls were made to take them to school with them on Tuesdays and Thursday. The batteries were made of glass and had metal carrying handles, they were hung over the handlebars and they had to be careful not to let them bang against their knees as the cycled, or let the acid touch their clothes. They liked cycling down to Pearce's garage as it gave them a chance to look around the town. The consequences of falling off and breaking the battery did not bear thinking about, so they always took their time on the journey home. There were many after school activities, Hannah asked if she could join the choir and stay over on a Tuesday for half an hour but Dorothy said absolutely not. Hannah argued that they fetched the battery and that made them late so why not the choir.

"Aye but you dawdle back with the battery taking your time" said Dorothy. Hannah felt it was time to stand up to her Mother and said "We do not. It is not fair; you could change it when you and Dad go shopping". Dorothy scowled at her and a blazing row developed, in the end Hannah fled the kitchen to the safety of the granary.

Mary found her sitting on the bags nibbling the sweet pieces from the cattle feed.

"You're in for it" she said "Mam has been and got a new nut stick she says she is going to spiflicate you". It had been a while since any of them had been on the receiving end of their Mother's stick which she kept on the drying rack above the range. It was about three foot long and has to whistle when she waves it in the air. If it did not a new one was cut that did whistle. Hannah recalled the swish that the stick made before it hit her legs.

"Don't you think that it's mean of our Man not to let us stay after school and join the choir or do other things after lessons?"

"Yes and now you know why I like getting away to the Half way house at a weekend." Mary went and carried on with her work. Grace paid a visit to Hannah she was unhappy with their Mother as well.

"I wanted to stay after school to play tennis but I can't ask now, she is going to be in this mood for weeks."

"Oh Lordy, why is she so mean?"

"She gets it from Granddad, he is the same" said Grace. "Anyway Dad says you have to go and see him now, he wants to know what is going on." Hannah was scared.

Fred did not approve of using sticks to hit children or animals. He had never hit them and if he was in the kitchen when Dorothy got the stick he would open the door so they could escape onto the back yard. They would stand round the corner and listen to Dorothy shouting and raving.

"What's Dad said?"

"Nothing yet but he has heard Mam's side." Hannah went down to the cowshed and carefully told her Dad about the things that went on after school and how they always were careful not to risk the battery.

"I'll give you a shout when I am going in and you come in with me" he said. "You don't say anything just head up to your room and one of us will bring you some tea later."

"Thanks Dad" said Hannah; she knew everything would be all right now.

Hannah and Grace had homework to do and usually worked on the kitchen table by the light from the big brass paraffin lamp after tea was finished. Dorothy made it awkward for them by complaining that she could not see to read or sew. She would move the lamp to her side of the table and if they said anything or moved it back they were sent upstairs where there was a lamp but nowhere to put the books down.

They had to constantly avoid confrontation with their Mother as the slightest thing caused a row. They each had two pairs of white socks that Dorothy considered sufficient to last them a week. However if the roads were wet and muddy, cycling the three miles to school meant the socks would be filthy by the time they got home.

Dorothy did the weekly wash but after that she would not bother so the two girls had to wash them during the week when her back was turned. They would hurriedly wash a pair in the kitchen sink using the bar of sunlight soap to get the worst of the dirt out. They dare not use the Rinso washing powder in case Dorothy found out and it caused a row. Once the socks were clean they were put on newspaper in the oven to dry ready for the next morning. Fred would see the socks drying when he put the morning sticks to dry or when banking the fire up before retiring for the night, he would chuckle and turn them over to make sure they dried properly for the morning.

September was a bad month for the Allies; the war was definitely not going to be over for Christmas. After early gains in the Low Countries and an incursion into Germany near Aachen they failed to secure the Scheldt estuary. This denied them the capability of bringing supplies into Antwerp and delaying the push into Germany.

On the 17th Operation Market Garden was launched and bridges at Eindoven and Nijmegan were captured but the third bridge at Arnhem was a disaster. Ken Winter was away most of the month and when he returned he was terribly depressed. He and Imogen had been hoping that this was the breakthrough to free the Dutch people but now it was looking unlikely, the occupying Germans were too strong. In the last week of September Fred told the family that he intended to start lifting the new potato crop from what had been the rough fields under the Wrekin. He expected the task to take up to two weeks and therefore the girls were to tell their teachers that this was the reason why they would not be attending school. Hannah and Grace were dismayed; they were enjoying school despite the trip morning and night.

"Why does Dad need us? He has the tractor and I heard he can ask for help."

"He won't want to pay for help when he can keep us here will he? At this rate we will not be qualified enough to get a decent job by the time we leave school. What are we going to do?"

"I suppose we have to help. Miss Etches will ask for a written note to explain why I am not going to be in class for a week or more. I know exactly what Mam will write back. She will say what she always says, that there is a shortage of labour and if the potato crop is not lifted it will rot in the ground and then we will be prosecuted." Grace sighed "Not more time off, Miss Talbot is going to be so disappointed. She had promised me a part in the school play and rehearsing was to start next week. If any of us do not make an effort or don't turn up we will be dropped and not be able to take part. Just my luck!"

Both of them tried reasoning with their parents but to no avail, the work had to go ahead. Monday morning the weather was dry and cold, the sun would come out later, ideal weather for lifting root crops. Dorothy complained that she had more than enough to do making sandwiches and filling bottles with tea for them to take to the field. Fred would not stop work while he had the daylight they would work through till five. Dorothy would have an evening meal cooked ready for when they came home. Fred had collected a large number of empty corn sacks from Turner's the local corn merchant who would also take the crop in the evening. He put them into the trailer behind the tractor with all the buckets and bags he could find in and around the farm buildings. The girls, with William and Gunter, climbed into the trailer to ride to the field, each clutching a paper bag with a couple of sandwiches.

Fred drove the tractor and trailer to the field where a ridge plough was waiting. While the girls set out the bags around the edges, Gunter and Fred hitched up the plough and Fred turned over the first rows against the wood, as he progressed the girls began collecting. They worked in pairs filling the buckets, putting large in one medium in another and the small ones, referred to as 'pig potatoes' in a third. Sometimes it was easier to leave the third bucket in one spot and throw the potatoes near it to be gathered up later. Fred got down off the tractor and picked up a bucket, there were not many potatoes at all. He was disappointed, "Either poachers or a poor crop" he said. As he looked along the strip he had uncovered it was clear that there were more potatoes emerging further into the field. He left the bucket and went back to the tractor. Four more rows and things were looking better. Fred knew that someone had been helping themselves but there was little that he could do about it. He could not have had the fields watched twenty four hours a day. There were two ways the potatoes were taken whether by poachers or just folk taking advantage of the remote location of Fred's fields. Those trying not to attract attention would dig into the ridge with their hands remove the large potatoes at the root and then replace the soil and break up any footprints before leaving. The field would look just as before and the plant would carry on growing just with less of a crop. Others would pull the whole plant out and kick the soil back into place to make it look as though it had never been there at all. They would then throw the leafy tops away into the bushes but there would be gaps appearing in the rows and the discarded plants were found by the likes of the gamekeeper or Ted Lockett.

Fred helped with the picking, working his way back from the tractor. When the buckets were full they were carried to the edge of the field and emptied into the sacks. The large and medium potatoes were put into the corn sacks. The small potatoes were bagged in any old sacks. The morning progressed slowly, it was back breaking work and coats were soon discarded. Bags were put further in the field to save walking to the edge. There was little to talk about as they worked, they knew better than to moan about potato picking in front of their Dad. He rarely said anything but if he told their Mother there would be trouble. William was a constant source of amusement as he carried potatoes back and forth. Dorothy had said he should start and learn about farming at an early age. Mary wondered if sitting on the ground sucking the soil off a potato was teaching him much. Fred called the breaks when they were to take a bite to eat.

As they sat on the sacks and looked over the field Grace again asked "Why doesn't Dad get more help this will take days?"

"I know what you mean," said Mary "if there were more pickers the tractor would be moving more instead of being stood there. It isn't much better than the horses. Perhaps one day they will invent a machine that picks them and puts them in the bags".

"Well, they will never buy one while they have us working for free."

"That's true, we have to earn our keep remember."

Hannah had been gazing at the tractor now she got up and went over to where her father sat.

"Dad, Is the tractor safe out there?"

"Of course lass why do you ask?"

"Well the Thunderbolts fly so low they could knock the exhaust off."

"I have heard that story lass. The beggars are known for hedge hopping but don't worry, I have been keeping an eye open and anyway they could not get down in here."

Hannah looked around; she could see her father's point. The woods would make it very difficult to fly down to the fields.

"I see what you mean" she said and went back to join her sisters. Fred winked at William, "The Yanks may be daft but they are not stupid are they lad?" William grinned. "No Dad."

In the afternoon Fred ploughed a good few rows then re-hitched the trailer and with Gunter's help began collecting the bags from around the field. When the trailer was full they took them down to the white gate and put them against the hedge just in the field. Turner's were to send a lorry for collection before the end of the day. The potatoes could not be left out all night as they would most likely go missing. At the end of the day the trailer was taken around to collect the buckets, part filled and empty sacks then finally the girls and William. When they got down in the farmyard they looked like little old aged pensioners, their backs were aching so badly that they could hardly stand up straight. Fred left the tractor where it was and they all went inside for a quick wash and cup of tea before starting all the feeding and milking. Before Fred had time to drink his tea there was a lorry at the front gate.

"Surry I thought I'd at least get chance for a cup of tea."

He went off down the drive it was Turners come to collect the sacks of potatoes.

The sacks were tallied and Fred was given a receipt, which he brought in and gave to Dorothy for safekeeping.

"I hope none of those sacks goes missing. The driver is not beyond counting a few short, you know what they are like you can't trust anyone these days" she said.

"It's written down there lass. I will be in their office on the double if the numbers don't tally." He went to the back door and fetched in a bucket with a sample from the field for Dorothy to see. "Who would have thought that a blackberry patch like that could have grown potatoes as good as this?"

Dorothy picked up a couple of the potatoes and looked at them.

"These are better than the ones we grew under the Hatch. My goodness Fred, you should get a good price if they are all as good as these."

"They are Dot, they are."

When all was finally done for the day everyone sat around the kitchen table and listened to the radio. The Arnhem disaster was still in the news. "It won't be over by Christmas after all" said Mary. The girls all went to bed early taking up bowls of warm water to wash in as the dairy was too cold. Fred sat in his favourite chair puffing on his pipe as the music played. Dorothy noticed he was smiling from ear to ear.

"What are you smiling about? You should be worn out after today."

"I was just thinking about those King Edwards we have lifted today, they have done well. I think they have turned out far above the average yield and they have lifted so cleanly. I could see where the poachers had taken a few but there is not much we can do about them."

"How long do you reckon it will take to finish. The longer they are up there the more will go missing."

"We should have the lot done by the end of the week. Mr Jones will tell us how many sacks we are allowed to keep back for ourselves. There are a few pig potatoes but not a lot. After he has had a look at the field I will run the arrows over it and there should be quite a few more for us, those that we don't keep I can soon get rid of on the side" he said, still smiling.

"You be careful Fred Thomas we don't want anyone talking now do we. You know that Mr Jones can make life very difficult for us."

"Don't you worry about that; the amount that he has allowed us is more than we shall need. There are some round here that have no problem getting what they need, like Percy Podmore. I hear the amount of meat he puts on the plates at those functions is far more than would be expected but then you only have to look who is eating it. The yanks can get pretty well anything they want when they go there and I'll bet that Bill Corfield takes more than enough milk when he goes round."

"Yes I know all that, our Lizzy let's drop some of the things that go on but I don't want us getting caught" she said.

"Lass, there is plenty of wheeling and dealing going on everywhere. I will have no difficulty getting rid of a few surplus potatoes."

"All right I will go along with you but be careful, let us see what the final tally is." Fred pondered for a moment "You know Dot it will be grand when we can buy a barrel of cider again. A barrel used to last us to the end of the hay harvest. We could do with a drink of cider this week; I can almost taste it you know."

"Sorry all we have is the spring water and you do not want to trade potatoes for cider."

"Just wishful thinking."

After ten days the girls were able to go back to school but there was a lot of catching up to do. Grace was so disappointed she was no longer able to part take in the school drama performance, another girl she did not like had taken her place.

"It's just not fair, I miss out on everything I like doing" she complained.

"It's the same for me, I have been left out of the choir because they were practicing for the Christmas carol service" replied Hannah.

"I often wonder, if I was still in the school drama group I might have become a real actress and think of how rich I might have become".

"Who knows, the worst thing is we have to catch up with the class work. I am going to borrow Jane Ford's books and copy it up." Grace was not listening "Imagine that we were able to go to school all the time, just think how clever we could be, just think what good jobs we might get".

"Yes just think about it. Why did I bother with taking the Eleven plus Exam if I have got to stay at home and pick potatoes? I don't need to pass exams to pick spuds."

"Well Dad has said nothing about lifting the swedes or mangolds so we had better keep quiet or we will miss even more school."

"Oh Lordy" said Hannah.

Exercise books were expensive and the girls knew that they would be given detention if pages were torn from their books. Dorothy did not care and several times she made them take out pages giving them to Helen and William to draw on.

"Let 'em have a bit of paper, the teacher won't notice a couple of pages missing."

"They will" said Grace "and then we will get detention".

"Nonsense!" Dorothy retorted "I pay enough for you to go there, a few pages won't hurt".

The teachers were quick to recognize when pages had been torn from books, and soon it was noticed that Hannah's books were thinner the staples looser. The next day Grace's books were checked, neither of the girls could say what had really happened so they were given detention, fortunately both were kept back on the same evening. When they finally arrived home they were fed up and to make matters worse Dorothy was in a bad mood.

"Where have you been to until now? You are to be up this road by four o'clock, there is work to be done". The two girls stood there then Grace said loudly "You got us put in detention by taking the pages from our books we have to stay over tomorrow night as well".

"It's only a bit of paper what's wrong with them teachers?"

"Miss Bygott said if you write her a note with an explanation she might let us off" said Grace.

"We have a farm to run, what is a bit of paper?" Dorothy said. "I'll be writing no notes you have jobs to do now get changed and get on."

Upstairs the two girls were fuming, Grace summed it up "So it is all right to get us in trouble and all right to complain when we are late but not all right to tell the truth, this is so unfair". Hannah could not argue with that, it was unfair. They changed and went outside; as they walked across the farmyard Grace stopped and turned to Hannah "I've had enough of her moaning I'm going to see Mrs Podmore about earning some money for myself".

"You can't" said Hannah looking around in case anyone was listening.

"I can. I'm going to call at the Glen and see Mrs. Podmore. I will ask her if there is any work for me to do perhaps in the evenings and at the weekends."

"Are you going to ask Mam first?"

"No. I will see if they will have me first and if not I will find something else. Perhaps a Saturday job in Wellington. Only then will I tell her what I'm proposing to do."

"Oh dear, Oh Lordy" exclaimed Hannah "rather you than me".

"You worry too much, can't you see we are not kids anymore. We are growing up. I hate this place, all the muck and wet. One day I will leave for good."

Hannah was astonished to hear Grace go on like this.

The next day they had detention again and after school, as they got their bikes Grace was still complaining. "This is the last straw, tomorrow I will be late, but not because of Mam. You will have to go on without me when we get to the Glen."

"Are you going to ask for a job?"

"Yes. You can tell Mam I'm waiting for Lizzy if you want." As they walked out of the gate Grace kicked the wall lightly.

"You don't see many of the other girls wearing shoes like these. I want some money of my own to buy proper girl's shoes."

That night she spoke to Lizzy who thought it a good idea. The following evening they stopped outside the Forest Glen. Lizzy came out, she had been waiting for them and was hoping that Grace might get a job there and was looking forward to company on the trip home.

"You get on back" Lizzy said to Hannah. "You can tell Mam that Grace will come back with me." Hannah set off not looking forward to telling their Mother.

Dorothy saw Hannah coming up the drive on her own.

"Now where is that Grace?" she said out loud, Helen was back already and looking after William. As soon as Hannah got through the door she shouted.

"Where's your sister? Has she got detention again? You know you have to come back together."

'She is coming" Hannah replied. She noticed the pile of dirty dishes in the sink waiting to be washed, normally one of Grace's jobs.

"What do you mean, coming?"

"She has called at the Glen. She said to tell you that she would be coming home with Lizzy."

"Oh she has, has she? We'll see about that. Get out of them fancy clothes and get the jobs seen to." Hannah was glad not to have to do the washing up. She ran upstairs and changed from her school uniform into an old dress. As soon as she was outside she went and found Mary.

"What is the rush? Has Mam made a drink?" asked Mary.

"I didn't stop to see got out as soon as I could."

"Why what have you done now?"

"Not me. Grace has stopped off at the Glen, says she's going to get a job there."

"What's Mam say to her getting a job?"

"I haven't told her why she had stayed; I only said that she had stopped off at the Glen and that she would be coming home with Lizzy."

"Oh this should be interesting; there'll be a row tonight."

There was an atmosphere as the two girls walked in. Dorothy was on her own it was if a thundercloud hung over her head.

"Where have you been till now madam? I expect you back here on time not this late." Grace expected this and was not worried about not having her tea, she had a cooked school dinner and Margaret Podmore had given her a cup of tea and a piece of cake at 4 o'clock with Lizzy. If she was hungry later on she would go down to the kitchen after everyone had gone to bed.

"Mrs Podmore says that I can go and work at the Glen to help out if I want" Grace blurted out.

"She does, does she?"

"Yes, two hours some nights and weekends they are very busy. She says that I can then come home with Lizzy so she is not alone in the dark."

"And what if I say you're not."

Grace moved towards the back door before answering.

"I will go just the same."

"Don't you tell me what you will do, young lady" Dorothy screamed. Lizzy knew to get out of the way and headed off to the front room. She would get her tea when the shouting had stopped. She had warned Grace that there would be a row she could have waited till they had eaten their tea at least.

Dorothy was in full flow but Grace interrupted and told her that she was going to have her own money.

"I'll not have forty words from you" Dorothy yelled. "If I say you're not to go you will not go."

Grace was already out through the back door to find her Father. She found him in the stackyard and told him what she was proposing to do as he lit his pipe and listened.

"Talk to her" she pleaded with him.

"I'll see what I can do. But how come they need help, aren't there enough of them?"

"There are dinner dances and weddings and social things. Lizzy says there is more to do when the day staff has gone. I just want some money."

"Your Mam's just worried about the work getting done around here."

"It always gets done, we work hard don't we? I can go to the Glen at weekends can't I?"

"I expect so" he said wearily. He knew the only way to placate Dorothy would be to mention money.

"You won't be asking your Mam for so much if you get this job I take it?" he asked.

"Oh no I will be able to get my own things I promise."

"I reckon so then, I will have a word later."

"Thanks Dad" she said and skipped off towards the house. She went in and before Dorothy could start on her she said, "Dad says it's all right" and ran off upstairs.

Dorothy sat at the table fuming. They needed a full time farmhand she thought, then the sooner those girls left school and earned their own money the better. What they did for a living she was not bothered but she would make them pay for their keep then. Her only interest was William and what could be done for him. She thought things over, Grace would have her food at the Forest Glen on weekends and the money she would earn would stop her whining about having her hair cut properly. She had not liked asking Grace to do any shopping for her because any change that came her way she had spent on herself much to Dorothy's annoyance, she considered the spending frivolous and wasteful. She could put a bit towards clothes and school things too, so why should she object?

She looked at the sink full of washing up still waiting to be done. If she wants washing up she can start here she thought.

No way was she going to let Grace think she approved of her washing dishes.

Later in the evening when all the work was done and everyone was listening to the wireless Grace joined Hannah at the table to write an essay as part of her English homework. Dorothy let her settle down, then when there was a break in the broadcast she said "I'm not working myself to death so that you can have a good education and then you end up washing dishes for the likes of Mrs Podmore."

Grace wanted to answer back that she was going to get a really good job with lots of money but thought better of it.

"And another thing there will be no stopping until the early hours of the mornings for you" Grace concentrated on her writing. Dorothy gave up "you mark my words" she said and went back to her reading, pulling the lamp closer to her making it difficult for Grace to see.

When they went to bed Grace said to Hannah "Why is she so mean? Why can't we have things like other girls have? Do you really think that they are so hard up for money? All we hear about is what has to be done for William".

"You are lucky. I did not think you would get away with it. She is still talking about rearing more and more poultry and that will mean more plucking and dressing to be done."

"Well I will not be helping unless I get paid and the chances of that are pretty unlikely."

"None of us will get paid. She will say that the money made at the butchers will pay for Christmas."

"No it is all for our schooling remember and she won't let us forget it."

"Oh. Maybe we will get something nice from our grandmas this time."

"Don't hold your breath" said Grace "it has been a long day and I want to sleep".

Saturday morning Grace was up early with Lizzy. She washed in the bedroom taking up warm water in a bowl. Only William and Helen were bathed in front of the kitchen range now. The older girls felt embarrassed stripping off in front of each other and so they used the bowl emptying it into a bucket when they had finished. After dressing she brushed her hair and was ready to go. Downstairs was quiet, Fred was outside with Mary and their Mother was still in bed. Grace and Lizzy had breakfast and cycled off to the Forest Glen. It was bitter cold so they kept their scarves tight around their necks, the cold wind cut through their gloves chilling their fingers but it was not long before they were in the warm. Grace loved it from the moment she set foot inside. It was so warm and clean, a little like being at school but far smaller. The work was straightforward and easily paced. At the end of the day Margaret was pleased with her and said to return on the Sunday for a few hours.

When she got home and told Hannah and Helen they were not pleased.

"So it is down to us two to do yours and Mary's work and look after William is it?" As it was Mary did all her usual work as the trade at the cottage was down considerably because of the cold weather.

Dorothy saw what was happening and insisted that Mary and Grace did not shirk their responsibilities.

"Thank you very much" said Grace at bedtime. "I got a right telling off. I can do my work all right, you will see. It is only looking after William and the washing up that you have extra and Helen can do most of that."

"I don't want to do any more work" said Helen defiantly.

"Well I think it is about time, we all get picked on here, you should know that. I had to do more work when Rebecca went and then on Sunday when Mary started up the Wrekin, it is just your turn to do more." Hannah was depressed "How did we find the time to walk the woods and pick flowers?" she said. "It seems so long ago now."

"Well I think we are growing up, you wait till you get a job it is brilliant. I can't see us going to university or such the way they make us stay off to help around here. I just hope Mam does not apply for me to leave school at fourteen to have me working here for a whole year it would not be fair."

"That is next year though" said Hannah.

"I know but they keep us off so much and I am fed up of it. We have not a cat in hell's chance of going to any university. I still want to make the most of what I can. It looks as if we have to get jobs for ourselves or we will never have any money of our own."

Hannah could not argue with her, she went to bed that night wondering what she would be doing when she left school. A teacher perhaps or a nurse, May be an ATS girl or an ambulance driver that would be fun, definitely not a land girl, one of those already" she mumbled as she fell asleep.

On Sunday Margaret Podmore told Grace there were two dinner dances booked for the coming week and she could work for two hours on each of the two nights if she wanted. Grace said yes immediately, the thought of some more money so soon was very tempting. On Monday Grace stopped off while Hannah continued home alone. Grace had a uniform that she kept there and set to work arranging tables and chairs, then setting the cutlery and adding any decorations. Margaret found Grace to be very useful; she was so keen and would work for little and be gone as soon as she was not needed without needing a lift. Yes, the Thomas girls were very useful and no trouble at all. She had insisted that Grace left just after eight o'clock. She had seen the guests arriving and it was clear that she had enjoyed it. "I don't think the Thomas girls have seen much of life stuck up on that farm" she said to Percy. "It suits us as they are such hard workers but I wonder where they will end up when they are older."

On Tuesday Hannah and Grace went straight home, it was Lizzy's day off and there were no dinner parties that night, the next was Thursday. Hannah was unhappy with that as it meant she would have to get the battery and cycle back alone as Grace said she must not be late for work. As they passed the Forest Glen, Hannah said. "So you are back there on Thursday are you?"

"Yes and I can't wait, I shall see an actual band playing like Lizzy has told us." Hannah had no enthusiasm for the conversation so simply said, "That should be nice for you" and cycled on in silence until it was too steep and they had to walk.

The nights were dark and they had no lights, trusting to their excellent night vision and familiarity of the roads. Creatures scurried in the undergrowth but it did not bother them at all.

"It is going to be lonely on my own. I have never been to school without anyone before" said Hannah.

"You soon get used to it; at least your bike is less of a wreck than this thing. You never know they might let you have some lights if the war ends."

At home there were the jobs to be done and then it was homework on the kitchen table. After a week Grace loved her job, she saw how beautiful the ladies were dressed and with her own money she went shopping after school on the nights she did not have to work. Although it was very little she was able to spend it as she wished. It made Dorothy furious, buying fancy things like ribbons and slides for her hair, little trinkets of no value just ornamental. Dorothy hinted that she should give her the money to help pay for her keep rather than waste it. Grace had no intentions of doing any such thing and took no notice.

Hannah missed having Grace for company. They were in different classes at school and Grace went her own way at the end of the school day. The batteries were now left for Hannah to sort out and carry home. Grace was behind in her homework and fell out with her Mother so much that she worked upstairs alone much as she had always done when reading her books. Dorothy was not prepared to give any praise for coping with school, homework and a part time job.

Hannah became so lonely struggling back alone she complained to Dorothy, it did not go down well. She told

Fred her problems while helping with the feeding, how hard she worked and how lonely she felt. A week later arriving home cold wet and miserable, Dorothy told her that if all went well and she worked hard she could go and stay with her Grandma at the Manor for a couple of weeks next summer. Hannah was thrilled to bits with the thought that she could visit Grandma and see Rebecca again. She had made only one short visit to the Manor since Rebecca had left all that time ago. She had gone along with her parents in the car and had been met by Rebecca as soon as they arrived. They had such a good time that Hannah had often asked when she could next go out there but with petrol rationing there was no possibility of any more social visits.

The Dinner dances at the Forest Glen had become extremely popular with the forces and there was plenty of work for everyone. Typically there would be over a hundred guests seated with more expected later for the dancing. Everyone ate a lavish meal by wartime standards, much of it supplied locally. After the meal was over the men left the tables to replenish their beer glasses at the well stocked bar. As long as everyone was having a good time there were no questions asked how it was acquired. There was plenty of money to pay for it, and how many of these men were going to be alive at the war's end. For the dancing, space had to be made As soon as places were vacated the waitresses, including Lizzy, came and cleared away the dirty dishes and removed the tablecloths. Percy took the empty tables folded them and then stacked them in the anteroom next door. When two thirds of the tables had gone the remaining chairs were moved to the outside of the room ready for the dancing to commence. The musician's, who were usually smartly dressed in black dinner jackets, were set up in the far corner of the room and played all the popular tunes of the day both American and British. Everyone had a good time. There was always a little friction when the services got together but rarely at the Forest Glen. The girls were almost as outgoing as many of the men. As the evening progressed, many couples paired off and went outside to get closer. Some went as far as the wooded slopes nearby, to make love in the moonlight. It was times like this that inhibitions were put aside none could be certain where they would be in six months time or even if they would be alive. Inside there were many calls to drink to those abroad or who had lost their lives. Men from the 495th Fighter Training Group often attended and during the night would be heard to call for a toast to their fallen comrades. So many had been involved in crashes in the area, two had died in a mid-air crash right above the Wrekin in September.

The dancing would continue late into the night and when the band finished there was always an encore something slow and then those not already drunk would cram as much down as they could before Percy shut the bar. Sometimes they would buy the bottles from behind the bar which was always a worry in case they were broken where people had to walk the following day. They would stagger out into the night air where the transport was waiting. Often they were so drunk that they did not know what they were doing or whom they were doing it with.

Even though the weather deteriorated there was no let up in the popularity of these dances. The young soldiers made passes at all the girls, Lizzy and the other waitresses kept out of the way once the tables were cleared. It was one such evening when Jane from Wellington slammed a tray down.

"Do I look like a doll?" she said sarcastically. "Am I a babe or a broad?"

"I don't know" said Lizzy "are they getting rowdy?"

"They all think they are movie stars or something, even our lads are talking like Yanks with their stupid boozed up egos. All trying to prove something to the lasses." Jane was in her late thirties and did not consider herself a babe at least not from some young soldier who looked as though he had only just started shaving that week!

As the night went on, couples left the pavilion to get more intimate sometimes things went too far and that was the case that evening.

Early the next morning an open backed lorry was being driven carefully along the frozen Ercall, everywhere was white over with frost. It was on its way to the Maddocks Hill Quarry and in the back there were a group of men huddled against the cold. As it trundled downhill toward the Forest Glen one of the men in the back saw something. "What's that?" he said standing up as the lorry swayed, he banged on the cab roof "stop, stop" he yelled. The lorry shuddered to a stop and the men in the back were thrown forward.

"What's wrong?" several asked.

"There's a woman lying in the bushes back there" said the man standing up craning his neck to see over the back at the undergrowth at the side of the road. Several others stood up and looked; they were almost on the bend and could not see anything. The driver shouted up to them "What the bloody hell's the matter with you lot, can't you go before you come out, and wait until we get to the hut or have you got the bloody trots?" "Jim's seen something in the wood back there, back her up a bit" one of the other men shouted. The driver obliged and began reversing; nobody was that bothered losing a bit of time. "There!" shouted one of the other men who'd stood up to see if he could spot anything. The lorry stopped, now all the men in the back took notice. "See. There's someone lying on the ground in the bracken, looks like a woman." Several of the men now saw her.

"Probably left behind from one of those dances at the Glen, just sleeping it off."

"It's bloody freezing. No one would be sleeping out here in this weather. Let's get up there." As they made their way up the bank they could see the figure was indeed a woman face down, her long dark hair coated in frost.

"Yeah just sleeping it off I expect" said one of the men nervously as they got nearer. "I've heard of what goes on at the Glen these days" the first of the men reached the prone figure. "Come on now wake up lass" he said as he bent down and shook her shoulder. "This doesn't look right" he said.

"She's only a young girl" said the next man and reached for her outstretched hand, it was grey and frozen to the touch. "See if you can sit her up, she needs help."

"Come on Miss, this is no place for a young girl to be sleeping" he turned her over and met the blank stare.

"She is dead" he said.

The men all stepped back this was something they had not bargained on.

"She's not dead is she?"

"Don't touch her any more; we had better ring for a bobby. There's a phone at the Glen."

They made their way down to the road, none of them wanting to stay with the corpse.

The driver did not believe them and went up to see for himself.

"She's been done in" he said when he returned. "Best get down to the Glen and knock them up."

"But who could have done it?" said one of the men.

"Probably one of them Yanks they get up here for the dances."

"More likely to be one of them Gerry's from the camp" said another.

"No time to waste" said the driver, "Jim, Bob you found her first so get down to the Glen and get the Bobbies out. We will make sure nobody messes with her". The two men set off down the road and around the corner to the Forest Glen where they went round the back and banged on the door.

"Stop that banging you will wake everyone up" said Percy as he opened the door to the quarrymen, still in his tweed dressing gown. He looked at them "What do you want? Cigarettes? We don't open until nine".

"Sorry to knock you up Gaffer, there is a dead girl up the road" Percy shook his head in disbelief. "Dead girl! What? A dead girl?"

"That is right, so mister, can you ring for a bobby?"

"Yes of course" he said alarmed, "go around to the front I will let you in. They will probably want to talk to you".

He rushed through to the front and was opening the door as Margaret came through "What is going on Percy?" she asked.

"There is nothing for you to worry about dear, go back to bed" he said and turned back to the quarrymen.

"Been a murder missus, up the road a piece" said one of the quarrymen.

"A murder!" she swayed visibly. "Oh I feel so faint" Percy cursed quietly.

"Margaret, put a kettle to boil and make some tea" he ordered. "These men could probably do with a strong cuppa while I phone for the Police."

"Never mind the tea, I'm going back to me mates" said Bob.

"You hang about" said Jim "I need a cuppa after that".

Percy was almost at the phone when Margaret shouted "Lizzy! Oh lord no, it can't be Lizzy! Percy she was here last night till late, oh no."

Percy looked at the men who clearly wished they were somewhere else.

"What does she look like?" Percy said very slowly.

The two men looked at each other.

"Smart dressed with long dark hair and make up."

Margaret and Percy sighed with relief, "Of course it's not Lizzy" he said, "She's at home tucked up still in bed. It could be lass from last night's dance. I will telephone then, go and see for myself".

"Look I'm off back to the lorry," said Bob "you ring for the Bobbies" He turned and left.

"Take no notice" said Jim "make the call mister".

Percy called the police; they said they would be there as soon as they could. Margaret was in the kitchen waiting for the kettle to boil.

"I am just going to get dressed" he said. When he returned Margaret was sat at the kitchen table, hands trembling as she tried to drink the freshly made tea. "I will just go up and take a look" Percy said to her.

"Don't leave me on my own. The murderer could be hiding in the backyard."

"You're all right dear; lock the door as I leave. Don't open it to anyone. I won't be long."

He went through to the front and fetched Jim through, locking the front door first.

"Please don't stay there" Margaret said from the kitchen.

"Just lock the door after me, I won't be long" and with Jim he slipped out of the back door into the cold morning air.

Fifteen minutes later he returned banging on the door and reassuring Margaret before she let him in. He had brought the rest of the men except Bob who stayed with the lorry. Percy put a pot of tea out for them and returned to the kitchen with Margaret.

"Have you seen her" asked Margaret closing the door.

"Yes I think she was here last night."

"They won't blame us, will they? Oh Percy they will not take our licence away would they? Oh dear, Oh dear."

"Calm down dear, the Police will be here soon. There will be a lot of questions to be answered. It will be nothing to do with us".

She was worried "What could have happened?"

"Who knows, the police will have to sort it out. But for now it could be that she passed out drunk and froze" he did not want to worry her. Then he heard his name being called, "The police have arrived by the sound of it, go and get dressed dear". He went to leave, "Oh Percy please don't go" she said, "I think she has been murdered".

"Now dear don't be silly. We don't know anything yet." She was not listening, "Do you think he's still here hiding" she said.

"Who?"

"The man who has murdered that poor girl."

"Calm down and let me speak to the police."

"Oh Percy" she moaned, "how dreadful" she lifted her tired, heavy body from the stool and made her way to the bedroom.

Later Hannah and Grace arrived at the Forest Glen on their way to school, two policemen stood in the road barring them from going up the Ercall. "We have to go to school" said Grace "let us through please".

"Sorry girls, no one is going through here. Go down to Cluddely."

"What is going on?"

"Just do as you are told" said the policeman impassively.

The girls turned their bikes and set off down the Cluddely Road. They looked over their shoulders and saw there was a lot of activity on the road they were meant to be traveling.

"What is going on down there?" said Hannah slowing almost to a stop.

"I don't know looks like a car accident" Grace answered. "Keep going or we are going to be late." They pedaled on down the road leading to Cluddely, they would then have to cycle along the main road into town and they did not want to be late for school.

The Police kept the road closed all morning, moving the girl's body to the Wellington mortuary and combing the area for evidence. The quarrymen were soon sent on their way and everyone at the Forest Glen was interviewed during the day. Lizzy arrived early; there were police and several military vehicles on the car park, so she rushed in through the back door. Margaret Podmore told her the news and she was mortified. The girl had been identified as serving in the forces and the case was handed over to the military police. The local police were no longer to continue with the investigation.

The news spread quickly during the day. Wilf Wilkins was told by one of the quarrymen who was convinced one of the German prisoners from the camp was responsible. This worried Wilf, what if there was a murderer on the loose? He rushed off back to the cottage to tell Joyce. The story was gathering momentum.

“Never, never;” Joyce exclaimed in disbelief. “Poor, poor girl, strangled and her neck broken you say, how awful, they must catch him. Oh dear Wilf I feel so faint.” She sat down on Wilf’s chair, something he would usually never allow her to do.

“Put the kettle to boil” she said. “My body has gone all limp. I don’t think that my legs will take my weight for one moment longer.”

“Are you all right dear? I did not mean to shock you so. It was what the fellow from the quarry said.”

“Wilf you keep that shotgun handy. This is terrible news; no one is safe while the killer is at large. We must lock the door tonight. I have told you and told that we should now lock the door at nights especially with the prison camp so close.” Yes dear” Wilf said as he made the tea. He was quite taken aback, she did not normally talk to him in this manner, and he gave the orders. When the tea was ready he took two cups and joined her, she was clearly agitated.

“Nobody is sure there is a killer on the loose, it’s only what the chap from the quarry said.”

“A girl is dead right on our doorstep.” She drank her tea and passed him the cup.

“Get me another please.” Wilf did as he was told without arguing. She regained her composure after drinking the second cup.

“Do they know down at the Willowmoor’s? Those girls, oh my goodness, all those girls and there’s Lizzy.”

“What about her?”

“She walks those roads at all hours. Two or three times a week, now they have so many of those dinner dances. It can be two in the morning before she gets home.”

"I wouldn't have a daughter of mine coming in at that time of the morning" said Wilf. "I would put a stop to that".

"You put a stop to us having a daughter" she said sharply. Wilf was dumbstruck. She got up "Where is my hat? I must go and warn Fred and Dorothy Thomas, yes I must, and I will take the thick stick." She put her coat and hat on then picked up a good strong walking stick from the oak stand by the door.

"Let him come near me and he'll have this around his backside good and proper." Wilf looked at her. He could see she was very serious

"Are you sure that you are all right to walk down those fields or should I come with you?" he said.

"Of course not, you must keep watch here we do not want the murderer creeping into the house while I am away and keep a watch on all sides of the house". Wilf stood there and watched her go. Out through the garden gate and off down the field she went, swinging her stick wildly about her as if swatting flies.

In the kitchen Dorothy saw her coming. Fred and Mary were sat taking a morning break.

"Come and look at this, it's Joyce Wilkins coming down the field but I don't know what she is doing."

Fred got up and took a look "There is not any wasps out at this time of year" he said puzzled at her antics. "Just look at the way she's swinging that stick." They watched her until she was coming up the yard then Fred went to the door and opened it.

"Good Morning Joyce" he said. "How are you and why are you swinging that stick like that?"

"Its murder, There's been a murder. Have you not heard?"

"Murder you say, come in and sit down."

"Murder! what murder?" Dorothy asked. Joyce went to the table and sat next to Mary. "A young girl, down at the Glen, last night! The quarrymen found her this morning."

"What young girl?"

"They told my Wilf that it was probably an ATS girl, one of those that go to those dinner dances" she was very agitated.

"Gunter said that there was a lot going on down there on the Ercall side of the Glen" Fred said. "He said it looked like a road accident." He thought for a second, "There was a dinner dance last night, our Lizzy has been home safe and gone back down this morning. She never said a word."

"You've let her go to work with a murderer on the loose."

"Just a minute, slow up a bit. Well she wouldn't know would she?" Joyce was not listening. "I've always told my Wilf that all young girls should be in bed by nine o'clock at night, not out dancing and drinking. They say it could be one of the prisoners from the camp and he could still be out there. Did she have to walk home last night?"

"She has her bike" said Mary "But she walks up the banks".

"I had better go and make sure that she has got there all right and the other two as well" said Fred worried.

"Now don't go panicking" said Dorothy. "A murder committed at the Forest Glen whatever next, let me get you a cup of tea."

Fred picked up the car keys from the mantle shelf.

"Wait a minute while I change my frock" said Mary "I'm coming with you."

"Alright but hurry up" he said and taking his coat and cap set off to the garage.

Dorothy poured tea for her and Joyce; the news had given her quite a fright. When they arrived at the Forest Glen there were still some police vehicles on the car park. They hurried to the back door and knocked, Percy Podmore opened the door surprised to see them. "Are you here about the incident Mr Thomas, or do you want to use the phone?"

"We have just heard Joyce Wilkins came running down the fields with the terrible news. We have come to make sure Lizzy got here all right this morning. I'd have brought her down myself this morning if we had known."

"She is fine, come on through" said Percy, they followed him through to the kitchen where they sat down.

"Do they know who's responsible?" asked Mary.

"Leaving all that to the police, I'm sure they will find whoever did it."

Lizzy came through from the middle kitchen, "What are you two doing here?" she asked. "Checking that you are all right lass, we've just heard about the murder. Are you coming home a bit earlier tonight?"

"Oh yes" confirmed Percy. "She finishes at six." Then he left them to talk for a while. Twenty minutes later he came back with the news that it was considered a military matter.

"Then we don't have a murderer running loose?" asked Fred.

"No it looks like it was someone who was here last night."

"That is a relief. The other two will be all right then."

"Yes" said Percy "there is no more threat around here". Fred and Mary returned with the news. Joyce was still there and at first did not believe what she was told. Then she said "It's those Yanks, I know it, and they have all the money. Those do's down at the Glen are bad, there is too much drinking and carrying on. It will happen again" and with that she got her coat and hat and set off back to the Hatch.

Fred watched her go "Wilf will get it in the neck now for sure" he said "anyway too much excitement for one day, best get on with it" and he went back to the farmyard.

That evening Grace called at the Forest Glen. Hannah carried on alone, unaware of the day's events. She was surprised that Mary was sat at the table with Dorothy, no sign of Helen and William.

"Haven't you any work to do" she asked Mary. Before Mary could speak Dorothy said "What news from the Glen? Have they caught him?"

"Caught who?" she said.

"The murderer" said Mary, "you know did you see it this morning?"

"I have no idea what you are talking about" said Hannah taking off her gloves and scarf. "There were policeman at the Glen; they made us go down the Cluddely way".

"A girl was found there this morning, dead, poor thing" said Dorothy. Hannah's mouth dropped open and she stood there aghast, then she said "We thought there had been an accident, or something, nobody has said anything at school. Is the murderer out there then?"

"They say not" said Mary "they say it was probably a soldier at the Glen last night".

"Oh Lordy it is terrible news. Grace has stopped off, is Lizzy here or still down there?"

"Everyone is going about their business as usual now; the police were there all morning. Dad and me went down there to see if Lizzy was all right and that is when we were told that it might be a soldier."

"But they don't know for sure, you said so, have we got to go to school tomorrow?"

"Of course it's too important to miss" said Dorothy.

"We just wondered if it was an American that did it" said Mary. Hannah was now all questions, Dorothy could see she had no news, so sent her to go and get changed; they would wait till Lizzy got home to find out the latest.

When Lizzy and Grace arrived home they were subdued and neither wanted to talk of the day's events. It had been determined that it was indeed a military matter and there was no civilian threat. Mary went up to the Hatch to tell Joyce Wilkins the latest news.

Later when Hannah got a chance she asked Lizzy what had happened as she had very little idea of what went on at a dinner dance. Grace had told her all about the jobs that had to be done but she was always gone when the party began so she asked "Did you se the girl who was murdered last night?"

"Not this morning but probably last night" said Lizzy wearily "she would have been at the tables or the bar".

"What did she look like?" asked Hannah without thinking.

"Look there is lots of people at the dances, we only look after the tables, and she could have been anyone."

"So what happened then?" asked Hannah, "was it an American soldier?"

Lizzy had heard enough, she was upset but did not want anyone to know. "It has been a long day and you know we don't really know much about the real world so leave it be and let's get on as normal." Hannah realized Lizzy did not want to talk and went off to pester Grace. The death of a person was not something any of the girls were familiar with. Animals died, they died all the time. People were different but everyday lives were lost, hundreds sometimes thousands, it was different though, always somewhere else and always somebody else, that was war. To Lizzy something had changed, the murder had struck a chord, even though it was not someone they knew. Someone had died yards from where she had been working; a girl's life had been taken away. One of the soldiers who looked such fun had turned into a killer. It opened her eyes.

Grace was cornered by Hannah and soon got fed up of the questions, she told her to stop being a nuisance.

"I am not a nuisance, what if the murderer is still out there, he might be at the next dance."

"Lizzy is upset and does not want Mam to know. She does not want Mam stopping her working at the Glen."

"Would she?"

"I don't know, but it would help if you did not go on so much."

"I am only asking it is not everyday that something like this happens, my friends are bound to ask me questions. You see, what would happen if the murderer was hiding in the barn? You have to think of these things don't you?"

"No. Anyway if there is anyone around whom we don't know Dad will see them off the bank with the shotgun."

For days after the girls kept their eyes open worried that somebody could be lurking around. Gossip was rife and there were some that said the Forest Glen should be stopped from holding the dances. But as it was confirmed that a soldier had been charged with the murder and the dances were so popular they carried on as before. The waitresses however were a little more cautious and Lizzy always made a point of checking she was not being followed when she set off for home at the end of the night.

In November a new threat to Britain emerged in a broadcast. Mr Churchill told of rockets called V2's that were now being launched from Holland against London with terrible results. As well as the V1 flying bomb it was clear that the Germans were not through with the civilian population. In December they flooded huge areas of Dutch countryside making liberation even less likely and then as Christmas drew near a sudden counter attack in the Ardenne region caught the Allies by surprise. The operation would become known as the Battle of the Bulge and for some time it looked as though the Germans would break through to Antwerp severing the Allies northern supply line. All through the Christmas period the fighting raged. The weather was severe and there was grave concern that the Germans might break the Allies down, but it was a last ditch effort and the overwhelming might of the Allies would win through.

At the Willowmoor farm Dorothy made quite an effort for Christmas as William was now three years old. There were presents for everyone, mostly clothes but also some treats that she had been saving the coupons up for. On Christmas Day they gave thanks to the Canadians, Americans and all the other nationalities braving the bitter winter weather to beat back the German armies. Ken and Imogen could see that the people of Holland were not going to be liberated; the aim was clearly to smash through to Berlin before the Russians. This worried them as they intended to return to Holland as soon as peace was established. It was not a happy Christmas for them.

CHAPTER 12

VICTORY

On the farm work was as any other in the New Year of 1945 but the weather was particularly harsh and water was a problem. The troughs were frozen and even though protected, the pump on the back yard froze solid, then the snow came. For several days there was no way out, all the roads were blocked. Eventually the road to Wellington was opened and the girls went back to school walking almost all the way because of the risk of falling off their bikes.

Jack Munslow had agreed for the threshing to be done early February. Due to demand there was no leeway, everything had to be ready for the agreed day. Fred was worried about getting the right amount of help on the day and had to offer more money than usual. He was seen as being wealthy and easily able to afford a few extra shillings, One-eyed Jack was the worst. "Just because I've got a tractor dunna mean I'm rich Jack" Fred told him.

"You have got to be, how else do you get one?" Jack replied. Fred could see he could not win. "Look how big our place is, we need the tractor to make use of the ground."

"Which makes you richer" said Jack triumphantly. "Thirty bob to help out I want."

Dorothy was not impressed when Fred told her. "We may as well get a lad from the village, may appreciate a bit of cash." Fred was torn, he did not want to upset Jack but neither did he want Dorothy's moaning about the cost. He already had two lads lined up as neither Joe Evans or his son could spare the time. In the end Jack turned up on the day for less than he demanded, but it was on the understanding that the radio would be kept on and any news would be brought out by one of the girls.

On the day everyone was on time, work went well and at lunchtime the news was of another gain in Germany. Everyone was sat around the kitchen table as Dorothy and the girls passed over the plates. "Keep going lads. Push them back" shouted Fred. Everyone agreed. After they had eaten and were drinking their tea, Wilf leant back in his chair "Let's not forget the lads in Burma, those Japs are worse than the Germans" he said. "Rubbish, them slant eyed little beggars are not worth bothering with" said Jack. There followed a heated debate that was starting to get serious when Fred called a halt and they went outside to get on.

After the threshing was done and the yard was clear, Fred breathed a sigh of relief. He was glad of the peace and quiet; he lit his pipe and sat on the granary steps. A bigger yield than ever before, a good supply of straw and plenty of dead rats!

Grace was getting along fine at the Forest Glen although she could only work limited hours to remain within the law as she was under fifteen years old. The murder had shaken everyone but demand was as great as ever, so things soon returned to normal. One evening after Grace had left Margaret passed comment to Percy "That Girl will never be content to stay at home and work on the farm, she hates having to miss lessons to help out. I reckon as soon as she has finished school she will be off to pastures new. I wonder what she will do".

"I agree with you Margaret. It is such a pity that she and Hannah have to miss so much school. They could go a long way Grace is such a hard little worker and can put her hand to most things. She seems very sure of herself as well which is a help these days. Has she said what interests her?"

"No, not really she is just glad to be earning some money like her sisters" she replied.

"That's right; Mary is helping out at the cottage now isn't she. Well Grace will be quite a good-looking young lady I am sure. Let us hope she finds a worthwhile profession despite missing so much school." He thought for a moment "I wonder what Lizzy would have done given half a chance."

"Lizzy is a totally different kettle of fish, I think that she is happy right here. Being a nervous girl I don't think she would have coped with the Girls' Modern School." She sighed "I wonder when this war will end?"

"Soon, I think the Germans and Japanese are not going to hold on much longer. Maybe we can get back to normal then. These dinner dances can be quite rowdy affairs."

"They have kept us afloat though. We have not done so badly."

"And when it is over we will do even better."

Lizzy was quite happy with her job and bringing back extra food from the functions always kept her in Dorothy's good books.

Dorothy was doing the accounts after they had received payment for the harvest. She had to tell Fred as it was the best she had ever seen, so she went to the kitchen where he was sitting.

"But am we all right?" he asked as usual.

"Of course. That is what I am saying we could pay a bit more off the tractor." He lit his pipe and sat back in his chair, "Why don't we get you that piano you have always wanted?"

"Really Fred that would be wonderful."

"Aye lass, best start looking in the papers."

"Don't you think it's a bit extravagant?"

"Dot, as soon as you see a good piano for sale you shall have it." She smiled at the recollection of her days at the Manor. "I hope I can remember how to play, it has been a very long time."

"Like riding a bike" he said "you will soon master it again. This war is coming to an end now I reckon and we have done well, better than most. However, it has been down to hard graft and a measure of good fortune, so let us see something for it."

A few weeks later Dorothy found out about a house clearance sale that included a piano. She could hardly wait to tell Fred but he cautioned her not to be too hasty in case it had been bashed and wrecked by children. On the day of the sale it turned out to have belonged to an old lady. It was beautifully polished and looked as if it was made of Mahogany, it was in perfect condition. All the notes sounded fine to Dorothy when she tried them, Fred couldn't tell but he could tell she wanted it by the smile on her face. The bidding was haphazard but on the piano it picked up and Fred was worried it might get too expensive. However the other contenders soon dropped out and his bid was accepted, he thought it was a good price to pay but felt a little concerned in case the other bidders knew something he did not.

"There you are lass. You now have a piano" he said as they drove away in the Wolseley, "Bought and paid for". She was smiling watching the scenery as they drove along.

"It is over this war, isn't it? You can tell, everyday a new battle is won or a town or city is liberated."

"Aye no doubt about it. They have Hitler on the run now" he said.

"I feel sorry for Imogen Winter though" said Dorothy. "Here we are buying pianos and she does not know if her family is even alive." Fred was surprised he did not think Dorothy cared too much for Imogen. She continued "And her husband Ken, he is always off here and there, she says it is important work he does".

"Aye indeed it is" said Fred. He thought very highly of Ken and spoke to him whenever he got the chance which was not often lately. After Montgomery's disastrous plan for a quick victory in Holland to be later known as a 'Bridge Too Far' Ken had been around a lot. The Battle of the Bulge and the slow progress being made across the salient had turned attention away from the relief of Holland. In December the Germans had flooded vast areas making progress impossible. Despite the awful bombing of the German cities and even the raising of Dresden to the ground, the dreaded V2 rockets still fell on London, mostly launched from The Hague. It was impossible to destroy them once they were launched, the only way to stop them was to halt supplies or capture the areas that were used for launching.

That night Fred made a point of talking to Ken who told him that the situation in Holland was severe. The people were suffering terrible hardship but while the Germans held on there was little he could do to help. "Its blood and bullets at the moment, no place for an old one like me" he said with a wry smile. He said Imogen was coping well, they knew her family was all right at the moment and that was the important thing.

That night Fred told Dorothy what Ken had said about Imogen's family.

"They will be off then when it is all over then" she said.

"Probably" he said "but who knows when that will be?"

The next day Fred took Mary and Gunter to collect the piano with the tractor and trailer. On their arrival back at the farm they decided to bring it in through the front door. By the time Fred backed the trailer up to the garden gate and got down, Dorothy already had the door and the wicket gate open, she could not wait. Carefully it was untied and the grain sacks put in place to protect it from the ropes were removed, then it was manhandled into the front room. There was a piano stool with it which had a lift up lid, forming a box to put the music papers in. To Dorothy's delight it was almost half full. As she ran her fingers along the sleek woodwork Fred could see she was thrilled to bits with it. "Go on lass, make some noise for us then" he said.

She pressed several of the keys lightly "I don't know if I can with you watching me" she said. "Mary, go and put the kettle on. Fred you go and put things away." As he went outside Fred thought he heard 'Little Brown Jug'. He grinned and wished that he had made the effort to buy one a long time ago. Dorothy practiced well and often on a Sunday evening the family would gather around the piano with the exception of Fred who sat in an armchair by the fire.

Everyone sang their loudest as their Mother played. Imogen joined them at times when Ken was away after Dorothy had sent one of the girls to get her. Even One-eyed Jack dropped in occasionally; glad of a bit of supper and a singsong. Since the bomb had dropped on his farm he had taken the war very seriously. He had worked at every threshing and harvest he could and now had a wireless of his own.

"I wants to know how them Germans like it" he said "when we drop bombs on them".

"I thought you said it was just propaganda" Fred said to him after he had gone on about taking an eye for an eye and so forth.

"Aye true" he said and paused for a moment, "but it's the right sort of propaganda you see". Fred shook his head and said no more.

Many were the songs they sang, were favourites like 'It's a long way to Tipperary', 'I will take you home again Kathleen' and 'The Old Rugged Cross'.

None of the girls were allowed to touch the piano unless it was to polish it. This annoyed them and occasionally when their parents were out shopping they would creep in, lift up the lid and try to play a tune without much luck.

There was no good news for Germany, the allies pressed on, the outcome was becoming inevitable. The bombing of Germany continued but even after the annihilation of the city of Dresden the resolve of the German people remained firm and the terrible revenge weapons the V1 and V2 still fell on London. Gunter was terribly upset at the news of Dresden, his family had moved into the city and no one had expected it to be hit, there was no strategic value there at all. He still came to the farm every day but he was withdrawn as he feared the worst. He told Fred and Mary that he had little to return to if the reports were true. He had been hoping that the war would have ended as soon as the allies crossed the Rhine. If only Hitler would give up. It would be better to surrender to the British and Americans before the Russians overran and destroyed the German people. Unfortunately for Gunter there was no sign of an end, it would be the end of March before the last V2 fell on England. The blackout was lifted and it was strange to see light after dark again, William had never known it.

April saw the assault on Berlin by the Russians, the end of Germany was imminent but the fighting continued. Holland remained under occupation then on 1st May the news was released from Berlin Hitler was dead. The news was marvelous, at last surely this was the end of the war, but there was no such statement. After hearing the news in the evening the kitchen was quiet. Fred broke the silence "Surry you think they would be ringing the bells or something".

"So is the war over Dad?" asked Grace.

"I suppose not lass; his armies have not given up. They have to surrender first for it to be over."

"Does that mean the fighting goes on?" asked Helen.

"Yes" said Hannah "but it should be over soon and then we might see Sam again, won't we Mam?"

"I dare say he will be back, that is if he is still alive" Dorothy replied.

"Aye you are right there Dot. He will not lose anytime getting back if he is able."

"Will it be different when the war is over?" asked Helen. She had been three years old when the war had started.

"No more rationing will be good" said Dorothy "I for one have had enough of rations and having to produce those damned ration books".

"If Sam was all right he would have written by now" Hannah said to Mary.

"Yes I think you are right, it does not look good."

Fred relit his pipe and pondered for a while. Dorothy tuned in the wireless to some music.

"We have not managed too badly with the rationing though, have we Dot?"

"You're not the one who has had to make it go around. Two ounces of this and four ounces of that, seven kids I have had to feed, that has not been easy. You lot have had it easy. I have hardly had a decent nights' sleep not knowing when those Germans were going to invade the country. Thank goodness this could be the end of it all." Fred was not convinced, "There are a lot that have had it much worse Dot, at least we are here to tell the tale and you have done well rearing this brood" he smiled at the children their faces lit by the light from the paraffin lamp.

"I think we can all sleep easier knowing Hitler is gone, it should not be long now." The next day Fred put the radio on when he got up, the news was the same so he switched it off. It was best not to start the day off with bad news he thought, in fact it was better to get the days work done, that way there was nothing to play on the mind. During the next few days Germany collapsed, the Russians had Berlin in their grasp and the civilian population was paying a high price. On the evening of the 4th May Ken and Imogen were home in record time, they went through to their room and switched on their wireless, this must be it. "Surely the Germans must give up now" said Ken as the set warmed up. The news was excellent, Holland was free, and the occupying German army had surrendered. Imogen wept, the joy was overwhelming. Ken sat her down and made some tea "We can go home soon" he said. "There will be so much to do, so much to put right." He knew that the truth would be too much for her at this time. Many people had vanished to the death camps and it would be some time before the enormity of what had befallen the citizens under Nazi rule would emerge. On the 6th May the German navy surrendered. That evening Fred was convinced it was over, Ken Winter had said the same thing earlier. There was clearly no point in the Germans continuing, their best hope was to surrender to the allies as the Russians would show little mercy. It was a surprise the next evening that the Germans were still resisting and it was reported that there were old folk and youngsters fighting to defend their homeland. There was little said of the news that night, it had been nearly a week since Hitler had committed suicide and still the fighting went on. That night everyone went to bed early as there was ploughing to be done and Fred wanted a good night's rest.

The following morning everyone got up as usual. It was the 8th May and the wireless was not switched on as was the rule. The day was as any other, Grace and Hannah set off to school for 8:30am as usual. When they arrived at school the two girls found none of the usual hustle and bustle of other girls entering the school gates, only one or two other girls arriving and going through the front entrance. Grace and Hannah took their bikes to the cycle sheds and there they met the caretaker who was much happier than usual. "What are you doing here?" he said smiling. "There is no school today young ladies, haven't you heard?"

"Heard what? Where is everybody today?" said Grace.

"Today is a holiday. Germany has finally surrendered, go back off home and celebrate."

The girls looked around, the school was indeed deserted.

"A holiday?" said Hannah.

"That's right; it was announced last night and again this morning. I'm not hanging around either, as soon as I lock the gates I am off myself. Has no one told you the news? It is all over."

"The war is really over" stammered Grace.

"Aye lass, it's all over by what I've heard. Unconditional surrender they say."

"What does that mean?" Hannah asked Grace.

They said goodbye and fetched their bikes then set off for home.

"To think we got up for nothing" Grace grumbled.

"What are we going to do now?" Hannah asked.

"Better go back and tell Mam, Dad and Mary in case they have not heard. They won't have put the wireless on."

"I'm not going back home", Grace declared. "I'm stopping off at the Glen. I might be able to earn a few shillings". They cycled along; there was no traffic on the road at all.

"No need to carry these dammed gas masks any more now that the war is over thank goodness" said Grace "Shall we throw them into the wood?"

"I don't think we ought to just yet, Mam might shout at us. Wait until we get back and see what she says."

"You are right but isn't it wonderful we are free, free at last" she shouted loudly. "We are free, we have won the war" Hannah joined in "we have won the war everybody listen, we have won the war" they laughed together as they peddled along.

"Things should be better now, perhaps there will be an end to rationing and Mam will stop moaning." Grace laughed "You have to be joking she will never stop moaning, it will simply be that everything is too expensive".

"You are right" agreed Hannah and they free wheeled down to the Forest Glen.

"Wait here while I ask if it's true" said Grace and ran inside. Hannah looked around, they had seen no Lorries from the quarry and now there was no noise, everywhere was at peace, it felt strange sitting on the wall the war was really over, perhaps now Sam would return. Grace returned she was not wearing her coat or hat. "It is true the war is over, everyone is going to celebrate so I am staying here. You had better get back home and let them know if they have not heard."

Hannah peddled as hard as she could zig zagging across the road to get as far up the banks as she could before dismounting. Through the gate and up to the garage she went throwing her bike against the garage wall, it crashed to the ground but she did not stop. She ran round to the back door and burst in; Dorothy was sat at the table with William on her lap. "What are you doing here you are supposed to be at school?" she said startled.

Hannah tried to speak but was too breathless.

"What has happened, where is Grace?"

Hannah got her breath and told Dorothy the news.

"Good lord!" She said as she put William down. The relief washed over her, she put her hands up to her face. "It's really over?"

"Yes Mam. The caretaker was locking the gates, the school's closed. Today is a holiday."

"Oh I don't believe it" she got up and switched the wireless on then went to the range and pulled the frying pan off.

"Get outside and tell your Dad, he is milking with Mary. Gunter has not turned up.

I hope those batteries you brought have not run down. Go and get them in. This had better be right". Hannah was already out of the door and around to the cowshed.

She went inside and down the aisle, they had been taught never to shout. She found her Father half way down engrossed in his work.

"Dad, it is over, the war is finished. Mam has put the wireless on and says for you to come in."

"Eeh Surry lass" he stood up awkwardly. "How did you find out?"

"It's a holiday Dad, the school is closed. We stopped at the Glen and they said it is true as well."

Fred walked to the door and took out his tobacco tin. He looked at the sky "Well we knew it was over when Hitler went but it is still a shock" he said, his blue eyes twinkling. "The beggars could not hold out much longer" he filled his pipe.

"Go find Mary, she is in the bottom shed, Gunter has not turned up today and I can see why now." Hannah found Mary; she wanted to hear it for herself and went off to the kitchen. Fred and Hannah followed, the milking was forgotten now.

Dorothy was stood at the range she looked upset the wireless was turned up quite loud.

"Surry lass are you all right" said Fred. "Is what our Hannah says right, is it over?"

Dorothy sat down in Fred's chair and started to cry, Fred went over to her. Hannah looked at Mary "What?" said Mary "I'm listening, put the kettle on will you" they had never seen their Mother cry and felt uncomfortable. Hannah put the kettle over the heat and stood by the sink.

"It is right, the war is over" she said crying with relief, and quickly dried her eyes on her apron. "Mr Churchill is going to speak to us later today". She looked at Hannah "Go and get out of those fancy clothes then get up to the Hatch and see if the Wilkins has heard the news."

"Aye that is a good idea. Mary get us some tea" said Fred. "Thank God it's over Dot, but it looked as if it was inevitable."

Dorothy lifted William up and sat him on her knee, he looked bewildered.

"Helen will be coming back soon. I want to hear what the Prime Minister says about this. I'll have the girls give me a hand and we will have a celebration dinner tonight." Helen came back pleased as punch, a day off. Then Dorothy told her to stop being silly, to get changed and help with the work.

Gunter arrived later in the morning, just as Fred and Mary were eating a late breakfast. He knocked on the kitchen door and waited until Dorothy opened it, she looked at him

"What do you want?" she asked.

"I have come to work, but I do not know if I am wanted now."

Dorothy did not know what to say so she left him standing on the yard and called Fred from his meal. Fred put on his boots and went outside. He was not sure of the situation so he advised Gunter to return to the camp and make the most of the big day. Gunter left with a very heavy heart, Fred, Dorothy and the girls had become his family.

After breakfast the essential work was done and a goose was killed. Helen and Hannah had to pluck it while Dorothy stayed indoors with William.

Mary asked Fred where Gunter had gone. She was not impressed that he had the day off while she worked. If Grace had come back she could have gone down town on the bike for an hour or so. It was not fair and if Gunter was no longer a prisoner it would certainly be more work for her.

In the afternoon Joyce and Wilf came down, they were taken into the front room for tea and they stayed there for over an hour, the girls were left to keep an eye on William and the evening meal. Mary complained to Hannah that Grace had not come back; it was not an evening she worked so Mary wanted the bike. Grace was celebrating with Lizzy and the staff from the Forest Glen. Percy had taken them all into town and had treated them to anything they wanted. The town was packed, everyone was in high spirits.

"Mam is going to go berserk with you for not going home with Hannah" said Lizzy to Grace. "I don't care, this is wonderful, and the war is over with Germany it is so good to be part of the celebrations."

"Don't let it go to your head; everything will be back to normal tomorrow."

"Don't remind me" said Grace "but I want to stay out and enjoy myself, if I go back there will be work to do and just for once I don't want to do it".

That evening as soon as the cows were milked and all the jobs were finished the family gathered around the kitchen table to listen to the wireless. Celebrations were in full swing, the whole nation was rejoicing. Grace and Lizzy had still not returned. They talked over the events that had occurred during the last six years, William had not even been born when it started and Helen had been three, the others felt very self-important talking with their parents.

At eight o'clock Dorothy put William and Helen to bed. When she returned she sat down and said "At last we can sleep safe in our beds and in peace. Thank goodness it is over now, where is our Grace?" she was annoyed that Grace had not returned all day. She turned to Hannah "Go out there and see that those hens, ducks and geese are fastened up for the night, nothing has changed here you know."

Hannah went off outside, this was such a day to remember and here she was trudging around the pens. "Nothing is about to change around here" she said out loud. "Nothing ever does."

At ten o'clock Hannah was sent to bed. Mary went as well, she was very annoyed, and she should be out celebrating not Grace. Fred and Dorothy decided to sit up for a while "So there it is lass, all over. What happens now?" Dorothy thought for a while watching the flames in the grate "I don't know, we still have to carry on as before I suppose. Perhaps we will see an end to rationing. I don't expect the subsidies or guaranteed prices to carry on; we could find things tougher as I see it".

"Surry do you think so?" She did not answer so he carried on "At least we have everything under the plough now if Gunter stays on and we get some help with the harvest we should be all right."

"I don't want Gunter here any more" she said sharply. "He's a German, he should be sent back to where he belongs. We don't need him here now, our own lads will be back and they will want work". Fred was shocked he and Gunter had worked side by side for so long a mutual respect had grown between them.

"Surry lass let's not be too hasty, he is a grand worker and I would be stuck without him."

"I just want him gone, it does not look as if our Sam is coming back but there must be somebody out there to do the work, how about one of the lads from the village?"

Fred was unsure what to say, "Let's sleep on it lass, it has been quite a day and we have no idea what is round the corner really." He changed the subject and they sat up talking over the war years, still conscious that there was still a long way to go until it would finally be over. When they went up to bed Dorothy was concerned that Grace was not in. "Where is that Grace, she has ideas above her station. She should be in bed at this time of night; it is well past everyone's bedtime."

"Dunna worry lass, let her alone, she is all right with our Lizzy."

"I hope you are right Fred Thomas, let us get upstairs, tomorrow it will seem like a dream."

It was well past midnight when Lizzy and Grace arrived home, everybody was in bed so they tiptoed upstairs. Hannah was still awake "Where on earth have you been?"

"Oh it has been wonderful, so much fun."

"Mary is going to kill you, she wanted the bike."

"Oh I think I had better keep out of the way then" she whispered, then she said brightly "never mind it was worth every minute, what a day you all missed." That night Grace and Lizzy slept with the sound of the singing still ringing in their ears.

The next morning Grace was up early to avoid her Mother thereby avoiding a confrontation over returning home late the night before. She waited for Hannah just inside the wood before they continued on their way to school. They were really happy and peddled along, Grace going over the previous day's events. As they came to the end of the Ercall the road began its descent to the A5 and Wellington a lorry was coming around the bend towards them so Hannah braked hard. There was a crunch and the front brake lever came back to the handle bar. She pulled as hard as she could on the back brake but it was not enough she was still going too fast. "Stop Hannah" Grace shouted but she was too scared to answer, she slid off the seat and put her feet on the ground turning the handle bars as she did but it only sent her further towards the back end of the lorry. Grace was frantic as she watched Hannah career across the road feet down then duck to go under the tailgate. To her horror she saw her hat go flying into the air.

"Oh my God, she has hit her head" thought Grace. Hannah carried on across the road and went down into the wood the gravel flying from under her bike wheel. Grace pulled up alongside to help her. Thankfully she was shaken but unhurt.

"Are you all right? Grace asked.

"Yes I think so. Where is my hat?" Grace went back up the road and retrieved it. Hannah was inspecting her bike, she saw the brake cable had snapped and she knew she had just had a very lucky escape.

After a few minutes they set off again cautiously. After school they went down to Pickering's bike shop and had a new cable fitted. When she got home, Hannah told her story and gave the bill to Dorothy who was annoyed. "Your Dad could have fixed it for less. You should have waited."

"I could have gone under another lorry?" replied Hannah.

Dorothy put the bill on the mantel shelf and told her to get on with her work.

"Nothing changes here does it?" Hannah said to Helen as she went to get changed.

After the morning milking, Fred and Mary went into town and bought the newspapers, which were full of the news of the fall of Germany and the world wide celebrations. Then they went to find a clock; not an ordinary clock, Fred wanted a grandmother clock. He found just what he was looking for, paid by cheque and took it back to the car where Mary was given the job of steadying it on the journey home.

"Why have you bought the clock?" she asked.

"To celebrate the end of the war lass, so it will be a reminder every time we look at it."

"Where are you going to put it then?" she said, thinking there were enough clocks in the house this was just another that would need winding.

"It's for your Mam so she will decide but I reckon in the kitchen would be good."

Back at the house the clock was carefully carried to the kitchen and set on the table. Dorothy was overjoyed and decided it would hang on the wall by the pantry door. "There you are, that is a clock that shows peacetime" Fred told Mary as they stood back to admire their handiwork. It ticked lazily as Fred sat down in his chair and lit his pipe then he smiled and rocked back and forth quite content.

With the ending of the war with Germany a new air of hope emerged but there was still the matter of the Japanese to be taken care of. There was still fierce fighting in Burma and the Americans were taking terrible losses. At home soldiers were being demobbed and were returning home to try and pick up the pieces of their former lives. At first nothing changed on the farm, cows still had to be milked, stock fed, ploughing done and soon the hay would be harvested. Gunter came each day for the first two weeks but he was desperately unhappy, He had no idea if his family was still alive after the bombing of Dresden. He had expected to hear something by now and feared the worst. Also he did want to return to his homeland as a former captive so he went to Fred cap in hand and asked if he could stay and work on the farm as he felt he had nothing to return to in Germany. Fred could not answer, he tried to reason with Dorothy but she was adamant that he had to go. She suggested that they would employ someone local rather than have him on 'the bank'. Fred was not happy with this as he and Gunter had worked side by side for many years now and a mutual respect had grown between them. He could not bring himself to tell Gunter so he had words with the Boss who was still involved with the prisoners' welfare. It was agreed that Gunter would be repatriated with the other prisoners and three weeks after VE day Gunter was gone. The girls were shocked, he had not been to say goodbye. They recalled the times they had shared with him, the little figures and aeroplanes he used to whittle for them. He would be missed for sure. Dorothy regretted his leaving immediately, when Fred insisted she help with the dairy in the morning. She was looking forward to the end of term when the girls could take over. She even suggested that Fred should consider buying a milking machine but he was not ready yet, he was sure they would manage, it was early days and Sam might be back.

One afternoon in June there was a knock at the kitchen door, puzzled Dorothy opened it and there was Bernie the lad from Birmingham.

"What brings you back?" she said. He was carrying his tent and a large battered case "I want to see the Gaffer," he said. Dorothy thought of how it was just like when Sam had arrived all those years ago but Sam had been twice Bernie's weight and several inches taller!

"What for?" she asked.

"This and that" he replied, looking at the floor.

"Well, he should be up on the bank with our Mary. Go on up there and give a shout, now be off with you." She pushed a curious hen away from the door, closed it and turned back to William sat at the table, scribbling on a piece of paper.

"He's a skinny little beggar isn't he lad? He will not be a lot of help, will he?" William smiled, he was growing fast and could talk quite well "No Mam" he said brightly. She went to the kitchen window and watched as Bernie went off to the back fields "I don't think that they give them enough to eat in the towns. You certainly will not end up like that" she said and went to the pantry.

Fred was pleased to see him, he could certainly do with the help so once again, Bernie was allowed to camp in the field next to the house and he picked up where he left off.

Dorothy was pleased and relieved, now she only had her chicks to look after and could spend more time indoors.

After a couple of days Bernie hinted to Fred that he would like to stay a lot longer this time, he had decided to leave school early so that he could get a job. Fred was not sure what to say as he still hoped Sam would return, he simply said that Bernie would be a great help with the harvest and should stick around to see how things were towards the autumn. Bernie was pleased with this as he had no intention of going back to Birmingham. He had fallen out with his parents who were far too busy drinking themselves stupid in the public houses. Half the time they did not know where he was and certainly did not care what he was up to his brother had returned wounded from the fighting and with no time for Bernie, life, had become unbearable.

Fred mentioned to Dorothy that Bernie wanted to stay permanently. "I suppose that you could manage with him for now, one more to feed does not make much difference, a few extra potatoes to peel and some vegetables that is all. Anyway he could do with feeding up."

"He might be thin but he's strong with it," said Fred. "I could bag an extra rabbit or two to help out as well I think he will be all right."

"Are you sure? He is no substitute for that Gunter or Sam if he ever comes back" she replied.

"Well Gunter's gone for good now and we have no idea of Sam's whereabouts. He wants to stay and help out so why not let him, I could certainly do with the help and the girls don't mind him, we will see what happens come autumn."

Ken Winter had gone to Holland as soon as the peace was established. Imogen carried on working at the post office keeping herself to herself and only speaking if spoken to. She always had time for Hannah though and would talk of life in Holland and how much she longed to return. Several days after Bernie's arrival Ken returned, he spent time with Fred telling him of the situation in Europe and how great a task it was to rebuild the infrastructure.

"We will be returning to Liverpool soon" he said "then when the time is right I am taking Imogen home to Holland, she needs to see her brothers and sister and visit her parents' graves."

"Surry I will be sorry to see you go not that we see much of you."

"I will miss this place too; the last few years have done us the world of good. I have never been fitter and feel ten years younger." In July two black cars arrived to take Ken and Imogen back to Liverpool. The drivers, both uniformed, helped them load up and after brief goodbyes they set off, the bicycles hanging out of the larger car.

"Well that was short and sweet" said Fred as he and Mary watched the two cars turn out of their drive and head off down the road. Dorothy was stood in the far room, it was strange, this room had been someone else's for so long, there was a perfectly good bed there what should they do with it? The room was left empty for a while then it was decided that perhaps if Bernie was serious about staying for a while the bed could be moved into the parlour for him and he could live in. As soon as Fred mentioned staying in the house Bernie leapt at the opportunity. He would be up early in the mornings to check the stock as Fred made the first cup of tea of the day. His enthusiasm reminded Fred of Sam in the early days and Mary was pleased as it gave her far less to do.

The need for an election had been agreed just days after the war's end. The date would be 5th July. All parties campaigned on the need for full employment despite the war still raging with Japan. The labour party however promised nationalization of the steel, iron and coal industries and a free health service. Only Dorothy and Fred could vote as the voting age was twenty one. Special arrangements were made for servicemen and women and on the day the nation went to the polls there was a good turnout. Fred and many folk believed Churchill had done a fine job but his personality did not save the day, many remembered it was the Conservatives that led the country to war. On the day it was a landslide victory for Labour. Dorothy was surprised when the result was announced "That is a kick in the teeth for Churchill after all he has done to lead us through this mess". She said

"Aye lass, this new lot reckon they are going to change everything for the better. I just wonder if the subsidies will be stopped."

"I really hope that they need us to go on producing as much as we can."

"Aye we have transformed this place through the help we got from the last government. They can't take that from us." Dorothy thought for a while "Yes first off they will want to get rid of rationing and they will need everything we can supply it's just the price that matters".

"Aye and talking of price, how are they going to pay for this free health service they are boasting of?"

"I don't care as long as we get it free; our Hannah has cost us a small fortune."

"Well we will have to see."

Hannah and Grace had been kept from school to help with the planting of the potatoes. They were also kept away from school for hay harvest, corn harvest, and potato picking in the autumn. Consequently, they had fallen behind with their schoolwork. Try as they might they had failed to catch up with the rest of the class, as had been expected. The teachers did not spend time with them preferring to coach those more reliable pupils.

Hannah was worried; she knew that the School had a reputation to keep up. Miss Bygott the Head Mistress would remind them every day at morning assembly. It had been every girl's duty, war or no war, to meet the expected standard. She would look sternly at the faces in front of her. "The future is in your hands, you have a responsibility to your school, your country and your family to do well." She expected a proportion of the pupils to go on to higher education. Hannah had tried to catch up but there was no time, she could not share books with her classmates and there was only a short time at school to copy missed work.

At the end of term Hannah and Grace returned home with their reports, they had lost too much time for one reason or another and the reports reflected this, neither of them could expect to go on to university. It would also be unlikely that they would become suitably qualified for a professional job. The two girls were very disappointed. When they complained to Dorothy all she said was that growing food for the country was far more important than books and paper. Hannah protested "but it is our future and now the war is over people with education will be needed. I could be a teacher or a nurse."

Dorothy did not listen "People need food and anyway we have no choice, we have to grow the crops or be turned out on to the street". She chose not to mention the good profits they were making and the cheap labour the girls provided, she would have no further argument.

When they were alone, Grace and Hannah talked about their reports; they had no idea what they would be able to do when they left school. The leaving age had gone up from fourteen to fifteen but there was an exemption for children living on the farms providing their last year was spent helping to provide food.

"Have you got any idea what you want to do when you leave school?" asked Hannah. "Mam could have made you leave this year if she wanted."

"I don't understand it; they keep us off which stops us getting good qualifications then let me carry on till I am fifteen."

"Maybe it is because Bernie helps out and Mary is always there."

"I see what you mean, but I've no idea what I will do. The only thing I want to do is to get away from this farm with all its mess and muck. What about you, have you got any ideas what you want to do?"

"I wanted to be a teacher like Mrs Hayward in the village or maybe a nurse."

"You would definitely have to stay on the extra year to do that and then you would be kept off so much."

"Yes I know, but I am sure that we will find something." She brightened "People are always advertising in the paper for young girls to be nannies".

"I reckon that we could manage a job like that" Grace agreed.

"Yes why not, I had not thought of anything like that and we have had plenty of practice with Helen and William."

"Well that is what we will do, we will show them one day you will see," said Grace and they left it at that.

Hannah had worked really hard during the hay harvest. She had been trusted to work on the dray with Bernie stacking the hay as it was pitched up to them. They had to build up the layers properly so that when fully loaded none slid off as it was taken back to the farm behind the tractor. She was so looking forward to her mother keeping her promise that she could go and stay at the Manor with Rebecca after the corn harvest. Then the whole world received a shock. On 6th August a city in Japan called Hiroshima ceased to exist in one single explosion, the atom bomb had arrived. The news was unbelievable how one bomb could do such a thing. On the 9th Nagasaki was also annihilated, the family were together in the kitchen when they heard. "Good lord" said Fred "where is this going to end?"

"Will Japan surrender now?" asked Hannah.

"I really hope so; our lads should get out of there now they have done their bit in Burma. It looks as if the Yanks can finish it on their own."

The focus of everyone's attention was switched back to the war in the Pacific; many folk had put this to the back of their minds since the defeat of Germany.

The Japanese surrendered on 15th August. That night a two day public holiday was announced but there was no holiday for the girls as it was a busy time, but at least there was an air of celebration in the house. Dorothy cooked them special teas and dug out some sweetened preserves that she had kept for just such a moment. Fred was so cheerful, the last threat had been removed and perhaps now the world could settle down. He knew there would be little change to their way of life. It was a well established routine now and the end of the war with Germany, although shifting the focus of the manufacturing industries, meant more work for the farmers if they were to keep up with demand especially as the soldiers, sailors and airmen returned to their homes and families. Hannah stuck her last few snippets in her war diaries and then closed them and put them in the bottom of a drawer. She wished Sam had come home but as their Dad had said, they simply had to get on with life, no dwelling in the past.

Dorothy had made the arrangements for the visit to the Manor. Hannah was thrilled to bits she could hardly wait. During the corn harvest she worked alongside her sisters and Bernie stacking and loading all the time reminding her father that she would be going to the Manor soon. He did not argue, his mind was on his work,

"Perhaps Mam will get me some nice clothes to take with me" she said to Grace one evening "Don't bank on it said Grace You won't get anything working here."

The day before Hannah was due to go, Dorothy packed her a bag. There was her best frock, which was now getting a bit small for her, two pair of clean knickers and some socks. Hannah looked at her belongings and was disappointed.

"Is that all I have?" she asked.

"No point in taking stuff only to bring it back for me to wash, your Grandma will see you all right for anything else you need."

"But that dress is getting too small for me, I will look silly."

"If they take you out, I am sure Beccy will be able to lend you a frock. She is bound to have one that is too small for her."

"I expect so" was all that Hannah could say. She really had hoped that with all the work she had put in that her Mother could have bought her a new frock at least. It was frustrating to always be dressed in 'hand me downs' especially when William always had new clothes bought for him. The next day she was taken to Wellington station in the Wolseley. Fred made sure she was on the right train and she soon arrived in Market Drayton where she was met on the platform by Rebecca. She was so happy to see her sister after so long and together they skipped out to the car park where Granddad and Grandma were waiting in their car. All the way back to the Manor the two girls chattered away in the back of the car. Sarah was pleased for Rebecca as she had few friends since she had left school. Bill was grumpy as usual and apart from a brief 'hello' he said nothing on the drive back. Rebecca took Hannah's bag and after a bite to eat took her outside to show her around, Rebecca wanted to know everything that was happening, particularly how their new brother was doing.

"William is a spoilt brat and gets all his own way" Hannah said. "He goes everywhere with Dad. Teaching him farming Mam says and then she feeds him chocolate and biscuits."

"Well it was always you that went with Dad in the old days when you were little. I used to think you were the lucky one. Except when you broke your arm that is."

"Well how is it here? I'll bet you get nice clothes."

"It is all right, the only problem is Granddad. He is so grumpy, always moaning about something."

"He sounds just like our Mam, she is getting worse lately, always falling out with Grace. Especially now she is earning her own money."

"In that case I am glad I am out here. It sounds like a new war is breaking out. Come on I will show you where folks go fishing." They set off together, happy in the warm sun.

CHAPTER 13

SECRETS

During the school holidays Grace was hardly around, spending most of her time at the Forest Glen.

The money that she earned she spent on herself, this annoyed Dorothy greatly. As it neared time for the girls to go back to school Dorothy thought Grace should be putting something towards the cost. When Grace bought new shoes and was parading them around in front of the other girls Dorothy rounded on her. "You should save your money rather than spend it on rubbish, those shoes will not last."

"It is my money and I have always wanted proper shoes" she replied and turned back to her sisters "and I've bought some nice underwear as well". Dorothy was furious. "Throwing every penny that you get on fancy things is no good. I've got you to keep; you should give it to me to help pay your way."

"I will not" said Grace and went upstairs. She kept out of the way for the next few days but the week before starting back to school she had her hair done at a proper hairdressers in Wellington. Dorothy was at the sink when she came in "What have you gone and done to your hair? How much did that cost?" She was furious not with the hairstyle which was very good and really suited her but with the fact that she had spent money having it done. Grace calmly reminded her Mother that it was her own money that she was spending and she did not consider it a waste of money.

"I've had it with your backchat" shouted Dorothy as she turned and seeing Grace stood by the range preening her hair was just too much. She had a half-pound bar of soap in her hand and threw it at Grace who ducked instinctively; there was a loud crash as the soap smashed through the small window sending glass in all directions.

"Get out of my sight" screamed Dorothy and Grace sped off upstairs; a torrent of abuse followed her. Later Dorothy told Fred the reason there was a large piece of cardboard over the window.

"That girl should not go back to school she does not deserve it. We should make her work here and earn her keep like our Mary. All that girl can think about is fancy clothes, she is never satisfied with what I buy her."

"Just likes to look smart" Fred said simply.

"But it won't last five minutes."

"Don't worry Dot, it's because she is mixing with those girls from the town." He knew how hard Grace worked and was conscious how much school time she and Hannah had lost helping with the farm work. He believed she deserved what she had worked for.

"I hope Hannah does not try to copy her," said Dorothy.

"Nay lass she is of a different nature, much more contented, she likes working outside more than inside." Dorothy dropped the subject.

When Hannah joined Grace upstairs in the evening she had some food for her as Dorothy had made it clear there was no tea for Grace. She declared that Grace should buy her own tea rather than waste money on fancy haircuts.

"Mam is bouncing off the walls down there," said Hannah. "She says you have to pay for the window."

"I'll give Dad something towards it but not Mam; she will only spend it on William. Do you like my hairdo?"

"Very nice, it suits you" Hannah replied. Grace knew that she was a very attractive young lady and was determined to make the most of herself. How envious she was of the girls that she saw attending the dances at the Forest Glen.

"One day I'm going to have a real ball gown and I am going to learn to dance properly just like other girls do. I am not going to be a skivvy all my life."

"It's all right for you to dream of nice things you have a job and some money I have none."

"Why don't you get one? Like I have."

"But where, I'm only thirteen. Do you think that Margaret Podmore would have me?"

"I wouldn't think so, but I can ask. There are already enough of us down there. Lizzy is working full time, Mary helps out when they have the dinners. I go after school and at weekends, no I should not think that they will take any more of us on." She had no intention of working with any more of her family.

"Why not ask Mary if they want any help up at the Wrekin Cottage that would be a better idea."

"Oh yes" agreed Hannah. Grace went to the mirror and looked at her hair.

"I will only get married to someone who can afford the things I like such as nice clothes and a car."

"Like our Wolseley?"

"No, a sports car. I have seen them and one day I am going to learn to drive."

"Oh Lordy, you drive a motor car!"

"Of course why ever not?"

"But it is the men who drive the cars, isn't it?"

"Rubbish, women can drive just as good as men."

"I bet our Mam can't, her hat would get in the way and she would ram everyone off the road." Grace pictured their Mother behind the wheel of the car and burst out laughing. When she stopped she sighed "Mary drives the tractor and she said Dad is going to let her have a go in the car but one day I will drive a really smart sports car you will see". Hannah left Grace daydreaming and went to find Mary; she would get a job as well.

She asked Mary about going to help out up the Wrekin but she too was hesitant "I don't know about that, what about the work that has to be done here?"

"Well Bernie helps out and there is Helen and William is growing up."

"All right I will ask at the weekend but you will have to get around Mam and Dad, and remember that you will not earn very much. It is the wrong time of year now."

Everyone had seen or heard of the German concentration camps as the allies had liberated the prisoners during the final days of the war, but few were ready for the awful truth that emerged later in the year. The number of dead was unimaginable. Dorothy put down the paper she had bought that day her face was ashen in the lamplight.

"Good lord, so it is right. There has been talk for some time but this beggar's belief. Is that what would have happened to us?"

"What's that lass?" said Fred. He was sat in his chair while the girls were sat around the kitchen table. They were listening to the radio; Dorothy had taken the lamp to her side of the table so there was little else they could do.

"It is about those concentration camps, you know there was talk of them being used to get rid of people. This is unbelievable what they say here, they say there were millions of Jews put in gas chambers and killed. They wiped out whole families without a thought. Fred, would they have done that if they had captured us?"

"Nay we would not have let them beat us, that is why we always said we would not surrender"

"You would have shot us all like Granddad said if they had come here" said Hannah "wouldn't you?"

Fed did not answer her. He spoke to Dorothy "As I see it lass there was a lot going on that we didn't know about. They called them all Nazis but I think they were a different lot to the ones fighting on the front line."

"Well it seems they killed thousands at a time, ordinary folk, and children as well it doesn't bear thinking about". Hannah thought of what Bernie had told them "Dad what they say, all those people killed has that been going on all the time?"

"Seems that way. It seems that while we were fighting their armies, others were doing all those terrible things"

"Was Sam there?" Hannah asked.

"Nay lass it was not our lads, they were treated all right. It looks as it was just the Jews and Russians. No wonder the Russians fought so hard, Bernie said there were thousands of

German soldiers captured at Stalingrad, what did the Russians do to them?"

"I hope we never find out" said Grace "it doesn't bear thinking about".

"True so let us drop the subject," said Dorothy. She was finding it hard to come to terms with the concept of thousands of women and children being gassed.

Later when the girls were in bed Dorothy raised the subject again "would that have happened to us if they had got over the channel?"

"Who knows but I agreed with your Father that it was best to shoot ourselves and not be taken prisoner. There was nothing like this in the Great War. Stories of villages being wiped out but always in small numbers, this is beyond comprehension; they say it is all down to the Nazis."

"I see now you would have been quite right. If they have gassed millions as they are saying, what would a few more like us be to them? They should never be forgiven for this, to think that we have given a job and food to one of their kind."

"Now steady on a bit Dot, Gunter was not a Nazi, he was just an ordinary German, one of the millions caught up in the war." She was not convinced. "What is happening to our lads against the Japanese? It is said they are worse than the Germans."

"So they say it leaves you cold it does. Let's not dwell on it, our lads are coming back now and those captured by the Germans have been treated fairly this other business has been directed at the Jews."

"It seems terrible how we have been moaning about the war and the rationing when so many have gone to their deaths, poor devils."

"Best not to think about it, you will only upset yourself. Let's think of the living and hope that there is an end to the war in the East, at least you can sleep easy knowing that these islands are now safe."

It was towards Christmas that an official letter arrived; Dorothy opened it and was shocked to read that Sam was alive and being cared for in a rehabilitation centre somewhere in the south of England. A law had been passed that meant employers had to re-hire those that had took up arms. Dorothy immediately thought that Sam was coming back but as she read on, it was clear there was a problem. Sam had been taken prisoner after being injured in heavy fighting and had been found in a German prison camp at the war's end. Years of captivity had taken its toll however and his mental health was poor, he would only be capable of menial work. Dorothy read and re-read the letter, this was not expected; Sam should be coming back as he left. She put the letter away deciding to wait until she was alone with Fred. During the day she thought hard on the situation, Bernie was a good worker, and so was Mary. Things were different now the tractor had changed things it needed skill to deal with mechanization. The farm was far different than when Sam went away. She made her decision and later when she had Fred alone she gave him the letter "It's about Sam" she said.

"Surry at long last, this is good news" he took the letter. She said nothing while he read it.

"This can't be right," he said, "what are they saying?" he turned the letter over looking for something else.

"We can't take on an invalid, we have enough to do as it is" she said adamantly.

Fred was very upset at her reaction he would have Sam back without a second thought no matter what state of health he was in. He had been like a son to him and he could not dismiss him just like that.

"Steady on lass let's not be hasty, he could get better, the letter does not say it is permanent."

"He will not be much use to you now especially as you have the tractor, there is a lot more going on now."

"Aye you have a point" he sighed. "Write back and tell them that if his state of mind improves we will certainly have him back" she thought for a moment, there was not much to be said.

"I will answer the letter as you say."

"And ask them to keep us informed as to how he gets on, so that we can go and visit him."

Dorothy had in her mind exactly what she was going to write back in answer to the letter. She decided that it would not be quite as Fred had wished. In her reply she pointed out that they had given the letter a great deal of consideration. Unfortunately they could not consider giving Sam a home as their present commitments were far too great. Also they were in no position to cope with him if he needed special attention. There was no reply to the letter and several months later the girls were told that Sam was being looked after by the army and would not be coming home; Fred's idea of visiting Sam was soon forgotten.

Rationing continued under the new government but there was some relaxation. The Forest Glen was doing very well; there was plenty of demand for the function room. In December Margaret Podmore hinted to Lizzy that she could do with a little more help with waiting tables at the dinners.

She had no intention of taking on a full time waitress and thought Mary might help out for a few shillings. It would only be the evening work so she could return with Lizzy.

Lizzy told Mary who said she would have to think about it, she was not one for being pushed into a quick decision. Grace was furious "What about me? I could do that work".

"But you are still at school and too young to be dealing with some of the ones we get in there."

Mary was quite surprised when she mentioned the offer over breakfast neither her Father nor Mother raised an eyebrow, Dorothy simply smiled and said "Why not?" After breakfast Mary set off to get some work done but Fred stayed a while to discussed Mary working at the Forest Glen.

They had Bernie working for nothing at the moment but it was Mary who did the most work and Fred now trusted her to drive the tractor. She certainly earned her keep, they did not pay her a proper wage just a little pocket money every now and then. If she left to take up a proper job they would have to pay someone as a labourer, Bernie would not cope alone.

The prospect of her working at the Forest Glen meant she would have more money to spend on top of what little she earned up at the Wrekin Cottage. Mary accepted the offer and after the first evenings work she walked home with Lizzy pushing the old bike Grace would use the next morning. She had enjoyed the work more than she had expected and the money in her pocket was a real bonus.

Dorothy had not felt well all through the previous autumn but she put it down to her 'time of life' as she called it. Her periods had stopped and she accepted that this was the menopause that folk talked about. She had not seen the doctor about it assuming her little knowledge was sufficient to get her through, anyway doctors cost money. It was difficult for Fred, there was little he could do and he understood nothing of what she was going through. Luckily she had William and she doted on him every waking hour. The only satisfaction she felt was that she considered every other woman, who had been through the change of life, as it was generally called, must have suffered just like herself. Fred tried to make her rest whenever she seemed irritable or tired but his time was taken working outside.

In the New Year Dorothy felt worse, her stomach was becoming distended; she was growing concerned and decided that she really must go to see the doctor. She did not want to worry Fred, so she made an appointment at the surgery while in town to do the shopping. The following week she told Fred she had to call in the surgery not saying why and he did not ask. She was on time and was sent through to see Doctor Williams straight away. It had been a while since any of the family had been in and Doctor Williams asked after the children. He was still amazed at Hannah's recovery from the whooping cough. Dorothy returned the small talk for a few minutes conscious of not being too long she did not want Fred worrying. She was sure that her problems were simply to do with her time of life. She briefly explained how unwell she felt, the doctor listened but there were too many issues for a quick answer so he decided to give her an examination. When he was finished Doctor Williams left her to get dressed behind the screen and returned to his desk. When she was ready Dorothy came out and sat down opposite him, she was surprised at the broad smile on his face. "You know what is wrong with you don't you?" he said, Dorothy looked vacant. "Can't you guess?"

"Guess what? What are you talking about" she was annoyed she did not see anything to laugh about. He saw her frown and so continued "You are perfectly healthy it is just that you are six months pregnant".

"Pregnant?" Dorothy raised her voice. "How on earth can I be pregnant at my age, I have not had the monthly cycle for ages now, nearly two years. Everybody says how you can't get pregnant when you've gone through the change. My friends said so."

"Well you clearly should not listen to people, friends or otherwise, there are too many old wives tales around."

"Well when is it due? This is unbelievable."

"I guess that you can expect this child at the end of April or may be sooner," he gave a little chuckle. "Because of your age, I will want to see you every two weeks to keep an eye on you. Perhaps you would make the appointments with Mrs Riley as you go out." She stood up to leave, as she reached the door she asked "Doctor, is it true what we have been reading in the papers, that the Government is going to give us all a free health service?"

"Ah yes, I have misgivings about the proposals but if it will enable the poor to get better treatment then who am I to oppose it?"

"Will it be of help for this baby?"

"From what I have read, by the time they have passed it through Parliament I will have retired and hung up my boots so to speak." Dorothy thanked him and went to make her next appointment as she was waiting to see the receptionist the doctor's words sunk in. She sat down hurriedly, this would be number eight and with Lizzy twenty in March what would folks think? But it was listening to other people that had got her in this predicament. No, it was that Fred Thomas's fault;

she had kept him at arm's length since the arrival of William and only given in when she had thought it safe to do so. She made her appointment and went about her shopping she was seething inside and kept it bottled up until the shopping was done and they were in the car. Then she told him of the baby he was so surprised the car banged the kerb and he had to pull up. His eyes were bright "Surry lass this is a surprise" he said. She then told him in no uncertain terms what she thought of him. How angry she was to have been so stupid listening to other women telling her that it was safe to give in to his desires.

"Aye lass but it might be another lad."

"It's another mouth to feed that's what it is, and when am I going to get any peace from washing blasted nappies. I did not want another child but it is too late now." She adjusted her hat pushing a loose strand of hair forcibly from her face a sure sign she was angry.

"Did you say April?" She nodded sharply.

"Well that is not far away you will have to put your feet up now." She was not talking anymore so he started the car again and they made their way back to the farm.

"Oh lord please let it be another lad," he thought, at least that would make her happy. As if she had read his mind she said, "If it turns out to be another girl I want nothing to do with it".

"Don't talk like that Dot, it's on the way now and you will cope."

"No I won't. If it is a girl Mary can see to it" Dorothy answered very sulkily.

"Mary! What do you mean Mary can look after it? She has to help me outside; I will not be able to spare her to look after a baby."

"You will just have to because if it is a girl I'll not have anything to do with it. Have I made myself clear?"

"Yes Dot, leave it for now, let us wait and see what happens". He felt thrown into a pit, this was not what they needed right now.

"What's up with Mam and Dad?" said Hannah that evening to Mary.

"I don't know but there is definitely something up with the pair of them because Dad usually cheers up when he is outside with the stock, but not today."

For the next week nobody said much, Dorothy was too irritable. She was so angry with Fred with his blue eyes and blond hair. Why had she given in to their desires, she should have not have taken such a risk. She was now forty three and had assumed that she was well past childbearing age.

In a way it had been such a relief to be told that she was pregnant. She had been worried that it was something serious that might require an operation and like many folk she was frightened of dying under the anaesthetic. Some of the things that had crossed her mind did not bear thinking about.

She had read that it could have been an ovarian cyst or worst, still, Cancer that had no cure. Cancer was not talked about. She knew of folk who had died from it but their relatives had said that it was pneumonia or a heart attack. She easily kept the pregnancy a secret from the rest of the family. She had put on quite a lot of weight in recent years and so by wearing loose fitting clothes no one suspected anything was untoward

As the weeks passed Dorothy began to rest more often. Mary knew something was going on

And Lizzy pointed out to her how much weight their Mother seemed to have put on recently they became suspicious.

The next few weeks passed very quickly for Dorothy she had so much to do at this time of year with the rearing of the poultry. She said nothing to any of the children.

At the end of February there was the National Farmers Union dinner dance at the Forest Glen. Fred bought tickets for himself and Dorothy and they were really looking forward to an evening out. Dorothy treated herself to a new dress that hid her condition very well and also looked very smart. Then the week before the dinner snow fell, the roads were soon cleared but the temperature dropped at night making driving difficult. On the night of the dinner the snow glittered in the moonlight, it was bitter cold. There were streaks of ice on the road so Fred was reluctant to take the car out in case he slid on it and they ended up in the woods. They decided they would walk so after wrapping up warm they set off early but they had only reached the road when Dorothy slipped and put her foot through some thin ice into a pothole filling her shoe with icy water. She was angry; she could not carry on with her foot soaked so they returned for her to change her stockings and shoes. It did not take long but when they set off again they were more careful and they arrived late. No vehicles had driven past them as they walked so Fred felt justified in not taking the car. Dorothy had not wanted to be late, she had hoped to be seated before most of the other farmers and their wives arrived. As it was the evening was a success, they had good company at their table and the meal was excellent. Both Mary and Lizzy were working that night and Dorothy was pleased to see them looking smart in their black dresses and white aprons. The two girls were finished and on their way home before the function was due to end. As they walked carefully along on the frozen road Lizzy again said how she thought their Mother had put on a lot of weight.

"Yes I noticed it as well; although she had that new dress on she is getting fatter and fatter. It's all the cake and stuff she eats when we are not looking. She buys extra and does not share it with us."

"I never see it around, where does she keep it?"

"She puts it in the cupboard in the front room. There's chocolate and biscuits too, that is why William gets far more than we do. She always has to give him the best as we all know, the spoilt brat," she ended sarcastically. Lizzy nodded and they walked on talking of all the different characters they had seen that night.

The winter was very harsh, the journey to and from school was dangerous and bitterly cold for Grace and Hannah but they persevered and were pleased when the weather picked up and the snowdrops appeared. Fred was pleased with the progress they were making. Mary was becoming quite capable of running the farm from day to day. She had learned to drive the tractor and the only real heavy work was shifting all the muck onto the fields. Bernie was a great help and Grace, Hannah and Helen helped out with the feeding before and after school. It was only the time taken milking that was a problem. He was thinking that maybe they should buy a milking machine with the profit from the grain they had harvested the previous year. He mentioned it to Dorothy, Mary and Bernie over breakfast. Mary and Bernie were enthusiastic. "That would be great Dad," said Mary. Dorothy did not agree.

"Don't you go getting ahead of yourself Fred Thomas, there are other things to think about and you know it." The look she gave him reminded him of the baby

"Aye lass, but think of the time we could save." She was not and the subject was quickly dropped. Fred was disappointed but one day he would get a milking machine, he had made his mind up.

That afternoon a cow began to calve and Mary, with the help of Bernie and Hannah had to do most of the milking and feeding. Grace was at the Forest Glen and Helen had been kept in to do the household jobs. When everything was done Mary went into the warm kitchen only to be reminded of the sheep. She was tired and had decided against checking them as they were up on the bank out of sight in the dark. Dorothy told her to go and check them and not to return until she had made sure they were all accounted for. Hannah wrapped up warm and joined Mary, glad to be away from her Mother's moaning. They set off up the fields, the moonlight reflecting off the frozen grass giving just enough light for them to see. Mary told Hannah about the plans for a milking machine and how there would be more free time.

"One day I am going to drive that car to town" she said "on my own as well". She had been having a go at driving the car, just backing it out of the garage when it was needed and putting it away again later. Dorothy was not too keen on her driving the car; she considered it belonged to her and Fred and that he should be the only one to drive it.

"Don't you need a licence" puffed Hannah, the bank was steep and the cold took her breath away, they crossed from one field to another.

"I suppose so but I am not going to bother. I can drive as good as anyone else with all the practice that I have had with the tractor, I think that I can manage to drive the car. Anyway I will say I have been driving through the war and that means I don't have to take a test."

"I don't think Mam will let you."

"Well apart from her poultry, she spends all her time eating and fussing over William. Be quiet now I can see the sheep." She could see them sheltering under a large thick holly bush in the corner of the field.

"I expect Grace will leave home and get a job of some sort, you can see she and Mam will never get on, they are always arguing over one thing or another."

"It's because Grace likes nice things and Mam says that they are too fancy. Now be quiet and stay where you are." Hannah stood still while Mary walked around the flock which remained calm, they were not afraid of the two girls.

"They are all here thank goodness" Mary said as she finished counting there were forty four now to keep an eye on and it was Mary's responsibility to count them every evening. She returned to Hannah and they walked back towards the house their feet crunching the crisp frozen grass. They pulled their woollen scarves tighter as there was a cold breeze against them and pushed their hands deeper into their pockets to keep them warm.

"So why don't you get another job, earn more money and buy a car for yourself?" asked Hannah. "That's what Grace wants to do."

"You are joking, I can't see that happening can you? They need me here until William is old enough then they will give it all to him."

"Oh yes, there is William, but he is so young that will mean you will be here for another ten years unless some handsome man comes and sweeps you off your feet."

"What nonsense you talk."

"You never know it happens in fairy stories."

"And in fairy stories only. You need to come down to earth girl and stop letting your imagination run away with you."

"I do not" retorted Hannah.

"You know that Dad is thinking of growing sugar beet this year? He intends to plant this spring just to see how well it grows on this type of soil" Mary said.

"Oh Lordy will that mean more time off from school? They could see the light from the kitchen window.

"I don't know. Dad is really doing well; I have little hope of getting away. I only hope we get more machinery to make it easier or he hires someone to help out when it gets busy; we are coping all right at the moment."

"It won't be long and the warmer weather will be here" said Hannah.

"Yes and the lambs, we will be busy then with the ploughing and all the rest of the work but at least I am not stuck indoors."

"Me neither, I will help once my schoolwork is done."

Hannah accompanied Mary whenever she could. The cold did not bother her, frost could be a nightly occurrence and there was always the possibility of snow falling at this time of year. Together they trudged back to the house. "Can I come and help out at the cottage? You said that I might be able to when the weather picks up."

"It won't be much, maybe a sixpence or a shilling."

"Yes but it would be my own" Hannah replied.

"Unless Mam takes it from you like she does whenever Granddad comes around."

"Can I come with you when you take the car out for a drive?" asked Hannah.

"Of course, but keep it quiet."

"Oh I will and when we go I will buy the pop with the money I am going to earn."

A free health service for everyone was the word in the papers and on the radio. The labour government laid out their plans for the 'National Health Service' as it was to be called. It sounded grand there would be no charges and everyone would have access to a doctor and treatment where and when they needed it.

"But who is going to pay for this new health system" said Fred. He disliked doctors at the best of times and was wary of anything offered as free.

"Oh we will pay there is no doubt about that" said Dorothy. "You, Mary and Lizzy will have to buy stamps every week and stick them on a card."

"It is not free then is it?" he said.

"Sort of, whenever we go to the doctors it will be because it is already paid for. I wish it had been around for our Hannah, that broken arm and the whooping cough cost a small fortune."

"Aye but that is the doctors, how will they make their money with this idea?"

"It says the government will pay them."

"If it is like the subsidies we got they will do all right then."

"Well I am sticking to the same place I had William" she said, "we know where we are then".

As April drew near Mary knew that her Mother was expecting, and mentioned it to Fred, he swore her to secrecy but she told Lizzy and swore her to secrecy too. None of the others suspected, sure that it was just too many big meals, cake and biscuits. Mary was keen for Fred to buy a milking machine but he said it would wait until the baby had settled in.

When Dorothy went into labour Fred took her to the nursing home where she had given birth to William. The doctor told him he could wait as it would not be long at all. Dorothy knew also, she said a prayer to the Lord that the child would not be born deformed or mentally ill on her way to the delivery room. Fred paced the corridors. The delivery was straightforward and there were no complications. It had been several hours and Fred was sitting not far from the delivery room when he saw a smiling nurse heading his way. "It has to be a boy" he said to himself, "it just has to be".

"Congratulations Mr Thomas it is a baby girl" it was a hammer blow. "Mr Thomas! Are you all right" the nurse said, suddenly concerned.

"Oh aye. I'm all right but how is Dot?"

"She is with the doctor at the moment; the baby is fine I thought you should know straight away."

"Thanks" said Fred and walked outside for some air. This did not look good.

An hour later he was with the doctor explaining all that had gone on before with Helen. The doctor was sympathetic but could not help him. Dorothy had reacted badly and they were having trouble getting her to feed the baby. They suggested she return home as soon as possible. After he had been to see her and the baby he returned home to break the news. Hannah and Helen were shocked, William did not understand fully but smiled and clapped his hands, a little sister.

Dorothy was very depressed she did not want folk to know about the birth. If it had been a boy she might have felt different but there was a stigma associated with having children so late in life. To many married women sex was something that finished once the family was established and that should certainly be the case of anyone aged over forty. Two days after the birth Fred came to collect her. As they drove along Watling Street she told him to go into the town centre to Bates and Hunts the chemist.

"What for lass?" he asked innocently, he had no money on him.

"A tin of Cow and Gate baby milk, a bottle and some teats. Two days of feeding it myself are enough. You lot can feed it from now on" she snapped. She had reasoned that powered baby milk would do all right. After all they took the calves from their mothers at two days old and fed them powered milk so why not the baby. She knew her milk would soon dry up as it had when she refused to feed Helen and she did not care what the doctor thought, her mind was made up. She gave Fred some money and he went and fetched what she asked for.

"Are you not going to feed the baby yourself?" he asked still not sure he understood what she was saying.

"No I am not" Dorothy snapped.

"Oh dear" thought Fred "I hope this is not a repeat of when she had Helen".

Back home she put the baby in the front room and told the children in no uncertain terms that they were not to mention the baby to any of their friends, no one was to know. She had wanted a brother for William. The poor lad had been reared with sisters and now another one. Dorothy was convinced that life was not fair to her at all. Why so many girls? She had heard that the only certain way of avoiding pregnancy was not to have sex in the first place also that it was something that could be done without. Now here she was with a new baby. That would raise a few eyebrows indeed. But if none of the family said anything to the neighbours no one would know she reasoned.

In the days that followed she had little to do with the baby. She made up the bottles of milk to the instructions. Always having one stood in a jug of warm water on the range ready for when the child woke. During the night she fed the child and changed its nappy but on waking she would simply wash and change her and then go back to bed that was all she was prepared to do. It was left to whichever of the girls was available. Often they would walk into the kitchen and hear the baby awake and crying to be fed. Dorothy was more interested in William and rearing her poultry. It was usually Mary who ended up feeding her when she came in from the farmyard. One afternoon the baby was crying and the bottle was sat on the range, Dorothy was sat rocking William in Fred's chair. Dorothy scowled at her "You go and pick her up and you feed her. I've got enough to do cooking and cleaning for you lot". Mary thought that it was unusual but did as she was told to keep the peace. She soon became quite good at feeding the baby and herself at the same time. She would hold the baby on her one arm with the bottle in that hand as she ate her dinner with a fork in her other hand. Mary began to take a great interest in the baby and put most of her spare time into looking after her.

The baby spent most of the day in William's old pram, which was still in good condition. No one knew why it had been kept, perhaps as a reminder of William's babyhood. If the baby began to cry when no one was about Dorothy pushed the pram into the far corner of the front room and closed the door so that she could not hear her. Nine times out of ten the baby went to sleep again until the next feed time. After a week Mary was doing very well at looking after the child. Even Lizzy helped whenever she could, usually washing the baby in the evening when she came home from work if Mary had not already done so.

Grace and Hannah had no time for their new sister they were far too busy looking after themselves. Each had homework to be done and their jobs around the farm. Grace was still working at the forest Glen. The baby was put in a second hand cot in the room they shared with Helen. They had two double sized beds in the biggest of the four bedrooms. As they lay in bed with the baby wriggling in its cot Grace said to Hannah "Our Mam does not have to worry, I am not going to say a word to anyone I know, especially at school. Having babies at her age! We are such a big family as it is. They would just laugh". For once Hannah was in agreement with Grace "I agree. Perhaps they wanted another little boy to be a brother to William. And like you I am saying nothing. It is just not worth it."

"Why does Mam always moan about the cost of everything saying they can't afford us, she seems to want the best for us and yet she is always complaining about the cost, I am just glad I earn my own money now," said Grace.

"And why have another one if we cost so much. If I ever get married I will see to it that I have no more than two" said Hannah.

"I wouldn't say that, you never know you could have twins" Grace said.

"Don't talk daft" Hannah replied.

"Glory only knows what we would be like if we did not look after ourselves. I am not going to have any children at all if I can help it" Grace said firmly.

"Don't you want to get married then?"

"Oh yes but only to a man that can afford to buy me the things I want, like a motor car. You'll see one day I will drive myself wherever I want to go."

"Tell me how do you propose meeting a man rich enough to buy you a motor car?"

"I will go to the dances at the Glen and at Sankey's ballroom. I will stand a much better chance of meeting someone worthwhile than at the village dances."

"Ooh, what if our Mother finds out what you are intending to do, she will hit the roof."

"She will not stop me. I will do what I want when I leave school. Anyway she is more interested in William than any of us." The baby stirred in her cot, the girls looked across "I suppose we will not be getting a lot of sleep from now on," said Hannah.

"You will find that you can ignore it after a while, I got used to you and Helen, and she could really scream."

"Will Mary come and see to her then?"

"Yes you would think she was hers the way she cares for her."

"Well Grace at least we know now that babies don't come from under a gooseberry bush as they say."

"Like I say I am not having any, I have seen enough of them."

At no time did either Fred or Dorothy discuss childbirth with any of them; there were no birds and bees lectures at home or at school. Dorothy's philosophy was simple although she had never bothered to share it with her daughters as yet. If any of them were to bring disgrace to the door then out on the street they would go with whoever got them into the mess.

Helen was often left to keep the baby quiet when everyone was busy, often she would rock the pram or wheel it around the back yard. One Sunday morning she went to the kitchen where Dorothy was preparing dinner.

"Mam, what name are you going to call her?"

"Who?" Dorothy snapped.

"The baby, we can't keep calling her just baby. Anyway she will need a name to be christened." As long as Helen kept the child quiet when she was at home and Mary gave her a bottle when she came in for her meals, her Mother gave the child very little thought.

"I had better think about it," Dorothy said.

"What about Sandra? There is a girl called Sandra in my class and she is ever so nice."

"Bit of a fancy name that" Dorothy mumbled.

"Yes but it sounds nice, Sandra Thomas" Helen said slowly.

"All right I will see what your Father says about it."

Helen went outside again, and rocked the pram. Then she decided to ask her Dad before he came in from milking. She knew if she asked him when he was busy, he would probably agree.

She left the pram on the concrete apron and found him in the bottom cowshed.

"Dad, can we call the baby Sandra?" she asked.

"Aye that sounds like a good name for the little mite," he said.

"Thanks Dad. It is a very nice name isn't it?"

"Aye" was all he said and carried on with his work. She went back outside and set off back to the house. Mary was in the dairy washing down, so Helen parked the pram and went inside "The baby is going to be called Sandra," she said.

"Since when? Has Mam said so?"

"Well not yet, but Dad says that it will be all right."

"Dad says that it will be all right? When did he say this?" Mary was annoyed no one had asked her.

"I have just asked him," said Helen happily.

"Oh you have. Tell me Helen, where has this name Sandra come from?"

"I asked Mam if we could call her that because we can't just call her baby, and I like the name, there is a girl at school called Sandra and she is ever so nice to me."

"I see. In that case she can have Jean for a second name. I have always liked the name Jean".

"Oh yes that would sound nice, Sandra Jean. Mam will have to agree it sounds just right."

"Well she should not argue it is us that do all the work looking after her. If I did not feed her I think that she would let her die of starvation."

"Will you get Mam to agree later tonight, if she is in a good mood?"

"Yes I will. But if Dad has agreed then we should be all right."

"Why do you bother, don't you have enough to do working outside all day?"

"Because no one else is going to worry about her like I do, certainly not our Mam." By the end of the evening it had been agreed that the baby would be Sandra Jean Thomas and that she would be registered in the following week. Fred was pleased; he insisted that a christening should now follow as soon as possible. Dorothy reluctantly agreed to write to the Reverend Barnfield again.

The christening was held on a Wednesday afternoon at Little Wenlock church. Only Fred, Dorothy, Mary and the vicar were there. Mary held her throughout the ceremony and the baby was christened Sandra Jean. There was no party and none of the family mentioned the event. Much to Dorothy's annoyance the Christening was reported in the monthly Parish Magazine, the gossip was soon around the village that there was a new baby at the Willowmoor Farm and everyone assumed that the child must have been Mary's. It came as a surprise to Joyce Wilkins when Wilf read the news. "Good heavens, this is a turn up for the books" he said, "Fred and Dorothy have a new daughter called Sandra. They should be ashamed of themselves, at their ages. Fornication that's what, it is surely they have enough children without one more." Joyce did not agree "People are never too old for such things. It is only you who never got started."

"Be quiet wife I will not have you talk about such things. We have had a very good life without squawking brats interfering" said Wilf and immediately regretted it; she would give him the cold shoulder for sure. He chose to keep his thoughts to himself. Soon the rumours was spreading that it was Mary's daughter and Dorothy being the mother was a cover up. It was the Wilkins who dispelled the rumours as they had seen Mary working the fields and had spoken to her right through the time that the child was born. Joyce was longing to know who had been Godparents to the new one she would have liked to have been asked.

When Hannah was thirteen she was offered some Sunday afternoon work collecting bottles and helping out with the fetching and carrying. Dorothy agreed as long as it was only the afternoon. Helen was there to look after William and the thought of another earning a little was very pleasing to her ears.

On the first Sunday of her new job as soon as she had swallowed her dinner and had done the washing up Hannah was off across the fields like a hare to the Half way house. The weather was good and there were lots of folks taking refreshments. She was met by Eric Watson, who seemed an awesome man, in his white baker's apron tied tightly around his huge stomach, the long drooping moustache was now waxed into position across his rounded face reaching from one ear to the other. Most of the time he sat in a wooden armchair in the corner of the kitchen giving out orders to the staff. Hannah's job was simple enough, all she had to do was to collect any empty mineral bottles, cups and tea trays which had been left lying on the hillside when people were too lazy to return them and collect the deposit which they had paid. She met his wife Gwen, she was very pale and her dark brown hair was tied back in a knot at the nape of her neck. She dressed very plainly and Hannah realized she must have been very beautiful when was younger. Mary had told her that Gwen was about fifteen years younger than her husband and could now be in her late twenties. She had started at the Cottage as a kitchen maid when she had left school. She had succumbed to her boss's lecherous advances and now had four children, two boys and two girls, the youngest still in nappies. Outside as she went around collecting the bottles, plates and litter she saw the three lads from Wrockwardine who worked regularly at the weekends. Charlie, Gwen's brother who was in his twenties, George who was eighteen and his brother Thomas sixteen. They cycled to the cottage early in the morning Between them they handled all the fetching and carrying and looked after the ponies and the swing boats when people wanted rides.

Eric Watson liked to seem busy; he was always giving orders often shouting. Hannah heard him throughout the afternoon, "More wood lads, and keep this range hot. The water has got to be hotter."

George and Thomas brought buckets of hot water from the boiler house, which was down by the bakery. "Keep those boats swinging? Have you given those ponies a drink of water? Don't let that dirty crockery build up. Chop more wood somebody, I have got enough to do in the week without having to cut wood. It is auction day tomorrow and I have to bake bread and cakes during the week". He made himself sound so important and busy. She got to meet Ivy the Mother of George and Thomas and Mrs Briggs who looked after the sinks.

She saw little of Gwen until late in the afternoon when she went inside for some tea. Gwen scurried from kitchen to kitchen keeping things ticking over as her husband wanted and at the same time keeping an eye on the children.

The staff had to use the public lavatories at the back of the house. The ladies lavatory was opposite the back door and the usual country type. It was a brick building and inside there was a wooden bench with two holes, one large for adults to use and smaller one for children and below there was a large pit. It was quite large inside and there was a brick settle on which there was a bucket of clean water, a jug and a bowl for washing hands. A roller towel was hung on the wall and a mirror that was in much need of repair. The men had to walk around the back of the big tearoom and go further downhill. Their lavatory was well out of the way to reduce the smell. Both of the lavatories only had a clean on Mondays, so on a Sunday afternoon the smell was pretty awful!

Hannah walked home with Mary, who had been there all day. It had been a very busy day but she had been paid one shilling and six pence and had her tea for free. Mary told her

"Mam won't pay for any chocolate or sweets that come into the house. She gives Lizzy or me the coupons and we pay it out of our earnings, Grace chips in as well so now you can." The ration was still two ounces per person per week and it had to be bought and taken home for Dorothy to share out equally. Hannah was unhappy with this but she had shared the sweets before so she could not argue. It annoyed her that her Mother made them buy the sweets, 'luxuries' as she called them to save her money so she could spoil William. Hannah wanted to buy oranges and bananas because they were now coming back into the shops. She wondered if Joyce Wilkins had any. Next time they saw her when chasing the sheep she would ask. To Mary it was not a problem; it was a small price to pay for a day's freedom. It was good now that Sandra was getting more attention from their Mother she did seem to be feeding her to keep her quiet.

Hannah forgot all about the sweet ration when it came time to go and visit Rebecca and her grandparents. As the year before she took her little case and went by train to Newport where she was collected and taken back to the Manor. The gout in Granddad's legs had grown steadily worse and so had his temper. He grumbled about the driving and everything else. He did say he was pleased Hannah was there, so she could help out while Rebecca saw to the milking. She was not too pleased at the prospect of running around fetching and carrying for him as she knew how awkward he was, so she went with Rebecca to help with the work outside. Rebecca had many jobs to do and she enjoyed Hannah's company and together they kept out of Bill's way. On the evening of her first day Hannah offered to help her sister to roll oats and other cereal in the corn shed, it was a job that Rebecca did not like much so she was glad of the help. They went up to the loft area where it was quite dark so Rebecca threw open the doors to let some light in. There were so many sacks Hannah could not believe her eyes, twice the size of the granary at home at least. The corn mill was quite a large machine powered by electricity. Rebecca switched it on and cut open a sack of oats. Together they shoveled the grain into the hopper from where it was rolled and fell into wooden bins below. It was not a heavy job and they soon had it done. Hannah looked in the bin and was pleased with the amount they had produced.

"Did you hear about our corn thief?" asked Rebecca?

"No" said Hannah puzzled.

"Well someone we both know was stealing it and I got in trouble for it" said Rebecca.

"What on earth do you mean?" said Hannah. Rebecca looked around to make sure no one was in earshot then she told her story. It had been earlier in the year and she had been rolling corn in the evenings but every now and again there would be far less the next morning. When this happened she simply went upstairs, started the mill and rolled some more. However one morning Bill heard the mill running and came to see why. As his gout had been particularly bad in the night, his temper was worse than usual and he stormed into the corn shed and bellowed at Rebecca, "How many times do I have to tell you to roll enough corn?"

"I do Granddad. But it gets taken overnight" she said trying to defend herself.

"Well the rats are not taking so much that you have to run the mill again," he shouted waving his stick around. She tried to say that someone must have been in during the night but he was not listening and in the end she gave up and let him have his say. Rebecca was really angry that she was being shouted at for simply doing her job. She asked all the men who worked there if they could shed any light on the missing corn but they could not help her. After some more went missing two days later she decided that she was going to find out who was paying a visit during the night. Two nights later when everyone was in bed she went out with a lamp and lay in wait. She made herself comfortable in between some sacks in the loft where she could look down through the trapdoor to the bin below. Her eyes soon adjusted to the dark. She found it very difficult to stay awake at first but then she heard the scurrying of rats on the wooden floor. They squealed to each other as they ran around picking up the loose corn. She could hear them gnawing at something and prayed they would not come near her, she was afraid of getting bitten. She cursed the farm cats and made a note to see they had less milk from the dairy. They should be eating rat for dinner instead of lazing around sleeping.

Several hours passed and the rats seemed to know she was there. Only once did one come near her. It paused a yard away on a sack then fled to where more squealing broke out. In the early hours of the morning she was rewarded for her trouble, a van drew alongside the corn house and someone got out, opened the door and came inside. Then the door was shut and the light was switched on, Rebecca leaned over to catch a glimpse of the intruder. To her amazement it was her Uncle Gordon. This was a turn up for the books. She watched as he filled some sacks with corn and put them by the door then he switched off the light, opened the door and put them into his van. It was as much as Rebecca could do to stay quiet and keep out of sight; the rats had fled as soon as the light came on. After the van had gone she switched on her torch and went back to the house for some well-earned sleep.

When Rebecca finished telling Hannah she smiled grinned a huge smile. "I bet you wouldn't have stayed up there in the dark with the rats would you?"

"No you must have been very brave. But Uncle Gordon has lots of money, why was he taking the corn?"

"I don't know. I never got to find out."

"So what did you do?"

"I Told Grandma and she sorted it out, Granddad has been a lot nicer to me since and no more corn goes missing. But we must not mention that it was Gordon."

"Oh right Mum's the word." Hannah felt privileged to share the secret she would not tell anyone.

After discovering that her uncle was taking the corn Rebecca had indeed told her Grandma. She had known that Granddad would never believe her and there would be more shouting so she had waited until he was out of the house then told her Grandma what had gone on in the night.

Sarah was quite shocked, Rebecca had to repeat her story adding that her Granddad would never believe her if she told him.

"He most certainly would not. He would never believe that his own son would steal from him."

"What can I do if more goes missing I will get into trouble again" said Rebecca.

"Don't you worry? Each night you grind the corn as usual and I will check how full the bins are before going to bed. Then first thing in the morning I will go round there and if there is any missing I will deal with it you can rest assured."

"What will you do?" asked Rebecca "Granddad gets so angry".

"As I say do not worry. It is the gout in his legs; it makes him unbearable at times."

"Most of the time" Rebecca said, laughingly.

Sarah kept her word. She checked the bins last thing at night and was out before the men arrived for work. There was no difference and Rebecca was disappointed. However Sarah was not perturbed and continued to check, then on the fifth day the corn was definitely much lower in the bins.

She was very angry to think that their own son would steal from them. If he needed some, all he had to do was ask, she was absolutely livid. She knew she could not confront Gordon or tell his Father as they had the same bad tempers and there would be the most almighty row. Catching him red handed as Rebecca had done was also out of the question because of his terrible temper. She would have to be more subtle. She decided to have a chat with Lucy, Gordon's wife next time they met up, that would be the day after tomorrow. Lucy was in the habit of dropping into the Copper Kettle café in Market Drayton and taking tea with her friends, it would be perfect. Rebecca was worried but Sarah told her to say nothing to anyone and trust her to put a stop to it.

On the Wednesday Sarah went early to the café and sure enough there was Lucy with one of her friends. She entered and made straight to their table.

"Oh there you are dear," she said to Lucy. "I am so glad that I have caught you, can I join you for a cup of tea?" She sat down ignoring Lucy's friend. "My poor old legs get so tired these days, there is so much to do at the Manor". Lucy looked at her friend and smiled "You should get a cleaning woman like I have. The Manor is such a big house; it is too much for you to do. I don't suppose Bill would consider moving into anything smaller though. You know Gordon is quite capable of running things for you."

"No he would not" Sarah said and ordered a pot of tea from the waitress hovering nearby. She turned back to Lucy "I can assure you that his Father will not hand over the Manor until he is six feet under, as you and Gordon know only too well". She could feel the anger rising, so decided to say no more until her tea had arrived, she surely needed it.

"Of course, we would not presume otherwise," said Lucy. Sarah sat back and waited for her tea while Lucy chatted idly to her friend. They had finished their tea already. When the tea arrived she drank a cup, it was so refreshing then she poured another. "That's better," she looked at Lucy's friend "I wonder if you would be good enough to excuse us dear. Lucy and I have one or two things to discuss. Just farm business you know" the friend got the hint and saying goodbye got up and left.

"We have enough problems at the moment without suggesting that we give up the farm. You see it's like this; we are having some of the corn stolen during the night. Now I do not want to worry Father he is likely to take matters into his own hands and we don't want somebody shot. So I was wondering if Gordon is about late at night. You know he may have seen something" Lucy looked surprised.

"Well of course he often is, there is always a cow calving or some other beast needing attention but he has never mentioned seeing anything untoward."

"The worst of it is that Father has been accusing Beccy of not doing her work properly. Poor girl she has been at the receiving end of his bad temper and she works so hard, I don't think that it is fair at all."

"No I have to agree. Do you have any idea yourself who is responsible?"

"Well yes, you see Beccy stayed up several nights ago hidden in the loft and she saw who it was but we dare not tell Father."

"Well who did she see?"

"Oh I would rather not say at this stage. Will you ask Gordon what he thinks we should do? I would like to get to the bottom of this without his Father knowing. He will know what I mean."

Lucy's suddenly realized what was being said, her face went bright red.

"If you will excuse me I have to get going, Gordon expects me back soon" she rose from the table.

"You won't forget to ask Gordon if he can help, now will you Lucy?" Sarah said as she went to leave.

"No I will make sure that I tell him" she said as she paid her bill and went out to the street. She knew what her mother-in-law was saying. It was Gordon taking the corn. But why tell her? She had not known where he went off to late at night. She had known he had been lying there was not a cow calving every night and why did he need to leave in the van? Now she knew, what a fool she had been, she should have said something. This could cost them the inheritance, that fool Gordon. When she got home there was a blazing row. At first Gordon denied taking the corn then when he realized that Lucy knew the truth he argued that it would not have been missed if not for Rebecca, this was the wrong thing to say and eventually he retreated to the farmyard.

Sarah said nothing to Bill until he mentioned that Rebecca had not started up the corn mill in the mornings recently. She told him that it was because there was no more being stolen, that she had dealt with it and Gordon thought he knew who it might have been and had promised to warn them off, she waited for his reaction. Bill thought for a while then said "Well I never, somebody stealing my corn. You know Sarah I would have shot the bugger if I had the chance".

"We know that, but next time, give Beccy a bit more credit. She is not one for telling lies."

Bill had to agree with her and no more was said. More importantly no more corn disappeared from then on. Sarah told Rebecca that Gordon would not be returning in the night.

"Thanks Grandma" she said, "does Granddad know?"

"Not who it was, but he should be a bit nicer now. Remember there is more than one way to skin a cat."

As the year was drawing to a close Fred was uneasy. On occasions he found himself staring at the clouds when they formed up around the top of the Wrekin, He decided to share his thoughts with Dorothy.

"I think that we should get Jack Munslow's crew to come and thresh this corn before Christmas this time. I reckon we could be in for a bad winter."

"What makes you think that?" she sounded concerned.

"Oh it's just the way the birds are behaving, the swallows have gone early. The magpies, the rooks and the crows are following the plough and whatever else we are doing in the fields. They seem to be in a hurry to fatten them up. I have seen them behave like this before and then a bad winter usually follows." Dorothy had noticed little signs as well "We haven't had a real bad one for nearly ten years now" she said. "I can remember when you and Sam had to dig all the way to the Glen." She hoped he was wrong, she did not want to face a really bad winter like that one again.

"That's right that was a job and a half. Anyway I would like to have the threshing done, so if the bad weather does come along we have the straw stacked and ready. It might be worthwhile sending Mary along to see Joe Timmins. I think that we should have that pig killed and hung up as well, just in case."

"I hope that you are wrong Fred Thomas but I will write to Jack Munslow anyway, I am sure that he will oblige. If it is really bad, we can always have a second killed. We will not starve like we almost did that last bad winter."

"We did not almost starve as you say, Sam and me managed to keep bringing a bit of grub for all the stock as well as ourselves. You killed off all your old boiler fowl and we managed" Fred said laughingly.

"Yes that I did and if the weather had not warmed up when it did and melted the snow I would have had to kill off the rest of the hens. I do not want a repeat of that winter, thank you very much."

The threshing was completed in the last week of November and Fred sold the grain for a really good price. Fred kept more oats back than he usually did and he sold the younger horse so there would only be Kit to feed. He had made up his mind to get rid of him when the horses had run away cutting the corn. The tractor would now have to do everything and all the implements would have to be adapted for use.

The snow started to fall at the beginning of December, winter had truly arrived. There was little let up over the Christmas period but the snow plough kept the road clear and the milk got away. Fred fitted the snow chains to the car wheels and was able to get to and from town with no problem.

Dorothy had managed to take up her market stall again and although she had little to sell, it kept her happy. The majority of her eggs were sent to the packing station. It was Helen's job to collect the eggs and to wash any dirty ones before packing them in special cardboard boxes provided by the egg packing station to await collection.

January brought more heavy snow and the frost was severe, especially at night. The snow blocked the roads and drifted up to twelve feet deep. There was no movement anywhere when Fred looked out of the window at it. He could see where the road ran but there was no way they would be getting to it without a lot of work. None of the children could go to school but they had so much work to do digging paths through to the pens and buildings. After three days the road was opened from Wellington but only to Fred's gate it was not possible to clear the bank. As soon as the road was passable, Hannah walked to school. She would try to work it so that she was by the Buckatree Hall just before Mr Hunt took his two daughters to college in Wellington. He was such a kindly man and was quite happy to give her a lift, as he had to drive past her school. She did not mind the walk home it would take her about an hour and by the time she was home she was hoping that Helen would have done some of her jobs. Grace did not bother. It would be quite a while until Helen and William could get up the bank.

The milk and eggs got away and with the chains on the car they carried on despite the weather. The house still had no proper water and the pump was often frozen solid. It was after Dorothy had been moaning about having to melt snow to keep going that Fred did some asking around on Market day.

Mary had just finished breaking the ice in the large trough at the bottom of the back fields when Fred joined her at the gate; he was gazing up the bank towards the Hatch. "I have been thinking that when the spring comes I'm going to see if we can't get mains water piped to us. We have had enough of carrying water around especially your Mam."

"But how would they get it here?" Mary asked, not that she was bothered as long as she would not have to lift the buckets into the tank for cooling the milk.

"Well I have been told that if we can persuade Wilf and Joyce to have it at their place the water board would take it up the lane from Miss Stewart's farm to them and then they would bring it down the field to us."

"Are you still getting a milking machine Dad?" she asked.

"Oh aye it's just that the water seems to be more important in case we have another bad winter next year." Mary knew it was because of the nagging but never mind she would remind her Mother how good electricity was when she went in.

As the days wore on, Fred became more concerned that they had not seen any sign of Joe Evans digging his way out from the Wrekin Farm. The drifts were too deep to attempt to walk in so he hoped that they had got out the other side where the track joined Spout Lane. Mary was the first to hear Joe's tractor. She could hear the engine noise echoing around the woods leading to his farm. She fetched Fred and they tried to see where it was but the snow was too deep.

"I reckon he is digging his way out like we had to do, all those years ago. Perhaps we ought to give a hand and start from the gate."

The next day they could hear Joe's tractor again so they began clearing a way towards the wood. After several hours they returned to the farm to get some of their own work done, they had got over halfway across the field.

Helen carried on watching from the house and late in the afternoon she brought the news that she could see Joe Evans making his way across the field, he had broken through. Fred went to meet him

"Surry, it is good to see you again. So you have managed to get through with the milk at last".

Joe was soaked in sweat but cheerful "I have spent the last two days digging this lane out. As soon as I can find the milk stand and unload I am going on into town for some essentials".

"I'll not keep you in that case" said Fred and together they dug the snow from the milk stand then unloaded the trailer of milk churns ready for collection the next day. As Joe got on the tractor to leave Fred looked at the sky "You be on your way sharpish. I think that the wind is about to change and we could have some more snow before a thaw starts to set in".

"Now don't you go saying things like that, it is the first time in weeks that I have been able to bring some milk away. I don't think I ever want to dig through snow drifts again as long as I live". Fred chuckled "We did it from here to the Glen so you haven't had it too bad".

"I'll grant you that, but that has been one hell of a job I can tell you." He set off for town and it was soon dark, that night the wind changed and it snowed and snowed. It was another week before Joe Evans was seen bringing his milk again.

The fresh snow compounded their problems, they had to dig all the paths again and the cold was relentless. A snow plough did get through from Dawley to Little Wenlock then down the bank past the farm and all the way to Wellington. They were able to get the milk and eggs away and Fred used the chains again to get them to town. The roads were very treacherous through packed snow and ice, the chains coped well but had to be removed when they reached the A5, driving with them on was unbearable on the tarmac road. The temperature stayed low though and whenever Fred went into the kitchen Dorothy would begin complaining but he turned a deaf ear as usual but he noticed the house was definitely getting colder.

"Surry it's not very warm in here lass" he said when he came in for his dinner, the children were wrapped up in pullovers and cardigans despite being indoors, she glared at him.

"We need more coal that's why, there is very little left and logs don't give out half as much heat you should try and fetch some from town." He could not argue with her, the upstairs rooms were now very cold and there was not enough coal to light fires in every room. The coal man had made no attempt to deliver since Christmas because he would not risk getting his lorry stuck once he left the road to go across the field to the house. Fred felt that he must do something; he could not do with her complaining.

"You are right Dot we will go tomorrow. Mary and I will take the tractor and trailer, Bernie can get on with the jobs here."

Fred found that it was quite straightforward driving the tractor and trailer into town as long as he kept in low gear. The return journey with the trailer loaded with more than a ton of coal was different kettle of fish! Mary sat on the wheel arch it was so cold. She would be glad when they were home. Fred drove through Cluddely to avoid the Ercall but when he reached the Forest Glen he could get no further, the tractor could not grip on the icy road surface with such a heavy load to pull. He had to reverse into the car park and go back taking the road around the bottom of the Wrekin. All went well until he came around to the far side, the snow had been very bad and was piled high on to the hedgerows leaving the way through very narrow. The sides of the trailer caught the sides of the frozen snow as Fred tried to keep the tractor going. It was proving very difficult. The tractor was sliding backwards more than it was going forwards; they were driving on solid ice. There was nothing they could do other than unload part of the coal from the trailer into the snow piled high each side of the road. The gateways were blocked with snow. It was now four o'clock, growing dark and they still had all the rest of the day's work to do when they got back home. Unloading the coal got their circulation going and they felt much better. Fred prayed and hoped that no one would steal it before they could return. With the load lightened they made it to Little Wenlock. Fred made Mary walk when they came to the Willowmoor Bank. He was worried what would happen if the trailer jack-knifed. All the way down he kept the tractor against the snow bank and eventually reached the farm, he drove in through the front gate and up to the house. Mary was not far behind but she was wet, cold and aching as she had fallen headlong on the ice and wished she had stayed with the trailer.

Dorothy came out to see how much coal they had brought back. She looked at the trailer and was very disappointed.

"Is that all that they would let you have? Just you wait until I go in to pay for it I will have something to say to that Mr Gough."

"Now wait a moment lass there is more, it is just that we had to leave it behind."

"Well you had better hurry and unload this or it will be too dark to see what you are doing. Took you two most of the day to fetch that bit, what have you been doing?"

"Go inside and put the kettle on Dot. Don't stand out here in the cold. Let's have Bernie give us a hand to unload. Mary you get in the warm you look all in." Mary was only too glad to get indoors, she was cold and her feet were frozen from the snow getting into her Wellingtons.

"He is with the cows," said Dorothy "I'll send Helen to fetch him and then she can fill the coal buckets for me. It will be good to have a decent fire burning in the grate tonight."

When the coal was unloaded Fred went in for a well-earned cup of tea and a cheese sandwich. He told Dorothy where the rest of the coal was. "You mean to tell me that you have dumped half a load of coal in Spout Lane?" she was almost shouting.

"Steady on a minute Dot, I reckon that you are lucky to have that much. I was sliding back further than I was getting forward when we were trying to come up from the Glen. We had no choice but to try the other way round. I will take Bernie tomorrow and fetch what we unloaded."

"That's if it is still there. You know that we will have to pay for it and I don't like paying for something that I have not had." Fred was tired from being out in the bitterly cold wind all day. He did not need to be reminded how much the coal cost. He drank his tea and finished his sandwich and was glad to get outside to the cowshed to do the nights milking. William went with him keen to hear of the day's events.

The next day Fred and Mary set off early and went back down to the Forest Glen and right round the Wrekin to Spout Lane where the coal was still in the snow where they left it. Dorothy was sure they would return empty handed and came storming out when they arrived back. Fred and Mary were grinning from ear to ear as Dorothy looked in the trailer and saw the coal.

"I don't know what you two are smirking for. It took two trips to get this. Just think of the fuel you wasted."

"Aye lass but we'll have a warm house now and I couldn't have fetched half as much with the horses in this weather." He thought he had the last word but she added, "It is no use in the trailer so stop grinning and get it unloaded. I'll get the kettle on" and went back inside.

"Our Mam is never happy," said Mary. Fred did not answer simply got his shovel and began unloading the coal; he was so pleased they made it safely back.

In the spring when the weather picked up, Eric Watson asked Hannah if she could come and start work at ten o'clock instead of two o'clock on Sundays in the run up to the Easter bank holiday.

Dorothy was unhappy with the idea, she considered she needed her help with the Sunday dinner and odd jobs. Hannah knew she could be spared; she could get up early with Mary, let the poultry out and get the feeding done as the mornings were much lighter now. She could still help with the milking and afterwards Bernie could carry on with cleaning the dairy or feeding the other stock.

There was no longer the family ritual of bathing on a Sunday morning and no one had gone to Sunday school for years. Therefore she argued that Helen, who would be eleven in June, could do her work in the house as well as look after Sandra. She could see no reason why William could not begin to help out just as they had at his age. Dorothy did not like backchat and told her so. Hannah retreated to the farmyard and no more was said for the day. That night Mary told her that she was able to go early after all.

"Does this mean William is going to fetch and carry for her?"

"Not on your life. Just think yourself lucky we can be over the road after breakfast and out of the way for the rest of the day."

Hannah did not ask what changed her Mother's mind and neither Bernie nor Helen seemed bothered so she did not raise the subject again but she was pleased when they arrived at the cottage nice and early on the Sunday. They both loved going there, the pay was very poor but it gave them a chance to get away from the farm and they were meeting people. Including the three lads from Wrockwardine, Charlie, George and Thomas. Hannah had not spoken to any of them much in the past but she found that they took more interest in what she was doing. Both she and Mary were quite flattered but were aware they had work to do. On their way home across the fields Mary raised the subject of the boys at the cottage

"I don't think we should talk to them really." She said

"Why not? It was quite fun" Hannah replied.

"Mrs Watson does not think so. I saw her scowling and I know Mr Watson told them to stop messing about." Mary said.

"I did not notice" said Hannah.

"Well you wouldn't, would you!" said Mary sharply. She was tired and was concerned about their baby sister Sandra. Their Mother was taking better care of her lately but she was nearly a year old now and showing no inclination to walk. All her sisters had been toddling around by that age but she seemed quite content simply to eat and sleep, taking little interest in what went on around her.

Mary did not feel comfortable being away too long during the day as Helen could only do so much to look after her.

"What's wrong?" Hannah asked. "You seem in a rush today."

"I just want to get back. Helen is looking after Sandra and I worry about her dropping her or something like that."

"Why, it is not your responsibility. Mam had her and she should look after her."

"Yes but she is more interested in William."

"Or hens."

"Exactly, now keep up."

Back in the house Mary took Sandra from her pram and changed her sodden nappy. The child was very docile; she had been fed and was quite content. Mary bounced Sandra on her knee, she was not a pretty baby, her face was too fat and she was clearly overweight. Mary looked at her eyes closely they did not seem to focus properly. When Dorothy came in Mary swung Sandra from side to side.

"Mam, do you think her eyes are all right?" Dorothy did not bother to look.

"Leave her alone, stop picking on her. If it is not you, it is one of the others. There is nothing wrong with her."

"No Mam, it is just her eyes don't seem right somehow."

"Since when have you been an expert? You have work to do, so do it."

Later that night Mary spoke to Lizzy about her concerns

"I think that Mother ought to have the Doctor take a look at Sandra's eyes."

"Why is that?" asked Lizzy.

"I think that there is something wrong, she does not seem to look properly, what's more she is quite happy to crawl about but she should make more effort to get on her feet and walk," said Mary

"She won't make much effort while our Mam keeps feeding her so much to keep her quiet," said Lizzy.

"Mam says that lots of babies don't walk until they are two but I don't believe her; none of us has been this lazy" said Mary. Lizzy sighed, "Haven't you seen what Mam is doing?"

"What making her lazy and fat? Not picking her up for a bit of love or a fuss?"

"Yes, but there is more to it than that." Lizzy went on "Mam sees to it that we have some sweet coupons so that we pay for the sweets out of what bit we earn. Then she shares them out but I have often wondered how she always had a bit of chocolate to give to Sandra and William. She is doing deals with Mrs Podmore at the Glen."

"What sort of deals?" said Mary intrigued

"One way is to sell a couple of cockerels or some potatoes really cheap in exchange for sweets without coupons. I have seen Mam on occasions at the Glen taking eggs or poultry in and leaving carrying a brown paper bag."

"What was in it?" Asked Mary

"Whenever I ask her, she usually says she has called in to see if the Podmores are all right for eggs or a bag of potatoes and keeps the bag out of sight."

"Sweets or chocolate then?" Said Mary

"Maybe, do you know, they stop off on the way back from the market?"

"No! What for?" Mary was really surprised at all this.

"Same thing, I saw her running back to the car last week trying to hide something after being in the tearoom with Mrs Podmore for less than five minutes."

"So that's where she gets the extra chocolate from." Said Mary

"Yes but it gets better. Why do the young ones get very few clothes?"

"That's easy; the coupons are used to get William clothes."

"Not all of them, Mam will exchange them with Mrs Podmore because she is always buying for her niece who she absolutely adores."

"How do you know this?"

"The Manageress of Mc Clures dress shop rings up when something special has come in. Our Mam swaps clothing coupons for sweet coupons."

"That is so sneaky and it is not fair."

"She reckons that Grace should buy her own clothes instead of wasting her money. Hannah and Helen can have 'hand me downs', or what Joyce Wilkins or Grandma buys. William is just spoilt."

Mary was speechless but it all added up. So that was why there was no shortage of sweet things for Sandra and William. She always looked after Sandra and it bothered her that she was so slow at picking things up. She mentioned her worries to their father but he was unconcerned. There was a lot of work to be done and the children were Dorothy's concern. He always let one of the little ones sit on his knee and he liked listening to them when he had time but he did not interfere. To Dorothy, Sandra had been an additional burden with the extra washing that had to be done. She hated the bucket of nappies soaking in the corner. The hard winter had been a nightmare for drying clothes and she had struggled to keep the house warm. She had pointed out to Fred that she was washing for ten of them and that the kitchen and far room was not warm enough, the house was wet and therefore cold. It was as she sat looking at the range she recalled first lighting it fourteen years before and the water leaking from the boiler. She decided it was time it was fixed or replaced. The early threshing had brought in a tidy sum and she felt that some of it should go into the house. Fred agreed and at the end of March the old range was ripped out and a brand new Rayburn cooker installed. It was cream enamel and only had to be washed to keep it clean. What a difference it made, the whole kitchen was brightened up. The girls were very impressed with the heat it gave out and it did not have to be black-leaded, a job they hated. Once it was stoked up the fire stayed in all night, keeping the kitchen so much warmer.

CHAPTER 14

A BREAK FROM ROUTINE

Easter was late, The Bank Holiday Monday came at the start of the second week of April, both Mary and Hannah had a very busy day at the Cottage. Neither of the girls was in a hurry to go back home they decided to take their time and go the long way home. At the Forest Glen they stopped chatting to Charlie, George and Thomas. They arrived home quite late, hoping there would be little work for them to do.

"Where have you two been until now?" said Dorothy, as they went into the kitchen. She was really angry.

"Coming" Mary answered.

"Coming, what do you mean, coming? Your father and I have been waiting for you." They looked at Fred sat in his usual chair. He was looking very pale and uncomfortable; he had one foot resting on a wooden kitchen chair.

"What is the matter?" asked Mary innocently.

"Your Dad's broken his leg! Showing that lad Bernie how to drive the tractor he was."

"He's what? Has no one fetched the Doctor?" Mary exclaimed.

"I went to the Glen to phone for a Doctor," Helen piped up. "They were ever so busy but Lizzy took care of it for me, and she did the telephoning."

"We are still waiting for the doctor to come" said Dorothy, "we have been waiting since it happened this afternoon. Now you two go and change those clothes and see if that lad Bernie has finished the work outside, I can't leave your Father on his own. In agony he is and that Doctor might come any minute".

"Where is Sandra?" Mary asked seeing that she was not there waiting to be put to bed. William was sat at the table playing with a toy tractor and trailer that Dorothy had bought for him at Christmas,

"I've put her to bed, I thought that you might be a bit late seeing that it is Bank Holiday and I wanted her from under my feet."

Mary and Hannah disappeared from the kitchen and asked no further questions about what had gone on. That could wait until later. They found Bernie in the cowshed, still very upset about what had happened.

"Well how did it happen?" Mary wanted to know.

"We were ploughing the bottom field and your Dad said that I could have a go at steering the tractor being as the field was not very hilly. He was standing on the back of the tractor and we were doing so well when the plough struck a boulder and caused the tractor to jerk. Your Dad almost fell off. His leg got caught on the wheel somehow and was broken when it was taken up to the mudguard. Oh Mary, I did not know what to do when I heard his screams. I just switched everything off. I unhitched the plough and took him back to the house, he sat on the back of the tractor and when I got him into the kitchen your mother was mighty angry. I did not know that it was going to happen, it just did."

"Well it was not your fault so don't worry about it. Our biggest worry is how we are going to cope with all the work. Thank goodness there is no school for you tomorrow Hannah, you can help out here."

"Oh Lordy," said Hannah "they are usually quite busy on the Tuesday after the Bank Holiday and I could have earned some money."

"Well you may be able to go next Sunday" said Mary "we will see how we get on, but there is going to be so much for us to do."

"I will work extra hard to help out," said Bernie.

"Good," said Mary "I will finish ploughing that field tomorrow while you two do the other jobs. It will have to be broken down and sown as soon as possible. Dad wants oats sown this week or it will be too late, he was only saying yesterday that the field is just dry enough to plough."

"He said that to me as well" said Bernie. "And that seed is very expensive and must be put in the ground or it would be wasted."

"Exactly, then all the more reason for me to get on with the ploughing," said Mary. Hannah was amazed how quickly Mary had taken control of things.

Back in the kitchen Fred was looking very grey about his face and was in a lot of pain.

"Should I go to the Glen again and telephone to see what has happened to the Doctor and make sure that he is coming tonight?" Mary asked her Mother.

"No don't bother, he will be here any minute now," said Dorothy "As our Helen has said, Lizzy phoned and told them and I am sure the doctor will not leave him sat here with a broken leg all night. You get some supper and go to bed I will stay with him until the Doctor arrives, there is going to be so much to do."

"Why don't I drive you both to the hospital so Dad can get some help?" suggested Mary.

"Don't talk so daft girl" Dorothy quickly replied. "We can't go doing things like that, what if the Doctor came while we were away and anyway you have not driven the car on the road before."

Mary said no more but thought to herself, "It looks as if I am going to have to drive it on the road before this next week is out. Mam won't miss the Thursday market, if I know her." She turned her attention to her Father. "I can finish ploughing that field tomorrow Dad; Bernie can take care of the rest. Don't you worry we will cope all right and have those oats sown by the end of the week if the weather stays good."

"But you have not done any ploughing with the tractor," said Fred hesitantly.

"I will be all right I have watched you do it enough times and I am sure that I can break it down, just leave it with us, Bernie will be here to help with the lifting. Hannah is on holiday from school this week and she can do some of the feeding. Besides you will have to have that leg put in plaster and we don't know how long that will take before you can work again."

"Get some supper and go to bed it is almost nine o'clock" Dorothy interrupted "sounding so morbid you are. Your Dad will be back on his feet in no time at all, you will see."

Lizzy and Grace came in from working at the Forest Glen.

"What's Dad doing still here?" Lizzy asked. "Its hours since I rang for that Doctor, I thought he would have sent him to hospital if his leg is broken. Why is he still sat there?"

"Because that doctor you rang for has not come as yet. Are you sure you made the right telephone call?" Dorothy replied.

"Of course I did, I spoke to his wife who said he would come as soon as he came in. She said he was out at the golf course and she would send him here as soon as he came in."

"Sounds to me as if he is still in the club house and has lost all trace of time, you know what these men are like when they get talking. You lot get yourselves to bed and I will stay here with your Dad until he comes.

Mary made herself a sandwich and a cup of cocoa then made her way to bed, when Lizzy joined her they discussed their Father's predicament.

"You would think I had not rung for the Doctor the way Mam's carrying on but I did and his wife was ever so nice and said he would come. Do you think Dad is in a lot of pain?" Lizzy sounded so concerned.

"Of course he is, it must be terrible to sit there with a broken leg and not be given anything for the pain, and I don't know how he can bear it. We had better get some sleep, there is going to be a lot more work for us to do" Mary was already yawning from fatigue having worked all day at the cottage.

"I can't stop away from work, not this week. I know the schools all have to be back in a week but Mrs Podmore says some of the factories are being given extra time off, some may be given a whole week and with pay. She says she does not know what things are coming to. Giving more than one day off at a Bank Holiday, I bet you she will not be complaining at the end of the week if we have been busy and she has taken a lot of money. She is staying open all day tomorrow, and said Grace and me can have the time off later in the year. I would have preferred to have been paid extra money; it would have been much more useful."

"You thank your lucky stars you get paid for what you do, not like it is here," said Mary. "All I get told if I ask Mam for any money is that they feed us and keep a roof over our heads and that is enough"

"I know, I hear it all the time," Said Lizzy stifling a yawn.

"What bit I get at the Cottage does not buy very much," Said Mary. "Thank goodness I can help you out at the Glen when you have those dinner dances."

"Let's not go on about money, we had better get some sleep it will soon be morning and Dad should be in hospital by then. Mam's right, there is nothing we can do for him just sitting looking at him. She will see to him if need be. I'm tired out". Lizzy pulled the sheet over her head, a habit of hers when she did not want to talk anymore.

Next morning both girls were woken by their Mother calling them to get up and come downstairs.

Mary was first to enter the kitchen and was surprised to see her father still sat in his chair, his right leg still on the wooden chair as they had left him the night before. He looked very pale and exhausted and when Mary asked he confirmed that he was in a great deal of pain.

"Sat here all night we have, and no Doctor has arrived as yet. Where is that Lizzy, I want her to get down that road and ring again and see if she can find out what is going on and why that Doctor Morris has not been to see your Father. I will have something to say about this, you mark my words, and you see if I don't. Been up all night I have but there is not much I can do for him. I have only got a few aspirin in the house and they are no good for the pain he is suffering, that leg is broken that is for sure. Here you drink this tea and have a look if everything is all right in the buildings." Dorothy passed a cup of tea to Mary and put another one at the back of the table for Lizzy.

"I have no idea how we are going to manage all the work. Trust your Father to go and do something like this when I've got so much poultry to take care of." She glared at Fred, and then asked if she could do anything to make him any more comfortable. Hannah came into the kitchen and took in the scene before her. Before she could say a word her Mother shouted,

"Hannah go and give that lad a shout or it will be dinner time before he gets up. Mary will want some help with the milking".

Lizzy was quickly washed, dressed and ready for work. By eight o'clock she was on her way to work. Her mother had instructed her to ask Mrs Podmore to telephone the doctor for her as soon as she got there

"I will be lucky if she has got out of bed. Still, perhaps Mr Podmore will be up and I am sure that he will telephone for me."

It was Percy Podmore who unlocked the back door to let Lizzy in when he heard her knocking.

"Elizabeth what are you doing here so early you do not start until nine o'clock. How is your Father? He looked down at Lizzy who was almost in tears.

"That's why I have come so early. Will you telephone the Doctor and ask him to come and see my Dad? He has not been to see him and Dad is in such terrible pain. Mam said that I was to ask you to do the telephoning for me then perhaps they would take more notice of you." Lizzy took a handkerchief from her pocket and wiped her nose. She did not want to start to cry, she had been really upset when she had seen her Dad earlier on when she had got ready to go to work.

"Come on in Elizabeth, I just cannot believe that no Doctor has been to see your Father as yet. My goodness it was yesterday afternoon when you telephoned for him to come out. Leave this with me, I will telephone at once and I will have something to say to whoever I speak to. Now you make a pot of tea and just relax for a while. Have you got to go back home and let your Mother know if the Doctor is coming to see your Father?"

"No my Mam said to stay at work once I had made the call and had an answer to say that the Doctor would go and look at my Dad. His leg is broken, Mr Podmore, the bone is broken right the way through, and he did it on the tractor somehow. They will take him to hospital to mend it and Mary says that he will be off work for weeks." Lizzy started to sniffle then blew her nose hard into her lace hanky.

"You sit there and don't worry; I will sort this out for you. It is Doctor Morris isn't it?"

"That's right he is the new one. Doctor Williams retired," she said

Percy left her and made the call, he was angry when he was told that the doctor had made no effort to come out. Lizzy could hear his raised voice through the open door, sound echoed well in the empty pavilion. When Percy returned he had calmed down a little. "The doctor will be on his way shortly," he said

Mary and Bernie got on with the milking of the cows. They carried the milk to the dairy and fed the calves, pigs and most of the poultry there was only the baby chicks for her mother to see to. It was Mary who called her when she had finished.

"Hannah, will you fetch the horses in? I think that you and Bernie can take a couple of loads of muck to the field across the road; Dad is planting swedes and mangolds on most of it this year.

"Surely you don't expect me to load manure." said Hannah thinking "Since when have you been the boss?"

"You can put the harnesses on ready for when we have had our breakfast. I will finish ploughing the bottom field so that we can sow that corn by the end of the week."

"You are going to be ploughing with the tractor?" Hannah said surprised.

"Yes, why not? I have used it before."

"But not like that, you have only used it for small jobs."

"Things are different now and it has to be done." It was obvious that Mary was the boss as far as getting the work done on the farm went.

"You can do your bit," said Mary. "Dad is going to be off work for weeks and there is so much to do. We can't let the muck pile up outside the cow shed doors." Hannah said no more and trudged off to find the horses. Fred used the tractor for shifting muck normally. The horses were kept for such jobs as sowing corn or binding. He had not altered all of the machinery to be pulled by the tractor preferring the steady pace of the horses. He still had Kit but Bonnie had gone and now he had Robin one of her foals, he came in handy when two horses were needed. Fred felt that horses did not flatten freshly broken down soil, as did the heavy wide wheels of the tractor restricting the new seed growth. It was usually the end of March before Fred's bottom fields were fit to cultivate after the winter months despite the drainage that had been done during the war. The horses moved much more slowly so that it was much easier for someone to follow the drill and keep an eye on the seed pipes and have the horses stopped if a pipe got clogged up or if a pipe hit a large stone and dislodged it.

Later Mary joined Hannah and Bernie to help them harness the horses to a cart.

"Where is Grace?" Hannah asked.

"I don't know," said Mary "probably gone to the Glen. You never know where she gets to these days and it is just as well as it saves her and Mam arguing all the time. I don't blame her, Mam seems to have something to say each time she comes through the door."

"It is not fair we have to do all the work. Has the doctor got here yet?"

"No and Mam is not happy, I wouldn't want to be in his shoes when he gets here."

Until the setting up of the NHS the family doctor had been Dr Williams. Visits to his surgery cost money and were only made when absolutely necessary. Dorothy had a whole range of cures available, some the girls were not so keen on, particularly the iodine or hot poultices. Dorothy was pleased when it was announced that the health service was to provide free care and medicine. The payment of the insurance stamp was something that she could see the benefit of. There would only be Fred and Mary to pay, leaving herself and five children free. When the details of the new surgery arrangements arrived in the post Dorothy had smiled.

"I will have a lady doctor" she said "I quite like the idea of that."

"Aye, well I don't think she will see me very often," chuckled Fred.

"You are to be seeing a Doctor Morris it says here and don't you go chuckling like that Fred Thomas. Do you remember the time you had that blackthorn in your leg and it went wrong ways. If Doctor Williams had not sent you to Shrewsbury you would have lost your leg for sure."

"Aye and it cost a pretty penny too." He had said thinking that if there was to be a next time there would be no hesitation.

Sitting there all night, with the pain throbbing through his leg Fred was reminded of that day. As the dawn came up he shifted and a stab of pain made him grimace. "Where is that bloody doctor," at least he was warm the Rayburn did a grand job.

Dorothy was dozing opposite him, sat in her chair wrapped in a blanket. He felt so proud of her; she had sat with him all night. He thought of all the times they had stayed up with animals, tending to them, sometimes to no avail. The pain was not that bad, perhaps he could manage to hobble outside. As soon as he raised himself a wave of nausea passed over him and he drew a breath sharply. Dorothy looked up. "Sit down Fred Thomas, the doctor will be here in a minute."

Dr Morris arrived about half past eleven, he had dealt with the morning surgery before going out on his rounds, by which time Dorothy was in a right state. He quickly examined Fred's leg and apologized for not visiting earlier. His excuse was that he had received the wrong message and that he had understood the farmer in question, meaning Fred, had only hurt his leg. He could not believe that Fred had been sat on the chair since the previous day.

"Well what were you told?" Dorothy wanted to know.

Dr Morris was very evasive, he said the leg was badly broken and assured her that he would have Fred admitted to

The Royal Salop Infirmary immediately. He quickly left and returned to Wellington to arrange for an ambulance to take Fred to hospital. Dorothy had no choice but to calm down when she realized that there was nothing else that could be done. "Even someone with two blind eyes could see how badly the leg was broken," Dorothy said to herself when Dr Morris had left.

A while later the ambulance came through the front gate. Hannah saw it, so, she quickly washed her wellingtons and went to see what was going on. Two men in uniform lifted Fred from the chair and laid him on a stretcher to be carried to the ambulance and made him as comfortable as they could. Dorothy had helped him to wash and shave and saw to it that he wore a clean shirt. She was fluttering around like a broody hen, making apologies for Fred's dirty trousers saying that the Doctor had told her not to try to remove them for fear of causing further damage to his leg which was well and truly broken.

After the ambulance had left Dorothy sent Hannah back to load the muck cart then she sat down in Fred's chair and cried with exhaustion. How were they going to cope with all the work she wondered, there seemed so much to be done There were cows due to calve, still more lambs to be born and she had more than enough to do with the amount of poultry she was now rearing.

Mary was already getting on with the ploughing on the bottom field when she saw the ambulance leave and go down the road. She felt rather annoyed that her Mother had not sent Hannah or Bernie to tell her so that she could speak with her Dad before he was taken away and reassure him that she would be able to cope with the work. Her Mother only had to look through the front room window and she would have seen both Hannah and Bernie loading the muck cart. Mary had felt a bit guilty asking Hannah to help Bernie but she had not got a lot of other work that he could do and she knew that if Hannah was with him he would work really hard. He liked showing off in front of them saying how strong a man he thought he was and not a weakling just because he came from the city.

Joyce Wilkins had seen the ambulance arrive from her window. She had bought a pair of binoculars and these came in very handy when she wanted to see exactly who was doing what at the Willowmoor farm. Wilf had commented that she was getting a right nosy parker but that did not bother or deter her. After all she thought what else did she have to take an interest in, absolutely nothing. Seeing Mary ploughing the bottom field with the tractor instead of Fred had caught her attention earlier. "Whatever next," she thought "Mary is ploughing with that tractor, I know some of the land army girls drive them but where is Fred, and he was doing it yesterday." The arrival of the ambulance gave her further cause for concern.

"Something has happened down at the farm," she told Wilf when he came in for his dinner. "An ambulance has been and gone, I think something has happened to Fred. Eat up your dinner, so that I can go down and find out." Wilf went to the window and looked down; he could see the tractor ploughing the field below.

"What are you talking about woman? That is Fred down there"

"That is Mary she has been ploughing all morning and it is the lad and another of the girls shifting muck. I thought it was odd Lizzy, going to work before eight this morning."

"Probably nothing to worry about." said Wilf and sat down to eat his dinner.

"Oh my goodness how will that family cope with all the work if Fred is not there to help them."

"They seem to be coping very well from what I can see. Anyway, it may not be Fred at all." He enjoyed knowing what went on to a certain extent but it did irritate him that she hardly missed a thing happening down at the Willowmoor farm.

"If it was someone else Fred would have taken them in the car." she said. "Oh yes, well you go on down then."

"As soon as you have finished I will."

"Yes you do that and offer any help they might need, not that I can be of much use. The arthritis is really playing up in this right leg of mine."

"It's been playing you up for years Wilf Wilkins but I reckon you could run as fast as any other man if a bull was chasing you."

"There is no need for your sarcasm wife; I have said that my leg is giving me a lot of pain. There is no law about making a statement as to ones health."

"Well in that ambulance there is probably somebody in a lot more pain than you."

"Oh be quiet woman and let me eat my dinner in peace. Is that too much to ask? When I have finished you can get yourself down there and find out exactly what has been going on."

Joyce was getting really angry at her husband's assumptions but decided to let the matter rest until their meal was finished and she had washed the dishes, she would never leave the washing up undone, then she would go down and find out for herself what had happened.

After Fred had been taken and Dorothy had a little cry, she decided to pull herself together. The word would soon get around the neighbours that Fred was in hospital. She smiled to herself as she thought that Joyce Wilkins would be the first to know except for the Podmores at the Forest Glen. She was not far wrong. Hannah and Bernie had been in for their dinner and then Hannah had taken some dinner in a basket to Mary in the field. "It's just as well she finishes ploughing that field before she comes back to the yard" Dorothy had argued with Hannah when she had protested at having to walk all the way to the far end of the bottom field.

"Bernie can carry on shifting muck while you are away. Just because your Dad is not here we still have to get on with the work."

Hannah decided the walk to take Mary her dinner was better than loading the muck cart, so she said no more.

Dorothy saw Joyce Wilkins coming down the field. "I thought as much. I'll bet the nosy beggar has been watching all morning. I could have well done without her company this afternoon, I feel so tired there seems to be no peace at all." She was so tired from being up all night, she had hoped to go to bed as soon as she had finished the dinner.

She quickly put a clean cloth on the kitchen table and put the kettle to boil on the hot plate of the Rayburn.

"Helen," she called "you can keep an eye on Sandra and William. Take them outside somewhere." Sandra was in her pram so Dorothy pushed it out onto the back yard. "While you are about you can pick up some wood for lighting the fires." Helen took William and the pram and went off to the stackyard to try and play hide and seek.

Dorothy turned her attention back to the boiling kettle. She fetched two of her best cups and saucers from the front room. She left the bowl of dirty dishes in the sink not bothered if Joyce Wilkins did notice. She felt that she had had enough to cope with for one morning without having to worry about a bit of washing up. Helen and Hannah could wash them later. She opened the door as soon as Joyce knocked.

"Hello Dorothy. I hope nothing too dreadful has happened. I glanced through the window and just happened to see an ambulance drive away from here, whatever has happened?

"Oh it is awful; Fred has broken his leg very badly. Snapped clean through it has."

Joyce sat down at the kitchen table uninvited.

"I saw Mary driving the tractor, such a clever girl and such a hard worker she is, I thought something was amiss." She noticed that Dorothy had not washed what few dishes had been used at dinnertime. "Just like Dorothy," she thought, "waiting for one of the girls to wash up later. It will still be there when Lizzy comes home I should not wonder."`

Dorothy started to sniffle and reached in her apron pocket for the piece of rag she was using for a hanky. She blew her nose.

"There. There, now don't you get upset. I am sure that Fred is in good hands now. Where have they taken him to?" Joyce was very sympathetic.

"They have taken him to The Royal Salop Infirmary. The Doctor thinks that he could be there a week and after that his leg could be in plaster for at least six weeks. There is so much work to be done I just doesn't know how we are going to manage. I really don't."

"Well thank goodness that you have Mary and that young lad to help. My Wilf told me to offer his help if you need it but his leg is not too good at the moment. The arthritis plays him up such a lot, he says that if the milking gets too much for him he will give it up and keep young stock or see the Estate manager about letting some other farmer rent the ground. I told him that it would be better to rent the ground because if he can't cope then I am sure that I can't." Dorothy put a cup of tea in front of her and she stopped talking.

Dorothy was thinking that if the Wilkins ground came up for rent, she and Fred would be the first to put an application in for it.

"I see," said Dorothy "do thank Wilf for offering his help, it is good to know that we can call on him should the need arise. I am sure that he will have nothing to worry about for quite a few years yet."

"Things can alter over night though," said Joyce "it only needs an accident like this and everything changes."

"True but we only have to get through this first week and hopefully Fred will be home, then at least he will be able to tell us how to do things. I will be glad when William is old enough to take over." She smiled at the thought of William controlling everything for her. Joyce noticed that there was not a word of praise for Mary out there doing the ploughing. The woman only thought of William.

"Tell me, how did Fred come to break his leg, what was he doing? Did a cow kick him or something? I noticed a strange car come here this morning."

"You don't miss much that goes to and from this place," thought Dorothy.

"He was standing on the back of the tractor showing that young lad Bernie how to drive it yesterday when the plough hit a large stone and, according to what he said the tractor jerked so hard his foot slipped and got caught under the mud guard somehow. The lad drove the tractor back to the yard with Fred sat on the back of it in agony. I really don't know what came over him letting that young lad have a go at driving a machine like that."

"But you just said that it happened yesterday, why has he only been taken to hospital today. Did you not know that his leg was broken and call for a Doctor? I wish you had let me know, I could have told you if his leg was broken or not." Joyce sounded so alarmed.

Dorothy started to feel angry, "Of course we sent for the Doctor, Helen ran all the way to the Forest Glen as soon as it happened and Lizzy telephoned for the Doctor to come. It turns out that the doctor's wife took the call and passed on the wrong message. He thought that there was nothing urgent for him to worry about so he did not come out. We waited and waited, in fact we waited all night expecting him to turn up but the devil did not. I sent Lizzy to work early this morning; she was to ask Mr Podmore to telephone the Doctor's surgery again. Poor Fred, he sat on his chair all night it was terrible for him."

"Oh my goodness, poor Fred, I feel so sorry for him I really do. Which doctor was it? He wants reporting to someone."

Again Dorothy took her hanky from her pocket and began to sniffle to let Joyce Wilkins know how upset she was.

"Doctor Morris one of these NHS doctors, his wife had said he was out at the golf club. Seems they don't like coming out on a Bank Holiday if they can help it. I suppose they do not have to worry about patients paying them any more."

"Poor Fred. Poor Fred. What sort of pain did he have to endure? Terrible it must have been. Wait until I tell my Wilf about this. He said it would not get better. The Government said that by folk paying their stamp everyone would get free health care. They did not say you had to wait in pain to get it. Doctors are paid for having patients that they may not see for years. They are taking advantage of us all. The old system was the best when they got nothing unless they did the work."

Joyce was quite irate, she drank her tea in one go then pushed her cup and saucer across the table to have it refilled. Dorothy refilled both their cups.

"There is only one good thing that has come from this new health system so far," said Dorothy. "We married women don't have to pay. It's about time we got thought of."

"Yes" agreed Joyce "and goodness only knows what it would have cost for your Fred to have this broken leg seen to in the past."

"We would have raised the money somehow, as you do in these sort of circumstances."

"Are you going to see him while he is there?" asked Joyce.

"I don't know yet, I have not had time to think about it or how I would get there. I will get Lizzy to ring tomorrow to see how he is and how long they are going to keep him in."

"Oh good, I hope he is all right. You know you are lucky to have these girls to run around for you. I often wondered how you coped with such a big family. But now I can see how useful they are helping with all the work."

"They have their uses" Dorothy replied.

"You should be very proud of them. I would have loved to have a family but my Wilf was adamant from the beginning and one did marry for better or for worse did we not."

"Yes well, be that as it may, we cannot do without Fred there is so much to do," said Dorothy.

"If they plaster him up he will be home within the week and then he will be able to supervise even if he can't help out with the work." Joyce finished her tea. "I must get off now; I would not like to overstay my welcome." She stood up. "I am sure you must be feeling very tired from being up all night."

"Yes indeed and thank you for coming," Dorothy answered. "Will you thank Wilf for his offer of help, you are quite right; I am very tired and will be glad to see my bed tonight."

After Joyce Wilkins had gone Dorothy sat herself down in Fred's chair again. She was glad that the schools were off for the week, at least she had the girls to help out apart from Grace that is. She thought of what Joyce had been saying about Mary. "Mary is so good," Dorothy said out loud mimicking Joyce's voice. "It's alright for her, she has not had them to wash and cook for."

Helen saw Joyce Wilkins going back up the field and decided to go back in. She took William and Sandra with her. As she opened the door Dorothy was muttering to herself.

"Who are you talking to Mam?" she asked.

"To myself. I have just got rid of that Joyce Wilkins. Been sat here for most of an hour hindering me, she has."

"Can I have a drink Mam?" asked William

"Of course lad," she said and turned to Helen "Get me some logs in and you can do that washing up before you sit down."

"Come on William, do as Mam says you can fetch some wood and coal while I get the washing up done." William made no effort to help and sat down at the table. Dorothy went off to the front room and returned with a packet of biscuits. She glanced at Sandra and shoved a biscuit into her tiny hand.

Helen turned from the sink, "Come on William get a move on, and you can fetch the logs surely." She spoke firmly and looked at her mother for support; Dorothy glared at her, "Give the lad a chance. He has only just sat down for a drink and a biscuit. You can sit down before you make a start if you want." She poured out some tea. Helen knew that it was best to keep quiet.

"It's been a long day for the little lad; he can do a bit when he has had a rest."

Helen drank her cup of tea and helped herself to a biscuit before William ate the lot.

She did the washing up and then remarked loudly that there was the coal and wood to get in.

"Well what are you standing there for?" said Dorothy. "Get a move on, it will soon be time for the milking to be done."

Mary finished the ploughing by four in the afternoon. She unhitched the plough and left it just inside the field; it could stay there until it was needed again. She looked across the field, what a sight, she felt very proud of her work.

If the weather would stay this fine for the next few days she would be able to get the soil broken down with the disc and spike harrows. It would then be ready for sowing. She drove the tractor into the yard and saw that the muckheap outside the top cow shed door was much smaller than it had been that morning. She parked the tractor alongside the binder in the cart shed.

"Thank goodness for that" she said to herself. "It must be almost five o'clock; I am having a cup of tea and a bite to eat before I start milking the cows." Helen joined her on the yard.

"How is it going Mary? Have you managed to finish ploughing the bottom field?"

"Yes. I have finished the ploughing and we can start breaking it down if this weather holds. We should have it sorted by Thursday night."

"You will be lucky; Mam will want to be taken into town to do her shopping. By the way do you remember how she said there were no biscuits left when I asked for one yesterday?"

"Yes."

"Well she found another packet for William to stuff himself with."

"Oh really. In that case I will go and see if I can have one with a cup of tea."

"You'll be lucky. What do you want me to do? I have told William to get the sticks and coal in ready for morning but I will have to do it myself."

"It's going to be strange first thing in the morning not having Dad about."

"True he will not be here for a while; I don't suppose that Mam will be getting up first. She has to have her cup of tea in bed as a rule."

"Not any more, she doesn't" Mary chuckled.

"She won't like that" said Helen and laughed, "She will be in a right mood first thing in the mornings. Thank goodness that I can go to school next week out of her way." Mary stopped laughing; there was still work to do.

"Perhaps you could go and check the sheep. Most of the ewes have lambs at the moment and that's how we want to keep it until Dad gets back. Keep an eye out for any ewes standing alone by the fences. It often means their lambs have got through to the other side and can't get back. You should find them all right. We don't want to leave a good supper for a fox."

Mary went and found Hannah and Bernie. They had taken care of bedding and most of the feeding there was really only the milking to do. She went to the kitchen for a cup of tea and a break.

"Is the ploughing done?" Dorothy asked as soon as she walked in.

"Of course it is "said Mary cockily.

"Well there is so much to do. How are we going to cope without your Dad?"

"We can manage. In fact we only have the milking and the locking up to do. Helen is checking the sheep right now. If we put the calves feed ready, she can feed them and the pigs when she gets back. Hannah and Bernie will be in for a drink in a minute."

"You seem to have it all organized, I see" Dorothy said sharply, she was quite miffed to see Mary had everything under control. "Well how I am going to get to Wellington on Thursday. Have you thought of that?"

"I will take you in the car" Mary said with a big grin. She had thought of it most of the afternoon.

"What? You drive the car but you are supposed to pass a driving test."

"Well why not? I have been driving the tractor all day there is not much difference."

"You have not driven in town. I really don't know about you driving the car".

"Well you think about it. If you go into town on Thursday, you will have to dress the poultry tomorrow. That is if you want to sell any this week. I have a provisional driving licence and unless you say anything different, no one will know that I have not passed the test." Dorothy did not have an answer, she poured some tea and Mary sat down at the table. There were only two biscuits left in the packet on the table so Mary took them both ignoring the look of annoyance that her Mother gave her.

Mary did not want her mother interfering with the work outside. She quickly went through her plans for the week adding "It's what Dad wants."

Dorothy told her of Wilf Wilkins offer to help out. They both agreed they could manage without bothering the neighbours unless it was absolutely necessary, it would be different if it was later in the year.

Dorothy thought of going to town on Thursday, it would be good if she could. She decided to wait and see how things were by the end of tomorrow afternoon and then she could kill the birds she intended to sell on Thursday. Helen and Hannah could pluck them she thought. Dorothy did not include Grace in her plans as she hardly ever saw her and it was clear she would leave home as soon as she finished school. She did not approve of anything Grace did, especially after finding out that she was going to the dances at Sankey's Ballroom in Hadley. But the more she argued with Grace the less she saw of her. Lizzy had telephoned the doctor from the Forest Glen and confirmed that Fred was in hospital and found out which ward he was on.

By lunchtime on Wednesday Mary was able to start breaking the ploughed field down ready for sowing. A warm spring wind was blowing and it was drying out really well.

"If the weather stays as good as this I reckon that we will be able to sow the seed on Friday." Mary told her Mother when she went in at the end of the day. "If I take you into town in the morning and then go over it with the spike arrows a couple of times it should be all right."

Dorothy had mixed feelings. She felt that it should be her organizing things. She had suggested to Fred that she should learn to drive the car but he would not hear of it, he was still a bit old fashioned in that respect. He would not have his wife driving him. It was all right for Mary though because she would only be driving when he wasn't able to.

"Just as you say" Dorothy answered. "I will see how well you drive tomorrow then perhaps we could go and see him on Sunday afternoon. It does not matter if you don't want to drive too near the hospital, we can walk some of the way if need be."

"All right," said Mary. The chance to drive to Shrewsbury pleased her, but there would be no going up to the cottage to earn a few pennies.

"Now we know your Dad is going to be all right we can relax a bit and get on with the work until he comes out. Lizzy is ringing the hospital again today to find out when. I am hoping it will be some time next week."

"Let's wait and see," said Mary. She was tired and wanted to go to bed. If she was to drive to Shrewsbury on Sunday Hannah would have to go to the cottage alone, Eric Watson would not like it if neither of them turned up.

Thursday morning, as soon as the milk churns were on the stand awaiting collection, Mary left the rest of the work to Bernie and Hannah to take care of. She took the car keys from the mantelshelf, went to the garage and opened the doors. She reversed the car out ready for Dorothy to load her dressed poultry and other produce to take to her stall in the market. There were no rabbits today; no one had time to reset the snares. She went back inside and quickly washed and changed then had a bite to eat. She was a little apprehensive when she started the car. She knew that her Mother had only trusted Fred to drive this car with her in it.

"What are you waiting for then," said Dorothy pushing her hair under her hat nervously. Mary put the car in gear and away they went.

"I hope you know what you are doing," Dorothy said as they drove out of the front gate and started off down the road.

"Of course I do Mam. Just you sit there and stay quiet so that you don't make me nervous. You have nothing to worry about. I will stop outside the market and help you unload and then you can tell me what time you want me to come back for you."

As soon as they started going downhill Mary found the car quite a handful. It began to run away with them so she pressed the brake really hard with her left foot but forgot to lift her right foot from the accelerator. She realized what she was doing and managed to slow the car down but then she tried to change gear and got it all wrong again and the car speeded up.

"For goodness sake girl," said Dorothy quite worried. Mary ignored her and hit the brakes again. They progressed in fits and starts to the Forest Glen where the road swept round to go up the Ercall. Mary thought it was safe to let the car speed up and put her foot on the accelerator. As they careered around the corner the tyres were squealing, she struggled to keep the car from going onto the grass verge, her head was against the window as she pulled on the steering wheel.

"For goodness slow down girl or you will have us both in the reservoir" Dorothy shouted clutching at her hat and leaning inward.

"You are perfectly safe Mam and don't shout like that again or in the reservoir we will surely end up. I know what I am doing, it's the car, and it goes much faster than the tractor and seems to have a mind of its own."

"Just get me there in one piece. It is bad enough having your Dad in hospital without us trying to join him there."

Mary said no more and managed to negotiate the bends down the Ercall without any further difficulty. She managed to park outside the market, a little further from the pavement than was normal. Dorothy gave a great sigh of relief and stuffed loose strands of her hair back under her hat. She did not speak as Mary helped her carry the dressed poultry and eggs to her stall inside the market hall. She was still shaking slightly from the ordeal. Mary started the car and carefully drove off. Not having her mother with her was so much easier, she could take her time and she soon began to enjoy the drive back home.

"This is lovely," she said to herself. "I am going to do this more often. Just imagine driving to Shrewsbury on Sunday. I suppose that I could even have a go at passing the driving test."

Later in the day she returned and helped with the shopping then drove her mother home without incident. As they got out of the car back at the farm Dorothy smiled.

"That was a lot better than the trip down," she said. "We can go to the hospital on Sunday if Lizzy has got us the visiting times."

Friday morning dawned fine Mary was up early. "If it will just stay this way all day we will have the oats in the ground this afternoon" she said to Dorothy. The horses were still used as Fred believed the tractor pressed the ground down too firmly. The horses were a lot lighter and also it made use of them, saving on precious fuel for the tractor. Mary found Hannah and asked her to get the two horses in and give them a bucket of corn. She would want them soon after breakfast. She had checked the seed drill in the stack yard and it seemed fine, she wanted to get the sowing done in one day.

"When we have had breakfast I want you to come with me and follow the drill so that you can keep an eye on the pipes," Mary told Hannah.

"Why me? Why can't Bernie do it? I will be worn out by the time you have finished, walking back and forth across the field.

"Because Bernie has not done it before and you have. I have lots of other jobs that Bernie can be getting on with."

"Such as?" Hannah wanted to know.

"Chopping wood for one thing, unless you would rather that you did it."

"No thank you, I have chopped enough wood for my life time already. What a bossy thing you are getting."

"Someone has to take control while Dad is not here. You pray and hope that no cows decide to calve in the night because if they do you will have to stay up all night and give me a hand. There are three due for calving so stop moaning and let's get a move on. If it rains it could be another week before we can sow that field." Hannah said nothing more and Mary went off to get the seed ready. Mary smiled to herself as she walked. "That's put her straight"

Mary and Bernie loaded the sacks of seed oats in the trailer and placed them along the outside edge of the field about every hundred yards. The wind had changed and blew quite coldly. Back at the farm Hannah began harnessing the horses to pull the seed drill. She was not looking forward to the day at all. She fetched her old school gabardine raincoat from the house and when Mary returned and everything was ready, they walked the two horses to the seed drill and put Kit on one side of the shaft and Robin the colt on the other. They then trundled over to the bottom field and through the narrow gate. While Mary poured seed into the long wooden box Hannah threw her raincoat onto the hedge to keep it off the soil and ready if it started to rain, thinking nothing of the tartan lining flapping in the wind. Mary took hold of the reigns and began leading the horses as they pulled the drill behind them. They started at the very bottom end of the field so that when the field was finished, it would make it much easier just to take the seed drill back to the buildings. There were no oats sown around the edge of the field, this was left for growing swedes or mangolds nearer to wintertime.

Everything was going so well, Mary had a tight hold of the horse's reigns and was able to get them both to cross the field in quite good straight lines. Hannah was keeping up with the drill watching to make sure everything was working properly. She had only stopped Mary a couple of times because of stones pushing the pipes out of their fittings. They were quite pleased with the way things were going for them; they had sown almost half of the field. As they were approaching the hedge ready to turn around and go back across the field the colt spotted the tartan lining of Hannah's raincoat blowing wildly in the wind. Mary saw it too and pulled on the reigns but the colt raised his head, snorted then bolted across the field taking Kit with him. Mary hung on as long as she could but they were careering towards the gateway and she did not want to get crushed against the post, she let go and threw herself away from the path of the bouncing seed drill. Hannah stood and watched in horror as the horses passed through the opening but a wheel struck the gate post so hard the shaft snapped and the seed drill was spun round tipping some of the grain out then it stopped, The horses stumbled, now caught up in the loose chains and the remains of the shaft. They eventually came to a stand still some distance from the wrecked seed drill.

"You idiot!" Mary shouted at Hannah as she looked across at the damage.

"Why! What have I done? I could not have stopped them from running away," Hannah was almost in tears.

"It was your entire fault. Fancy putting your raincoat on the hedge like that, you idiot."

"What was wrong with my raincoat? I always put a coat on the hedge to keep it off any wet grass."

"Well it was blowing about and you should have known that the horses would be scared of it" Mary was really angry.

"Well how was I supposed to know that?"

"Has Dad never told you?"

"No never and anyway Robin is over four years old, he should have known better."

"Oh for goodness sake stop arguing. Let's go and get hold of them and see what damage that they have done to the drill. What a great pity, we were doing so well and we would have finished the field today if this had not happened." They reached the seed drill, some of the seed was scattered around and there were several broken pieces of wood to be picked up.

"Lordy what will Mam say about this?" said Mary. "You had better keep quiet and let me tell her. I'll say a pheasant flew up and frightened them. We have to give a good reason for what frightened them or she will moan for days." Hannah was relieved. Mary went and retrieved the two horses.

"Well that has finished our work for today, you take Kit and I will bring Robin we will head back."

"You can have him. I have seen enough of him for one day," Hannah said as she took hold of Kit's bridle while Mary unfastened what was left of the shaft. "Come on Kit, let's go and settle you down." They returned to the farmyard and unharnessed the horses then went to the kitchen.

"You two are back before I expected" Dorothy said as they entered.

"We've had a bit of an accident" Mary stammered.

"What do you mean an accident?" Dorothy said sharply.

"A pheasant flew up out of the hedge and frightened Robin; he bolted taking Kit along with him. They ran into the next field catching the gate post as they went and they have broken the drill." Hannah thought it best to say nothing.

"What do you mean broke the drill? How bad is it? Can you still use it?"

"Very bad, and no, we can't use it. They have broken the shaft clean off. I'm putting the kettle on; I need a cup of tea." She went to the Rayburn and put the kettle onto the hot plate, then opened the door and gave the fire a good poking with the steel poker to get a bit more life in it. Dorothy noticed the soil marks where Mary had fallen.

"Yes sit down; you do need a drink after what has happened. How much of the field have you sown?"

"A good half of it. I think that we had better take up Wilf Wilkins offer of help. Perhaps he can fix the shaft so we can finish the job. When I have had a cup of tea I will go and tell him what has happened."

"Perhaps you should," said Dorothy. "Why did this have to happen when your Dad is not here, he will be pretty upset if we tell him when we go to see him on Sunday I was hoping to tell him that he had nothing to worry about. That gamekeeper wants to keep his pheasants in the woods. He can't be feeding them properly" Dorothy grumbled.

"If it does not rain, and if Wilf can fix the drill, the field will be finished by Sunday dinnertime." We can still go to see Dad and we don't have to tell him about the accident," Mary replied, pleased she was still in with a chance of driving the car.

Joyce Wilkins had been watching the two girls sowing the field and had seen the horses run away. She screamed abruptly startling Wilf who was resting in a chair by the table.

"Those two girls were lucky not to be killed. Their horses have just charged the gate," she said.

"What do you mean horses charging the gate?" he said, annoyed that she spent so much time watching what went on at the Thomas's place.

"Well I don't really know why but suddenly I saw the horses running away into the next field, they have left the seed drill in the gateway. The girls are going after them now; it looks like they may need some help. Don't be surprised if they come to us for help after all, you did tell me to offer your help despite your leg being so painful and that is what I did." His jaw dropped, "You did what woman? Have I not got enough to do? I told you that my leg was very painful did I not."

"Yes but you did offer" she said defensively.

A while later there was a knock at the door. Joyce had seen Mary on her way so the door was opened before Mary could knock for a second time.

"Is Mr Wilkins in? I'm afraid that we need his help. You see the horses ran away with us and they have broken the seed drill. If only we could mend it I could finish sowing the field before we go to see Dad on Sunday." Mary pleaded.

"Come in, my husband is here at the moment."

Wilf listened to Mary's problem. He gave a sigh of relief. At least he was only being asked to help repair the drill and not finish the sowing.

"Of course I will come and see what I can do but it will have to be tomorrow morning now. Can you tell me what tools I need to bring with me."

"You have changed your tune," thought Joyce but she did not voice her opinion.

"A good saw if you have one, Dad's does not cut very well. I think that I can find some nails and bits and pieces."

"You do that Mary, I am sure that between the both of us we can fix your Dad's drill."

"Thank you, I must get back now as we have the milking to get done and time is getting on" said Mary. She left and ran all the way back down the bank. Wilf pondered the situation.

"I had better take a few more tools with me and some bolts, just in case Mary can't find what I need," he said to Joyce. "A broken shaft! That should not take too long to fix. They should be able to start sowing again by dinner time."

"That is good of you to help. I feel so sorry for those girls always working so hard. Mary does the work of any man and more besides. She even has to clean that kitchen when her mother goes shopping."

"That is enough Wife, what goes on down there is none of our business, but you are quite right Mary does work extremely hard I will say that for her."

It was almost dinnertime when Wilf finished mending the broken seed drill. He had fashioned a new shaft and fastened it securely to the drill. A few nails had repaired some broken boards and everything seemed fine.

"There we are, I think that should hold," he said to Mary as he put the last nut on to the last bolt.

Hannah had already brought the horses to the stable ready to be harnessed.

"Thank you so much, we can finish the sowing now," she knew it would take a while but Bernie could get the cows in for her and start the milking.

Mary thanked Wilf again for his help and he went off to the kitchen to talk to Dorothy. Then she and Hannah harnessed up the horses and went to finish off what they had started the day before.

"Where is your gabardine Mac?" asked Mary "Nowhere near a hedge is it?"

"No I left it back in the house" Hannah had not dared to bring it with her, rain or no rain.

Mary smiled and they got to work there were no problems and the drill ran true. It was late when everything was finished that night. Dorothy was very pleased and made sure that everyone had a really good tea. Mary was so glad to get to bed and rest. When Lizzy came in she asked how they had got on. "I reckon that Dad should be pleased when we tell him what we have done."

"How are you going to see him tomorrow? By bus from Wellington?"

"No. Mam says that I can drive her in the car. I am sure we will be able to park somewhere near the hospital."

"Good grief. You are not thinking of actually driving all the way are you? It will not be like driving to Wellington there is so much more traffic in Shrewsbury."

"So what? I will be able to do it." Mary said defiantly.

"Well I hope you know what you are doing. What are we going to do if you and Mam land up in hospital?"

"Lizzy stop worrying and get some sleep I am worn out." She gave a loud yawn and turned over. Lizzy was concerned but decided not to say any more. It was hard to believe that their Mam had agreed to let Mary drive her. She had heard two walkers laughing about a black and yellow car on two wheels as it came around the bend by the Forest Glen, they said it was a miracle it made it at all.

On Sunday morning Hannah went to the cottage early. Mary had all her work done and Dorothy had the Sunday dinner ready so there would be plenty of visiting time at the hospital. She was taking William with them so that would leave Helen and Bernie to look after Sandra and see to the feeding. Mary told them that if they were late back to fetch the cows in and start the milking.

When they set off William was sat in the back, his constant chattering was distracting Mary so she told him to shut up and be quiet for a while.

"Leave the lad alone. You are always picking on him. Let him enjoy the ride. I've got some sweets here for him but I don't want to give him any until we are on the way back in case he makes a mess of his clean shirt." Mary was so annoyed, "Oh yes," she thought to herself "Mam must have sweets for William. She never buys any for us. If we want any we must pay for them out of our own money." She counted to ten and concentrated on the road and driving the car. As they neared Shrewsbury she could sense her mother getting a little nervous.

"Stop worrying Mam we have got this far safely. I will go up the main street and go around to the hospital."

"No need to go too close, we can get out and walk if you can see somewhere safe to park the car."

"I will take us all the way if I can, just sit there and relax. You just worry about holding on to William when we get out. You know what he is like, be across the road before we you can bat an eyelid." She was not expecting the response she got.

"There you go again, picking on the lad. He gets no peace at all. If it isn't one of you picking on him it's another. It's a good job he has Helen, she is the only one who seems to have anytime for the little lad. Grace is horrible to him even though she is hardly at home, always gallivanting off somewhere. I am so glad that we have brought him with us, your Dad will be so pleased to see him." Dorothy turned and smiled at William in the back, Mary noticed the smile on his face,

"Perhaps it's because you spoil him," she said. Dorothy did not reply. They found the hospital and there were spaces to park the car. Mary carefully positioned the car and backed into one of the spaces. She was very proud of herself. She had driven them through the town and parked up, all for the first time. No praise came from Dorothy; she was still annoyed at Mary's remark. They made their way inside and eventually to the ward where Fred was situated. There were six beds all occupied; he was at the far end. He was so pleased to see them; the first thing he asked was what was happening over the sowing. Mary told him the bottom field was now sown with oats, not mentioning the broken seed drill.

"Surry that's grand, I have been so worried, especially as the weather has been so good. Well done. It has certainly paid off letting you have a go on the tractor." Then he paused, "How did you get here?"

"In the car Dad. I drove all the way, she said with a grin from ear to ear.

"Surry what next?" he smiled and shook his head.

"What about you though?" said Dorothy. "When are you coming home?"

"End of next week all being well." He told them that the break in his leg had been a very nasty one and it would take at least six to eight weeks before he would be able to put any weight on it. The doctor had told him that he was extremely lucky that he had no infection due to the length of time before he was admitted to hospital. When he got home he would have to rest and not do anything.

"Well, once you are back home you can organize things and tell us what we have to do," said Dorothy. Mary did not like the way it sounded, she was in control.

"Nay, our Mary seems to have it under control. I will be taking it easy," Fred replied.

"Thanks Dad but it is Hannah Bernie and Helen that have worked so hard as well, we even have some muck shifted" Dorothy glared at her.

"Don't you forget William," she said. Mary did not answer, there was an awkward silence. William was fidgeting as he was bored. "I will take him for a walk" said Mary.

"Good idea, but don't go too far," said Dorothy.

Mary took him outside leaving their parents alone. She took hold of William's hand and they went along to Pride Hill where there were so many more shops to see. Everywhere was closed but they looked in the shop windows. In the window of Marks and Spencer she saw a lovely tailored costume in sage green.

"If only I had a decent wage, just think what I would be able to buy. That colour would suit me. I would look good in that with my dark hair." William looked bored he was only interested in tractors. He cheered up when they found a toyshop and he could gaze through the glass at all the different things. After a while they wandered back to the hospital. William began talking of the toyshop and it was Mary's turn to be bored.

Eventually Dorothy told him to stop as they should be getting back. Fred agreed, and then to Mary's surprise, he thanked her for driving the car all the way to Shrewsbury so he could see them, and for getting the field sown. She was as pleased as punch.

As she drove the car home, she told her mother of the clothes that she had seen in the shop windows.

"Well what do you want fancy clothes for unless you are going to a wedding or somewhere posh? I buy you everything you need don't I?" Mary went to speak but Dorothy carried on.

"You don't go short of much that I can see. You go to the Glen and the Cottage and you get to the village dances as well. What more do you want?"

Mary decided not to start an argument but she thought a new dress would be nice considering how hard she worked. It was not that they could not afford to buy her one. William only had to whimper and he was given anything that he asked for.

Dorothy took a paper bag of sweets from her handbag. She passed one to Mary, took one for herself and then gave the rest to William in the back; he did not even say thank you.

"Greedy little sod." Mary said to herself

Hannah arrived at the Cottage for ten o'clock. She went to the kitchen door and knocked as it was normally Mary who led the way. Eric Watson called; "Come in." she went inside. He was sat in his usual chair by the range.

"Is Mary not with you?" he asked.

"No, our Dad has broken his leg and is in Shrewsbury Hospital. Once she has done her work she is taking our Mam to see him," she stammered, expecting Eric Watson to shout at her because of Mary's absence.

"Sit down lass and tell me what has happened. I know we could do with Mary's help today, I guess we are going to be busy. But never mind we will cope I am sure. Pass a cup and I will fill it for you, there will be more for you to do today so you may as well have a cup of tea before you start work."

Hannah was surprised by his attitude. She sat down at the other side of the table. Gwen passed through on her way to the back kitchen and looked angrily at Hannah sat at the table drinking tea.

"Have you nothing to do?" she looked Hannah in the face.

"Leave her be for a moment, her father is in hospital and she is just telling me that Mary will not be here today."

"Oh really! In that case there is going to be much more for each of us to do. I suggest that you drink that tea and come and help out in the back kitchen as quickly as possible." The look she gave Eric was not a very friendly one. Hannah noticed, she decided she had better get a move on and start work, there was clearly an atmosphere. A trickle of people began to arrive. Hannah was asked to help prepare the trays for the waitresses, Elsie and Vera who's job it was to take the food and drinks through to the tearooms. It would be the afternoon when Mary would be really missed. It was hard work having to carry the heavy trays to the big tearoom that stood several yards from the main house it could seat at least one hundred people. The smaller tearoom was not too much trouble but without Mary, it meant there would be extra for the others to do. Most customers came for afternoon tea. A pot of tea, Eric's homemade bread spread with best butter, jam and homemade fruitcake. There were sandwiches, boiled eggs, meats and early in the day, breakfasts.

Gwen was kept busy preparing the food while keeping an eye on their four children. Ivy helped with the food and looked after the shop counter. Her daughter Judith had come along for the day so she was given Hannah's job doing the collecting. Mrs Briggs helped get the dinner as well as see to all the washing up. The afternoon was bedlam, it was the last day of the Easter week and schools would be back the next day. As the weather was fine, many folk had taken a last chance for a walk up the hill and a bite to eat. It had been a long and busy day for Hannah. At last the customers dwindled and the demand for food became less. She was asked to give a hand changing tablecloths, and stacking clean crockery onto the shelves in the larger of the two kitchens. There was a small kitchen of sorts that was for the private use of the Watson's. They had a bucket toilet for their own use, but staff had to use the smelly public one.

Hannah was glad when she was able to go home. As she walked onto the back yard, she met Mary returning from checking the sheep on the backfields.

"What did Eric have to say about me not turning up?" Mary asked.

"He was pretty good about it but you could tell that Gwen was a bit put out, she has been very grumpy all day long."

"Hmmm" said Mary "I think there is something going on there, I have heard rumours that it is to do with Mr Watson's drinking. What about the others?"

"Elsie and Vera were not pleased, especially Elsie. She had to see to the pavilion on her own, there were a lot of people hanging about and you know what it is like with a loaded tray. No matter how many times you say "excuse me, excuse me." She mimicked the busy women "they just don't move."

"Did you take Mam to see Dad?"

"Of course I did, I drove all the way to the Hospital without any problem."

"What did you do with Sandra and William?"

"Well we had to take William of course. Mam left Helen to keep an eye on Sandra until we got back. That child needs bathing properly; we will get it done later."

"Did you tell Dad about the horses running away?"

"Of course not, he would have been out of that bed like a hare running for the woods. He is very pleased, thinks that we are doing wonders. Except that our Mam tried to make out that she was doing most of the work."

"Well she would wouldn't she," said Hannah "no change there."

Mary thought of the shops that she had seen in town "Hannah, I went for a walk to look in the shops. There are some lovely clothes. I wish I had the money to buy something really nice. I have seen such a lovely dress today, but Mam would never buy it for me no matter how hard I work.

"I know exactly how you feel, it is not fair. Other girls who do nothing get fine clothes; I see them everyday at school. Cards and presents on their birthdays, we never get anything like that" Hannah checked that her wages were still in her pocket.

"Why are they so mean to us?" Mary continued "I'll bet William gets a new toy next time Mam goes shopping. It seems that if you want nice things you have to go out and earn the money yourself. I can see why Grace is so hard nosed."

"I heard Mam saying how they are too busy saving to buy the farm for William to waste money on us. She said this farm is his inheritance," said Hannah, Mary shook her head.

"You know how we have to buy our own sweets. Well on the way back she had a paper bag full. She gave me one and then let William gobble the rest."

"William. William. That is all she cares about. Thank goodness I go to a different school and anyway I will soon be old enough to leave."

"Then what are you going to do?"

"I really don't know anymore. I always wanted to be a school teacher but Mrs Turner the Math's teacher says I will not be good enough to go on to University. She was ever so nice about it, she said it was not my fault I had missed so much school. She said how if it had not been for the great effort we put in on the farms the country would have starved."

"I reckon Mam and Dad will expect you to stay at home, I don't think that they will be very pleased if you go and get a job working for someone else."

"I stay and work at home, not likely, that would never work. They do not pay any wages as you know. I can't see them letting me drive the car and anyway it will be William this and William that. Dad never says anything to make us think any different." Mary had to agree it was pointless to think otherwise.

"You are right; I think Grace has the right idea. She says she is leaving home as soon as she finishes school."

"I think it would be the best thing she could do. It would save any more arguments with our Mam." Hannah always left the room whenever Grace and Dorothy were together, as the rows were awful.

"Are you going to take your driving test now you have had a proper go?" asked Hannah.

"I asked Mam about that on the way back from Shrewsbury but she did not want to know. She said Dad will soon be able to drive again, so make the most of it."

"More likely she does not want to pay for you to take the test. How much is it now about?"

"Nineteen shillings?" said Mary.

"She will let you drive as long as it suits them. I intend to learn as soon as I can after leaving school but I only know what I can't do."

"So you are not going to be a nurse or teacher then?" Mary asked her.

"I doubt it. Grace has said how being a nanny is a good job."

"You won't need a car for that."

"I might. So many women are learning to drive now. One day everybody will own a motor car," Hannah said confidently.

"You have been letting your imagination run away with you as usual. Come on, let's get these jobs finished. There is only the fastening up of the hens to be done." said Mary. Together they finished up the work and went in. They both slept well that night.

Mary had heard that Gwen had a problem with Mondays. It was said that she could not abide Eric's drinking but it was the only time that she got any satisfaction. Everyone at the cottage knew that he always went to town on a Monday where most of his day was passed away in the Railway Inn. It was always late in the evening when he left for home and was usually totally drunk. He had to rely on his pony taking him home safely. Thank goodness the pony was familiar with the track and took him and the trap back as far as the buildings below the cottage. He would manage to take the harness off the pony and turn it loose into a field, leaving the tack on the floor. The last part of his journey was up the track to the cottage. He would stumble along shouting and singing at the top of his voice 'Show me the way to go home' or 'It's a long way to Tipperary'

Gwen hated it when he came home worse for drink but she did not grumble. When she had been a young girl they had enjoyed satisfying their sexual desires together but with the children she began to lose interest and tolerated, rather than enjoyed, their lovemaking. Now she had completely lost the desire to please him. He had become awkward and clumsy; his huge beer belly did nothing to improve the situation. When he staggered home drunk he would attempt to arouse her. It left her cold; she felt that he was just an old man trying to convince himself that he had not lost his ability to please her. After he had tumbled into the room and fallen on the bed he would struggle out of his clothes and clamber in reeking of stale beer and cigarettes. She would pretend to be fast asleep then grumble that he had awoken her and remind him of how much work would have to be done the next day and that the children were trying to sleep. She would refuse to let him touch her and after protesting at her refusals for a few minutes he would go into a deep sleep made worse from the effects of the beer he had drunk during the day. She knew from her childhood how drink could bring out the worst in people. Her father had liked his beer and many had been the beatings she and her family had received. She remembered the sense of relief when she had attended his funeral, he died an alcoholic.

Little did Eric know that Monday was the one day Gwen actually looked forward to? He rose quite early in the morning and lit the fires under the two copper boilers ready for Mrs Briggs to start the washing when she came at nine o'clock.

The boilers were always filled the day before, along with the spare water barrels for rinsing the washing.

He got changed and set off to town about ten, the day now belonged to Gwen and she made the most of it while he floated in his drunken haze in the pub. Mrs Briggs was the only member of staff that came on a Monday. She biked from Wrockwardine and was usually finished and off home by three o'clock in the afternoon. Gwen only had to manage the few customers that dropped in, during the day. There was a bell they rang at the shop to get service. She served tea, cake and sandwiches, which she made, requested. The two older children were collected from the bottom of the hill early in the morning by a small bus and taken to Wrockwardine School. They would arrive back later in the afternoon. At four in the afternoon Gwen closed the shop and locked the tearoom door. She was now at her happiest; after the children were fed she would put them to bed with all sorts of promises of an extra bar of chocolate or a bottle of pop. She made it clear that they must not say a word to their father it was his special night and they must behave otherwise there might be a smacking. He often threatened them with the belt when they misbehaved and they had also heard him shouting loudly when he was angry so it had the desired effect.

Gwen hurried and prepared a bath using rainwater from one of the tubs or barrels that collected rainwater from the roofs. She poured it into the galvanized bathtub and added hot water from the big copper tank in the kitchen. She would quickly run down to the spring and collect a bucket of clean water to replace the amount she had taken.

She knew not to let the tank on the range boil dry as it could split with the heat. If that happened there would certainly be trouble, Eric was mean with money unless it was for beer. He would not have approved of her tablet of perfumed soap and a cheap bottle of lavender scent.

Gwen would then relax in the warm water and let her body soak. After a while she washed her dark brown hair and rinsed it with clean soft rainwater. When she was done she dried herself thoroughly then put on clean underwear and her best dress. She emptied the bath and tidied up then brushed her hair until it was dry and shining and let it hang loose. She felt so young again, was it the same Gwen looking back at her from the mirror? Some face cream, a touch of face powder and a touch of pale pink lipstick. It all helped to emphasize the pallor of her skin against her dark brown hair. Monday evenings were the only time that she let her hair hang loose over her shoulders. "He likes it like this," she thought. He had told her that it made her look at least ten years younger, her 'Monday night man'. She often daydreamed at that point of the night. The thrill that her lover would soon be there for her. Once a week for a few hours until Eric came ranting up the bank she could enjoy herself. Her lover would satisfy all her needs and more besides and then slip quietly through the back door and away as soon as Eric's drunken renderings could be heard. Many was the time the lovers had nearly been caught, they always went to the front room as Eric would go straight to his bed on his return. Gwen would move fast and be up the stairs while Eric made his way in and took off his coat. She would throw her dress and pretty petticoat into the old oak wardrobe and slip into her winceyette night-dress. She was always in bed before Eric was even starting up the twisting stairs. She knew that if she were caught cheating he would give her such a beating she would be lucky to survive. She had seen him in a temper when things had not gone well for him. Once when a cow had kicked him on the leg he had taken a strap and beaten it until Gwen had pleaded with him to stop. She thanked her lucky stars that he came home drunk but she had to be careful she had her children to think about. However he was hardly likely to notice things and if he did notice the smell of lavender, Monday night was her bath night. Once he dropped off into his drunken sleep, she would lie there still tingling from the night's passion. This made her life up here on the side of the hill worthwhile.

Fred was brought home by ambulance at the end of the following week. His right leg was completely covered in plaster and what a fuss Dorothy made of him. She said that she felt such a great weight had been lifted off her shoulders now that he was home. Mary was really annoyed as she listened to her mother crowing on how he could resume responsibility. How, although he would not be able to do any manual work, he was there to keep an eye on things again and tell Mary in particular how to get the work done.

"It's me that has been doing it these last two weeks." Mary stormed "and I have done a proper job, even taking the car into town."

"Steady lass," said Fred "you've done a grand job and I will need you to carry on."

"Yes Dad" Mary said glaring at her mother. "I had better get on then." She got her coat and went outside, not daring to slam the door.

Within a day Fred could not stand being in the house he was used to moving about with crutches so he had Dorothy bind the foot with old cloth so that he did not get the plaster wet and dirty and then he was off around to the cow sheds. At first he liked to sit and watch as the cows were being milked but as the days went by, he could be found almost anywhere, even part way up the Willowmoor Bank one afternoon.

Then he began to get solemn and moody. It was near the hay harvest time and there was too much work for Mary to cope with, she was working far too hard and the pressure was beginning to tell. She began to row with her mother.

"What am I supposed to do?" Mary said "I've Dad moping around out there and you telling me we cannot afford any help with the hay harvest." She was really fed up

"It is because he is not able to do any work himself. He blames himself entirely for what happened when he broke his leg. Take no notice of him," said Dorothy.

"If that is the case why doesn't he stop in the house instead of coming and bothering us? We can't help but notice that he is so miserable. We need somebody to help pitch the hay this year; you cannot expect me to do it all, unless you want to come out yourself." Dorothy did not like her attitude but simply said "I will see."

Mary told Hannah that she felt like packing up and leaving home but there was no one else to do the work.

"If you could where would you go to?" Hannah asked.

"I don't know and I don't care. I know why Grace does not bother coming home any more than she has to. Another thing, our Mam is getting so mean with money it's not just when I ask for something. I am not going to tell her next time a hen looks really ill. The last one was awful it was diseased, yet she killed it and made us eat it saying that it saved buying meat. All she thinks about is saving up to buy this farm or some other just for William to inherit."

"I thought that hen was odd it was practically green," said Hannah.

"Yes if you see any sick poultry or even lambs just tell me and I will put them out of their misery without Mam knowing. I did not think that we were going to have that hen for dinner or I would not have taken it to the back door. I thought that she was just going to kill it and throw it away."

"I see what you mean; I suppose there is nothing much we can do though."

"No you are right. It is getting worse now that Dad is back home; we have to put up with him behaving like a bear with a sore head whenever he comes around to the buildings. Don't you think that we have had enough to cope with? At least he has not heard about the seed drill."

"He will see the new shaft next time we use it so we can tell him then," said Hannah."

Mary drove Fred to the hospital to have his plaster removed, the weeks of practice taking Dorothy to town had paid off and he was very impressed. With the plaster off he perked up, but he was under strict orders not to go putting too much weight on it for a while, so no pitching hay. Back home when Mary asked for some help Fred said he would have a go, but Dorothy was having none of it. "You can drive the tractor and nothing else." She told him.

"But there are three fields to harvest," Mary said, "who is going to do all the pitching. I can't do it all by myself and we only have Bernie."

"Hannah can stay off school and help," said Dorothy.

"Yes, with the stacking but not the pitching." Mary felt it was like banging her head against the wall.

"We will manage somehow," her Mother said. Mary was fuming.

"Nay lass" said Fred from his chair. "Let's get somebody in." Dorothy thought for a moment

"All right I will ask Jack Latham, old One-eyed Jack but I expect that we will have to fetch him in the car. Since the war ended he won't give any one a hand unless they fetch him and take him back, he will expect dinner and some pay, he's not as daft as folk make out. I don't think Wilf Wilkins is up to much these days."

"Well, any help is better than none at all," said Mary not mentioning how Wilf had moaned of his arthritis while fixing the seed drill. "How about Joe Evans from the Wrekin farm? He might just spare us a bit of time, should I go and ask him."

"No you leave it to me and your Dad. We will see how he gets on with his leg, a bit of practice driving the car should help." Mary wanted her Dad to say something; she could see her chance to drive the car again slipping away. He said nothing she was so disappointed.

Hannah was very annoyed at the thought of having to spend more time from school.

"What more time off! I might as well leave altogether. I don't expect she suggested that Grace stays off and gives a hand."

"Grace says that she is leaving school at the end of July and you will be leaving next year. So what if you do take a couple of weeks off? I can't see that it is going to matter that much. I was only eleven when the war started and I hardly went after that. I was not able to go to a posh girl's school like you two. I suppose Helen will be going as well next year. You lot forget about what I had to do." Mary was fed up of it all.

Hannah could see how frustrating it must be for Mary, everything she did was constantly being undermined. She thought for a moment.

"It's not that we have forgotten how you were kept here." She began "I know you only had two choices, either work here on the farm or go to work in the factories."

"Lizzy was lucky getting that job at the Glen when she did," Mary sighed.

"I agree" said Hannah "She could have ended up in a factory or stuck here. I reckon it was all down to the Glen having that big function room and Mrs Podmore needing someone living close by who was reliable."

"Mam still makes her work here on her day off, which is so unfair," said Mary.

"You could have both ended up in factories if the war had not ended."

"Well I suppose the war has messed up a lot of lives," said Mary "Our problems are small compared to some."

"Yes I wonder what happened to that soldier who murdered the ATS girl at the Glen?" asked Hannah.

"We will never know. It was all hushed up. That wasn't the only one, though they reckon there was another murder just down the road. A girl was thrown out of a lorry, now I'll bet you didn't know that."

"Oh Lordy. No, how terrible. Who told you?"

"Oh it is just a rumour, supposed to have happened some time ago they say."

Hannah changed the subject, "If I have to stay away from school for two weeks for the hay harvest. I am going to ask Mam if I can go and stay at Grandma's for a week before you start the corn harvest rather than wait until you have finished. It would be good to see Beccy again."

"She got it right," said Mary miserably "She has the best of everything. Grandma certainly looks after her"

"Yes but she still has to work very hard and Granddad is so horrible. He finds fault so quickly, you can see where Mam gets it from." Mary had to laugh at that remark

"See what Mam says first and don't forget you will lose your money from the cottage."

"All right but see if you can get me out of the hay making, I was hoping to get on with my lessons and maybe get a really good end of term report."

Fred was able to drive the tractor by using the crutch to help press the pedals down. Once he was moving he drove steady, very careful not to jerk his leg. By the end of the day his leg would be throbbing but he was almost back to his old self. Mary was pleased that he let her carry on taking her mother to do the shopping in the car. When the time was right to gather the hay, Hannah and Helen were kept from school to help out. William was kept at home but not to work, he went with Fred and sat on the tractor. He did not lift a finger to help while the girls gathered up the hay for loading. Helen asked why William was at home and was told that their mother did not want him walking up the bank on his own, she was dumbstruck. One evening she approached Dorothy

"Mam, William does not need to be off school as he does not help at all."

There are plenty of little jobs that he does for me," she said coldly "I still need a lot of coal fetching in."

"Really he does not seem to do much as far as I can see. Anyway he will have to go to school on his own next year when I leave to go to Wellington." Dorothy spoke slowly and with menace.

"It's a long way for a little lad to go on his own right now. Don't you go picking on him miss or you will not be going to any fancy school?" Helen did not push her luck any further.

Joe Evans came along and brought his tractor and trailer to lend a hand with the hay harvest. Mary fetched One-eyed Jack in the car and with Bernie and the girls the hay was gathered in before the rain set in. Dorothy was pleased with the amount gathered, it would see them a long way through the winter.

"Now we only have the corn harvest to get in and then we can relax a bit," she said hoping, Fred would agree.

"Nay lass, there is never time to relax. I hope my leg will all right by then. I should be able to drive the binder if one of them can ride the first horse."

"It's about time you had that binder fitted for the tractor to pull it and not still be using the horses."

"The horses do not flatten the corn down like the tractor does." Fred still wanted to keep the horses, he was not about to make them redundant and thereby have to let them go. After all he was a traditionalist even if he did have a shiny tractor.

CHAPTER 15

Independence

To Hannah, the day Grace left school was not that special? Grace had talked of this day and how wonderful it was going to be to walk out, never to return. On the day, all the leavers were given a specially prepared talk and the headmistress said goodbye to each of them, wishing them all the best for their future.

As the girls left the school building Grace threw her hat in the air, Hannah was waiting by the bike shed and watched while Grace retrieved her hat and hugged her friend goodbye.

"Let's go then. I won't be back again. The sooner I am away the better" said Grace as she got her bike from the rack. They walked to the road then mounted and set off.

"So what now?" Hannah asked "have you decided what you are going to do."

"Well I haven't got a full time job to go to but Mrs Podmore says I can work there over the holiday and maybe a bit longer. It doesn't pay much but it will do."

"Mam will expect you to help out at home. She is on about getting a deep litter shed meaning more hens and more eggs."

"Not for me. I don't mind helping with Sandra because she is not getting much care and attention. I am not working for Mam, all she does is moan and start rows."

"She will make sure you have jobs to do, just like the rest of us."

"Not if I am not around, she won't."

"So what were you told before you left?"

"All the usual stuff, they have told us over the years, how we must go out into the world as smart young women and do our best. Looking smart is one thing I can definitely do"

When they reached the Forest Glen, Grace stopped off and Hannah continued on, she knew she had work to do and she did not want to fall out with her mother as she wanted to go to the Manor in the holiday.

Grace returned around nine o'clock and fell out with her mother almost immediately. She told Hannah that their mother had told her what work she expected to be done.

"I am not staying around waiting for her to dream up jobs for me to do."

"Such as?" asked Hannah

"Well for starters, she wanted me to start mopping the kitchen floor every day and making beds and all that sort of stuff because you and Mary work outside."

"Well, you will have to if that is what she says."

"Not on your life, I am off to the Glen every chance I can get."

On Monday morning Grace was up and gone with Lizzy. Fred and Mary saw her briefly as she drank a cup of tea and then she was gone. Dorothy was annoyed but she did not make a fuss. They could manage without Grace but she felt that if she was not going to work like Mary, then she should contribute something for her keep and not fritter it away on cheap rubbish or just having a good time. In the evenings when she was in, Grace helped with Sandra and William and sat with the rest of the family sewing or reading. When her Mother was not around she would do her washing. Now that the war was over, more washing powder was coming into the shops, so Grace did not worry too much about using it.

The Wrekin Cottage was very busy during the summer holidays and another lad, nicknamed Snowy was taken on to help out with the ponies and the swing boats, which were very popular with the children. He was called Snowy because of his very blond hair and he came from somewhere in Wellington. He was thirteen and like Hannah and Mary he desperately wanted to earn a bit of money, it was his job to take the money for the rides and look after the ponies. Unlike the other three lads Charlie, George and Thomas, Snowy was reluctant to talk to anyone. He was always in a hurry to get home, for some reason. On the warm evenings the girls sometimes walked the long way back which was down the track to the bottom of the hill where it came out by the Forest Glen then right and all the way up past the lane to the quarry and then home. One evening Hannah and Mary arrived at the Forest Glen and there, outside the pavilion, were the three lads from the Cottage, sat on their bicycles.

"Let's stop for a chat," said Mary "We are in no rush are we?" Hannah did not know what to say.

"Bit out of your way aren't you?" said one of the lads.

"We fancied a walk that's all, our sister's work here," answered Mary

"How many sisters have you got?"

"Four here and one at the Manor," said Hannah, wondering if she should have counted Sandra.

"Blimey," said Charlie. He was the oldest and worked in a Quarry during the week; he talked for a few minutes of the days work at the Cottage, and then ran out of things to say. George lit a cigarette and casually blew smoke circles into the air. George was extremely good looking. He had dark wavy hair almost black, which was always combed and shone immaculately. He worked as a carpenter for a local undertaker and had learned to drive a car. Mary could see that he really fancied himself as he sat there. His brother Thomas did not say much at the best of times, he was not as good looking as George but he too was training to be a carpenter. It was George with his grizzly tales of dead bodies

And coffins that impressed the girls, they were so enthralled they forgot the time and were still there when Grace and Lizzy came out to go home. Mary and Hannah scurried off and the lads went off home laughing.

Later that night as they went to bed, Hannah told Grace about the chat with the boys outside the Forest Glen.

"Strikes me, that George is a proper show off," Grace teased Hannah. "I expect he is like that with all the girls he talks to. Now his brother sounds a much nicer lad."

"He is very quiet though, he hardly says anything and George has seen dead people" Grace was not listening.

"Do you think Mary fancies Charlie then?"

"I hope not Mam says that we are all to marry farmer's sons."

"Well don't you go getting fancy ideas about George. Mam would never allow you to marry someone as common as he is." She enjoyed making Hannah uncomfortable.

"Don't talk daft Grace I am only fourteen, I don't want to think about marrying anyone, well at least not for years. Perhaps when I am twenty and that is a long way off. Anyway how do you know that Mam says we are only to marry farmer's sons?"

"Lizzy told me. Did you know she is smiling at a lad who comes to the Glen bringing milk from his uncle's farm? You must have seen him around, his name is Noel, and he works for his uncle, Bill Corfield who has that big farm at Cluddely."

"I know the one, Dad has sent me down with a note on several occasions" said Hannah.

"That's it; well this Noel sometimes brings the milk when his uncle is out doing what they call his veterinary work. I think that Lizzy really fancies him."

"So, does Mam know about this?"

"No of course not, and don't you say anything or we will both be in trouble with Lizzy."

"What veterinary work does Bill Corfield do then?"

"He goes around the farms castrating the animals. You know, you have seen him here often enough doing the pigs for Dad."
"I've seen him. Sometimes Mary has to hold them for him, she says it is a horrible job, not only the blood but they mess all over her as they try to get away."

"Well I intend to get a job that does not involve being messed and bled on."

"You might do, if you get a job looking after children and they are sick on you. That won't be very nice. Anyway why do they do that to the piglets?"

"It is so that they will grow lazy and fat and make more money when they go to the auction." Hannah was thinking of the farm at Cluddely

"When I have been there, that Mrs Corfield has looked down her nose at me. I always go to the back door and she tries to talk posh 'I will tell my Husband that your Father wishes him to pay you a visit in due course' that's how she talks" said Hannah, mimicking Mrs Corfield, causing Grace to chuckle. "So is this Noel a farmer's son?"

"I think his Dad has a small holding somewhere at Ketley, the other side of Wellington, he drives his own car so he must be pretty well off."

"Well fancy that! Our Lizzy, but then she is twenty one," said Hannah.

"I will have a boyfriend much sooner. I am going to make sure that mine has a motor car as well, I have had enough of cycling everywhere."

"Are you working at the Glen all the time now?"

"Oh no, I go to my friends in town. I don't come home otherwise I get shouted at. I have been thinking of getting a job as a nanny or a housekeeper for an old lady where I can live in. I want a proper weekly wage. In fact I have already been looking in the vacancy column of the papers; I can't wait to get away from here."

"Don't let Mam know. But then I don't think they would miss you all that much. Except when it comes to picking potatoes and such."

"If it had not been for all the wretched farm work that caused us to miss so much school, I would have been able to qualify for something decent. I would not be looking for just any job to get away from here."

"The war had a lot to do with it. Things could have been different, Dad could have had Sam still working for him."

"Maybe, but Dad would not have a tractor or be harvesting so much if it had not been for all the money he got from the

Government, and think how much they have saved. Sam used to get a wage. A farm worker should get, at least ten shillings a week and what do we get nothing. What is more Mam gets to being driven about in a fancy motor car."

"Oh Grace you can be horrid at times."

"No Hannah, you are so naïve, you don't notice what goes on. You live in fantasyland, when will you decide to grow up a bit." Hannah did not like Grace's sarcasm, but there was nothing to say unless she wanted a bigger argument. She shrugged her shoulders.

"The sooner I am out of here the better" said Grace closing the conversation.

Hannah did not share Graces feelings, being quite happy working outside when not at school. She also had her yearly trip to the Manor as an incentive so it was a tremendous disappointed when she was told there would be no visit this year as she was needed to ride the leader horse when they started cutting the corn. She was told it was because Fred's leg was still giving trouble and she would have to be around all the time throughout the holidays, just in case. Hannah was adamant that she was going and asked if she could go before they started, she was told no. She tried arguing and pleading but to no avail, her mother had to make the necessary arrangements for her to be picked up from the station if she went and it was clear she had no intention of doing so. Hannah tried to get Mary to arrange a visit for her and was told that she probably wouldn't be needed after all but without someone to meet her it was too late.

"You can drive me all the way now you have the car," said Hannah brightly.

"I wouldn't dare, there has already been enough moaning about the petrol ration. They don't want me using the car unless it is to ferry them around," said Mary. After a day or so however she thought it was worth a try so she asked if she could take Hannah over in the car. Dorothy changed her mind about not needing Hannah at home in a flash and was adamant that she would stay around after all.

"I will go on my bike then," Hannah said to this new development.

"It is too far to bike. You must be mad; it has got to be twenty miles at least." Mary was amazed at her suggestion.

"So, I can do it, you will see," Mary shook her head.

The harvest still required the use of horses as the binder was not modified for the tractor yet. Hannah was to ride the first horse so that Mary was free to help stooking the corn.

Hannah constantly pestered Fred to let her go to the Manor after they were finished harvesting but he did not want to go against Dorothy's wishes. The first day of the harvest was no exception.

"If we get this done on time, I can go, can't I Dad?" Fred shook his head "Wait and see lass, there's many a slip as they say."

It was usual to have a rabbit shoot at harvest time and Fred had invited a few men he knew to come along some for some sport. The cutting was hardly underway when they appeared with their guns. Fred was on the binder and when he came level with them Hannah brought the horses to a halt and waited while he talked to them.

"You're a bit early, he said "we have quite a way to go and then we will have to stand the horses and unhitch them." He looked at the group, Wilf and a few friends from town were there to join in the fun but he was annoyed that his old friend Harold had two strangers with him.

Fred was very wary of folk he did not know and did not encourage them onto the farm. He gave them strict instructions that shooting would only begin when they neared the centre of the field and that would be quite some time away. The little group went and sat at the side of the field, the newcomers were clearly impatient.

Progress was steady, the stooks were mounting up. Mary, Bernie and Helen worked well but there was no sign of William he was elsewhere. After a couple of hours there was a large square in the middle of the field left to do. Fred stopped the horses; the rabbits would now be concentrated in that one area and eager to run for the woods.

"None of you are to fire a shot until I give the signal," he said. The men took up position with their guns and waited. Fred walked around to the front of the machine to unfasten the horses while Hannah waited patiently astride the lead horse. Suddenly a shot rang out and then another, someone had fired a gun without being given the all clear by Fred. The horses panicked and surged forward. Fred was in the most dangerous situation possible. He had no time to disconnect the harness chains and he had put the long reigns to one side well out of his reach. "Stop," he shouted.

Hannah glanced back and saw the predicament he was in, he was in front of the blades of the cutting knife against the shaft, as the horses moved forward, and the huge reel began to revolve to pull him in. Fred had to run behind the horses or he would be caught and cut to ribbons on the clattering blades. Out of pure instinct Hannah turned her horse across the path of the other two causing them to stop abruptly. Fred threw himself clear as the clattering binder stopped. The horses were agitated, their ears were twitching and they had a look of panic in their eyes.

"Surry that was a close thing, said Fred. "What bloody idiot let that gun off?" He talked to the horses and they calmed down. Hannah dismounted.

"If I get my hands on whoever loosed that shot off I will bloody kill him" He quickly unhitched the binder then together they took the horses to the side of the field and tethered them up. Leaving them to calm down they returned to the centre of the field. "What with breaking my leg and now nearly having them chopped off this is getting a dangerous business," he said to Hannah as the shock subsided.

"There are rules on a farm and they have to be obeyed or someone gets killed."

"I can see that Dad, I think it was one of the strangers."

"I reckon so too. Well they will not come on 'the bank' again I will see to that." They walked back to where the group of men was standing. One of the strangers was looking at the ground. He was obviously the one who fired the shots. Fred told them in no uncertain terms how stupid they had been and the consequences, had it not been for Hannah's quick thinking.

He made them spread out facing the woods so as the rabbits were driven from the remainder of the corn no gun will be fired towards anyone.

"You shoot as they run for cover, if you miss, and then that is your own fault. I reckon there are at least fifty in there. Now do as you are told or leave the field, is that clear?" The men all agreed and Mary and Bernie then began scaring the rabbits out of the corn. The gunshots echoed as the rabbits zig zagged for the woods, lead flying around them. Quite a few were shot and the men were very happy with the final tally. Before they left they paid their respects to Fred and apologized for the earlier incident. The horses were hitched up and the remaining corn was cut and stacked.

At the end of the day as they walked back, Fred told them all to say nothing to Dorothy of the incident earlier. "If she saw from the window then say nothing about the danger I was in." He walked in silence for a while then said, "I have been thinking, we will not use the horses next year. I will get a new binder, one that can be pulled with the tractor. It should be a lot safer."

"What happens to the horses then?" asked Mary.

"One will have to go."

"You would not sell Kit would you Dad?" Hannah asked not wanting her father to part with the horse that she had known all her life.

"No lass. I will never sell her; she has been too good to us over the years. It's that young one that will have to go; he's too jumpy and temperamental. He will up and run at the slightest opportunity.

"That's true," said Hannah not thinking. Fred smiled, "By the way girls, I have seen the seed drill has been repaired. Someone has fitted another shaft and nailed a few bits and pieces together. So what happened?" Mary looked at Hannah, what could they say?

"Don't worry," he said "I asked your Mam about it and she told me how the horses ran away with you, it's lucky neither of you were killed, I was lucky today as well. I suppose you told Wilf Wilkins to keep quiet about it while I was in hospital?" he looked at Mary.

"Didn't want to worry you that's all and we managed to get the field sown, so there was no point in telling you; was there?"

"No there was not. If I had have known they would not have been able to keep me in the hospital. I will thank Wilf next time I see him." Hannah and Mary relaxed then Fred added "I have been thinking that we can sow sugar beet next year. The government is still paying a good subsidy for growing it."

Mary had been so pleased to hear a word of praise for her work but she was not happy at the thought of growing sugar beet. The weeds had to be removed and that meant walking between the rows with a hoe chopping the weeds off as they went.

"Dad don't you think that we have enough hoeing with the swedes and the mangolds".

"We can manage a bit of beet hoeing I am sure" Fred chuckled. He filled his pipe from his tobacco tin and lit it.

"Sugar beet, oh Lordy" said Hannah as they went to the kitchen for a cup of tea before starting the milking. "There is no end to it."

The next day Hannah resumed her pestering to go to the Manor.

"Aye lass, why not, Mary says you want to bike all the way?"

"Oh, yes, right," said Hannah completely thrown. "I really want to go."

"Well why not," he said smiling "I owe you one for yesterday. As soon as the harvest is in you can go." Hannah was speechless, it was twenty miles, what had she done.

On the morning she was to set off, Hannah made sure that her bicycle tyres were properly pumped up and that everything was working properly, especially the brakes. She clipped the pump into place praying that she would not get a puncture during the journey.

Fred came round to the garage with her when it was time to leave.

"Now lass you be careful, I would have run you out but the petrol ration will not stand it."

"I know Dad, and don't worry I am quite looking forward to this."

She had a duffel bag on her back with some belongings and some sandwiches. She had decided to go to Newport and head for Market Drayton where she would find the signpost for Cheswardine, then she would not have far to go. This was the way her Dad had driven on the rare occasions that they had visited their Grandparents.

Hannah reached her journeys end at about two o'clock. Her legs were aching and she was very saddle sore but it was worth it just to see the smile on Rebecca's face.

Her grandmother was pleased to see her and made such a fuss about taking such a long journey on her bike, even Granddad was impressed.

"You must really have wanted to visit to ride all that way," he said "it is nice to see you." Hannah's mouth fell open even Rebecca was surprised.

"You are honoured," she said "but then he is a lot better recently. Anyway I have another surprise for you; I have an admirer let's go for a walk." Beccy was so glad of Hannah's company and wanted to know all that had happened at the Willowmoor Farm. Hannah told her of their father's accident which Rebecca knew nothing of. She was concerned as she still missed her Dad and wanted to visit sometime.

As they walked down the sandy lane that ran alongside the estate they met a very nice young man who stopped for a chat with them. Rebecca was all smiles as she knew him from the village dances and it was obvious that he wanted to get to know her much better. After a while he went on his way. Rebecca was happy, "He waits for me down here in the afternoons as he knows I often go down to the reservoir to check on the fishermen. It is quite silly really as he pretends to be just passing. Sometimes I wait at the top and watch him, and then when I show myself he starts walking towards me".

"You are blushing," said Hannah.

"I know it is silly really but great fun."

"What are you going to do when you leave school?" Rebecca asked, changing the subject.

"I don't know but I don't want to stay at home and work on the farm. Mam has grown so miserable and mean; all she thinks about is William. She says how everything that is being done is for his inheritance.

"What is it all about? It is the same here. Gordon this and Gordon that. He must have his inheritance and yet last year he was pinching the corn."

"Mam says we keep picking on William but he simply does nothing to help. Are you going to stay and work for Granddad until you get married?"

"I suppose so. That is if a fellow comes along who wants to marry me."

"I am sure there will be one who wants you, how about the lad we just met?"

"Good lord no. Has Mam explained about having boyfriends to you yet?" Hannah was embarrassed and did not reply.

"Or about your monthly cycle." Hannah felt trapped these were not things openly discussed.

"Err. No she has told me nothing. She does not have any interest in that sort of thing."

"She will certainly have views when it comes to boys."

"I have been listening to the other girls at school, but I don't really learn anything. They come from the town and have some strange ideas."

"I see," said Beccy. "Have neither Lizzy nor Mary told you what to expect with the cycle". Hannah looked blank. She wondered if this was right. "You know, that you can buy proper towels from the chemist now. They are called sanitary towels and you can buy a belt, which has two hooks, so that you can wear them in comfort not like the old days when you had to make your own."

"So that is what those little bits of towel are that Lizzy washes and hides away in her drawer. They look like tiny nappies. How on earth does she keep them in place? "

"With two safety pins I expect, but you have no need to do that. Grandma has been so helpful she has explained it all to me and all about where babies come from and how to avoid getting pregnant"

"Mary could have told me, I work a lot with her. That explains what she is burning every so often when Mam has gone to town. Grace has never discussed anything like this. Will we have to wear those corsets like Mam wears to keep our stockings up? They look so uncomfortable. Does Grandma wear them?

"Yes Grandma does wear a corset but not as big as the ones Mam wears. Grandma says she must wear one to protect her back from too much strain and it keeps her stockings up. We don't need them we will use a suspender belt. Save some of your money if you can and buy one when you decide to wear stockings."

Hannah found it easy talking to Rebecca who was seventeen. Unlike her other sisters or mother she was open minded to all the problems a girl could face. She told Beccy about the boys who worked at the Cottage and how good looking she thought George was.

"Don't you get too friendly with them, Mam might not like it" Rebecca warned, "you are only fourteen and still at school."

"Mam is not interested in what we do outside of the farm. She only thinks of William. Sandra would have starved if it were not for Mary and Helen. You know, I think that when Helen goes to school at Wellington, William will stay at home as often as he wants."

"Really, do you think that Helen will pass the Eleven Plus?"

"Probably but I don't know what she will do, she does not say a lot"

"I could have had a go at that when I first came to live here but I did not bother, I was quite happy going to the school at Drayton."

"Well they have opened a big new school in Wellington for those that are over eleven and have not taken the Eleven Plus exam. It is to be called the 'Wellington Senior School for Boys and Girls' and I think Helen would prefer to go to it. It is to be very modern with all the latest equipment in the gymnasium and laboratories. She was telling me that because she lives three miles from the school, she would be given a new bike to go to school on free of charge."

For the rest of the week no stone was left unturned, no subject was too embarrassing. Hannah returned home with a whole new outlook, she had grown up in many ways.

On her arrival back at the Willowmoor Farm she found everyone in good spirits. The corn harvest was stacked safely in the brick barns, waiting for a visit of Jack Munslow's threshing machine later in the New Year. Fred and Mary were pleased, the quality of the crops were far better because of using the tractor. They had been able to get more muck to the fields and then plough it in much deeper with the double furrowed plough, burying the muck much better, as well as any weeds.

Two days after Hannah had arrived home- work began on erecting a deep litter shed down by the orchard. It was basically a very large shed and got its name from the floor being covered in a deep layer of straw which could be cleaned out every so often. The hens were kept inside at all times, no longer did they roam about laying their eggs in places where only rats, hedgehogs and foxes could find them. The shed had special nesting boxes for the hens to lay their eggs in, which were accessible from outside making collection simple. The eggs were much cleaner so there was far less to be washed before sending to the packing station.

Dorothy was over the moon and ordered sacks of grit to provide the essential minerals the hens would no longer get through foraging. The grit arrived in hundred weight bags and Dorothy had it stacked in one of the old pens that she had refused to have knocked down by arguing that they would be very useful for keeping sickly animals in. Hannah and Helen were given the job of looking after the shed. They had to carry buckets of water off the back yard and fetch corn from the granary to fill the large galvanized troughs set on the ground. They had to spread the grit over the floor for the hens to scratch up, keeping themselves busy. Dorothy stressed that the hens in the shed had to have plenty of corn and grit as without grit, the shells would be brittle and without corn they would eat the eggs if hungry. Hannah and Helen thought that this new way of working with the hens was wonderful compared to the old method. They were able to collect the eggs without entering the pen and cleaning out was less regular and a job for Bernie. He was welcome to the white poultry fleas that jumped about when moving the litter. They were no real danger but could be a nuisance causing itching and discomfort.

No longer did they have to clean the wooden poultry pens, a job that they had not liked. The hen muck stuck to the wooden floor boards and it was a tough job to remove it with spades and load the wheelbarrow.

At first Fred had been reluctant about the whole idea of housing hens that had previously run free and then feeding them corn and the same stuff they had picked up off the ground. He was further concerned when Dorothy told him she would be buying chicks in at a few days old, already sexed, and at a hundred at a time. There would be no need of the incubator as she would not have any fertile eggs to hatch. She said that she would still have a few cockerels as one or two always turned up in the batches of chicks. They would be easy to fatten up and could go to the market stall when ready. Fred was worried what the size of the corn bill would be like and he was less than happy that grit was being bought when the hens used to get this from the ground for free, along with bugs and grubs.

Since the ending of the war, packing stations had gone into private ownership and were taking all the eggs farmers were able to produce. The eggs were now graded into different categories, the largest and the best were sold to the shops and the small ones were sold to the catering trade or turned into egg powder, which was much easier to distribute across the country or send for export. The best prices were paid for the large brown eggs, which were more popular with the public than the white ones. The benefits soon became apparent and Fred stopped worrying, he had enough to do as it was.

Hannah started her last year at school in the September. She now cycled on her own each day, it was lonely at first but she soon began to enjoy the journey speeding up or slowing down, as she wanted. She now had to take the battery for recharging and it was quite a worry because her handlebars were not suited to carrying things. With Helen and Hannah back at school Dorothy only had Sandra to cope with and at last she was starting to catch up. The egg collecting and packing was quite a job and Dorothy had Mary help out when she was free. She had hoped that Grace would have taken on that work leaving her free to prepare the dinner. It annoyed her that they had not seen that much of Grace since she had left school. She had dodged the harvesting and would probably get out of potato picking. It was a good job that Hannah and Helen had turned out to be such good workers although not as good as Mary; as yet.

Grace carried on working full time at the Forest Glen while she decided exactly what she wanted to do. She kept going through the job listings but, while the Forest Glen was busy she worked every chance she got. Her money was spent on herself much to Dorothy's annoyance but Grace knew what she was doing. If she bought good, well fitting clothes that suited her then she stood a good chance of meeting the right man for her. She knew that she was fast becoming a very attractive young lady despite not being sixteen until October. The monthly dances at the Little Wenlock village hall were not for her. She and her friend from Wellington went to the dances at the Majestic Ballroom in Wellington, and Sankey's ballroom in Hadley. The girls easily passed as eighteen and these were much better places to go to have a good time. Also there were far more nice young men than at the village dances. Grace would come home at all hours. If Dorothy asked what time she had got in Grace would shrug and say she had been at the Glen.

For one of the dances Grace bought a full length blue taffeta dress. She sneaked into the house and waited till bedtime to try it on. Hannah was there and had not seen anything like it before.

On the one shoulder was fastened a beautiful pink taffeta rose. Grace slipped it on and twirled around. She was very pleased.

"Where are you going to wear that?" asked Hannah, her big brown eyes almost popping out of her head.

"There is a big dance at Sankey's and I want to look my best."

"You are lucky, I wouldn't dare go to such a place and anyway I can't dance" Grace was not interested.

"I am going to get a job where I can live in. I can't stick it here any longer."

"You would not leave home would you Grace."

"I am. You would think that our Mam would be proud of me and pleased that I am making an effort to look nice but no, all she does is moan. I will meet lots of men at this dance. Good dancers, so different from the village yokels. Oh yes! There is a big wide world out there Hannah."

Grace picked up a paper bag and took out an elasticated body belt.

"Oh Lordy what is that?" said Hannah.

"This is a roll on, little sister. Watch and learn." She rolled it up over her legs under the dress and onto her stomach. It had suspenders sewn onto it for keeping stockings up.

"There! What do you think?" Hannah grinned; she did not know what to think. Grace dipped back into the bag.

"I have nylons too," she said holding out the dark flimsy stockings, "not those Lyle things Lizzy and Mary, wear they are too thick, more like socks."

"What else have you got in there?" asked Hannah.

"Just new knickers and this" said Grace with a huge grin, "It is a brassier. A thing that Mary and Lizzy do not need, seeing as how they are as thin and flat chested as sticks."

"But why do you need one?" said Hannah.

"I have a bit more up top and everyone's breasts need support otherwise you lose the shape of your figure far too soon, just like Mam has. You can't wear nice dresses if you have lost your shape, you will look dreadful," Grace said smugly.

"Good grief and all this to go to a dance! Is it worth it? I mean, Mary has a suspender belt what is wrong with that?"

"I intend to have the best. I will be away from here you mark my words" said Grace and twirled across the floor as if dancing with a beau. Hannah put on her cotton nightie and got into bed. Growing up was a complicated business indeed.

In the autumn Hannah and Helen were kept off school to help with the potato picking. It was hard work and the girls were exhausted at the end of the day. Hannah and Helen told Grace how hard they had worked when she came home but she was not interested.

"If I had been at home I would have been mopping out the kitchen and cleaning for Mam while she did her poultry, and then had to help in the fields."

"But we could have done with your help, William does nothing, it is left to Bernie, Mary, Helen and me."

"My job at the Glen is far more important. If I don't work, I don't get paid" she said simply.

"That hardly seems fair" Hannah said. "We work, don't get paid and worse we get behind at school."

Quite right," said Helen "I want to get good qualifications and have a really good job."

"Where have we heard that before?" said Grace sarcastically.

Grace decided that she was going to look for a job in town where she would be able to live in. After Christmas she began searching the papers and applying for jobs. She was tired of having to put a hard day's work in at the Forest Glen and then being expected to start again when she came home at night. She could not understand how Lizzy had put up with it for so long. If it was not put the younger ones to bed, it was fill the coal buckets, get sticks in and oh, that sink full of dirty dishes waiting to be washed and put away. On their day off Dorothy had insisted that the family wash had to be done and it was late in the afternoon before they could go into town to do any shopping. "No," she thought "I've had enough."

It was an evening after the Easter Bank Holiday when everyone was sat round the table that Grace announced she was giving up her job at the Forest Glen.

"Guess what? I am leaving the Glen and starting a proper job," she said.

"What doing?" asked Fred?

"I am going to be a nanny."

"You are a bit young for that," said Dorothy.

"No, I am not and the best bit is I will be living in."

"You are leaving home?" said Helen.

"That's right, very soon."

"Well there's a turn up for the books," said Mary. Neither Fred nor Dorothy said anything, her sisters bombarded her with questions but she did not elaborate much, only saying she had definitely got the job and there was no turning back.

Later that night in their bedroom, Grace gave Hannah and Helen more detail. She was moving in with a family called Reynolds who lived in Wellington. Her job would be to look after their daughter while her parents ran their fruit and vegetable business. They were always very busy having to be in different towns to attend the markets.

"So how much will you get paid?" asked Helen?

"A lot more than Mary does and I still get a roof over my head."

"Won't you miss us?"

"I suppose so, but look how we soon forgot about Beccy when she left. I am hardly here as it is."

"I still miss Beccy" said Hannah "so we will miss you." Grace felt a little sad at that remark. Her motive was to get away from the farm and the rows. She would miss her sisters but she knew that she had made her decision.

"I am tired and I want to sleep," she said, not wanting to continue with the conversation.

When the girls were in bed Fred and Dorothy sat for a while listening to the wireless lost in their own thoughts. After a while Dorothy turned the wireless off to save on the batteries. They sat quiet for a while, and then she said, "I don't suppose we will miss her that much once she has gone. She does little to help as it is."

"She hasn't been a bad lass though, she helped out when things got bad" said Fred.

"Yes but she would rather have been down the town shopping. That girl will never save any money that is for sure."

"Aye but she worked hard for it stopping off at the Glen," he replied lighting his pipe.

"Money burns holes in her pockets it does. As soon as she has any it is gone. That blue taffeta dress did you see it? What a waste of money. I only hope that one day she meets someone who can afford to keep her."

"Aye well she is the first to go of her own accord, we will have to give her that, an independent lass without a doubt."

"Oh she is independent all right, sneaking about behind my back to do her washing. Not good enough to have her stuff washed with the rest." Her voice was rising, the more she thought about it and the better it would be when Grace was gone. "Don't think I haven't noticed the things she does. And when was the last time she put something towards the washing powder or soap she uses?"

"Surry lass, I thought you would be glad having less to do." Too late Fred realized his mistake. It was ten minutes before Dorothy calmed down. Silence descended like a curtain, just the ticking of the clock. Dorothy would not admit that Grace looked pretty when she was dressed up and reminded her of herself when she was young. She decided to go to bed and, as her final remark to Fred she said, "She has made her mind up about this so it will be on her own head. There is no point in our trying to persuade her to stay."

"Aye lass," Fred sighed.

Upstairs Grace felt lonely and isolated from the rest of the family. The prospect of leaving was daunting but if she wanted a better way of life she had to go. Also she had talked so much to her sisters of this moment that there was no turning back. In her heart she knew it was the right thing to do. She waited until she heard her mother going to bed then got quietly out of bed, trying not to disturb Hannah and tip toed downstairs.

Fred was banking up the fire in the Rayburn before going to bed. The fire would stay in during the night and the kitchen would be nice and warm next morning. It was so different to the old days, when he had to re-light the black-leaded range every morning.

The door at the back of the table leading to the stairs opened, Grace came into the kitchen, a coat covering her nightie. She went to the table and sat down. She looked pale by the lamplight. He was concerned she looked quite depressed.

"What is the matter lass, are you all right?" he asked.

"Just can't get to sleep Dad. I am all right. I heard Mam go to bed and thought I would come down for a minute." He guessed that she wanted somebody to talk to.

"Well how about a hot drink lass. And I will have one with you before I turn in."

"Yes I could do with a cup of tea but I will make it, you sit down." She got up and went to the Rayburn and put the kettle to boil. She went to the sink, knowing his cup would be there and rinsed it out with some clean water. She went to the kitchen cupboard and found a cup for herself and sugar for him, as like her sisters she had not taken sugar in tea since it had been rationed. As she went to the larder for some milk, Fred thought of the time so long ago when his mother had decided to leave. This was so similar; the way she put the milk on the table and put the teapot ready brought the memories flooding back. She pulled a chair up to the Rayburn and sat down.

"What is it lass that's bothering you?"

"I want you to understand things Dad. Mam and me can never see eye to eye. All of the things I like make her mad and I don't think it is fair; it's not as if I didn't do my share in the past. It has only been recently and that is because nothing I do is appreciated."

"Aye lass I can see that. I see how you two rub each other up the wrong way." He smiled "You two can be as obstinate as a pair of awkward old ewe at times". She smiled, "I will miss you Dad".

"Well you think of this," he said warmly. "We would not be where we are today if it had not been for you girls and the way you worked in the fields. With the war on and Sam gone I was done for but you all stood behind me and got on with it. We could have gone down the road like old Morkin but we made it. No one can ever take that from us, we made this place what it is as a family. You did your bit and for that I will always be grateful."

"Thanks Dad" she said and got up to make the tea. She felt too emotional to speak for a while and concentrated on the brew while Fred relit his pipe.

When they each had a drink, Fred said to her, "So are these folk going to look after you proper?"

"Oh yes they are ever so nice and have a lovely house." She did not mention that she was pleased with what she had seen at her interview, electric light, hot and cold water and a bathroom.

"Well you are only moving to Wellington it is not the end of the earth. You can always come and see us, you know that."

"One day I will have a car and then I will drive and see you," she said.

"Full of big ideas lass, but there's no harm in it. Just keep your feet on the ground that's all I ask." A thought struck him, "You just remember our saying," he paused.

"The brook runs free?" she said.

"That's it. It's what my old Dad used to say. That the brook must run free or you have trouble. In your case keep your eyes open, don't ignore that which is around you and your brook will run free."

Grace thought of this for a while. "I will try Dad, but I want to have a good time and it's not easy sometimes to see the effect I have on others. I will miss my sisters, even Sandra. Maybe things could have been different if it hadn't been for the war."

"Aye well as I said, the war has made this place but remember what your mother always wanted was to have a son and heir. One day, you will understand for yourself what a struggle it has been for her."

Grace drank her tea. She felt a closeness that could only exist between fathers and daughters. He was their rock, always there for them when their mother was not.

"Thanks Dad. I know I am doing the right thing" she stood up and put her cup in the sink.

"You see that you take care of yourself lass" said Fred a little choked. "The outside world can be hard at times you know."

"I know Dad, but don't worry about me." She put her arms around him and gave him a hug, something she had not done for years. "Goodnight Dad" she said and went back to bed.

Fred sat for a while in the quiet kitchen, the clock ticking softly. He struggled with his emotions; they had come so far since the days when Grace had sat on his knee back at the old farm. After a while he rose and put his cup in the sink. "Oh well, tomorrows, another day" he said softly to himself. Taking a last look around the kitchen he picked up the brass lamp and went to the door. "So where do we go from here?" and then he went upstairs to bed.

Lightning Source UK Ltd.
Milton Keynes UK
24 February 2010

150546UK00001B/1/P